TASTE

TASTE

CHERYL KAHN

CONTENTS

"To do injustice is more disgraceful than to suffer it."
—PLATO, *Gorgias*

I.

STARS

POINTS OF LIGHT HOVERED ABOVE MY NOSE.

Smaller flecks drifted in the distance.

The shining dots spread, flickering out, into the surrounding blackness.

Brightening. Dimming.

Twinkling.

Like stars.

A sky full of stars. Floating over me, all around me, as I floated out of sleep.

For a moment, no pain.

For one rare moment, peace.

My eyelids heavy, I blinked, waiting for the stars to fade, for the outline of the bed rails, the machines, the rest of the lab to appear out of the darkness. Nothing changed. I glanced to where the mirror should be, searching for the glint of the exam table in its reflection. No sheen of metal. No glow from the defibrillator's control panel, always on, nearby. Nothing. My eyelids fluttered, then drooped. A fog pushed down, clouding my head. My mind fuzzy—fuzzier than when I last woke—I sank into a cocoon between wake and sleep.

And still stars twinkled.

Everywhere.

I swayed, wrapped in a thick haze, among them.

In deathly quiet. A faint beat, thudding slow. Unsteady.

Thump-thump.

Pulsing up, from my chest. Pulsing louder.

Faster.

My heart beat. Why so loud?

Why no beep from the heart rate monitor?

I wasn't in the lab. They'd done it again. Must have drugged me through my IV. My eyes shot open, the thumps quickened, drumming in my ears. Where was I? Another hallucination?

No. Though it was much too loud, the pulsing, pounding—racing of my heart—was no hallucination.

They'd moved me again.

I widened my eyes, resisting the fog, every inch of me struggling to wake. Really wake. In blackness. Calm down. You're okay. Focus.

On my back, I floated.

Wet. Oh god, I was wet.

I shivered.

I tried to sit up. Couldn't.

My hands, arms, chest were caught in an unyielding web.

Heavy.

Sodden.

Trapped. Trapped in water. My heart burned, throbbing. The pounding exploded, hammering in my head. Amplified, held in—by? Water. Oh god. Water, jostling in the shell of my ear, flowing down my neck. Water everywhere.

Stay calm. It's just something new they're trying. You have to stay calm and learn more.

I relaxed a bit.

The web loosened, freeing me to float again.

I tensed, and it pulled back. My ribs ached. I willed what was left of my legs to work, thrashing out. My ankles jerked; my spine wrenched. Tied up, hand, foot, head, body. I swore my eyes were open, but the stars disappeared. Then reappeared, twinkling again. I clenched my eyes shut, opened them wide. Blinked.

A wall of darkness. No stars. Then a few drifted in, exploding into many.

I repeated the test, waiting.

Blackness first.

Then bits of light, fading in and out. Just like they had in that room. That tiny, pitch-black room. These stars, too, must be my nerves firing randomly. In total darkness, they offered me false light.

Sensory deprivation again. An isolation chamber. A *different* isolation chamber.

Now Nurse Violet's words made sense. Three days ago— maybe four?—I'd woken during the blood draw, the needle burning. Nurse Violet turned toward one of the speakers in the wall. "No vein. Should I try another central line?"

"No. Can't risk another infection." The speaker crackled. "Too dehydrated?"

"More than ever."

Muffled words, as if whoever was on the other end had turned away.

"We need baselines." I barely caught the new voice.

The first voice screeched back, computer-altered, tinny. "Try again."

Nurse Violet did, and I whimpered. Her one eye widened. The sunken pocket of skin where her other should've been stretched, and she'd dropped the syringe to the tray with a clatter. "I'll give her a subcutaneous infusion first." She'd tugged my gown, slid me to the edge of the bed, and scooped me into the wheelchair, whispering, "Charlie." I'd thought I was imagining it, wishing for her to speak to me again, like when I first arrived. So, I'd let my eyelids droop, drifting back into unconsciousness, where I could be free of the pain.

"Charlie," she'd breathed again, right into my ear. I'd wished she would use my real name. How long had it been since anyone called me Ellis?

As she wheeled me across the lab, I'd forced myself to answer the only safe way—looking at the mirrored wall, avoiding the figure slouched in the chair, as if never seeing myself would negate what I'd become. I glanced at her reflection instead, her lanky body hunched to push me.

Her thin lips had barely moved. "It'll be okay, Charlie."

I still didn't understand why they called me that, but I understood they watched. Always. Cameras encased behind black domes in the corners stood sentry. Judging by her glances to the mirror, they must watch behind the silver surface too. "Don't be scared." Nurse Violet had tucked her heart-shaped chin into her chest, her hair sweeping low, concealing her young face. They must have been listening. She'd risked murmuring, "It'll be different. But you'll be okay." Her hand slid to my shoulder. "He promised." Her fingers trembled.

Even without her fear, I'd known better than to ask what would be different or who "he" was. Just more questions to torture me, lying awake after they turned out the lights at night.

Not that I could ever tell day from night in the lab, much less in here, in this new, endless blackness. Couldn't see. Couldn't move. Couldn't hear anything except my heart. Like before. The old panic seeped inside. My heart hammered, pounding like the grenades had that night. My mind flashed to the swirling depths of the pool, the dark waves swelling as I sank deeper and deeper.

I shivered.

No. Not like the pool. That was before this place, the last thing before. Here—in whatever this place is—they're in control.

They're in control, and they don't want me dead.

This is like that isolation room. Not the pool.

Still, my empty stomach ached with that remembered helplessness, stirring up acid. I forced myself to repeat Nurse Violet's assurance. *It'll be okay.* She must've meant, *The water will be okay.* Someone had promised her the water would be okay.

Be calm. If I could breathe, it wasn't like the pool. Breathing meant my head floated above the surface.

Keep breathing.

That's it.

Even if the water's there, all around, ready to flood in, suffocate me with its weight. *No!* Not again.

Oh god. I panted. In, out, in, out. Calm down. Save energy. Your heart can't handle this. Oh no. The air over my mouth thickened, heavy with warmth. Dampness hit my tongue, and a copper taste soured it. Moisture mixed with blood, dried blood from my cracked lips, and beaded around my mouth. Even as a breeze cooled the tip of my nose. Dense air swirled over my face, smothering it as crisp air cut under my nose.

Something trapped my breath and simultaneously wafted in fresh oxygen. How had I not noticed? Now my panting made it impossible to miss, this *something*, reflecting my breath. Gripping my cheeks, pinching my forehead, cradling my chin. Not more restraints.

A mask?

Yes. They'd fitted me with a breathing mask while unconscious. When they put me here… underwater.

They drugged me and put me *under* the water.

I struggled against the restraints. Acid blazed up my chest.

Don't panic! Nurse Violet said I'd be okay. Because they don't want me dead… Do they? My chin trembled, shaking the mask. The hose that fed it stirred the water. A current caressed my body, stroking my skin. Skin? They'd put me in here naked? Another tremble of my chin. More currents skimmed my sides, to my toes, whirling around to my face. Like tipping a snow globe, jostling a fish tank. Dizzy. I felt dizzy, even with the fog of drugs lifting. Dull pain crept in. My head drifted, light, but bound. The familiar tug of sensors pulled at my scalp where my hair used to be.

My beautiful hair. Gone.

The price of keeping secrets.

This was meant to break me, right? Just like that tiny room. How many days would they keep me here? A shudder stirred inside me. It tore out. Without willing it, I thrashed again. Convulsing. The restraints slowed my movements. Would this break me? Pain radiated in my chest, below my left breast. My heart wouldn't make it. Not this time. I didn't want to die in the water.

You're not dying in the water! You're getting through this. The pain means you're alive, and awake for once. You're not dying. Stop thinking like this. Like you're crazy. Talking to yourself. Calm down.

Slowly my body quieted, giving in to exhaustion.

My skin prickled, fear turning to cold goose-pimples. So cold, even with sweet warmth from the heated water tickling my toes. That was good. Great, even. Because if I was finally awake and aware enough to take all this in, then maybe I could figure a way out.

2
VOICES

WHIR.

The sound pulled me from sleep. *Whir, whir* echoed, above and below me. A faint mechanical noise. Steady and soothing. It must have been there before, but my heart had been too loud. The thought of my heart sharpened its beats. I pushed out the sound to focus on the whirring. It was easy.

Emboldened by my improved control, which I hoped might help me figure a way out of here, I focused harder. *Whir, whir* over my feet. Pumps, pushing in warm currents. *Whir, whir* under my head. More pumps, pulling out colder water. The whirs melted into separate frequencies, as satisfying as music. Like falling asleep to the tinkling of Mom's music box after she opened it to put her great-grandmother's ring away.

Desperate for more knowledge, my ears searched outside this tiny space, and footsteps walked right out of the humming and into my consciousness.

Thud, thud, thud, against concrete. Not the lab's tile floor.

The sound of footfalls sharpened, coming into focus. How could I hear them so clearly? Was I hallucinating? Or was I trapped in a coma like Nurse Violet had warned the speaker voices about?

Real or imaginary, the steps bounced off enclosing walls. A hall. I concentrated, and the volume increased. Two sets of steps. Someone in heavy dress shoes walked slowly. Deliberately. *Tap.*

Tap. Tap. Confident, older. Firm, thudding boots—youthful, energetic—overtook the dress shoes.

"Dr. Craig?" I was sure this was the younger, though his voice was deep and world-weary. "Got a moment?"

The scrape of a shoe pivoting. "Jackson." The older man's tone was warm, though his voice was unremarkable. "Always a moment for you. What do you need?"

"Sir, it's not my job." The young man exhaled a measured breath. "But since I arrived, I can't help but notice."

"Notice what?" They stood, unmoving, in the hall.

"The way they treat the detainees."

Detainees, plural? My head spun. They had others like me here? What if I was really overhearing my captors for the first time? Not filtered speaker voices with strange questions, badgering, lies, but really them. Was Dr. Craig or Jackson the mysterious "he" Nurse Violet referred to?

"I know we've done worse." The young man cleared his throat, a forced, uneasy sound. "When we've had to. But here, some things don't make sense. Whatever the mission."

"You've come to me with this first?"

"Of course." Jackson sounded surprised.

"Good. In this business, the wrong question raises doubt. I warned you it would be a demanding post." The older man's tone remained gentle despite the reprimand. "And I shouldn't say it, but I've had concerns myself. Even knowing the mission."

For a moment, silence.

"This damn program," the older man grumbled. "Officially, I'm just an inter-agency observer." Inter-agency observer? "But now that I'm on site, nothing untoward will go on."

"It's just—" I barely caught Jackson's lowered, husky words. "The water." Water? The water *I'm* in? "I mean"—his boot tapped on concrete—"she's so weak." The last word faded into a sigh. He sounded concerned… about me?

"She'll be okay. Whatever they want from her there. I'll go now, make sure of it."

The tapping slowed. "Thank you, sir." The tapping ceased. "I needed to hear that. It's just, well, she's… She's not eating." So, it *was* me he was worrying about. "Struggling."

"Jackson?"

The young man stuttered. "I mean, no one seems to know why."

"I know what you're trying to say. She's declining fast, despite their efforts. I'm bypassing them. If there's something that can be done, I'll do it. For mercy's sake, as well as the project."

"Thank you, sir." A long breath passed through his lips. "I shouldn't have doubted you." His boots planted, scuffing the floor.

"Just refocus on your job. Surveillance." The older man's tone hardened only a moment. "I mean, it was smart befriending the head tech." This place needed a head tech? "With security so lax. But you're distracted."

"The girl's distracted me, yes." The young man swallowed, an awkward sound. "But Scott? Just a friend."

"You always did have a soft spot for that sort." The old man huffed. "You've been wasting time talking to your other friend. Don't make me regret pulling those strings."

"No, sir. I'm grateful you did."

"Then focus. Surveillance. Leave the mission to me." Was I imagining the soft clap of this Dr. Craig's hand on Jackson's shoulder? Was I imagining this whole conversation?

The hallucinations, even the worst, had never been this detailed.

The footsteps resumed. They sounded as real as the whirring pumps. The steps parted. The younger man, Jackson, continued on his course, but the older doctor changed his, coming toward me.

Jackson… was concerned about me. Dr. Craig's response felt like proof that they wanted me alive? But "they" sounded much more structured, much more bureaucratic, than who I'd thought was holding me.

Distracted, the sounds of both men vanished.

No footsteps. No voices. This time, I really had lost them. I was all alone, back in the water. My body sagged beneath the web. My hearing redirected to the sounds of the tank. *Thump-thump. Whir.* I strained to hear more. *THUMP-THUMP. WHIR.* Louder. Blasting like a foghorn. I screamed in my head. My hands jerked, pulling at restraints, wanting to plug my ears. I focused on tuning the noises out, as if I could turn them down. They needed to stop.

THUMP-THUMP. WHIR.

Please stop.

Slowly they softened. That's better, just a bit more. When I commanded it, the sounds obeyed. *This was insane.* Hearing my heartbeat and distant voices. Controlling their volume on command. All while stuck underwater.

Underwater...

It must have something to do with my relic.

How? I'd lost my guidestone in the pool. And despite Uncle Alec's best efforts, I'd almost stopped believing "my" relic—the water relic—actually existed. Or if it did, that I could do anything with it, much less everything prophesied. Still, if underwater hearing was one helpful thing from the crazy path Mom and Dad chose for us, I'd take it.

I focused again. My heart, the pumps. I had to hear past them.

Bubbles, popping within the warmth swirling over my feet.

Outside, machines beeping, switches clicking. More distant, fingers tapping on a keyboard. Farther away, clinking of metal, rapping on wood, rattles of indistinct movement. Voices, running together. A cacophony of noises and babbling. My ears pulsed; my skull ached. Slowly, I focused.

At last, I had some semblance of control here.

As naturally as shifting my eyes around one of my painted landscapes, I moved through this prison, room by room, using sound as my guide. Where the voices were strongest, chairs squeaked, papers rustled, and overhead fans purred. Was it hot out? I was taken in summer, but that must've been months ago.

Beyond the voices, the confusion of activity, the faint stirrings of machines, in the uttermost distance, the scream of a bird. A hawk? Filtering in through an open door, a cracked window. The bird wouldn't get me out of the water. I returned to the voices.

"Security Group Two, report with current status. Over." A new man. Young, but he spoke with an authoritative, clipped tone like he'd already reached the end of his patience.

"Roger. Security Group Two, reporting. On the mountain. North Quadrant secure. No sign of the anomaly, over." This voice had the rasp of a smoker.

"I knew it was a faulty heat sensor."

"Sensors always on the fritz."

"Leave it to AJ to waste everyone's time," Mr. Impatient growled. A pause. "Local Group Three, supplies at the main gate. Cafeteria shipment. New saline for Charlie too. Need it stat. Who wants to take a tunnel run? Over."

Clues. Finally!

A gruff, older voice spoke up, "Shipment's large. Better attach trailers to the UTVs." Hope quickened my breath. I'd driven an UTV before. Uncle Alec had taught me. My legs stirred against their restraints, spasming and bursting with pain. Would the muscles, atrophied, still be strong enough to drive?

"Control forgot the extra receiver battery again," Smoker groaned.

"Roger that," said a chipper, female voice. "I'll radio Test-Site HQ about scheduling a Janet flight. Who's meeting the next shift by the airstrip?"

Clues melded together, forming a picture of how massive this operation must be. So many people involved in my imprisonment, holding others like me.

Even if I could slip away, crawl to a UTV undetected, where would I go? This place was remote, if it took flights and airstrips to get people and supplies in and out. I wasn't up against a few humans influenced by the Summum Malum or a desperate alternate race group after the relics, like Uncle Alec had warned us about, either. It seemed the government—*my* government—was doing this. Why? Did they know about the relics? How? My heart jumped. I'd kept my vow to never mention them. And other alternates would too, right? And wouldn't the government want me free, if they knew what I was supposed to do?

A sharpness amplified a nearby voice. "I'm the MD in this room." The familiar, nasal voice of Dr. Hurst sent a painful shudder through my atrophied muscles. "And I'm telling you, *Doctor* Craig, we've pushed Charlie hard enough." Craig? The older man from the hall. Jackson's confidant.

"Stop calling her that. She's a girl." *Yeah. Tell him, Dr. Craig.* "Her name's Ellis." For an instant, my heart beat easier. "Ellis Zephyrus." My name brought a smile, squeezing my cheeks into the mask. How long since I'd smiled? "Besides, you may play doctor during interrogations, but you haven't practiced in years. I'm telling you, this'll get positive results."

"We've got a perfectly good isolation suite." Dr. Hurst sniffed. "Fully instrumented, high and dry. Didn't produce a thing." A faint scraping sound, like when Dr. Hurst scratched the bald spot on the back of his head. "Other than a vomiting fit." I flinched. "Of course, she probably would've done that anyway." A whoosh as his arm fell to his side. He omitted that he'd left me covered in my puke, until what seemed like days later. "Yet, you *have* to have this?" Dr. Hurst scoffed.

Dr. Craig was responsible for the water torture? If so, he'd lied to the young man—Jackson—in the hall. Or he really thought he was doing me a favor, keeping me here?

"You're calling that room an isolation suite?" Dr. Craig's voice maintained that same unfluctuating calm. "That was a tricked-out broom closet. You just wanted to scare her into talking."

"Our orders are to extract information. By any means." Hurst bit out the words. "Anything for the program. There are no guidelines."

"Your damn program." Even Dr. Craig's curse stayed cool and

collected. "This is bigger than Psy-Ops." A Psy-Ops program? "She needs to regain her strength. And don't worry about the cost. I've spoken with the Secretary's office. It won't come from your budget."

"Screw the cost. I'm no goddamn bean counter." A loud bang. "The IV's barely helping. She's beyond dehydrated. Her veins barely functioning. Her heart weak. At this rate, she'll be dead in days."

"Not if you follow my protocol. That's precisely why I requested the—"

"Save it," snarled Dr. Hurst. "After the last report, what happened to Bravo, it's not happening like this."

"Stop with the code. She was just a girl too, right? Kit Katana."

"Whatever. You weren't here. After what happened to Bravo, I'm not losing Charlie. Especially not over your wild theories." What happened to Bravo? To Kit, I corrected myself.

"My 'wild theories' might have saved the Katana girl, too, had I been here. Ellis is perfectly safe in the water. More than safe. Warm. Hydrated. If her veins will take it. I had that tank specially built. And maybe… maybe you're right, she's dying. If we can't fix her fluid intake and nutrient deficiency, we can at least learn more."

"Hmph. We've barely learned a thing. This won't be different." Dr. Hurst paused. A softer bang. "Just monitor her, dammit. Be careful."

"Of course."

The men lapsed into silence.

Beep. Pause. *Beep,* over keyboard taps.

Long pause.

Beep. In time with my heart. My shivers picked up. "And get your boy under control. Let Test-Site security do their job." Dr. Hurst's voice lost its sharpness, turning wispy, more nasally.

"What?"

"A.J. almost flipped." A third voice. Clipped. Hard. Mr. Impatient. "An animal tripped the perimeter sensors." A chuckle. "I thought he was going to hunt it down, use those skills you keep hyping."

"What kind of animal?" Dr. Craig asked.

"God knows. Just tell him to cool it," Mr. Impatient griped. I pictured him closer to my age, wearing a classic antagonist's sneer. "Last year, a bunch of bighorns wandered in from the Sheep Mountains. Had Weapons' boys running around with their hair on fire." He snorted. "Dr. Hurst runs a tighter ship."

"I certainly do," Dr. Hurst piped up.

"When? When did this happen?" Dr. Craig kept his cool but seemed fixated on the incident.

"I don't know, early this morning," Mr. Impatient answered. "You're missing the point. Remind A.J. who's in charge."

"Don't mean to step on Security's toes, but I need to know of every perimeter breach." Dr. Craig paused, as if to let that sink in. "If *Jackson* wants to investigate, let him. We're here to help."

"Cut the crap. Whatever you and your precious A.J. are here for, it's not to help Psy-Ops," Dr. Hurst said.

"Jackson," said Dr. Craig, voice hard. "I don't much appreciate Mr. Reyes' petulant little nickname. In fact, I'd prefer you call him Special Agent Hunter."

"When he earns it," Mr. Impatient—Reyes, presumably—cut in.

"Earns it?" Dr. Craig asked, his tone hardening.

"Yes." Reyes hesitated.

"That's right. You're challenging a superior. Consider your next words carefully."

"He's not your superior. I am," Dr. Hurst jumped in.

"You were saying?" Dr. Craig asked. "You'll call Jackson by his title when he earns it?"

"Yes. But I don't see how. A.J.'s damaged. Just like the nurse."

"Jackson." A grinding, as if Dr. Craig gritted his teeth. "Special Agent Hunter can do more with his *damaged* hands than you can do with yours. He came at Command's request. So accept orders. Work with us."

"As if you're working with me," Dr. Hurst said. "I've run my own tests. The results are back on Delta. Despite what you said, we have something. Finally." I pictured a satisfied smirk. "A real subject."

Oh no, a new detainee at Hurst's sadistic disposal.

Kit—Bravo.

Me—Charlie.

The newest—Delta.

Bravo, Charlie, Delta… three of us… before whatever happened to Kit. Maybe one more before us and more planned, if they were using the phonetic alphabet Uncle Alec had taught us as part of our radio training.

"You have no idea what you're getting into," Dr. Craig said.

"Hmphh," Dr. Hurst snorted. "I'm the one tasked with figuring out this damn mind control thing. And Delta won't be weak long. Stop wasting time."

"There'll be time for your tests."

"Dammit," Dr. Hurst snapped. "That's what I'm talking about. If you cared about Psy-Ops,"—Psy-Ops, Psy-Ops… psychology something?—"you'd know Delta resists all mind control precautions." Mind control, mind control… Did they want alternate races who could control people's minds? Which meant… compelling people.

How many races could do that?

Only one that I knew of.

A dying race with two survivors. Uncle Alec—Alexander Zephyrus—and his son, Vin. Uncle Alec and Vin, who'd give me their name, protected me, Cyn, and Lana, and treated us like family. Tried to keep us safe from those who'd kill and burn every last alternate girl. A lump swelled in my throat. They were my family, maybe the only family I had left.

My chin trembled against the mask.

From the instant the flash grenades—the *government's* flash grenades—had knocked me into the pool, I'd had it totally backward. This had nothing to do with the Summum Malum, the relics' purpose, or me and my sisters' alleged "destiny." I'd been taken to learn more about Uncle Alec and Vin. They probably even thought

I was really related. Uncle Alec certainly tried to make it appear that way. But my only ability was an ultra-heightened sense of taste and a corresponding ability to survive on little food. And now, it seemed, I had ultra-heightened hearing underwater.

But none of their interrogations revolved around my eating habits; they thought I was starving myself because of the trauma. No, when I examined the pieces, it started coming together. For weeks, they'd worn masks, kept me strapped down, and treated me like a major threat, only sending in Nurse Violet, who barely looked at me with the one eye she had. Dr. Hurst stopped bringing his mask into interrogations eventually, but they still used those speakers. Because they thought they'd captured someone who could compel them, just by looking at them. Like Uncle Alec and Vin could. Now it seemed like they'd captured a real member of their race.

Thump-thump, thump-thump, my heart awoke.

But how could Uncle Alec or Vin be captured? If one of them was the new detainee, Dr. Hurst was right: they wouldn't be weak long. Once they regained their strength, maybe they could compel their way out of here, escape. Maybe… maybe I could help. I had to help. *THUMP-THUMP, THUMP-THUMP,* hammering in my ears. I lowered the volume. My heart still raced. Adrenaline brought me back to life. With renewed strength, I struggled to break free. I couldn't move.

I had to move.

I focused on my stronger right leg. Back, forth. Back, forth. Finally, all those afternoons Vin pulled me away from painting to play soccer paid off. The restraint loosened. My heel struck something hard. *Bang.* Achingly loud. I kicked harder. *Bang.* Louder.

"Dammit, do you hear that?" Dr. Hurst asked.

He could hear me? Good. I kicked again.

Bang.

If they thought I was damaging their tank, maybe they'd come get me out.

No, their attention was on a different sound. I heard it too. A rhythmic pulse far away. I fixed onto it, struggling to hone this new ability, related not to taste, but my connection to water. A blaring buzz. An alarm. Suddenly, chaos. Panicked voices, shouts for help, bellowed instructions for emergency evacuation. Heavy breaths falling on top of one another. Thundering footsteps. Running. A piercing cry. "Fire!" More running. "Where?" Another voice. "Tunnel entrance into corridors two and three, spreading fast."

My heart seized. Was I going to burn instead of drown after all?

The shouts converged and overlapped. "Call Control."—"I'll get Charlie!"—"Evacuate the Warehouse."—"Get to emergency posts." A pause. The alarm stopped, then blared again, taking on a different tone. "Power's out."

"How?"

"Fix it!"—"I'm securing Delta."—"Run, run!"—"Put it out! End of the hall!" I grabbed onto a familiar tone, deep and distinct, floating above the rest. "I can't believe it. But I know what I saw." Jackson. Faint and far away.

Like a lifeline, I hung on. I tried to picture him. Would he be a hardened soldier type, like Captain Williams in that WWII drama series Uncle Alec always watched, with cropped hair, hulking arms, and a chiseled jaw that contrasted warm eyes? Or was he a conflicted, "bad boy with a heart of gold" type, with purposefully disheveled hair, tattoos, and a crooked grin? Like Shane Greenvale in *Farraway Heights*, my all-time favorite teen fantasy show? Please be a Shane. Please be a Shane.

"No one else is going to believe me either."

"Don't worry. I believe you, Jax." Another male voice, softer, out of breath. "And playback will show it." Booted feet pummeled concrete.

"It doesn't make sense. They said transformer fire?"

"More like"—gasp—"explosion."

"Well, playback won't show a thing. Whatever happened took out the recording system." A deep exhale. "Repeater's down, radios almost useless. Take the next turn, check on the backup generator. I'm headed to the main bay."

A sharper alarm rang over the first.

"Scott?" Jackson's footsteps slowed.

"The high alert alarm. They spotted whoever you saw." Who had Jackson seen? "Come on, maybe we can nab him!"

"I have to check on someone." Jackson's voice deepened with worry. "Scott, get to the repeater. Get it back up. I'll be right behind you. Go, go."

Then only footsteps running and alarms blaring. I tensed in the web. Don't panic! One voice had said they'd get me—Charlie—away from the fire, right? Just stay with Jackson. His even breaths, his steady gait. They eased my tension. I followed each sound he made, the long draws of air passing in through his nose, out through his mouth, the brush of his arms swinging at his sides, the beat of his boots pounding the concrete, each step sounding a bit louder, as if he was coming here, to the water. Was I the "someone" he'd worried about? Maybe he'd get me out of this tank. And then… then I could convince him to take me to the new detainee. Maybe he'd help get me and Uncle Alec or Vin out of this place, and then maybe, maybe we could find some way to fix whatever was wrong with me. I could eat something. Drink something. Recover my strength.

Fantasy. Desperation.

As if I needed proof, the hawk screamed again, enticing me to join him flying free in a far-off place. I latched onto the false promise of a way out of this hell, and I lost track of Jackson.

Metal boomed, right on top of me, the sound exploding in my ears.

Someone or something had struck my tank.

For an instant, I floated in utter blackness, ears ringing.

Then the stars reappeared.

3

SOMEONE TO SAVE ME

THE STARS TWINKLED IN WILD PATTERNS, JOSTLED BY another thunderous boom above my head.

The mask muffled my scream.

A softer boom pulsed through the tank, picking up speed. A would-be rescuer hard at work? I hoped. Unable to tune out the monstrous sound, I tensed against the restraints. Calm down. Someone was coming to save me from the fire, even if it wasn't Jackson. I waited and tried to relax into the web's embrace. Metal parts ground and strained, unleashing an ear-piercing sound. Water crashed all around. The darkness lifted away. Light slivers streamed through the plastic mask covering my face. A massive lid rose. Bright rays transformed the darkness into blinding white flashes. I flinched and squeezed my eyes shut, waiting.

The grinding stopped. Something dropped into the water and swished by my shoulder. A hand? Yes. Fingertips touched my collarbone. Nails dug into my sternum, then climbed the column of my neck. Fingers fumbled under my chin, knocking the mask. Scratching, tugging, yanking.

Yanking?

"You don't need this." The cacophonous whisper overwhelmed my sensitive, submerged ears.

I don't need my mask—what!? I wasn't out yet! My eyes flashed open. Blinded by a halo of burning light, I shut them. The mask peeled away from my chin. Pungent fumes of chlorine filled my nose. Water bubbled up, gurgling over my mouth. The water swept in, tickled the skin below my nostrils. On instinct, I took one last sharp inhale, flooding my lungs with air.

The mask lifted away.

Water closed over my face.

"There. That's better." The voice lightened.

Someone was trying to drown me? *Oh my God.* My arms flailed. The restraints pulled back. I kicked with my loose foot, but nothing broke the surface. The sounds of my struggle roared in my ears.

Beyond it, a breath crooned.

Someone watching me.

Watching me drown.

My struggles slowed. I forced my eyes open. A shadow wavered through a mist of steam, hovering. A boxy figure, a basketball-shaped head, outlined in coils of moisture and blazing light. The figure's breath played across the ripples, their face inches from mine.

But I couldn't breathe! Warm water bubbled into my nose, stung my eyes. I clamped them shut. That last breath I took, how long could it last? How long had it lasted in the pool? When I thought they wanted me dead. Someone wanted me dead now! But I wasn't losing consciousness like in the pool. I had my wits. I pulled, twisted. Each attempt was weaker than the last as my attacker breathed across the water. Evenly. Calmly.

I kicked again with my right foot. The strap moved but held firm. I drew it back, building momentum. My leg barely floated forward this time. The adrenaline was gone. Nothing in my belly to fuel me, not even the tiny bits of food I ate growing up. But I had a mission now, even if it was nearly hopeless. I had to try to reach Uncle Alec or Vin, whichever was Delta. What air remained had to free me.

I thrashed again. Nothing.

My lungs tingled.

Not too bad yet. Stay calm.

The mask floated, hissing over my face.

The air hose was filling with water, like I would be soon.

The plastic dipped, sank, and pressed onto my sunken belly. My chest throbbed, burning. The impulse to breathe in intensified. My body wilted into the web. I tried to listen, connecting to anything above the water.

Breath on the surface.

A faint crackle.

The hiss of a radio. "Can't hold—" mumbled words "—too much… one, the… walked through fire." Could one of the alt races do that? Of course, Cyn was supposed to bond with the fire relic, but Cyn must be dead. She wouldn't have left me so long if she was alive.

"Repeat," demanded the looming figure.

More mumbling. A few garbled words, "Ignited… over twenty… They're all trapped… wall of fire."

"Hold position! I need to observe and assess."

I opened my eyes as the lowering lid obscured the boxy shadow. My hearing weakened, but a sliver of light remained. Then footsteps rang on metal. Clang, clang, clang… silence.

Whoever it was, was gone.

The urge to breathe was overwhelming, despite knowing the consequence. Bracing for the water's weight, I screamed in a last-ditch effort for help. The stale air left my lungs, compounding the urge to breathe to unbearable heights. Somehow, I clamped my lips before water entered.

Silence.

I heard so little now.

I screamed louder, *AHHH!* I clamped my lips again. Not fast enough. Water flooded my mouth. Bubbles streamed from my nose, brushing my cheeks, floating away.

Silence.

Even my final scream had seemed silent. No reverberation.

I knew what was coming. I'd been here before, at the bottom of a pool. Instinct took over, and I inhaled. Water hit the back of my throat and raced to fill my lungs. It plunged deep, and my mouth fell open, choking. Pressure built in my lungs, and I sank like the mask. A spasm, which would've been a cough if I'd had any air, racked my chest. Then a gurgle, a slow splutter, pushed out the last trace of breath.

And it felt better with just the water inside.

Warmer and heavier than I'd been in so long.

My lungs didn't even burn anymore. Strange.

Maybe I was blacking out, like I had when I sank in the pool. Or maybe this was just what drowning felt like. Surprisingly pain-less. A silent way to go. Pleasant. Lazy. Like sipping a glass of iced tea sat out in the sun too long, while sunbathing by the pool's edge.

Heavy steps clanged. The hearing I'd lost in my fight against drowning returned. I strained to hear more. Shouts in the distance. I could make out each voice now.

"Who's got eyes on the big guy?"

"Don't know, but if he comes in after her, we'll be ready."

"I'll go after her."

"Hold that. I just need to rewire this last piece." Jackson's friend! Was Jackson there?

I heard even better filled with water, when I didn't resist it, which was crazy.

The closest steps quickened, drawing nearer. A thud, as if some-one had dropped to their knees. A gasp, right above my ear. "What the—?" A deep, intense voice.

Jackson. He wasn't with his friend after all. He had come!

Jackson's arm, contoured with muscle, cut through the gap of light left in the lid. I struggled to keep my eyes open as his shoulder wedged against the lid, inching it open. His hand reached down, three fingers jutting out. A strange, black tattoo swirled in his palm. Despite missing a ring finger and pinkie, he made short work of the tangled mask straps and threw them to the side. Next he wrenched the mask off the hose and threw it out. His arm returned, and two fingertips found the small of my back. His palm drew me up. I strained, trying to help. Useless. The web dragged me back down.

His warm hand brushed my ribcage, searching. He tugged at one wrist, then the other. Nothing budged. The water in my chest slowed, settling. Too heavy now. My eyelids slid shut. My body slackened, lifeless.

I heard water trickling onto the surface. The faint *thump-thump* of my weakened heart. Nothing else.

Where had Jackson gone?

I forced my eyes open, using my last iota of strength to swivel my head, search for his outline above. Nothing.

Had he given up? Left me for dead. Oh god, did I look dead?

Help, I mouthed.

It made no noise. I had no air. I couldn't even whimper.

Help. I tried to raise a hand, let him know I was alive, but only sank deeper in the web.

I don't want to die.

Come back. Please.

A metallic screech assaulted my ears. My eyes cracked open. Light gleamed through dancing waves.

Jackson had thrown the lid all the way back. He hadn't left me. His shadow appeared above—taller, broader than the other had been.

Help, not too late. My jaw gaped wide open without sound. I flickered my eyelids for proof of life. As if answering, his arm swept into the water. His large hand enclosed mine as he plunged in, up to the waist. His other hand—missing two fingers as well—was closed around a black handle. A flick of the thumb, and a knife blade, long and jagged, popped free. A dull snap near my wrist. My right arm drifted free of the webbing, but I had no strength to move it. A warmth grasped my left hand. *Snap.* The light changed as his silhouette shifted toward my calves—*snap, snap*—then returned to my chest. My legs rose, and straps around my neck and chest fell away.

He pulled at my shoulders and waist, wrenching me from netting, bumping my hip into the wall of the tank. One arm scooped under my knees, and he lifted. Water poured off me. Air chilled my skin, but I couldn't breathe it. Couldn't take anything into my lungs. My side hit something hard. No air.

He turned me on my stomach, crushing my chest against frigid metal.

My lungs still weren't burning. Insane.

I'd somehow survived drowning, and it hadn't hurt. But I was out of the water now, and I still wasn't breathing.

A hand smacked between my shoulder blades. Smacked again. Water gushed up from my chest, then forced its way past my throat to spill from my lips. Drops splashed back, warm on my face. I was warm inside. A good sign? Or was it just the heated water of the tank? I coughed. More water. I coughed again. Air. I really wasn't going to drown. After the coughing and gasping came the stinging, as my lungs struggled to rediscover the air.

Warm hands shifted me onto my back. My head fell to the side. I squinted, glimpsing a dim vastness spread out below, cluttered with shadows, streaked with harsh, pale amber lighting, interspersed with flickering red. The huge panels of fluorescent bulbs hanging from the ceiling were out. The light came from somewhere along the walls. Emergency lighting. Crates and shelves materialized from the dim. Stacks of black cases, like huge toolboxes. Or massive gun cases. Huddled shapes draped with canvas sheets and plastic tarps. I lay on a metal platform perched between a domed ceiling and the floor.

A broad chest, plastered with a soaked green t-shirt, moved over me, blocking the view. Knees scooted in and nudged my side. A head tipped toward my chest, an ear rested across my left breast, and for an instant, there was silence. But with warmth pressing into it, my heart took on rhythms of life again. *Thump-thump.*

Long pause.

Thump-thump.

A face moved over mine.

Thump-thump, Thump-thump. Water caught in my throat.

Jackson was striking. The same black tattoo marking his right hand swirled at his right temple. Short, black hair, dark skin, bold eyebrows, an angular chin. This was really him? Jackson? Special Agent Hunter? He looked too young. Too captivating. Too determined. Too much like Shane Greenvale. Like I'd made him up—a handsome, tattooed knight to come rescue me. Yet he had to be real. I hadn't gotten out of the tank on my own. It had to be Jackson, even if he looked barely older than me. I'd recognized his voice, my hearing strong when he'd arrived. His uniform was different from the others I'd seen—his t-shirt stamped with a logo of an eagle, globe, and anchor over the left breast; camouflaged cargo pants with patches of brown, green, beige. Dog tags hung on a chain around his neck, dangling over my face:

HUNTER
A. J. O NEG
USMC M
323 77 5190
NO PREF

He leaned away. His dark eyes scanned my body. His lips mouthed words I strained to hear, catching only the muffled pulse of the alarms. In the water, I'd heard so much. Was I deaf now, back in the air?

God, oh god, he was speaking to me. I couldn't hear anything except for the faint alarms.

He pressed his lips into a hard line and tilted his head. His right eyebrow rose, drawing the tattoo up with it. Was I breathing? I thought so.

He glanced between my chest and mouth, as though my breath wasn't deep enough to tell.

I parted my lips, preparing to speak, but my throat burned. Far from healthy, drowning had made it worse. But I had to speak. Just two words: *I'm okay.*

I started to form the first and choked. I sputtered and struggled for air.

His jaw quivered, ticking a nervous tempo. He shifted to sit by my shoulder and slipped his hands under my head. His fingers brushed a sore at the back of my skull.

I flinched.

He mouthed a curse, then carefully moved his hands away from the damage and cupped the sides of my head. His fingers brushed right above my ears, where suction-cup sensors still clung, and gently lifted my head into his lap. His mouth moved several more times. His eyes softened around the edges as he stared into mine. Sadness clouded them, accentuating the dark rings of exhaustion beneath. His unguarded look and gentle grip shot a signal through me: relax.

Everything about him said I would be all right.

Though I knew it was another fantasy, born of desperation, I sank deeper into his hold.

His lips pressed together, a debate playing out behind his eyes. Then his mouth moved toward mine, its destination and intent crystal clear. Though I knew he meant to offer life-giving oxygen, a crazy, foolish, yet powerful thought hit me.

I'd never kissed a boy before.

When I'd dreamt of what I'd do if I ever got out of this place, I ignored all the responsibilities Mom and Dad had forced on us, everything I was supposed to be. Instead, I imagined, as I always had, living like people on TV do. I'd turned eighteen in here. Locked up. Never been on a date. Never been kissed. If I died in this place, would mouth-to-mouth resuscitation count? Would this be the closest I ever came?

Using his left hand to pinch my nose closed, he gripped my shoulder with his right. His eyes fell shut. His mouth slanted over mine, and he breathed into me. For an instant, the air flowed to the back of my throat and filled my lungs, then nothing. Again, he breathed in, his nostrils flaring. His dark cheeks hollowed as he blew air I didn't feel.

But it was there. Its sweet taste hit my tongue—sugary notes overlaid with a sharp, herbal quality. Ginger.

So complex, so satisfying—my first real taste in weeks beyond the empty, dry bitterness of my own mouth or the tang of blood from my lips. I almost whined when he pulled back, his eyes fluttering.

His left hand dropped from my nose to my arm. His eyes bounced around the swell above my breasts, as if trying to figure out if I was okay.

My chest struggled to rise and fall.

He stared at my chest, his ears flushing a bashful red, even as his hand clenched in his lap. He frowned at the staggered rhythm of my shallow breathing, hitching between each minimal inhale. His head jerked in an awkward nod, as if convincing himself of something. Then he swallowed hard before leaning in, eyes closing as his lips pressed against mine once more. That same gingery taste burst through my mouth, and I drank it in greedily.

4
BLOOD

GINGER. SUGARED GINGER. INTENSE. SPARKING OFF MY overactive taste buds like miniature fireworks. More satisfying than a forkful of the modest, under-seasoned dinners Uncle Alec made special for me.

His lips pressing against mine was the only sensation strong enough to cut through the flavors sinking into me. He coaxed another breath into my mouth. Part of it flowed toward my lungs, and the rest spread out, melting like caramel on my tongue.

My next independent exhale felt stronger, flowed evenly. I should say or do something to tell him he could stop. But I needed this more than pride. His heat and his taste, coming on the tail of hypothermia and starvation, brought me to life again.

Ginger. Sugar. On that next breath, a yearning spread up my chest. It swelled into an ache at the back of my throat. As instinctively as coming up for air during a swim, my lips sought his, pressing back.

He stiffened, and his eyes popped open.

My own eyes fluttered closed.

His fingers slipped from my nose to cup my shoulder, and he withheld his breath, frozen over me as my mouth widened against his.

Without thought, I pulled his bottom lip into my mouth.

He gasped, his taste flooding me again.

Like sneaking one of Lana's gingerbread men right out of the oven at Christmastime, before she'd adorned them with intricate icing. The flavors danced along my taste buds, spicy and sweet, stirring up more than memories. Hunger—absent for so long, now insistent and feral. My front teeth clamped over his bottom lip. My stomach growled, rumbling under my bottom rib. Months of gnawing hunger swelled up, aching after weeks of absence. My body had abandoned hunger pangs, giving up, beyond starved, beyond drained, beyond hope. With fresh hope, the urge to sustain myself, the will to live, returned.

My stomach convulsed, and my teeth bit down.

A thick liquid filled my mouth. Silky. Warm. How long since I'd been able to eat or drink anything? Instinctually, I swallowed.

Tangy. Metallic. Copper.

Blood. Oh God. Not my blood. His. I'd tasted mine so much from my cracked lips. His tasted sweeter. Delicious and mellow, like wild honey, yet my body didn't reject it, as it had always rejected any overly flavorful morsel. Sometimes even water was too bitter—but I'd stayed healthy because I absorbed abnormal amounts of nutrition from very little. Until I'd gotten to this place and couldn't eat or drink a thing. But as I swallowed, a bit of liquid flowed into me, trickling down, and my body allowed it, welcomed it.

He pushed on my shoulders, drawing back, but his lip was locked between mine. He couldn't move. Neither could I as, all at once, something else, something almost intangible, flooded over me. Emotions. Stark and cold. What?

Loneliness. I shivered.

Blinding rage. My arms tensed.

Mom, Dad, Cyn, they'd always told me I needed to control my emotions. Here in this place, I thought I'd succeeded bottling them tight. What was happening to me?

Regret. Shame. Guilt. Pain exploded in my stomach, an old, forgotten symptom of self-loathing. That bit of hate I felt when I looked in the mirror, wanting to be better, smarter, prettier, obsessing over my looks in hopes they would make me confident like my parents wanted me to be, strong like my sisters, Uncle Alec, and Vin needed me to be.

I felt all that now, in the span of a heartbeat. Coming from him?

His fingers moved to my jaw. My hands shook, trying to wrap around my waist, the dark emotions tearing at me. *Ahhh.*

As quick as they came, they faded. Thank the Priestesses. Better, new emotions replaced them in an equally swift wave. Warm adoration. Acceptance. Respect. Love. Familiar but distinctly not mine, they rinsed out the darkness, swept away the self-loathing. Love, palpable love (For a friend? Authority figure? Both?), spread comforting heat through my chest. As if Cyn had just hugged me.

God, what would I give if Cyn could hug me?

Using what had to be borrowed affection, I let myself imagine that she was, that Cyn's strong arms embraced me, that her soft curls brushed my face. That she whispered comforting words, about how we'd get Uncle Alec or Vin out of here and get to all the relics if our sisters couldn't, together. Tears clouded my eyes. My shoulders shook. My lips held on, ignoring Jackson's coaxing squeeze to my cheeks, begging for release. His feelings melded with mine, summoning those remembered sensations.

But how was this possible? His emotions in my brain? Insane, and yet, the questions I really wanted answered were, Why did he feel such shame? And who did he love so much?

He squeezed my shoulders next, and when I looked into his watering eyes, I released. But not before I swallowed one more time.

As he jerked back, my heart thudded in my chest, beating with more ease, picking up speed. Steady. Strong. With each beat, with each swallow, energy poured through my veins. My legs shook against the platform. For the first time in weeks, I felt alive. Then reality sank in. I'd drank his blood.

I gagged.

He'd shoved my shoulders down against his leg. My neck

strained over his knee. My throat shook, releasing a whimper I didn't hear. What was wrong with my ears?

Using his hands on the platform, he propelled himself away.

My head rolled off his lap.

He scooted back until he hitched against the outside of the tank, wrapped in thick, white padding. He leaned against it and shook his head. He didn't understand what had just happened. Neither did I.

My lips twitched. My throat ached. "I—I'm sorry." My voice wavered, out of practice. Worse, it sounded echoey and muted, like when I wore earplugs while Uncle Alec taught us to shoot. "I'm sorry I bit you."

He pressed his large body deeper into the padding and wiped his palms on his cargo pants. His upper torso was soaked, his t-shirt clinging to his chest. A camouflaged button-down shirt lay just feet away, buttons scattered around it, as if he'd torn it off while running to me. A small radio lay by a pocket. A cell peeked out from another. He glanced at both, his fingers twitching as though desperate to use them. Maybe to check on his friend, maybe to get out of here, maybe to warn people about how crazy I'd become. *What had I done?* He'd just saved my life. Sure, he was one of them, part of the program that put me in that tank. But he was also the only person who'd bothered to come for me, pulling me from a watery grave and giving me air, and I'd attacked him, bit him, swallowed his blood. Swallowed his blood?!

God, had he noticed that part?

What was wrong with me? What was wrong with my voice? My ears. Could he hear me? "I'm sorry," I shouted. My voice rang in my head. "Jackson, right? I didn't mean to hurt you." My throat throbbed.

He stiffened and cemented his jaw into firm lines. They broke as his mouth parted and blood seeped from his bottom lip. He mouthed several words, but I only caught "Jackson." He frowned. He was asking how I knew his name?

How could I explain?

He mouthed faster, lifting his chin. More blood seeped out. I had to do something—anything—to show him I wasn't some sort of animal, a nutcase. I needed him to help me, needed him to know that I was sincerely grateful and that the bite had been an accident.

Had it been? I'd swallowed his blood easily enough. What had this place done to me?

I sat up easily. Where had the energy come from? His blood?

I licked my lips, tasting it again. Without thought, I gulped it down. My throat calmed. My chest lifted. My breath deepened. I licked again.

His eyes widened.

Oh no. I wiped my mouth, trying to remove any traces of his blood.

His fingers dug into his thighs.

"I'm sorry!" I crawled closer and stretched out my fingers for one of his wrists, my arm shaking.

He let me take hold.

I sat back on my heels, pulling his hand toward me, and smoothed out the tension in his fingers, trying to communicate my regret.

His gaze wouldn't meet mine.

I gulped in a strained breath. Though I couldn't hear it, I must've made some sound.

His face softened. His dark eyes twitched toward my mouth, burning with an intensity I couldn't read.

I inhaled sharply, my chest lifting, drawing his eyes for an instant. Then he tugged his hand out of my grasp and plucked up his knife from the platform. I jerked back, making fists on the metal platform. *Enemy! One of them!* roared through my synapses.

He slipped it into a leather band strapped to his leg, and I breathed again. A thick belt with a canteen and a gun—it looked like Uncle Alec's Glock—hung low on narrow hips. He faced me again, his mouth moving fast, angry, questioning me, his focus on his boots.

He wanted some sort of answer, but though I strained to hear, there was only silence. Complete and utter silence. Outside, just the faint pulse of the alarms. Inside, just the rush of my own breath. *Why can't I hear him?*

My fingertips found my ears. Malleable barriers were jammed deep into each. I wiggled both earplugs loose, and sounds poured back in. Both the fire alarm and the high alert alarm blared from the farthest corner of the massive room.

Jackson's radio hissed and spat out, "Jackson, where are you? I'm back in the main tunnel. Primary fire's contained. But I can't get the backup generator online."

I dropped the earplugs to the platform.

His breath caught. "You can hear me now?" He watched the earplugs roll away instead of looking at me.

I nodded but wasn't sure he saw it.

He reached for the radio. "Scott, thanks for trying with the generator. Maybe you can get the repeater online. I'll be there soon."

"Got it, Jackson. Over. Out."

He set the radio down, and his eyes flew to a spot over my shoulder. "Are you okay?"

"Yes." I cleared my throat.

"Sure?"

"Yes, I'm—" I coughed.

His gaze wavered toward me, a hand drifting to the canteen on his belt. "I'd offer you a drink, but you can't drink it?" He slid the canteen out. "You've been in there for hours. Maybe you should try?"

I'd drank his blood, but water? My stomach lurched, and I waved the canteen away.

He slid it back into place. "Okay, we'll get you back on an IV." He dropped his head to the tank behind him, looking up. "I'm glad you're out of there."

"Thanks so much for getting me out." I started to reach out to him but remembering his previous reaction stopped me. "Are you okay? Your lip?"

Part of me—a part that often took on Cyn's voice—snarled, *He's fine. A busted lip is nothing compared to what he and his bosses and the rest of these assholes have put me through.*

True, but a louder part of me was so horrified by the thought of *biting* someone like a wild animal that I had to apologize, explain. But I couldn't even explain it to myself.

"I'll be fine." He dropped his chin and swiped at his bottom lip. "But what were you…" He lowered his hand to his thigh and blood streaked onto his pants. "I mean, what happened?" He scanned the tank, as if wondering if it had made me crazy.

"I don't know." My voice barely carried over the alarms. "I—" I started to speak up, but the alarms fell silent.

My shoulders fell. "I didn't mean to bite you."

"I believe you." He said it so softly, I believed he did.

He leaned in. "Sure you're okay?" He scanned my body, quickly darting his eyes away. "I'll help if I can."

I shrugged. "There was this tiny, dark room they—you guys— put me in once."

He nodded like he knew the place.

"I went a little insane in there, too." I tried to keep an edge in my voice, but the truth frightened me as much as I was certain it would him. The taste of his blood had driven me wild with hunger. My tongue fumbled the words while my brain worked overtime.

Still, he sagged and fiddled with a thread on his pants. Guilt? Maybe I could use that. I needed to get out of here, and he was my only real ticket.

"I swear I've never done anything like that before." I cringed. "You must think I'm a…" The reflection I'd worked to avoid for weeks came back to me. "A monster."

A muscle ticked by Jackson's facial tattoo. "Don't say that."

I brushed a hand over my scalp, irritating the bumps of raw skin and blisters. I jerked it away.

His tongue flitted over the cuts on his lip. "After what you've been through, anyone would feel crazy. I'm just glad you pulled through." He broke his vow not to look at me, letting his gaze hover around my sunken collarbone for just an instant. I rubbed above my heart, and his scrutiny jumped to my scalp. "Did I hurt you?" He scooted in, pointing toward the damaged skin. It matched the bed sores on my hips, ankles, and heels.

"No. It's fine."

"Can I look?"

"If you have to." At least he'd asked permission. Nurse Violet and Dr. Hurst never had.

"I need to make sure you're okay in case we have to move." After a glance toward the emergency lights, he took my chin. "It's my job." He half-smiled, adding, "Well, my job's security, but that means looking out for everyone here, including you. We're safe here for now, so let's take a look." He gently tilted my head down, thumbs brushing my cheeks.

"It's disgusting." I twisted away.

"It's not." His grip tightened. "You're not."

I scoffed.

"No." His voice sharpened. "I know what you're thinking. Don't call yourself those things. Disgusting. Monster." He released my jaw and splayed out his hands in front of me. His six fingers clenched up, and he grimaced. "Don't think of yourself that way." He frowned and this time, looked right into my eyes. "As far as I can tell, none of this is your fault." His expression gentled, but his eyes fell away from me.

He didn't want to look at me.

He seemed sympathetic, though. And I had to try to get to Delta, even if the chaos of the fire was waning. "You're right. No one deserves to be tortured," I said, keeping my tone hard but not accusatory.

It worked. He chewed his lip.

"Including Delta," I ventured.

"You're right," he said through a stiff jaw. "But…" He twisted farther away.

Any farther and he'd be facing the tank. Maybe he didn't want to look at me for the same reason I no longer wanted to look at myself. It couldn't be more ironic, after all the efforts I used to make, all the time spent gazing in the mirror and at girls online. My protruding bones, where once I'd had soft curves, scared me. They probably scared him too.

My body rounded in on itself. I shouldn't care what I looked like to this boy, this man, not when I was on the verge of death. I tried to straighten up. My hands shook. I clasped them around my legs. It didn't help. My throat clogged. I swallowed a choked sound, and he looked back over, scanning me.

My body tightened. Goose bumps broke out along my arms.

"You're cold." His eyes flashed from my forearms over my shoulder. Avoiding me again or seeking something or someone in the corner of the room? The huge room—a warehouse, really—was empty of anyone else. Unless they hid among the rows and stacks of boxes, crates, and machinery littering the floor. But we were unlikely to be alone much longer. Where had Dr. Hurst been monitoring me from? A panel of windows hovered across from us, built into the concrete wall. They revealed some sort of office or control room filled with desks, computers, and monitors, cast into shadows by the emergency lights. Empty. For now.

"I should check in." He grabbed his radio, turned a knob, and held it to his ear.

A faint crackle and low, garbled voices.

"Fire's under control. But we need to get your IV hooked up again." He pointed to the tube he'd cut, attached to the needle sticking out of my arm. "Need to get you checked on." He stood and scanned the platform's narrow length, over the edge to whatever was below. "Let me find something to, um, cover you."

Cover me? Oh god. Was that why he'd stopped looking at me?

I'd forgotten I'd felt naked inside the tank. I unwrapped myself from around my knees and looked down. A black brief clung to my hips and a thin strip of the same material hung under my arms. What was left of one of my breasts was out. Heat flooded my face.

The damp strip was molded to the covered half of my chest and sagged under the uncovered half, showcasing just how nonexistent every part of me had become.

I fumbled the material up, but the jerky movements snapped the wet material back into the wrong place. My cheeks burned.

His head low, Jackson knelt in close. His knee bumped my hip, and he quickly reached over and pulled the top back up. "There."

"Thanks." My toes curled up.

"You're welcome." His arms fell to his sides, but he stayed close and looked at me now.

It took every ounce of will not to tighten into a ball again.

"I should've said something before." He offered another apologetic cringe, rubbing at his neck. "I just… Well, it was…"

"Incredibly awkward?" I volunteered.

"That's the one," he said with a mild smile.

My hands shook against the sunken flesh of my waist, and my stomach gurgled.

"Is there any food you think you can keep down? An old favorite, maybe, to get your strength back?"

With the beginnings of a grin twitching my mouth, I almost said melomakarona, the syrup-soaked Greek cookies Vin used to make. Then he said, "You already seem a little stronger. Somehow."

Guilt and revulsion bubbled up in my stomach. How could I confess my suspicion? That drinking his blood gave me energy. If he knew it wasn't an accident, but that I'd swallowed his blood down like food, he'd lock me away again. Nausea washed over me, dulling my hunger. My head throbbed with doubt. My stomach hurt, and my limbs convulsed with cold. I pressed a hand to my aching guts as I inched toward the heat of his leg. My knees bumped into his thigh, and he held stock still, barely breathing, as we touched.

I couldn't help myself, I leaned into his leg.

Neither of us breathed, and after a moment that felt like forever, he angled his chest toward mine. I inched closer. It was more than just for his heat or needing his help to get to Delta. That feeling I'd had when tasting him, that everything would be okay—being close to him sparked it again. I could let go of all my fears, like when I was with Cyn.

I gulped and dropped my head to his shoulder.

He hesitantly curved his upper body around me and rested a hand between my shoulders. I nudged my forehead into the side of his neck, letting myself rest. My face brushed his hot neck, and tiny beads of his sweat clung to my lips. They tasted like the cinnamon sugar that Cyn put in her hot chocolate. I ignored my inner voice (*The hell is going on?!*) and let the taste take me back to all the nights Cyn had stood at the stove, stirring the mixture, telling me there was nothing to fear, that this would help me sleep without nightmares. It always calmed me down, even though I could only take a few sips.

He created warming friction on my upper back, seeming unfazed by my jutting bones, and the massive warehouse seemed to shrink. Like a camera zooming in, all focus funneled onto the platform, and all sensation ceased except in the places where his skin touched mine.

We inhaled at the same time and suddenly our breaths deepened, making a soft sound together. Another. It took me further back in time, before Uncle Alec and Vin moved to the States for us orphans, back to our first home—our only home with our parents—reminding me of how our horse Bosco sighed when I stroked his neck. A contented sound. Jackson turned his head, the stubble on his cheek scraping my scalp, and I let myself imagine I was giving him as much comfort as he was giving me. He was my only chance. The only shred of good I'd seen in this hellish place.

But I had to ask him about Delta. I prepared myself to pull away. I just needed one more moment. I inhaled again.

A blare cut off the next soft sigh of our breaths.

The high alert alarm.

5
TROUBLE

JACKSON'S HEAD POPPED UP, THE MUSCLE BY HIS FACIAL tattoo ticking in the flashing light. The fire alarm shrieked next, mingling with the high alert siren like the peal of church bells.

Jackson's grip tightened painfully, and for a horrible moment, I thought he was going to throw me back into the tank. *So much for saving Delta.* Then I heard through the sirens the faint clang of feet on metal below us.

Jackson braced himself (For combat? For a reprimand?) as a bald head, not as bald as mine, appeared between two looping ladder handles. Jackson released me. Thick fingers gripped the sides of the ladder, and a large, whiskered face preceded a middle-aged man's rounded midsection.

"Thank goodness. She's out of the tank. We need to get her out of here." The man's voice was almost fatherly. Nondescript, yet familiar.

"Sir." Jackson shot to his feet.

"Jackson, why are you here? We need you out there." The alarms echoed his words.

Jackson inched away from me.

The older man heaved himself onto the platform, stood awkwardly, and stumbled a few steps toward us. His head barely reached Jackson's shoulder. I'd never seen him before. He was in standard doctor garb, except his white coat and dress shirt sleeves were rolled up way past his elbow. An odd look for a professional.

Jackson snapped to attention when he spoke, but relief was clear on his face. Like when your dad (or Uncle Alec) shows up to get you out of trouble. There was love there, even amid the scolding. The love I'd felt from Jackson before, maybe? Love for this man? Who must be Dr. Craig.

Nurse Violet's blond bob popped up between the ladder rungs, and she climbed onto the platform. She towered over the doctor as they asked, over top of each other, "Is Charlie—" "Is Ellis okay?"

"Ellis." Jackson repeated my name. He shook his head. "Yes, Charlie—Ellis—is okay. I think. She wasn't when I arrived." He tugged his belt higher on his hips.

"Good. But what are you doing here?" Dr. Craig asked.

Jackson's face lost a bit of color. "You said not to worry about her. But I—" He stopped and squared shoulders. "Sir, someone needed to come. I found her drowning. Her mask was off." He nodded to where it lay in a puddle of water.

"We'll deal with this. Then we need to go." Dr. Craig rushed to the top of the tank. "What happened?" Dr. Craig asked me, kneeling by a plastic tub. He opened it, tugged out a blanket, and shuffled over to drape the grey wool across my back. "I know you've been through a lot, but tell us, Ellis. Please."

Recalling it, my throat dried up. I swallowed hard, barely able to push out the words. "My mask. It was yanked off. Someone tried drowning me." *Trying to kill me.* The questions flooded back. How was I alive? Why hadn't my lungs burned? Why hadn't I blacked out? Could a person's body get used to drowning? No. But then, I wasn't exactly a normal person.

All their faces registered surprise, shock, anger, interrupting my confusing thoughts.

"Who?" Dr. Craig laid a hand on my shoulder blade. "You saw them?"

"No. Just a shadow." I tried to explain. "After so long in the dark, the light was blinding."

"And Dr. Hurst drugged you this morning." Dr. Craig ran a hand through his remaining strip of thinning hair. "More than normal. Said you needed it for the transfer." This didn't seem to be the time to mention I had overheard the conversation with Hurst and knew I'd been transferred into this tank at Dr. Craig's request. How would I even explain that?

He and Jackson shared a glance I couldn't read.

"Then… how can you be sure of what happened?" Jackson's facial tattoo crinkled as he shot me an apologetic cringe.

"I felt someone's hand pulling at the mask." God, I wished I could tell him about the voice and prove my attacker's intentions were clear. They waited for me to drown. But Jackson knew about the ear plugs. How could I explain they didn't affect my hearing in the water?

"We'll figure this out later." Dr. Craig's head jerked toward the mounted alarm lights. "Stay here," he ordered Nurse Violet. "Keep her safe."

Jackson stepped toward me.

Dr. Craig continued in a rush, preempting any objection. "This is the safest place to be, fire's not coming this way. I hate to leave her like this, if someone's trying to harm her, but they need us."

Jackson opened his mouth, but "Jax, help!" scratched over the radio. A soft voice, out of breath. His friend.

"Scott." Jackson's whole body jerked toward the warehouse's exit.

"You have to help him," said Nurse Violet. "You know how he is. All those brains and still charging into trouble like a dummy." She rushed to my side, her mouth taut and eyes wide. "I'll take care of her. You go." Dummy or not, she was worried about this Scott guy.

"But if someone comes after her?" Jackson kicked the mask, spilling water from it.

"I have this." Nurse Violet pulled a thin, pronged object from her jacket. Her stun gun. She'd used it on me that first week to try to get me to eat, urged on by shouted commands over the speaker.

I trembled, unable to look away from the prongs, remembering the blue flash that vibrated my bones and convulsed my aching, wasted body.

"I won't use it on her again," Nurse Violet assured Jackson, who was scrutinizing the device. "I'm sorry about that. I promise, I'll keep her safe."

"I know." Jackson rested a hand on her shoulder. "Thanks, Vi."

"Of course." A soft look passed between them.

It was more than a look between co-workers. Her glance held a yearning, his a sadness. Both spoke of a history. A romance?

She blushed, and he turned to me with a jumpy movement. "Let me just…" He cleared his throat and scrubbed a hand over his face. Kneeling, he squeezed his eyes shut, lifted his right hand, and pressed all three fingers to my neck. The blood in my artery pushed back, steady and strong. His eyes shot open, the dark depths flashing. "Get some rest, okay, Ellis." He pulled the ends of the blanket together, tugging my hands up to replace his, and brushed his lips to my ear as Dr. Craig neared the ladder. "I'll be back soon."

"Jackson." Dr. Craig swung a leg down.

"Vi, here." Jackson pointed to his radio and cell. "You might need them. Repeater's still down, cell's probably still blocked, but try Dr. Craig if you need us." He jumped to his feet, strode to the ladder as the doctor's head disappeared, and backed down the rungs, glancing between Violet and me. With his eyes breaching the platform, he shot me a look I couldn't read, but he spoke to her. "Take care of her, Vi." His dark hair disappeared as he descended, and footsteps faded away.

Nurse Violet reached for my hand. "I should check too." She placed two fingers on the inside of my wrist and stared at her watch. "If we need, there's emergency equipment below." She waited, counting the beats of my heart. "It's better." Her fingers pressed deeper, her eyebrows pinching together. "A lot better." Her fingers wrapped up my arm. "You feel warmer too." She clapped a hand over my forehead and gasped. "Almost feverish, compared to this morning."

I shrugged. There was no way I could tell her the truth, especially if she and Jackson were close. Was she the one Dr. Craig had mentioned pulling strings for, for Jackson? Did they have a thing? It would make for good TV. The dedicated nurse and the reserved soldier, kept apart by his fear of bringing her into his dangerous world. An unfamiliar bitterness built in my gut and seized my throat, and I sputtered on a bit of watery blood.

She patted my back and took a thermometer from her breast pocket. As if by command, my mouth fell open. She stared hard at the temperature reading and stiffened. Then she did something she'd never done before. She showed it to me. 99.0°. No denying it now. Drinking Jackson's blood had made me stronger. The strongest I'd been since losing my guidestone.

Nurse Violet and I stared at each other for a strained moment then glanced away. We hadn't spoken since the first few weeks, but silent communication had passed between us for months. Now that we could talk, what would we say?

"I'm glad." She released a deep breath. "So glad you're better. I thought this would only make you worse." She cocked her head at the tank. "I don't know why the hell he needed it, or why he made me promise I wouldn't tell Jax it was his idea." Her chin fell.

Would confirming "he" was Dr. Craig remind her she shouldn't be talking?

"I guess he told the truth, though. It wasn't about breaking you. He doesn't share that goal with the others." She gulped. "Every day I wished I could explain why." She swallowed her words. "Why I didn't do something to help, when I knew what they were doing to you—having me do to you—was wrong. I'm sorry." She slumped, and her head dropped closer to mine.

"It's okay." An automatic response.

Was it really okay to follow along with something you knew was wrong?

"My dad's sick." She pushed back the collar of her scrubs and tugged on the chain I'd caught glimpses of before. Pulling it out, she revealed a locket on the end. "My mom's." She clicked it open and showed me a picture of a young couple wrapped in an embrace, smiling at each other. "She died in a car accident. Rushing to the hospital after I lost my eye." She shuddered. "My dad, he's all I have left. He has cancer now. The bills. I need work. No one wants to hire me. No unit commander wants me assigned." She snapped the locket shut, dropped it back down her shirt, and reached up to the sunken pocket of skin where her eye had been. "Dr. Hurst thought this was an advantage at first. I need this position."

"I understand." I coughed out. And I did understand, even though I'd never had to take care of anyone else, or myself for that matter. Uncle Alec, Vin, Cyn, they'd always been there to take care of me.

She hugged herself.

"It's okay." Another automatic response, though I did want to comfort her. She'd been kind to me when she could. I placed a hand on her knee, feeling like the strong one. How long would that last? Better not take it for granted. I steeled myself and coaxed, "There's a new detainee, Delta."

Her brows jumped, then she squinted sideways at me. "How did you hear about Delta?"

"Is it a young man? Please, I might know him."

Her lips pressed together. "Well, all I know is, he's old."

Old? Definitely not Vin. Probably not Uncle Alec either. I mean, Uncle Alec was old, but he didn't look that way. "How old?"

She glanced around like we were back in the lab. Her voice lowered. "I haven't seen him. Just heard things."

If she'd never seen him, maybe what she'd heard was wrong. Even if he was a stranger, I had to help, or at least try. "Is he okay?"

She tilted her head. "I want to help you. I do. I regret so much. I don't want to regret more. But Delta?"

"I think this could be the man who raised me." Saying it out loud—trusting her—went against everything Uncle Alec had taught us.

"If that's who it is, I'm sorry." She shook her head slowly. "He's in bad shape."

"Explain," I croaked on a shortened breath.

"Not as bad as you."

I breathed more deeply.

"But not good. They're taking this so much farther than I'd thought." She shook her head harder, her bob swaying. "They have these precautions." Her thin lips set into a grim line. "He's been kept weak, more closely guarded than you."

"Since when?"

"Since he was captured."

"When?"

"Well, they ambushed him outside the facility right around my dad's surgery. So… a week ago. No, more."

More than a week? If it was Uncle Alec, their precautions were working, or he would've just compelled us both out of here. "Where is he?"

She chewed on her bottom lip. "I'll tell you. But I don't see what good it will do. Even if you somehow get to that corridor, you'll never make it. They'll stop you." She said it like it was inevitable. "But I get wanting to see him." She brushed her fingertips over her locket chain and sighed. "Maybe you can at least peek at him on a monitor. There's a corridor leading to a holding facility. Like for you. Just harder to get through."

"Where?" I could help him. I had to. Bolstered by fresh determination and my newfound energy, I forced my legs under me and pushed myself up.

She gasped, just a bit more surprised by my legs bearing my weight than me.

"Where?" I locked my knees out.

"What if the person who did this comes after you?" She pointed at the mask.

I stared her down. "This is the only family I have left. You said you were sorry. Help."

"Yes." She clutched at her locket through her shirt. "Yes, if you're lucky, maybe you can see him, before you—" She eyed my forearms, where she often struggled to find veins, then my hollowed stomach. Before I—die? She released her locket, and her words tumbled out. "Get to the main hall." She pointed to the far corner of the warehouse, in the direction Jackson and Dr. Craig had looked. "It's wide, usually lots of traffic, but everyone's been drawn away. You only need to make it about a dozen yards. Take the second left, and then the first right will lead you downstairs, where you'll go right again. Corridor fifteen. Where the holding areas are. You'll know the one for Delta—four—when you see it. There's a huge sign." She uncrossed her legs and stood. "Watch out for the guards. Even with the fire, they'll be back to their posts soon. Be careful."

"I will." I raised my chin. God, I'd never been out of the lab or that room. "Can you come?" My chin trembled.

"I want to."

A strangled sound of hope filled my throat.

Her eye filled with tears. "But no. I can't risk it." She swiped at a tear rolling down her cheek. "I'll have to tell them you recovered your strength, overpowered me."

"Okay." I swallowed down enough of my fear, and my chin stopped shaking.

"I'll do my best. Give you as long as I can." Her eye locked onto mine. "I hope it isn't your family. But if it is, stay strong." She patted her fingertips above her locket. "Good luck. I'll see you soon."

Again, she was assuming I'd get captured. That was, if I didn't run into whoever wanted me dead. My palms dampened with sweat.

Jackson's radio hissed. "Anyone… we need Test-Site…" A pause. "Anyone heard from Test-Site Control… over… backup…"

I stumbled over and snatched up the radio. It could be useful. So could some clothing. I set the radio on the edge of the tank and snagged Jackson's shirt, catching a whiff of the stale odor rising from whatever was below us. I slipped on the rough material and worked a few of the remaining buttons at the top through holes. Jackson's sweet scent enfolded me. Cinnamon, like his sweat. Ginger, like his breath. I tucked my nose into the collar.

I stood taller and looped the radio's strap around my right wrist. Nurse Violet pursed her lips and nodded.

I grabbed the bulk of the radio in my right hand, pushed off from the tank with my left, and jolted my legs into action. "Wait." She pulled out the stun gun. "I'll tell them you got it away." She was risking a lot. No one was likely to believe that.

I took it from her, gripping it tightly, using more energy than I should.

But it would be a precious commodity if I ran into the person who'd tried to drown me. I lifted it to my chest. My throat closed, but she seemed to understand my gesture.

"You're welcome." She squeezed my forearm and helped me to the edge of the platform.

My fingertips found Jackson's cell in one pocket. I stuffed the stun gun in the other. I peered over the ladder. Far below, concrete waited. The radio weighting down one hand, I hobbled down the rungs. A far-off screech punctuated the piercing tones of the alarms. The hawk? Its call was faint now. Where was it? I turned my head, slipped, and fell. *Whack.* Pain slammed through my heels, and I sank to my knees.

"Oh no!" Nurse Violet called.

I crawled to a crate and pulled myself up. "It's okay."

She leaned over the rungs.

"I'll be okay." I staggered forward. My ankles throbbed. My leg muscles cramped up, barely holding. I forced one foot ahead, then the other. No sign of a bird, no noise but the alarms, I weaved through a maze of machinery, equipment, and objects draped in tarps. The largest were topped with blades, fanned out near the ceiling. Helicopters? Labels on the crates proclaimed, "Area 51."

Area 51? The classified air force base? So restricted it prompted theories of UFOs, government conspiracies, and testing of secret weapons. They'd brought me here just to understand the abilities of Uncle Alec's race?

I neared the corner of the warehouse, where a triple-wide garage door rose up one wall, panels of double doors along the other, and hope filled me. I'd made it this far. Still, I felt watched by that empty panel of windows hovering above. I raced to a door, pushed through it, and stumbled into a dark closet. No, an entry into a vast hall, wider than any I'd ever seen. It was broader than a two-lane highway and stretched for miles. Emergency lights sparked an amber trail ending in billows of smoke, ballooning from dark depths. Footsteps echoed over the alarms, storming up and down to one side. More shouts. "Load that hose. Back to the entrance."

Jackson's radio hissed.

I turned it off and stumbled forward. The smell of smoke hit my nose, burning my lungs. I coughed it out, and it stung my mouth, like I'd swallowed vinegar. More thundering footsteps. Which way were they coming from? Amid the haze, I started to turn in what I hoped was the opposite direction but found myself staring into the depths of the smoke cloud. Red-orange tongues of flame shone at its heart, jumping for the ceiling, licking the walls, heading straight for me.

6
CONTAINMENT AREA FOUR

I ROTATED, RACING AWAY FROM THE FIRE WITH MY MOUTH AND nose in the crook of my elbow. Garbled shouts followed me until I took my next turn down a sloping hall feeding deeper into the bowels of the facility. Another turn took me down a staircase that left the smoke behind, and as I turned the final corner I hoped Nurse Violet meant, the lingering, acrid scent faded. I gulped in cleaner air, washing the bitter taste from my mouth. The alarms pulsed faintly behind me, breaking the silence. My legs grew weaker with every step. I tripped down the slanted hall, running one hand along the wall for support while the other clutched the radio. My bare feet slapped concrete, not making a sound. I didn't weigh enough.

My left ankle throbbed. My head spun.

The radio slipped, and I fumbled it, knocking it into the end of the IV tube. I shivered with nausea. Slowing my pace for a moment, I cradled the radio, pulled the needle out, and flung it away. Blood seeped out of my bruised forearm. I licked it to stop the flow, intending to spit it out. But the velvet warmth and briny tang of salt enticed my stomach, and I swallowed, distracted by a gush of emotion blossoming somewhere near my diaphragm. I knew these feelings well. They were mine, and they brought memories with them. Degrees of love, all with different shapes that made faces swim in my mind's eye. Familial love. Alanna's gentle tones and touches on my back; Cyndra's buck-up speeches and whoops of praise; Dad's eyes lifting from a book to ask me "What's wrong, cupcake?"; Mom's laugh, so fuzzy now that I wasn't sure if it was hers or something my mind adopted from a movie. Platonic love. Vin's teasing pokes in the ribs. Pain. Old and new. Physical and psychological. Hiding in a closet, pressed against Cyndra's knobby knees and wet with Alanna's tears on my shoulder. Leaving an empty house, a pink roller suitcase in my small hand. Needles. Fear. So much suffering.

No time.

With the fire fresh in my mind and mouth, the alarms held more urgent meaning. Their echoes prodded my ankles and muscles to push harder. *Run. Run.* But what was I running to? Unlike the other corridors, there were no doors or halls branching off this one that I could see between the scattered amber cone lights. *Run. Run.* An alcove appeared from the shifting gloom. I peeked inside. A mounted metal rack held stun guns and plastic riot shields. I kept running until a narrow passage appeared from the gray. I forced myself into the dark tunnel and ran smack into a row of metal bars. They didn't budge. A lock was welded in the split of a floor-to-ceiling gate. A sign overhead:

Containment Area 1.

Permit C Only.

Check In and Check Out Required.

The first holding area. I limped back out. Further into the corridor's depths, another darkened passage appeared. This black tunnel led to another sign: Containment Area 2. Also barred off to those without a *C* Permit. Right past it, a door marked "Supplies." I opened it and found a closet stuffed with mops, brooms, buckets, folded linen, and the like. Limping even further, I passed another alcove filled with more guns and shields.

Then another passage. Containment Area 3. The same damn bars, the same damn lock, the same damn sign. Was I going to fail before even seeing who Delta was? I forced my ankles to hold, rushed deeper into the corridor, past another alcove, another supply closet.

At last, Containment Area 4, just like Nurse Violet said. Below the typical warning, an even larger sign hung:

PROTECTIVE FACIAL EQUIPMENT MANDATORY.

AT ALL TIMES.

NO EXCEPTIONS.

Footsteps echoed beyond the bars. I pressed flat against the wall and peeked around the post where the gate attached to the wall, squinting into the depths beyond the bars. A cordless, battery-powered lantern sat on a desk, emitting a dull yellow glow that revealed two pacing men. They wore matching khaki uniforms—no camo, no dog tags, nothing like Jackson. One wore something on his head. A closer look revealed a thicker version of the plastic masks worn by Dr. Hurst and the team that kidnapped me. It reminded me of the welding visor Uncle Alec had worn when he installed a security gate at our new home. The dark screen reached down to the collar of the guard's uniform. The other guard, bare headed, stalked around the small room, muttering to himself. "What the hell are we doing here?" he said, coming to a squeaking halt.

"The Director's orders. Maintain post," the visored-one said.

"But we could be trapped!" The other started pacing again. "There's only the two exits. Or the one. Did they seal the utility access again?" Utility access? "They finished with the tank. Maybe they did." He froze, and a sheen of sweat along his forehead caught the stark lantern light.

"Maybe." The visored-one reached beneath the mask screen and tugged the collar of his uniform. "Doesn't matter. We maintain post. And get your headgear back on." He pointed to another visor on the desk. "The Director won't let anything happen to this prisoner anyway. If we need to evacuate, he'll radio."

"Are you kidding me?" The bare-headed one turned to a bank of electronic equipment against the wall. All the monitors were black. "Power's still out. Damn repeater's out. Radio's barely working."

Jackson had mentioned the repeater too. Repeater, repeater… I'd heard that before, though. A cop show? Uncle Alec's war drama?

Something about bouncing signals, no, relaying, making them reach greater distances?

The visored-one took a deep breath. "He said he'd get close enough. Radio if needed."

Yes, they could only hear nearby communications.

"Haven't heard shit. Not since he checked on his V.I.P."

"V.I.P.?"

"Very important prisoner," he spat.

The other one laughed.

"No joke. He treats this one like he's gold." He glanced behind him to a metal hatch in the wall, with a huge lever serving as a door handle. Somehow, I had to get the gate open, get past these guards, and help whoever was behind it. I needed help. Or something to help. I stuffed my hand in Jackson's pocket. The stun gun. But there were two of them. Then I thought of it.

The radio!

I shuffled back into the hall and slid into the last supply closest, hoping they couldn't hear the radio's hiss as I turned it on. I lowered the volume. Recalling what I'd heard in the tank, I summoned my deepest, most authoritative voice and pressed the talk button. "This is Test-Site." I paused. "Control," I threw in for good measure. "Repeater's online. Running diagnostics." I gulped. "Only essential communications." I paused again, thinking. "Need a response from Containment Area Four. Over." Would it work?

"Roger, roger. Containment Area Four. Over," the bare-headed one answered.

Now where to send them? Maybe to my old holding cell? I was the third prisoner, so… "Need your guards to assist at Containment Area Three. Over."

"Roger."

"Remain until further ordered."

"Roger."

A scuffle, as if the visored guard grabbed the radio. "Okay to leave Delta then? Over."

"Delta is secure. Need you at Containment Area Three. Over."

"Charlie heading back to containment? Over."

"Affirmative." Please let that be the right choice of word.

"Roger."

I dropped the radio to my side, cracked open the door, and pressed my ear to the opening.

There was the click of a lock turning, a squeak of the gate opening, then the footfalls paused.

"You don't think that was weird?" the visored guard asked.

"This whole thing's bullshit. What are you talking about?"

"Just seems weird they'd prioritize Charlie like that. The Director acted like he was about to cut her loose cause she's got no ESP or whatever. Said she was just draining resources."

What did "cut her loose" mean? Surely not let me go. I didn't think I wanted to know. But maybe I'd already found out, back in the tank. The shadowy figure. The Director?

The bare-headed guard scoffed. "Charlie's in transport. Higher risk. Makes sense to me. You're paranoid, man."

"It's this job," Visor said with a jumpy laugh. Their footsteps started up again.

I didn't hear the gate close. They'd left it open. Thank the Priestesses and all their gods.

They strode down the corridor, passed me in the closet, and disappeared into the darkness. I shot out of the closet and sprinted into the tunnel, panting as I hobbled through the gap they'd left in the gate. I scurried around the desk and threw my weight on the hatch lever. Nothing. I lifted and pulled. Nothing. A small keyhole taunted me.

Panic set in, and the rapid, cartoonish thumping of my heart became white noise in my ears. I spun in place, searching. To the side of the electronic equipment, a narrow shelf was built deep into the wall, covered by bars and seemingly secured by a keypad affixed to the wall beside it. I inspected the curious, guarded shelf, and saw a tiny gold key dangling on a metal loop inside. It was impossible to tell which keys were depressed on the pad. No way to guess the code. But my hands had always been small, and malnourishment had made them downright tiny. I squeezed my fingertips between the narrow bars, momentarily hitching at the knuckles. I scraped the skin as I pushed them through. My index finger brushed the key's jagged edge. Wiggle, wiggle. The key swayed. I looked over my shoulder. The lamp blinded me to the darkness beyond the gate. *They're coming!* my mind screamed at me, though there'd been no sound, and my breathing shallowed.

I jammed my wrist through with bruising force, my fumbling fingers knocked the key too hard. The loop slid from the post. No!

I snagged it and gulped a huge breath as I extracted myself and the key. Rushing back to the hatch, I twisted it in, pushed down on the lever, and the thick metal creaked open outward.

I slipped in, pushing the door open further to shed a strip of lantern light on the utter blackness of the long, narrow room.

A mirrored wall ran its length. An exam table, monitors, and medical equipment were scattered around the floor. It was like my lab, except where the bed should've been, bars jutted out. They'd built a jail cell in this lab.

I flipped a light switch by the hatch. Nothing. Lighting banks running across the ceiling stayed dark. My hand trembled as it fell to my side. "Uncle Alec? Vin?"

A scuffling sound answered from the cage.

I backed up, hitting the edge of the hatch. "Hello?" I croaked through a tightening windpipe as I forced myself to take a small step forward.

"Ellis?" The voice was even weaker than mine. Nothing like Uncle Alec's or Vin's rich tenor. "Ellis, is that you?" But the smooth accent was theirs.

I hurried forward, feet smacking the tile.

"Wait!" The word ended in a harsh cough.

I froze.

"Prop the door open. It will lock behind you."

I spun around. The hatch swung back toward me, hinging closed. I shot over to give it a push. "What do I do?"

More coughing. The calm tone was actually Uncle Alec's, just stripped of its signature strength. "Find something to hold it."

I raced to a metal stool, dragged it over, and propped it up against the hatch. "I've taken care of it, Uncle Alec." I stumbled my way through the lab, ran into the wall of bars, and peered between them, trying to see the back of the cell. Metal squeaked, as if he'd shifted on the hospital bed. I pressed my forehead between two bars.

Another cough. "I can't believe you found me. Made it to me." No more sound from the bed, like he wasn't even trying to get up. Was he strapped down? Or maybe he didn't want to get too close to me. He'd never wanted us too close, keeping to his elegant office, circling the outskirts of the training field, sitting at the far head of the long, white dining table—all so he never accidentally enforced his will upon us three girls with the barest of smiles. I pressed my whole body to the bars, trying to see into the shadows, and he gasped. I couldn't see him, but he must have seen me. "Oh, Ellis. What have they done to you?"

What did the lantern light show him? Please, please don't let him be able to see it all.

But he'd see it soon enough.

I pictured my last forced glance into the mirror, and my head fell. My long, beautiful hair gone. Bones jutting. Veins popping through papery skin and what remained of a fine coating of white hair along my arms and neck. Nurse Violet had told the wall speaker that the tiny hairs were a symptom of my body's deep starvation, an attempt to retain heat. When I'd started losing them a week ago, Nurse Violet had reported that my body must be in its end stages. Yet, besides my shaved scalp covered with sensor sores, my captors weren't to blame. Not as far as I could tell. They weren't responsible for the starvation.

"It wasn't them. Not all of it." There was so much to tell him.

"Uncle Alec, I can't eat a thing now. Or drink. Not even the portions I used to. I don't know what's wrong."

"Your guidestone. You need it." His tone was certain, but his voice caught at the end. He cleared his throat. "I'll tell you where it is, how to get to Vin. Though I have a feeling that Vin is behind what's happening right now. So you have to take advantage of it. You have to get yourself out of here."

"You're coming too."

"I can't." A feeble cough.

I stepped to the side and more of the lantern light touched the cell. I finally made out his figure. It was the silhouette of an old man, riddled with aches and pains, not my sharp, spry guardian. His thick salt and pepper hair was gone, stolen for the sake of the sensors that had left their puckered red marks behind. He looked way too thin, except for where a fat cast circled his right leg. "Uncle Alec, are you okay?"

He cupped the IV attachment on his forearm, shifted in the shadows, and winced.

"What happened?" My hand found the lever to his cell and shook it.

"It was a bad fight, and I'm not used to losing," he said with an attempt at a smirk. "They're trying to get something from me. They want to learn how to control my ability." He hesitated. "I've been better, but seeing you, I'm okay now." His eyes scrunched up, lifting his cheeks a fraction, but his other facial muscles froze, his lips remaining in a tight line. His version of a smile, trying not to influence me. "I'm okay," he repeated softly.

But as my eyes adjusted, it became apparent he wasn't okay at all. On top of the cast he was bandaged around his right ear and right hand. A loose-fitting scrub shirt covered his torso, but his exposed limbs and face were littered with bruises and angry abrasions. Still, most disturbing was how old and weary he looked. I mean he was old, sure—well over a hundred because of his race's unique aging process. But I'd never really questioned his exact age because he'd always looked young. When I'd first met him as a child, he'd driven up to our desecrated family home in a white car—a handsome, olive-skinned knight, with the lustrous hair of an Adonis and a romantic Greek accent, come to rescue me in his modern steed. That vision of him had never wavered. Our genteel knight, who'd dropped everything in his homeland and moved to a foreign country to take in frightened orphans and treat them as his own. Now he looked the part of an aged, dying king. His stubble was silvery and wrinkles drug down his face. His tall, lithe figure now hunched in on itself. "Oh, Uncle Alec, what did they do?"

"Don't worry about me. When I'm overtaxed, my age shows. I'll recover with a little rest." A lot. It looked like he needed a lot of rest. "Don't worry." He tried to catch my gaze in the dimness. "Just listen." His cheeks lifted higher, the corners of his lips curving, and I knew what was coming. He was going to compel me. I knew I should look away, but I couldn't. He struggled to lift his unbandaged hand. "Even if I could walk. I can't come." His index finger pointed to a recess in the wall. "It needs a passcode. It changes daily. They call it out over speakers when they come to get me." Another barred shelf, another dangling key and imposing keypad.

"I've got this."

"But how?"

I hurried to slip my hand inside, ignoring the pain on my damaged knuckles as I pulled out the key.

He gasped. "I still can't make it."

"You can, I'll help." I strode to the lever and pushed the key into the lock.

"I'll slow you down."

I threw open the cell and hurried to his side. "We're going together."

His jaw tightened, his smile growing into the famous charmer he'd passed to his son.

I looked away. "Together."

"Please, look at me. Listen, Ellis—"

I twisted my head away.

"Okay, together."

I risked glancing at his face. His features had relaxed.

"Can you think of how we might get out?" he asked.

He'd given in easily. Maybe too easily.

"I only know of the tunnel entrance," he continued. "There'd be no place to hide there. Vin and I theorized there might be passages connecting the underground buildings to the aboveground facilities, but there's a higher risk of foot traffic there. But I think there's an equipment entrance for the larger items they can't bring up through the tunnels. I saw a dirt road climbing up the mountain, a small power line, a small concrete building, maybe an old guard post. It looked abandoned. I just don't know how to get there."

I racked my brain for any useful information I'd heard in the tank. Yes, a tunnel entrance, like Uncle Alec said. It sounded too far away, too close to the fire, to be safe. But the hawk's cry had come from elsewhere. Maybe that was the equipment entrance? The utility access that one guard had mentioned?

"There might be a way." I reached for his unbandaged hand, unsure if he'd let me take it. Even if the fading bruises didn't hurt, he'd always kept his distance.

He surprised me, inching his arm toward me, palm up.

I clasped his hand.

He squeezed back.

"We can do this, Uncle Alec. We have to."

"You're right." He pushed himself up, wincing as his bandaged hand bore weight.

I used our joined hands to pull him the rest of the way. He swung his good leg around and I released his hand to help shift his cast toward the floor. He scooted to the edge of the bed and slid down, his cast hitting first. His knees buckled, and I looped one of his arms over my shoulder, lifting him up. "Did they give you a shoe?" I pointed to his other foot.

"No, but you made it here. You don't have any shoes." He hopped forward and wobbled.

I cinched an arm around his waist. "This way." I guided him toward the hatch.

He tilted away at first, but after several staggers, he sighed and leaned against me. We limped along, out the hatch, past the desk, through the gate, around the corner, and back down the hall. As we passed the supply closest, the sour smell of smoke greeted us, stronger than before. "Smell that?" A voice echoed from ahead.

I backed Uncle Alec toward the closest, painstakingly slow.

"Yeah." Another familiar voice answered.

"What if they diverted Charlie to the entrance? We should confirm orders directly with the Director, no middlemen this time."

I had my hand on the closet door handle when the bare-headed guard appeared ahead, the visored one right after him. "Hey!" They chorused together and charged us.

7
REYES

AT THAT ONE SHOUTED, "HEY!" PANIC SET IN, AND I BECAME a kid again, huddled against Uncle Alec to protect me from monsters. But this time, my pitiful weight nearly toppled him sideways.

"Hey, yourself." Uncle Alec pulled out of my strangling hold, stood tall, and smiled wide and bright. "Back away."

The bare-headed guard froze. The visored one didn't.

"Pull your friend's visor off," Uncle Alec directed at the bare-headed guard.

The bare-headed guard lunged at his friend from behind and tackled him to the ground, tugging off the headgear.

They both scrambled to their feet.

"Back away." Uncle Alec repeated firmly, smile unwavering and unnatural. "Go. You didn't see us. Hide in the supply closet until someone finds you."

I'd only witnessed the power of Uncle Alec's ability a handful of times over the last eleven years of living with him, and each time I was left in awe. The guards' eyes glazed over, and they stared ahead, past us into the corridor. They plodded forward, limbs limp, feet dragging. They brushed by Uncle Alec without any indication they knew we were there. He could tell them to stand on their heads and do the chicken dance if he wanted.

They'd cough up top secret information at a word.

"Wait," I hissed in an urgent whisper. "Ask them to tell us who the Director is."

Uncle Alec shot me a questioning look before focusing on the men's backs. "You, with the mustache." The previously visored guard slowed and looked back, head lolling like a sleepwalker. "Tell me, who is your Director? Their full name."

"Doctor Everett Hurst," the guard droned, then drifted after his fellow.

I should have known. Hurst had pulled all the strings, ordering my torture, conducting my most intensive interrogations. If he was who wanted to "cut me loose," did that mean he was the shadowy figure who pulled off my mask?

Uncle Alec sagged against me, but I dragged him along at a faster clip, glancing behind to see the guards swing open the supply closest door, zombie walk inside, and shut it behind them.

"You should leave me, Ellis." Uncle Alec tried to pull away. "I'm even weaker now."

"Together. We're doing this together." I clutched him to me and ignored the shaking in my ankles.

"What was all that about the Director?" he asked between pants. "Does that mean something to you?"

"Oh, I just wanted to know who tried to kill me," I said bitterly. "Know thine enemy, and all that."

"Kill you? Ellis, you really must leave me—"

Jackson's radio crackled in my pocket. "Firestarter captured. Repeat. Firestarter in custody. Reyes reporting." A voice I'd heard earlier today. The words clipped, haughty. *Remind A.J. who's in charge.* Mr. Impatient.

Uncle Alec and I exchanged wide-eyed glances. Our (possible) would-be rescuer had been captured. What if it was Vin?

"Roger that, Reyes. Bring detainee to quadrant seven."

"Roger. Lopez is delivering detainee. I'm grabbing bigger tranqs and going after the big son of a bitch."

The radio went silent.

"Two people?" I asked Uncle Alec. "Do you think one's Vin? Who would he get to—"

"It doesn't matter," Uncle Alec interrupted, but the gravel in his voice and the pained crinkle around his eyes said otherwise. "You have to get out, now more than ever. No one's coming for you anymore, if they ever were."

My protest locked behind my gritted teeth. He was right. Uncle Alec was always right. And I didn't know where quadrant seven was anyway. I had to follow my hunch and lead Uncle Alec back the way I'd come.

We turned one corner, then a second. The smell of smoke was stronger. The fire had spread, or at least its suffocating fumes had. One more turn and we'd be way too close for comfort. I scoured the passage for alternate routes.

"There," I whispered to Uncle Alec, pulling him toward a narrower hall branching off the main passage. It ended in a fork. I looked to Uncle Alec for answers, but he just shrugged. Only half the doors we'd passed had labels, and there was no proper signage denoting where the halls led.

I played a rapid game of eenie-meeni-miney-mo and chose the right. I regretted it after only a few feet. I heard the thudding boots too late, beneath the pulsing alarm beats.

A camo-clad, twenty-something guard rounded the corner at top speed, skidded at the sight of us, then unholstered a gun in a flash.

"What are you rats doing out of a cage?" His classically handsome face, complete with square jaw and slightly cleft chin, twisted into an ugly leer. His voice—this was Mr. Impatient in the flesh. Agent Reyes, who didn't think Jackson deserved the same title. And he was wet. His sleeves and his shirt front were dark with water. Like he'd leaned over the side of a tub (*or a tank?*) and plunged his arms in.

"Drop your weapon," Uncle Alec wheezed.

The agent's finger slid off the trigger, but he broke out in a sweat and screwed up his face like he'd sucked a lemon. The gun wavered, up and down. He was fighting Uncle Alec's influence.

"Put the weapon on the floor." Uncle Alec bared more teeth in his smile.

Reyes crouched and put the gun down.

"Kick it to me."

Instead of kicking it, he crouched for it.

"No!" Uncle Alec shouted, and the agent tumbled to his knees, fingers twitching but unable to grab the gun.

"Dammit." Uncle Alec breathed hard. "I thought I'd be strong enough. This is why—" This was why he'd come with me. He didn't have to say it. He was only here to make sure I got out. But he was hurting and weak. Compelling the solider down on his knees was making him ashen.

I pulled out the stun gun and approached cautiously. Reyes turned his eyes up at me and snarled, but his arms stayed stuck to his sides, fingers twitching. I zapped him in the neck, and then everything twitched.

While he spasmed like a beached fish, I picked up his weapon. It was odd. Too light. It had a bulbous pin at the back, an unusual chamber. I popped it open and saw a feathered dart inside.

"Ellis!" Uncle Alec's warning came too late.

Reyes' leg swept out, and the world turned. I barely got my arm underneath me to keep from smacking my head on the floor. I whimpered as pain radiated from wrist to shoulder blade, and out from my hip down my thigh. My unbruised arm searched for the dart gun. It was under me.

Reyes staggered to his feet and pulled a baton from his belt. Head down and weapon raised, he stumbled toward Uncle Alec, who was swaying on his feet, wheezing, "Stop. Stop."

I lashed out at his knee with a vicious kick. There was a soft *pop* and then a much louder shriek. He dropped, clutching his leg. I rolled back upright and fired a dart into his ass. He flailed around and pulled it out, but his movements were sluggish.

He looked back at me, and spittle flew from his slack mouth as he said, "You little bitch. I'll…"

His eyes rolled back, and he slouched to the floor like a rag doll.

"Ellis, get those shoes on." Uncle Alec pointed toward the young agent's shoes.

I ignored my aching arm and loosed the ties before wrestling off the big boots. "What about shoes for you?" I asked, thinking these would fit him better.

"Put on the socks. You've got over ten miles to travel, probably twice that given the topography."

Wrinkling my nose against the eggy smell, I pulled off the thick socks and tugged them on, wincing at the sting of the bedsores on my heels.

"Take his pants too. It's cold in the desert at night."

Awkward, but okay. It was a task getting him rolled over so I could undo his belt and zipper. His legs were dead, uncooperative weights.

"Hurry," urged Uncle Alec, leaning against the wall.

I got the pants off him and then wiggled my way into them, cinching the belt as tight as the holes allowed. As I returned to Uncle Alec's side, I dug around in the many pockets, showing him my new goodies: a wallet with an electronic ID badge in addition to money and cards, a set of keys, a pen, and a pocketknife.

I didn't find more dart ammo, so I abandoned the gun and took the fallen baton instead.

"Give me that pen." Uncle Alec motioned. "And your arm."

I obeyed, and he wrote out a series of numbers on my arm. Longitude and latitude. He'd made sure we could read them years ago, and use a compass, even though I told him that was super outdated.

"What's that to?" I asked. "Why are you giving me that?"

"A safehouse in Colorado. I set it all up before I was captured. But first, you'll need to meet up with a friend of mine."

Uncle Alec had safehouses all over the country, maybe the

world, but friends were rare. The alt life was isolating. Very little trust, even for someone as respected as renowned Grecian art dealer and philanthropist to the alt races Alec Zephyrus.

More running feet. Multiple people. Low voices, words indistinguishable.

My heart sank. Neither of us was up for another fight. My everything hurt, and Uncle Alec was way too drained to influence several people at once, in any capacity.

"Come on," I urged him, ignoring more of his protests about me leaving him.

Using memory, a few false starts, and some dumb luck, I led him to the only place I had a chance of finding a semi-friendly face and a potential way out of here. The warehouse, and the tank. It took a while, and that main, double-wide corridor about gave me an anxiety attack—way too big and open—but we made it unscathed.

Nothing seemed to have changed in the vast space. It was dead quiet now. Lit by glaring emergency lights high on the walls, which cast long shadows and left pools of darkness out among the rows of stacked crates and tarp-shrouded equipment.

At the bottom of the ladder, I squeaked, "Nurse Violet?"

Nothing. No sounds of movement. No "hello."

Was she gone? Could someone else be waiting for me up there? Jackson's deep-set eyes appeared in my mind, and I imagined them peeking over that ledge, his swirling tattoo bunching at his temple when he smiled at me. But if he'd returned, he would've responded. I doubted I'd find anyone or anything so inviting at the top of that ladder.

I had to chance it. On our mad kind-of-dash back here, I'd had an idea, but I needed the stupid tank to pull it off.

"Wait here," I told Uncle Alec.

He just nodded, and I started my climb. When the top neared, I pulled out the stun gun before peeking over the lip.

Nobody in sight.

I hurried to the tank and dunked my head in the warm water.

Sounds flooded in, but I pushed them away and searched for one in particular. The hawk. I waited and searched, searched and waited. No hawk. I tried to imagine the outdoors, where the hawk would fly, instead.

There!

No hawk's cry, but a whooshing. The rhythm was natural, not overly steady or artificial. A breeze through a cracked window or door. It was close. Somewhere… to my right.

I climbed back down the ladder, told Uncle Alec to keep resting, and then moved to the right wall. I tracked my hand along it in the dark, and my fingers eventually bumped a handle. I opened the door with ease, stuck my head into the passage beyond, and listened. Was I imagining it, or was that fresh air on my face?

"I think I found a way out," I said, hurrying back to Uncle Alec.

"Excellent."

He let me loop his arm over my shoulder, and I led him through the door. The unlit tunnel beyond slanted slightly upward. A real bitch when you're trying to help a guy in a cast, but I powered on, fueled by hope. Up meant out. When we rounded a bend and a strong breeze chilled my arms, a laughed slipped through my teeth.

"We did it. We really did it," I breathed, as a garage-style door with windows greeted us a few feet down the hall. Air whooshed under the door, puffing sand onto the floor. The seal at the base was frayed and loose, letting in the wind.

I propped Uncle Alec against the wall before sliding the agent's keycard into the keypad by the door. It lit green, and the door raised.

"This is it! We're out!" I said, turning to him with a massive smile.

He smiled back, big and bright, and I froze.

"No," I whispered, already feeling that false serenity sweep over me.

"It's time to listen."

I shook my head, gulping back a sob.

"We're in Nevada. The Mohave Desert. On the western slope

of Bald Mountain, near an area of restricted airspace surrounding Groom Lake. Area 51. Some people call it Dreamland." He took a deep breath, rushing on. "Stay away from the access roads. The mountain is behind us." He pointed to a peak. "We're facing west. Move across the mountain, northwest."

"Northwest?" I pulled Jackson's cell from my pocket and started searching for a GPS app.

"What's that? Who gave that to you?" Uncle Alec asked.

"It's an agent's. He helped me. He gave me—"

"It can be traced. Give it to me. You don't need it. Use the stars." I handed it over.

"Follow the sloped hills right down to the highway. A few miles before town, look for a small trailer in a pull-off not far from the road. Carl Simmons."

"Carl Simmons?" My voice cracked.

"Only black man you're likely to see in Rachel. Bald, salt and pepper beard. He's been our eyes and ears around here. A friend. Your best bet if you don't manage to meet up with Vin first."

"You don't have to tell me all this now." It spilled out in one breath.

"Yes, I do."

"I can't get away without you. I can't leave without you."

"Don't worry. Vin will find you. He's either behind this distraction and will find his way back out, to Carl, or he'll meet you at the safehouse."

"I love you, Uncle Alec. I could never leave you behind." My lower lip trembled.

"You have to."

I started to sob. I'd thought that, for once, I could save our knight, but here he was again, sacrificing his own needs for me and my broken family.

He lowered his chin and looked straight into my eyes. "Shh, shh." He hushed me. Tears ran down my cheeks, but with my gaze locked in his focus, my throat relaxed. My sobs quieted.

"Slow your heart." His voice was firm, almost cold. "Deepen your breath."

I swallowed a gulp of air.

"Do it again."

I did.

"Again."

One more, until my heart no longer felt like a hummingbird flying in my chest.

"I know you love me. I love you too." His accent thickened, sounding like it had when I first met him. "I've loved all of you. Though I may have never showed it." His eyes shimmered, and a single tear ran down his cheek. He wiped it away. "I asked so much of you. Too much." He shook his head. "Now I've failed you when you really needed me."

"No. You haven't." I clutched his shoulders. "But I can't do it. Not on my own."

"You have to. We need you to." He stared right into my eyes, and I knew I was being compelled, but it was okay.

I wouldn't fight it.

Because I wasn't strong enough to do what needed to be done without him ordering me. I held onto him as he stared harder into my eyes. His cold tone returned, though I didn't really hear the words. Thoughts flooded my head, giving me prompts that were not my own. *Go. Get your guidestone. Get your relic. Leave Uncle Alec.* I didn't move at first. *Leave.* My feet shuffled back in the sand on the floor. *Leave.* My feet shuffled again, to follow his bidding, but I forced my arms to hold onto him. I pulled him close and buried my face in the crook of his neck.

He wrapped his arms around me too. I think this was the first time he'd ever hugged me, always taking precautions against his abilities, but I couldn't process all that now. He gave me one last squeeze and pushed me away. "You can do it. Go. While there's still time."

He turned away and trudged back inside to press the button that would close the door.

As his face disappeared, "don't go" leapt to the tip of my tongue, and my hand raised, reaching for... what? I turned to survey the cloudless night, wiping at tears dampening my cheeks. Why? I'd lost something. Something precious. Maybe it was that way.

As I trotted past an abandoned concrete guard post...

Wait? How do I know it's abandoned? I wondered.

Did Uncle Alec say that?

I crouched low and stiffened, but something in my foggy brain urged me not to worry, to keep going, past the barbed wire fence.

Wait. Uncle Alec. He'd stayed behind. That was best. I wanted to turn and say goodbye. Did I already say goodbye? But I had to go now. While there's still time.

As I scanned the keycard again and slipped through the heavy outer gate, I wanted to tell him things I'd learned in the tank. He needed to know about Jackson and Nurse Violet. Maybe they'd help him, too.

These doubts, I had to erase them from my mind. Because I had to go now. While there's still time.

8
HUNGER

NIGHT IN THE DESERT WAS COLDER THAN I EXPECTED. Darker, too. I thought there would be more stars, with no city lights to clog the atmosphere. Maybe on most nights there were. Tonight, though, the sky was a void dotted by smoky clouds. The stars and moon were out of sight. Out of reach.

Too bad. I could have used their company, their direction. I would have to use the landmarks Uncle Alec had given me as my guides. As the serenity of Uncle Alec's influence wore away, I craved their light, too, wished it could help chase away the growing sense of helplessness. I was prey in more ways than one out here, running and hiding without a burrow or den for shelter.

I shuffled over rocky terrain dotted by half-dead shrubs and mountains that cast shadows on the midnight sky. I'd left the slope of Bald Mountain behind for the desert below. Like Uncle Alec had warned, I stayed away from anything that looked like a road and ventured the way he'd pointed.

"S-sloped hills. A highway. Just b-before town, a pull off and a t-trailer," I murmured, my teeth chattering. A reminder that I had a destination. A reminder that Uncle Alec had done his best to guide me. Or a prayer, maybe. A prayer I'd make it there before the soldiers found me.

Even with Jackson's military shirt buttoned all the way and my arms wrapped around my torso, the wind cut through the heavy cotton. The pants I'd stolen from Reyes back at the compound swallowed me whole. I'd rolled the hems five times over and retightened the black belt, but they still slipped off my too-thin hips every few yards.

I stopped. Readjusted. Kept moving.

The agent's boots kept my toes warm, but they were too big for my feet. Every step sent my foot shifting and sliding inside the leather. Every time I lifted my leg, the sores on my ankles and heels rubbed against the scratchy wool socks still soaked by Reyes' sweat.

I couldn't stop, though. I had to keep moving as fast as my damaged feet could carry me. Even when the wet socks turned sticky with my blood. Even when the pain began to dull into a tingling ache.

After an hour, the numbness set in.

After two hours, I lost all sensation.

I couldn't do anything but scuffle forward, kicking up dust beneath feet I could no longer feel.

I kept my pace steady, trying not to worry that it was painfully slow. I was well beyond the perimeter fence now. Surely they didn't have outposts this far outside the safety of the facility's perimeter.

Surely all the commotion back at the base was working in my favor, too.

The two guards Uncle Alec compelled into that closet might have been found, though. How long after that until Hurst realized I was gone? How long until Jackson or Dr. Craig returned to the warehouse? Had they already, before I left? Was that why Nurse Violet was gone—she'd already given her story about being overpowered? Would they realize I'd gotten out, or would they search for me inside first? How long?

Eventually, I had to cast the thoughts away and focus on maintaining sufficient lung capacity, on putting one foot in front of the other.

The night hung so absolute that I imagined the shadows were moving. The first few times I caught movement in my peripheral, I jerked around with a squeak, staring long and hard into the dark.

Shadow paranoia was nothing new to me. When the Summum Malum crossed over, back into the plane of the living, they entered as Shadows. Moving, shadowy figures that watched and reported to the living cult members. They whispered in the ears of those whose hearts were already inclined to devilry and encouraged them to act on their urges. It was from the Shadows we had fled, to the house in the countryside that was no real shelter at all. The place where we lost Mom, Dad, Aurora, and Persephone. All the watching and the hiding and avoiding the dark had done no good. The Shadows had whispered, and the Shadows had won.

But out here, I was more likely to run across the shadow of a predator with claws and fangs. I had no idea what monsters lived out here, but they were bound to be hungry, stranded in this desolate terrain. I was hungry too. More so by the minute. The kind of hunger that tore at your gut and made you tremble, awakened by a small taste of Jackson's blood.

The next dozen times I saw the darkness twitch, I ignored it. What good would it do to spend my entire journey jumping at shadows?

I had to keep moving. Keep walking. As far as my feet could go. *While there's still time.*

If I didn't, I'd die of starvation and dehydration, or they'd find me. I knew they would. The Psy-Ops doctors and their security team wouldn't let their experiment walk away so easily. The Director, Dr. Hurst, might have tried to kill me—or sent his attack dog Reyes to do it—but he'd still want confirmation of my death. I refused to give him the satisfaction. And there was nowhere to hide long term. A few boulders, some strange hill formations formed of brown rocks, and a few scraggly bushes. The camouflage might help, but only wide-open desert stretched out before me.

I wasn't safe here.

But I'd be safe if I could reach Vin.

A safehouse in Colorado.

Just to assure myself it was still there, I slid up the sleeve on my right arm and stared down at the coordinates Uncle Alec had inked onto my skin. That collection of numbers was all I had to go on. It was my past, present, and future all at once. The single most important piece of information I had.

I was in the middle of nowhere Nevada, and somehow, some way, I needed to reach Colorado. The idea seemed ludicrous and absolutely out of reach, even with the promise of this Carl Simmons guy to help.

No real money. No real clothes. The bit of strength Jackson's blood had offered, that had helped me feel normal again, was waning. I was never strong to begin with. Not strong enough to trek across a thousand miles of empty desert to find a tiny cabin in the Colorado mountains.

Not with numb feet.

Colorado might as well be half a world away.

But the promise of my guidestone waiting for me kept me moving, even when I felt like I couldn't go any further. I'd thought my guidestone was gone for good. I'd thought I would die before I ever saw it again, wasting away without its help to keep food and water down.

Leaving Uncle Alec behind seemed a little less devastating knowing that he'd protected my guidestone. He'd believed I'd be free one day.

And I was. Free and adrift and scared.

Which was stupid. All those months in the program, deprived of my senses, treated like a sub-human experiment, fear had been a constant companion but not a close one. More like a lurking presence at my back. Maybe sensory deprivation took away what turned fear into terror—the sensations, the sounds, the smells.

Now, I was alone in the desert. Alone and far, far away from Vin and the guidestone. The sensations came back, front and center, overwhelming.

"Just reach Carl Simmons," I muttered as I stumbled over the dry ground. I mumbled along with the recording of Uncle Alec's final instructions playing on repeat in my head, because hearing my own voice in the vast emptiness of the desert helped curb the terror. "Vin will meet me at Carl Simmons' trailer. If he doesn't meet me there, he'll meet me at the safe house. Vin will meet me…"

And what about Uncle Alec? He was still in trouble. Still trapped by those horrific people in whatever mad scientist program they were running. Plus, whoever set that fire to save us, they'd been caught. I'd left them both behind for freedom, and the thought made bile burn my throat.

What if it was Vin? What if I was on my own?

I could go back.

No, that was stupid. What good was I without my guidestone? What good was I after months of torture? I was hardly half a person anymore. I needed my guidestone, and I needed to get strong again. Then I could come back with whatever resources and allies I could muster and, hopefully, pull off a jail break. We'd bust everybody out. I could be a regular action hero. The thought was laughable. But, hey, I'd try, anyway.

The cold desert wind burned against my bare fingers, so I shoved them deep in the pockets of Jackson's shirt.

My fingertips brushed against all the things I'd stolen.

I extracted Reyes' wallet and decided to distract myself from my hunger by counting the cash inside. Two hundred bucks. I fantasized about all the food I could buy with that, and eat very slowly, in small increments. Vanilla ice cream. Nilla wafers. A plain cheeseburger, maybe. A couple fries. And veggies. Lots of good ol' unseasoned, straight from the ground veggies. They never bothered my stomach, so long as I only ate a few and didn't butter them or anything. I imagined sweet corn kernels bursting on my tongue. Earthy carrots roasted in olive oil. Potatoes! Oh god, potatoes! Baked and fluffy with a little salt—a mellow, two-note flavor. Or sliced thin and crisped in the air fryer—decadent and flaky. So much for distracting myself.

But could I eat any of that anymore? I mean, I was so hungry

I'd drank blood, for god's sake. Surely, away from that awful place, I could stomach some real food now, just a few bites, even without my guidestone. Right?

I rummaged in my other pockets for a better distraction. Didn't work. But having the stun gun and the pocketknife at least offered some semblance of protection from wildlife out here. Wouldn't put a dent in any soldiers who showed up with firepower, though.

I curled my fingers into fists inside Jackson's shirt and continued walking.

So cold. So hungry. My teeth chattered, and my body ached. The further I walked, the more I felt detached from my body. Soon, I couldn't move my arms. My legs were too heavy to lift, my toes numb and brittle. Every step felt like it might be the one that shattered them. My vision narrowed on the path ahead. I couldn't focus on anything else.

I tripped over an exposed root and went down hard, taking the force of the blow on my knees and hands. Pain lanced up my thighs and wrists, but it should have hurt worse.

It was probably bad that it didn't hurt worse.

I managed to get my feet back under me and stand. When I tried to take a step forward, I fell again. This time, I didn't have the presence of mind to catch myself. I landed on my shoulder and cried out.

Hot tears stung my cold, wind-chapped cheeks. I lay still, staring off into the inky desert night. How screwed up would it be if I escaped that place only to die in the desert? Maybe Dr. Hurst would find me dead after all. Despite my best efforts, I slipped into a hazy half-sleep. Dreams merged with reality until I wasn't sure if I was awake or not. A tumbleweed rolled by. It could have been real. But the river of water that followed it most certainly wasn't. Not here. I reached for it anyway, wishing I could dip my fingers in the water. But no—I jerked my hand away. No more water.

Not after the pool. The tank in the lab.

Too late anyway. The water was gone.

A light flashed—a near-perfect circle, like a lens flare. I froze, heart dropping into my stomach with a painful *thunk*. A flashlight! They'd found me!

No…

This was softer, a soothing gold tone. It didn't sweep side to side, but hovered, bobbing like a buoy. I tried to raise my head into its warm glow. Too sleepy. It winked at me, flitting around like Tinkerbell greeting Peter Pan. And then it vanished, leaving me to wonder if I'd imagined it—an angel created by misfiring synapsis.

A spider crawled over the cracked dirt near my face. He was big but didn't seem to care that I was there. He was real, right? I thought I glimpsed another light in the sky, but my eyelids were too heavy to look up. Lightning? Falling star? No way to tell if it was a dream. Oh, the clouds had cleared. The moon was shining down on me.

Something moved. I expected a tumbleweed or the spider, but an animal materialized from the night's shadows. A bobcat. She stalked toward me with a bloody rabbit dangling from her vicious teeth, her dark eyes gleaming.

Was I dreaming again?

A twig cracked under her paw. Very real.

Terror forced me to my knees. I stumbled away on all fours. I fell on my butt and shoved a hand into my pocket, fumbling for the stun gun.

"Stay away!" I snarled, pointing it at the big cat. I pressed the button in a threat, and blue light danced between the prongs.

The bobcat stopped and sat. She dropped the dead rabbit on the ground and tilted her head at me.

My hands trembled, but I didn't drop the stun gun. I did release the button.

She was beautiful. Black, tufted ears. Spotted coat. A fluffy face and over-large paws. Perhaps cutest of all, three symmetrical white lines ran parallel through the fur of her forehead, stopping between her big brown eyes, giving the illusion of scrunching her brow with curiosity or skepticism. The bobcat leaned down and nudged the dead rabbit several inches over the dusty ground.

In my direction, with an almost human-like motion.

I shivered as a cold wind cut through me. Dust and twigs fluttered on the current, and I closed my eyes against the onslaught.

When I opened them again, the bobcat had dropped the rabbit right at my feet.

She sat down, looking ridiculously similar to a housecat, and nudged the rabbit with a paw.

I caught the scent of blood on the air, and it called to the ache in my stomach.

My mouth watered.

The bobcat bobbed her head like she was encouraging me.

"Desperate t-times call for d-desperate measures." My teeth chattered.

A strange clicking sound came from the bobcat, followed by… purring?

"Could today get any weirder?"

I picked up the dead bunny.

I considered my options. I could try to eat it raw. But just the thought of the skin tearing beneath my teeth and entering my body made me retch. My body didn't want the skin or muscle.

My body wanted the blood.

A revolting thought, but I relished the warm scent hanging on the air, potent. Decadent. I'd never craved anything so much, even as my conscience writhed in horrified discomfort. My fingers curled into the rabbit's soft, gray coat, and I twisted its body until I found the large wound where the bobcat's jaws had broken its neck.

The rabbit's coat glistened with red. Nothing had ever been so beautiful.

I closed my eyes to silence the voice in the back of my head screaming "Ew, ew! Please, no!" Taking a deep breath, I pressed my lips to the gash.

Blood oozed over my tongue. Coppery. Tangy. Another flavor

appeared underneath. Crisp, clean. Like water. That refreshing note helped me swallow, but with it came fear. All-encompassing, life-or-death, fight-or-flight terror. Potent fear. The emotion tore through me, stark. Naked.

The rabbit's emotions in the moment before its death, the bobcat on its heels.

I sobbed with its distress, but my trembling fingers clutched the rabbit harder, urging its defeated body to give up more blood. Every swallow made me feel stronger. Warmer. Less hazy. I fought the urge to get up and run, to continue the flight to the safety of the rabbit's hole.

When the blood stopped flowing, I let the poor rabbit's limp body fall into my lap.

I lifted my teary eyes and looked right into the bobcat's, an inch from me.

My breath caught. I jerked back my head, and then her furry head rubbed my arm. She curled up beside me, still purring, and her heat suffused my body.

She was sharing her warmth with me.

"What is happening?" I whispered.

Her purr deepened, and she *cuddled* me.

I reached out slowly, trying not spook her. My fingers slid into the fluff on top of her head, and she leaned into my touch, closing her eyes.

A dead rabbit on my knees, my fingers in a bobcat's fur. It wasn't exactly how I'd imagined my desert trek going, but it was certainly an improvement.

She jerked her head from my rubbing fingers and growled. I gasped and reached toward the forgotten stun gun—but she wasn't growling at me. She whirled toward a scraggly bush that hugged a boulder, her hackles rising all along her back. Shimmying her shoulders, she crouched and hissed.

I squinted between her perked ears, and I saw it, too. A shifting, inky shadow, darker than the moonlit rock it was cast upon.

Summmum Malum! They'd found me. How long until they sent some-one to slaughter and burn—

"Ellis?" A familiar, deep voice cut through the eerie silence of the desert night.

I jumped, and the bobcat swatted a paw in a warning, growling louder, as a figure stepped out from behind the boulder.

But… it was on the other side from the—no, the shadow was gone. A trick of the moonlight? A shadow from the bush that had vanished with the shifting of the clouds?

Special Agent Jackson Hunter stepped around the bush and into the silvery spotlight of the moon.

Not an improvement. I'd been caught.

9
THE COLD NIGHT

I N THE MOONLIGHT, JACKSON'S DARK GAZE SWEPT OVER ME, the bobcat, and the dead rabbit.

It must look weird. I mean, there was nothing normal about this situation. Any of it—past, present, or even what waited in my future.

If I even had a future at this point.

He was alone, at least. But what was he going to do with me?

Jackson's expression gave nothing away. He'd replaced the shirt I stole with one just like it—buttoned to the top and sporting a patch that read *Hunter*. His dog tags hung outside the lapels. He had a Glock holstered at his hip and a black backpack on his shoulders. There was a new hardness to his eyes. He looked bigger in the middle of the desert than he had on the floor outside the tank.

I had no doubt he could throw me over his shoulder and take me back to the base. My fear made a reappearance, mingling with the rabbit's leftover emotions. I struggled to stand, intending to run like hell, but my brief rest had brought on the return of searing pain in my feet. The rabbit fell off my lap, and I collapsed to the dirt, breathing through the agony. My new bobcat friend made a small sound and rushed to my side.

"You're hurt," Jackson said gruffly. He whipped the backpack off his shoulders and dropped it to the ground, then went down on one knee beside me.

The bobcat growled, low and even, and wedged her upper body between us. She swiped at him, narrowly missing his face.

Jackson arched his back away from her and raised a thick eyebrow at the cat, hands up in surrender. To calm her or to calm me. Maybe both.

He glanced past the cat to me. "Where are you hurt?"

I ignored his question. "How did you find me?"

"Is it your leg? Knee?" His fingers latched onto the hem of my pants, but his gaze stayed on mine.

I crab-walked backward, away from his hands. The bobcat hissed and planted her paws, ready to spring. He'd have to go through her to reach me again.

Her presence gave me courage.

"Answer me," I demanded. "How did you find me? Are more coming?"

Jackson sighed and rested his arm over his raised knee. "I tracked you. Alone."

"*In the dark*? Can your friends do that too?"

"Does it matter?"

Curling my knees into my chest, I stared him down. After months in sensory deprivation, months of *listening* instead of speaking, I could outlast him.

He met my glare moment for moment with brooding silence. Finally, when it became obvious I wasn't going to crack, he rubbed his brow and said, "I'm an expert tracker. It's an... innate ability. The tactical training helps, though."

Innate ability? What the heck did that mean? Innate ability like my heightened sense of taste that allowed me to feel emotions? In my world, innate ability was precognition or special powers.

Regular people, non-alts, didn't have innate abilities. Not that the rules of my world were the standard. Maybe he just meant a talent.

I glanced through the dark, not gleaning much. "So, is anyone else coming?"

He shook his head. "Only me."

It was my turn to raise an eyebrow. "Really?"

Jackson glanced off into the darkness. "Gut instinct."

Something was up. Why track me alone? Why so confident no one else was coming? Not that I was complaining.

Silence fell between us. The bobcat's hackles lowered, and she returned to my side, nudging me until I buried my fingers in her soft fur. I felt lingering tension in her muscles, but the way she calmed made me think Jackson was telling the truth about being alone. That no one else waited in the shadows.

She still eyed him warily, though, yowling when he moved too suddenly to scratch his nose. Kitty cat had an attitude.

"You can't take me back there," I said, voice hard. "I won't let you. You'll have to kill me first."

He nodded. "Okay."

A pang of surprise thrummed through my chest. "Are you going to kill me?"

"Of course not," he said impatiently. "Why would I save you from drowning just to kill you?"

"Fair point."

Another beat of silence passed between us, then he motioned to the rabbit on the ground. "How did you intend on eating that?"

"I wasn't—I don't know." I didn't want to tell him about the blood. I flushed at the memory of his lip between mine, my teeth piercing his skin, the rush of his blood and emotions. A far better experience than with the rabbit.

Staring hard at me, Jackson nodded, as if answering a question he'd asked himself. He stood, leaving his pack on the ground as he walked away.

I exchanged looks with the bobcat. I wasn't a mind reader, but her eyes seemed to say she was just as confused—and cautious— as me.

He returned a moment later with his arms full of brush. He worked quickly, building a circle out of stones, then piling the debris inside. Using a lighter from his backpack, he lit a dried, dead branch of some desert plant to use as kindling, then sat for a few moments more, feeding the flames.

I watched the thick tendrils of smoke rise from the ring, then narrowed my eyes at him in suspicion. "Won't that, like, call people to our location?" Was he leaving a trail for his buddies? I should grab the stun gun and—

"Nobody is out looking to see this. They can't spare the resources they'd need to find you in the dark. They're preoccupied with the damage, the paperwork, and dealing with whoever is responsible for the fire. But mostly,"—he winced an apology—"they don't think you'll get very far. They expect to collect a body for research in the morning."

"Oh." It was all I could say. The Cyndra in my head told me to ditch him at the first opportunity, use the stun gun if necessary, but I'd never had her kind of follow-through. The fire was a necessity, my feet were in shambles, and... if he was even telling half the truth, he was my best hope of survival. Otherwise, Dr. Hurst and his minions *would* find a body out here. It had nearly happened already.

The fire grew, and I slowly slid toward the warmth, keeping one eye on Jackson. One yard, and my skin warmed. Another yard, and I could feel the heat through the bottom of my boots. A third yard, and I was close enough to hold out my hands and let the heat wash over me like water.

I crisscrossed my legs, careful of my aching feet, and kept my fingers splayed dangerously close to the flames. Slowly but surely, they began to thaw and tingle back to life.

The bobcat leaned against me with the firelight flickering in her eyes. In the orange glow, the spots on her back turned the color of milk chocolate, and the cream of her coat was like the wafer inside a KitKat bar.

I hadn't thought of KitKats in years. I loved them when I was younger. I snuck them so often it drove my mother mad, considering the battles it took to make me eat real food. Of course, that was before my abilities—my *curse*—took away that small, simple pleasure.

Kit. Wasn't that the name of the girl they'd called Bravo? Kit Katana. Gone forever, lost to somebody out there. Funny that I should think of KitKats at a time like this.

"I'm going to call you KitKat," I whispered to the bobcat. "Is that okay?"

She purred.

Jackson glanced up from where he was building a makeshift grill over the flames. "Picked up a friend, I see."

"I think she picked me."

He grunted in response as he reached for the dead rabbit. "She bring you this?"

I nodded.

His gaze slid over KitKat with something akin to suspicion, but he just turned back to the fire and started skinning the rabbit.

I swallowed rising bile at the sight and sound of the rabbit's pelt tearing off. To give me something else to focus on, I started loosening the laces on my borrowed boots. My feet were swollen. I just managed to pull the shoes off. I peeled away the thick woolen socks one at a time, fighting the urge to scream as dried blood and scabs peeled away with them.

Jackson paused his butchering and stared at my feet, illuminated by the firelight. "We need to clean those."

I shrugged. "It's fine." I'd had worse. Recently, in fact. Thanks to creepy doctors, like his buddy Craig, and their soldier drones, like him. He didn't need another look at how gross I was, anyway. "The warmth is helping."

"It's fine until gangrene sets in," Jackson retorted.

Ew. Not helping. I countered his scolding look with a wrinkled nose.

He finished dressing the rabbit and settled the body over the flames on his stick grill. Then he snatched his pack off the ground and came to sit beside me.

"What are you doing?" I leaned away from him. I wanted to trust him. He'd saved me once already, so why couldn't he be doing it again now, no strings attached? But he was still a soldier. Still an employee of that… place.

"I'm going to clean and bandage your feet." He pulled a small, white duffel bag from inside his backpack. "Don't argue with me," he added when I opened my mouth.

I clenched my teeth and glared at him, but I didn't argue. The word gangrene was still bouncing around in my head, thanks to him.

Jackson's fingers were gentle as he lifted my right foot onto his lap, angling so that he could see the worst of the sores in the firelight. "This is probably going to hurt."

"I'll be fine."

He glanced up. With his back to the flames, shadows turned his striking face into deep valleys and strong highlights. "I know you will be."

Jackson ripped open a square packet, and the sharp scent of antiseptic drifted to my nose. The first swipe of the wet cloth over my sores felt like he'd thrust my heel into the flames.

I gasped, came up off the ground, and flailed for something to hold onto while Jackson clutched my ankle in a vise grip. My hands found KitKat's fur, and I buried my face in her shoulders, hiding my tears.

"Sorry," Jackson said quietly. "Told you it would hurt."

His fingers loosened but remained against my skin. When the alcohol pad rubbed against my sores again, I managed to stay put by focusing on his fingers: Thumb. Forefinger. Middle finger. They were soft on my ankle but slightly callused.

The missing ones didn't look amputated. They didn't have a prominent knuckle or short nubs, just smooth skin in the vacant spaces. Four fingers short across two hands. The disability didn't seem to slow him down at all. He'd built the fire and skinned the rabbit with efficiency. Now he cleaned my wounds with the same speed and care.

I cleared my throat. "Can I ask you a personal question?"

"Sure," he said, never pausing his work.

"Did you lose your fingers in an accident?"

His head popped up long enough to flash me a smile. "Nope. No gritty, traumatic backstory. I was born without them."

"Oh," I said, a grin playing at my mouth. Now I just hoped I hadn't opened the door for him to ask me personal questions. I had plenty I didn't want to tell him.

After cleaning the sores, he coated my heel in ointment, then expertly bandaged me up. He wrapped the white gauze in a crisscross pattern around my ankle and heel, anchoring it in place with an inordinate amount of surgical tape. Then he moved on to my other foot.

While he cleaned, he tried to distract me from the pain with an uplifting speech. "If I hadn't found you, you probably would have died of hypothermia tonight."

Gee, thanks. I lifted my head from KitKat's fur to look at him. "Maybe not."

His gaze remained on my foot. "The desert can drop below freezing at night."

"I have KitKat."

Jackson pursed his lips but dropped the subject. "Where are you headed?"

"If I tell you, are you going to turn me in?"

The hand holding the alcohol pad fell away from my foot, and he looked at me, exasperated. "I already told you I wasn't going to do that."

"Technically, you just said you weren't going to kill me."

The firelight flickered off his eyes. "They're one and the same, aren't they? You were going to die back there. You would have. Eventually."

I traced my fingers over KitKat's spots. "I thought you worked for them."

"I did," he agreed, turning back to his cleaning. "I worked for them. But I have a mind of my own. I saw what was happening."

"You didn't agree with it." I thought of what I'd heard him say while I was underwater.

"I didn't agree with it," Jackson parroted. He opened the antibiotic ointment and slathered it over my heel, his face guarded.

Hmm. Maybe he was even more of a "tough guy with a heart of gold" than I'd thought.

This time, it was Alanna's soft voice that echoed through my head. *All people are capable of good, Ell. It's a matter of choosing it. And lots of people do—more than what this life… our situation… would have you think.*

"So, what happens now?" I asked.

"What do you mean?"

I watched the way he spread the ointment, surprised at how much I liked the sight of his hands on my skin. "Are you going to help me?"

"Tell me what's going on and what your plan is, and we'll go from there."

How much could I tell him? Not about Uncle Alec or my powers or my relic, if it even existed. Good or not, he was an outsider to my cautious, perpetually suspicious, unnatural life. There was no way he'd believe any of it anyway. He'd probably change his mind on helping me, thinking the lab was the best place for an insane person.

But if he'd just get me to Carl Simmons…

"I have a friend. An ally," I amended, since I couldn't even pretend to know what Carl looked like beyond Uncle Alec's *the only black man in Rachel* comment. "He lives in Rachel. On the outskirts of town in a trailer. I need to reach him."

Jackson wound the gauze around my ankle, glancing up as he asked, "And when you reach him?"

"When I reach him, I'll be okay," I said firmly. "He can get me to safety. Then you can go back to work before anyone knows you went rogue."

He placed surgical tape along the edge of the gauze. "Where is safety? Home?"

I shook my head. "It's just… It's a place in Colorado. I have family there. Or I will. My cousin, Vin." If Vin had actually been related to me, he'd be more like a brother, but that didn't need to be explained; I'd probably said too much already. "He'll come for me."

Jackson nodded. "Okay. I'll get you to Rachel. It's close. Half a day's walk at the most."

Relief flashed through me. He'd bought it without any weird looks. I leaned in to put my hand on his shoulder, to add weight to my "Thank you."

But the gesture put us close. Very close. My leg was still draped over his lap, my other leg crossed beneath me and pressed against his muscular thigh. Those few inches had brought me close enough to feel the warmth coming off his body. I got a whiff of cinnamon sugar, and it elicited such feelings of home in me that I wanted to wrap my arms around him and hold him here. Forever. For the night, at least. Both my homes, the idyllic fairytale image my mind had created of my early childhood house and the relaxed haven that was the Zephyrus house, were gone now. Both were in my past forever. I could never go back, except in this feeling brought on by the scent on a stranger's shirt.

In the ambient glow of the fire, his umber eyes turned chestnut, the pupils shot through with miniature Milky Ways of orange and yellow. He was beautiful. A beautiful savior.

Jackson's lips parted, and his gaze slid to my mouth.

My breath hitched in my throat. I remembered the taste of him. Ginger and wild honey. I could close the rest of the space between us and taste that again. Maybe get a bit of blood from the cut I'd left on his lip. Taste his emotions, taste everything that made Jackson Hunter who he was.

KitKat growled.

I sucked in a breath and pulled away, tucking my hand back in my lap as I extracted my leg from his grasp. The bobcat stared into the night, her hackles rippling.

Jackson popped up to his feet, following KitKat's gaze over the desert. "We should find a different place to rest for the night. It's too open here. I know Hurst's official order was to wait till morning, but maybe Reyes…" He shook his head like the thought was silly, but my blood went cold, and not just because he'd stepped away, taking his blissful warmth with him. "Either way. We should move."

"Couldn't we just keep going to Carl's trailer?" I asked.

"You need to rest those feet unless you want to lose them," Jackson replied, tucking the spent alcohol wipes back into the first aid kit. "We'll find a hiding spot and rest. Leave at first light when things start to warm up."

While Jackson packed his things and wrapped the cooked rabbit in a towel from his bag, I shoved my bandaged feet back into Reyes' socks and boots. The ointment must have had a numbing agent in it. KitKat helped me to my feet, and I tested out walking. Still painful but not debilitating. The thick bandages around my heels had the added benefit of making the boots fit more snugly. No more rubbing.

Jackson passed the wrapped meat to me, then kicked dirt onto the fire while I tried to hold the rabbit far enough away from my body that I wouldn't smell it. The little bit of blood I'd managed to drink before he showed up had gone a long way toward giving me strength. The last thing I wanted to do was catch a whiff of physical food and vomit up the only dinner I could stomach.

Once the fire was out, he put an arm around my waist, and we set off at a slow hobble. KitKat followed, staying close to my other side.

Jackson was right. We didn't make it far before my feet began to protest. There was no way I'd be walking a half day to Carl Simmons' trailer tonight. I let Jackson take the lead and focused on breathing through the pain. If I had any luck at all, the rabbit's blood and a couple hours of sleep would help me get past the worst of it.

Jackson jerked us to a stop, fingers squeezing my side. "Do you hear that?" He perked up like a pointer hound, surveying the area in front of us without moving an inch. He barely breathed.

KitKat let out a hellish, screaming yowl, and I almost didn't hear the rattle. Like a maraca.

"Rattler," Jackson said.

"Where?" I breathed, then snapped my fingers at the bobcat, hissing, "KitKat, come here. Don't get bit." She was crouching like she wanted to pounce on the viper, her hackles spiked along her spine.

"There." Jackson pointed to a scrub bush growing up a craggy rock formation. "In the crevice beneath the rock, behind that bush. See it coiling up? The sand's moving."

I followed his directions and spotted the fat, scaly head poised atop two loops of its coiled body. It rattled again and opened its jaws wide, popping out its formidable fangs. KitKat growled, low and seething like she had a vendetta, but she inched back two paces, bumping her stump tail into my shin.

"Come on, we'll just give it space." Jackson urged me forward with the arm wrapped around my back.

The snake uncoiled and slithered out from its rock, but we hurried past it in a wide semicircle and kept walking a mile or so before Jackson found a makeshift cave in one of the rocky hills. It was exposed on two sides, but the wind's strength and chill were halved once we got under shelter. The three of us sandwiched together in the cramped space. Jackson's cinnamon-laced body heat was a relished blanket against the cold… until KitKat wriggled in between us with several unladylike grunts, bonking her skull against Jackson's chest until he scooted to admit her.

Jackson shook his head at her on a long, audible exhale, then unwrapped the rabbit and began peeling off strips.

I tried not to gag, but it wasn't easy to move back with half of KitKat's body draped over me like a throw blanket, her fat paw on my shoulder. At least the earthy musk of her fur cut through some of the cloying barbeque smell. Her head twisted at an alarming degree to keep a watchful eye on Jackson. This bobcat was something else. Unnaturally smart, intuitive, and tame—toward me anyway.

Unnatural, like me. Maybe that was why we'd found each other. Maybe she'd been someone's pet? Maybe a trained circus animal? Maybe there was more to it. Something of my world, the alt world. Something—

"It won't be fine cuisine, but it'll give you a little strength," Jackson said, yanking me from my study of KitKat by offering me the thready meat.

Holding my breath, I accepted it from his fingers and thanked anybody who was listening that it was almost pitch black beneath the stones. While Jackson tore into his own piece, I surreptitiously fed mine to KitKat.

Jackson polished off the rest of the edible meat, then wrapped the remains back in the towel and shoved it in the bottom of his backpack. At my questioning look, he shrugged. "We don't want wildlife coming for our scraps."

Away from the wind, the cave seemed eerily hushed.

I shivered and shoved my hands into my pockets, wishing we could have a fire again. KitKat snuggled me, crawling into my lap, her muzzle pressed to my neck like she could warm me up by osmosis, and her weight tipped me sideways into Jackson.

He readjusted, wrapping his arm around my shoulders. Cinnamon sugar wrapped around me, too. "Best we stay close. Share body heat."

I nodded. "Right."

Body heat was fine and all, but I cared more about how being so close to him made me feel.

KitKat, on the other hand, growled as his fingers touched her fur. She snapped at him. A warning, not meant to hurt him, but it drove his fingers away.

"I don't think your pet likes me," Jackson muttered, curling his fingers around my shoulder to keep them away from the bobcat.

"She's not my pet," I said, "and she doesn't trust you."

His gaze met mine in the dark. All I could see of his eyes was the faint reflection of the night sky. "Do you?"

"Jury's still out."

I didn't think I'd be able to fall asleep wedged against a stone wall under Jackson's arm, but I must have. When I opened my eyes next, dawn tinged the horizon outside the opening in the cave walls, and Jackson was squeezing back inside, bathed in the rosy light of morning.

"Let's get moving," he said, shoving something deeper in his pocket.

"What were you doing out there?" I tried for a playful smirk, though unease made my heart skip beats.

"Had to do a little, uh, business," he said, cringing slightly.

"Oh." I blushed. "Of course." I cleared my throat. "Yeah, I'm ready. Let's go."

Traveling through the desert in the early morning was a much nicer experience than at night. The sun warmed the land until the cold was a bitter memory, yet the hottest part of the day was hours away still, so we wouldn't burn to a crisp, either.

We remained mostly silent for the journey, which suited me. My feet weren't one hundred percent yet. Though they *did* feel a little better. I still had to concentrate on making sure I didn't fall on my face. Jackson seemed on high alert, his rich brown eyes missing nothing of our surroundings.

Once, to distract myself from the discomfort in my heels, I almost asked about him and Nurse Violet. If they were dating, friends, whatever. But I decided I didn't need to get to know him or make casual conversation.

Not if I wanted to walk away from him at the end of this journey. Besides, I didn't know if I'd like his answer.

We left the hills behind by mid-morning and stayed off the highway as we took the road toward town. There wasn't much to hide behind, but there weren't many cars passing, either.

The turn off came up on us suddenly, just past a sign that read *Rachel, 2 mi.*

Dust billowed beneath our feet as we took the small gravel drive through a thick copse of juniper trees. On the other side, the tress parted to reveal a dingy, white, single-wide trailer.

Just like Uncle Alec said.

Not that I'd mistrusted his guidance. Not in the least. I was just relieved to be here, one step closer to Vin and my guidestone.

Jackson motioned for me to hang back, then stepped onto the concrete stoop and knocked on the door. It shuffled in its frame, making the knock more alarming. When Jackson's fist lowered, the door opened several inches and hung there, revealing a strip of dark interior.

He glanced back at me, raising an eyebrow. I shrugged.

In the anticipatory silence, I waited with bated breath. The chittering of birds and the *whoosh* of distant cars were the only answer to Jackson's knock.

"Hello?" Jackson called. He peered into the trailer. "Anybody home?"

No answer.

He glanced back at me once before disappearing inside.

KitKat pressed against my legs, and I petted the three white lines on her head, my heart racing.

Carl Simmons was supposed to be here.

Carl Simmons was supposed to get me to Vin.

Jackson returned a moment later, his face grim. "No one home."

"Maybe he's just out," I said, crestfallen.

Jackson took my elbow, glanced around the clearing, and then started to lead me away. "No, Ellis. I don't think so. There's blood. Everywhere."

10

MORE BLOOD

CHILLS TURNED MY SKIN TO ICE DESPITE THE BEAMING sunshine.

I stared up at Jackson's profile as he pulled me away from the trailer. The sky didn't seem real. It was too bright. Too harsh. The sun glared around his head like a halo, and it felt like a lie.

So did everything he'd just said.

This trailer and Carl Simmons were the only leads I had to help me reach Vin, so I planted my heels in the grass. I immediately regretted my decision. Pain lanced up my legs from my blistered soles, and I stumbled onto my toes for relief. KitKat danced around us, growling and nipping at Jackson's knees.

"Blood?" I said sharply. "What do you mean there's blood?"

Ignoring KitKat's attempts to punish him for touching me, Jackson readjusted his grip on my arm and leaned down to speak in a low, hushed tone. "I mean, something bad went down in that trailer. We need to get out of here."

He marched onward, dragging me along. His gaze darted around the clearing like he expected an attack at any moment, and his free hand hovered near his gun. Like some hidden enemy might be lying in wait.

But there was no one around. We'd walked right up to this trailer from the desert, miles outside town, and hadn't seen a single person on our way. We'd seen one car. Maybe two.

Nothing looked out of the ordinary. No weapons. No signs of a struggle. No body.

"No," I said, yanking against Jackson's hold. "No, it's just a set up."

Jackson raised his eyebrow. "A set up. Are you serious right now? Ellis, there is *blood* in that trailer, and no dead body to go with it. We aren't safe here."

"There's *no dead body*," I repeated pointedly. "It's staged. To keep people away. Carl's in there. Hiding."

Jackson rubbed the bridge of his nose with his free hand. "It's not staged. That's real blood."

"How do you know? It could be from a blood bag."

"It's not. Because it's not staged. I know."

He couldn't though.

He couldn't know how dangerous my life was. He couldn't know that the idea of staging a murder scene wasn't out of the norm for an alt always on the run from intangible, unknowable enemies. I imagined there were no lengths my family wouldn't go to in the name of protecting me and my sisters from the Summum Malum.

Jackson couldn't know the difference between fake blood and real blood because he didn't have some special power to scent blood.

Not like I did.

I tugged my arm out of his grasp and ran. Back to the trailer. Up the two concrete stairs. Over the threshold.

The moment I stepped inside, shadows enveloped me, as dark and unforgiving as the desert last night. I wavered just inside the doorway, loathe to walk away from the only light I had.

The interior smelled stale. Musty, like it had been sitting empty for a while. Under the dust, I smelled a hint of mildew, and something else. Something that made my stomach gurgle and brought my hunger back full force.

Blood.

Real blood.

Jackson was right.

A slim beam of light spilled over my arm. Jackson's presence loomed behind me, blocking most of the sunlight, but his tiny flashlight chased away the shadows. I felt better with him at my side.

The beam illuminated a saggy, overstuffed couch in a garish orange floral pattern, an old-fashioned box TV with a detached antennae sitting on a cheap particle-board table, and a bare, warped coffee table made of wooden pallets.

Dried blood spatter covered all of it.

A delicate arc across the back of the couch, as if an artery had been severed. Thick, rusty drops down the cushions and the television screen. What looked like a handprint on the table, as if the victim had used it to catch their fall.

"See what I mean?" Jackson murmured close to my ear.

"We need to search anyway. Please," I added, embarrassed at how small my voice sounded.

What if something had happened to Carl? Or even worse, Vin?

"There's not a lot of blood," I said. "Not enough to prove someone died here. Let's double check."

Jackson stared at me in the ambient glow of his flashlight for a long moment, then he swiveled his pack around and dug inside, withdrawing a second flashlight. He offered it to me without comment, then slid past me into the trailer.

KitKat poked her head into the doorway, and I pointed back out into the sunlight.

"Wait outside, girl," I told her. "Keep watch."

She glared at me—an honest to goodness human glare. She had to be tied to the old magic somehow. Maybe a descendant of one of the beasts in Uncle Alec's ancient Greek and Egyptian texts, which he claimed hinted at what life was like before the Priestesses made the relics, if you looked close enough and read between the lines.

Despite her sass, KitKat backed up and sat on her haunches by the concrete stoop, staring off across the yard.

The trailer wasn't big. Single wide, every room connected and only separated by half-partitions, except for the bathroom, which had its own accordion door. The furniture was sparse—a bed and a dresser in the bedroom, a single chair and a folding card table in the kitchen, and a couch and TV stand in the main living area.

Not many places to hide.

I opened every cabinet in the kitchen, though most of them weren't even large enough to hide a toddler. I found three plates, two bowls, a coffee mug, and a bottle of Svedka vodka. Carl apparently didn't go big on belongings. The trash can only held three crushed beer cans and the contents of an ashtray. A dorm-sized fridge was unplugged from the wall and held only a half-empty bottle of mustard.

In the bedroom, I dropped to my knees on thin, well-trafficked carpet and peeked beneath the bed. I found a suitcase—empty—and about three inches of dust, but no hidden Carl. The dresser drawers held more clothes than I expected, after the ghost town that was the kitchen.

If he'd packed up and left, surely the suitcase would be gone. There would be holes in the drawers where he picked out clothes for his trip.

So where was Carl Simmons?

As I was walking back toward the front of the trailer, Jackson emerged from the bathroom.

"Clear," he said in a crisp, militaristic voice. "Three-in-one shampoo. No towel. A dry toilet."

I stepped past him and sank into the metal chair at the makeshift kitchen table. "No running water. In the desert. Another bad sign, huh?"

Jackson came to stand before me, hands clasped behind his back. He looked through the open partition into the living room where a sharp angle of daylight fell across the bloody coffee table. "I'm sorry, Ellis, but your friend isn't here. Quite frankly, I'd hate to even guess what happened to him."

I swallowed hard to unclog my windpipe, thinking about last night, right before Jackson showed. That shadow. Maybe I had really seen it after all. What if it was Summum Malum? They might have sent someone in the dead of night. Was it my fault? Had they overheard where I was headed?

Jackson cleared his throat, startling me. "I hate to ask, but… was this guy mixed up with anything shady?"

"No," I said sharply. "He was a friend of my uncle's."

"How well did you know him?" Jackson asked. "Because… this looks like a hit or something. It wasn't an animal. No tracks. Could be drug related."

I didn't know Carl at all, but I didn't want to admit that, didn't want to have to explain that the only connection I had to Carl was our alt blood.

So, instead, I said, "It's still not enough blood to prove death. A human body holds way more than what's there."

"I'll give you that, though I'm unsure how you could possibly know the blood content of a human body."

"Around five liters," I muttered, more to myself than to Jackson.

"Uh…"

"I like police procedurals," I said with a shrug. "The fictional ones. Like *Criminal Minds*."

"Really?" His disbelieving smile crinkled his nose.

"Derek Morgan's a babe, all right."

"And the truth comes out." Jackson's smile grew, and all the air whooshed from my lungs. It was the first real smile I'd seen, outside of his knowing smirks. It tugged at his face and reached all the way to his eyes, transforming him. The strong, tough soldier became a playful kid in a split second.

But it was hard to maintain a smile in such a grim setting, and both our faces fell slowly, observing the trailer like some new clue might pop out and hit us in the face.

"Carl's okay. He has to be," I said softly.

As Jackson continued to eye the empty trailer, I stared at the swirling black tattoo on his temple, mesmerized by the depth of it on his skin. I wondered if he'd gotten it before becoming a soldier or after. It seemed like the kind of thing the military would look down on. But he looked so young. Had he gotten it in high school?

I thought it was beautiful.

"Do you have a back-up plan?" he asked.

I slouched in the cold metal chair and crossed my arms over my dusty shirt. Jackson's dusty shirt. "No. All I can do is wait and hope my cousin shows up."

"You know for sure he's coming?"

I laughed, but it wasn't a happy sound. Bitterness took the place of mirth. "I don't know anything. I'm running blind."

"Does your cousin have a phone number?"

I nodded slowly. "Yeah. But I don't have a phone."

He blinked at me. "What happened to mine? I've been meaning to ask."

I cringed. "Sorry. I don't know what happened to it."

I did. But I decided to keep that information to myself. "Maybe Nurse Violet picked it up."

"Maybe."

"So, I'm guessing you don't have a spare."

He snorted. "No. My contract only pays for the one."

I scanned the walls of the kitchenette. "Even if this place has one, I doubt it works."

Jackson offered me a hand. "Let's go. There's a one-stop shop down the road that has a pay phone outside. Last I passed through, at any rate."

I motioned to my clothes. "I can't go in public like this. These clearly aren't mine. I look like I've escaped from a secret governmental facility where I tranqed a guard in the ass for his things."

"Did you really?" Jackson asked, but then he closed his eyes and held up both hands. "No. Don't answer that. I'll keep my plausible deniability."

"If I'd fled the base in the tiny scraps they dressed me in, I really would have died of hypothermia," I pointed out. "Reyes is fine. He'll walk it off."

"Reyes, huh?" Jackson grinned again, a real one that melted a piece of my chest. "You're fearless, Ellis. Anybody ever told you that before?"

No. Cyn was the fearless one. "I'm a survivor. There's a difference."

Jackson grunted. "I think there's a thin line between those."

That thin line seemed a chasm to me, but it was nice to think I could be compared to Cyn.

"Let's head to town," he went on. "You can try to call your cousin, and I'll find you some less conspicuous clothes."

I needed those. Carl's weren't going to work. Whoever he was, he must have been twice the size of Reyes and built like an ox.

"Maybe grab some food, too."

I refrained from telling him I wanted nothing to do with food, because my growling stomach made it sound otherwise. I wasn't ready to tell the blood-sucking truth yet, either.

Currently, Jackson Hunter was the only ally I had. Best to not scare him off.

"What if someone sees me?" I asked.

"It's the wrong time of year for Rachel to be busy. We can get in and out. It's a plan, at least," he said.

"The only one we have," I murmured.

He offered me his hand again, and this time, I took it.

The Little A'Le'Inn sat right on the main road that ran through Rachel—a ranch-style building with a corrugated metal roof and a giant UFO painted beside the front door. A green alien statue the size of a young child stood on the sidewalk out front holding a sign announcing, "Welcome Earthlings," while the large road sign promised a combination bar, motel, and restaurant.

"You have got to be kidding me," I said as we approached the door.

Jackson chuckled. "Welcome to alien country."

"Is there not another, more *normal* store to shop at?"

He shook his head and shoved his hands in his pockets with a smirk. "On the bright side, you really won't look *that* out of place at a restaurant that caters to people dressed up like little green men."

I rolled my eyes, but I laughed anyway. And it felt good. Foreign and strange, but good. Like my time at the base had made the muscles in my throat atrophy just as bad as my legs. Or was it the tiny knot of fear in my diaphragm that made the sound stutter? Despite Jackson's assurances, I didn't like waltzing out into the open looking like a lab rat, especially not this close to the military base.

Jackson took the lead, bypassing the front door to circle around the side of the building. A weathered picnic table sat off in the sparse grass, but otherwise, the area was bare.

No pay phone.

"Dammit," Jackson muttered. "I could have sworn it was here."

"It's probably in an antique store somewhere now," I quipped. Uncle Alec never let us venture out much, but even I knew pay phones had gone the way of the dinosaurs. Thank the Priestesses for TV, or I'd have gone the same way, completely out of the loop, disconnected from the world.

It was Jackson's turn to laugh. "Touché. They probably have a phone inside you could borrow."

"I don't know… It seems risky. What if the base comes looking for me? The workers are going to remember a malnourished girl with a shaved head wearing giant military fatigues."

My stomach twisted at the image—a reminder that Jackson had been seeing me at my worst.

I couldn't shove away the burning shame trailing up my neck to my cheeks.

Jackson planted his hands on his hips and shook his head, glancing off at the mountains like he could see the base. "Nah. The alien community has a healthy mistrust of the soldiers. I think we'll be fine."

"If you say so," I muttered and followed him through the nondescript front door, hoping he was right.

The interior was part gift shop, part restaurant, and all crazy. Hundreds of dollar bills clung to the ceiling over the wooden bar in some strange ritual I didn't understand. Tables dotted the open floor, and even the hotel-grade furniture had UFO patterns on the cushions. Jackson pointed me to the bar, where a guy in a white apron stood polishing a glass.

"Go ask if you can use the phone," Jackson said. "I'll find clothes."

I picked my way around the scattered tables, thankful the place was empty this early in the day. But crowds or not, a Humvee could drive by at any moment. A soldier could get the urge to come in for a drink. Any number of things could go wrong and send me right back into Dr. Hurst's clutches.

I'd die before that happened.

The bartender watched me approach with a passive expression on his round face. He was young, mid-twenties maybe, with a head full of black hair I was jealous of and skin so pale it seemed translucent. He sat the cleaned glass on a shelf as I slipped onto a bar stool.

"Need a menu?" he asked, bored.

He didn't give my get-up more than a glance.

"No, no menu," I replied. "I was wondering if I could borrow your phone."

The guy shrugged. He tossed his rag over his shoulder and turned to grab a cordless handset mounted on the back wall.

I took it from his sausage-like fingers. "It's not a local number."

"No worries. Free long distance."

He headed down the bar to give me some semblance of privacy, and I stared at the keypad, searching my memory banks for Vin's phone number. Cellphones made things so much easier—one click and go. But Uncle Alec prepared us for the inevitability of being stranded and alone, without our belongings. I'd been forced to memorize his number, plus Vin's, Cyn's, and Lana's.

Crazy that it had come to pass. Crazy that only two of the numbers went anywhere now, and Uncle Alec couldn't even answer his.

I gulped back a swell of emotion that threatened to clog my throat, then dialed.

Instead of ringing, the line let out a series of garish tones, and the robotic operator told me the number was disconnected.

"*What?*" My heart stopped beating. I double checked the numbers I'd entered.

I'd transposed one.

The surge of fear and adrenaline ebbed, but I was still a puddle of anxiety.

I took a steadying breath, hung up, and then redialed with shaking fingers, careful to hit the right buttons this time.

The line rang six times before an automated message told me the mailbox was full.

Dammit. And strange. Why would so many people need to reach Vin at once? Had something gone down in the alt community while I was locked away?

I tried three more times, but Vin didn't answer.

Dejected, I called out a "thanks" to the bartender and left a wrinkled five-dollar bill on the counter from Reyes' wallet.

When I found Jackson, he was standing in a narrow alcove packed full of souvenirs and touristy items. He held up two t-shirts, one with a cartoon alien head on the front and the other white with red lettering: "Area 51 Warning Deadly Force Authorized."

"They're both horrific," I said.

"Take your pick. This is your selection. Only one kind of shorts that would fit you, too," Jackson added, tossing me a pair of purple cotton basketball shorts marked with an alien head and the Little A'Le'Inn name.

"Kill me now," I muttered. Uncle Alec's stay-at-home tendencies meant I'd grown accustomed to an unlimited online selection when shopping. I was still dying to shop at a real, physical mall, but this was far from the glitz and sparkle of a bustling galleria. "Shoes?"

"No go. You're stuck with the boots for now. But if you want clean socks…" He pointed at a rack near my knees.

I sighed and swiped the *Warning* t-shirt from his fingers, then crouched to pick out a pair of socks. "As if I haven't already suffered a dozen indignities."

Jackson grimaced. He reached out and gave my shoulder a comforting squeeze. "I'm sorry, Ellis. What they did to you… There's no excuse."

I shrugged, staring down at the Area 51 t-shirt so he wouldn't see the hot tears stinging my eyes. "Yeah. You know. I'll get over it with years of therapy."

"Hey." His hand moved, and his fingers pressed against my chin, angling my face up so he could look me in the eye. "Quit doing that."

"Doing what?" I demanded, irrationally furious that he'd exposed my watery eyes.

"Covering up your pain with jokes. You need to deal with what happened."

"I will. When I'm safe with my cousin back home." Though there was no going back to our old home, we'd make another place a home. I blinked away the tears before they could spill over my cheeks, then snagged the socks with the least amount of cartoon aliens on them. "Let's get out of here."

On the way to the register, I grabbed a cheap vinyl sling satchel with the motel's logo on it. I needed something to carry the wallet, knife, and stun gun. I also snagged a pen to write the safehouse coordinates somewhere safer than my arm, especially with the day's heat building. Wouldn't do me good to sweat away my only other lead to Vin. Maybe he wasn't picking up, but I knew I could rely on him to come searching for me or meet me in Colorado if something went awry, no matter what. Unless he'd been the "firestarter" they captured at the base. But I brushed the thought away. Vin could influence others, within the facility, to break me out. He probably never stepped foot inside. He was smart.

The bartender left the bar as we ventured up to the cash register.

He wore that same passive, bored expression the entire time he rang up our purchases. Jackson tossed a few bags of food on the counter: some single-serving bags of chips, a package of beef jerky, and a bag of candy that I didn't quite see before the clerk shoved it in a plastic bag. He added a couple bottles of water, too.

I blanched, knowing he was going to force me to drink one.

He knew how dehydrated I got back at the base.

The bartender totaled the order and looked at Jackson. "That'll be $125.60."

I balked. "For a bag, a t-shirt, some shorts, and some chips?"

The bartender shrugged. "I don't set the prices."

I peeled off five twenties and three tens from the stash in the guard's wallet, grimacing at handing over more than half my total amount in one go. The bartender passed me some change, then Jackson picked up our bags and we booked it out of there.

"That was sheer robbery," I griped when we were back on the road toward Carl's trailer.

"I could have put it on my card."

"Why, so the government could track us to the Little A'Le'Inn?" I scoffed. "No, it's best you don't leave a paper trail. When Vin comes for me, you need to walk away clean." I glanced over my shoulder at the store. "That place was weird."

Then I did a doubletake.

The bartender had followed us outside.

He stood just outside the front door, a smoking cigarette dangling from his lips as he watched us walk away.

"Don't look," I hissed at Jackson, "but that clerk followed us outside. He's watching us."

Jackson's shoulders tensed. He surreptitiously swept his gaze over the empty fields to our left, then casually glanced at the bartender.

"Do you think the base has put out some kind of bulletin?" I whispered.

"No. Not with the Inn," Jackson said, though his tone betrayed his unease. "But maybe we should get out of town. Hole up some-where else while you try to get in touch with your cousin. Just in case."

"No. We wait here," I said firmly. "Vin is coming for me."

Jackson turned his enigmatic gaze on me. "What if he isn't?"

I didn't have a response to that. I was trying really hard not to entertain that possibility.

Because it seemed *way* too possible.

11

THE WARM NIGHT

As we climbed the inclined drive to the trailer, I heard KitKat mewl. I'd been afraid I'd come back to find her gone, and my relief was surprisingly strong. But when she called the second time, I registered fear in the sound. I raced ahead, but Jackson quickly paced me as we came over the rise.

KitKat was backed against the trailer, hissing and swatting at a semi-circle of advancing snakes.

"Holy shit." I turned in a circle, scanning the ground for a rock to bash the serpents' heads.

"Stay back," Jackson said and broke a branch off a juniper tree. "I'll handle it."

He crept up on the ring of snakes in three silent strides and scooped a big black one up on his stick. Tossing it aside like dirty laundry, he lifted a brown one and gave it the same treatment. It flew a few feet, landed with a thump, and slithered back into the copse of trees. The remaining snakes wriggled their heads around, rearing at the new threat. Jackson trapped the head of a coppery, patterned viper with his stick and then stomped it into the dust with the heel of his boot. KitKat took care of the final black snake, pouncing it with a snarl and ripping open its scales in a flurry of claws.

I drew a full inhale. "Well, that was dramatic."

"That was *weird*," Jackson said. "Snakes aren't pack animals."

He poked the crushed snake with his stick. "Thank God only that one was venomous. I think."

KitKat rubbed her side against Jackson's leg, purring, momentarily forgetting her wariness of him in her gratitude. Then she pranced over to greet me.

I kneeled to hug her, nuzzling her fur. She smelled of sunshine and grass. "Thank goodness you're all right."

She purred loudly, side-eyeing Jackson as he set the bags on a stump in the yard.

He shuffled through one of the bags and retrieved one bottle of water, the beef jerky, and some corn chips. "You know, normal bobcats don't behave like that. If you tried to hug a wild bobcat, it'd probably rip your face off."

"Your face, maybe," I replied, baring my teeth in a saucy grin. "KitKat is my friend. She would never."

He frowned but didn't press further. "Do you want to wash up before you change?" He motioned toward the copse of trees sectioning the trailer off from the road. "There's a well pump there. Shampoo in the trailer. If the guard cat stays with you, I'll go wait on the other side of the trailer while you wash."

If the guard cat stays with you. It made me feel all warm and fuzzy to know he worried about leaving me alone. Even though the bartender hadn't followed us, the weird way he'd watched us walk away still stuck in my mind.

"A bath would actually be really great." I glanced at the rust-red pump. It popped out of the ground, looking like an overgrown wrench with a spade attached. "How does it work?"

Jackson grabbed the three-in-one shampoo from Carl's shower, then gave me a crash course in how to pump the well. Afterward, he dug down into his pack for the leftover pieces of rabbit, which he tossed onto the ground for KitKat before he disappeared around the trailer with his stash of food. KitKat happily grabbed the unidentifiable leftovers and lay down a few paces away from the well to gnaw on them.

I peeled off the heavy boots, wishing I had something more comfortable to wear. At least I could trash the gross, bloody wool socks I'd stolen off Reyes. I tossed them into the brush, then unbuttoned Jackson's shirt. I stored the wallet and other sundry stolen items in my Little A'Le'Inn sling bag before pulling his shirt off my shoulders. I brushed my thumb over the patch that declared his last name, then carefully folded it and put it in the plastic bag that held the rest of the food.

Reyes' pants ended up in the brush with the socks, along with the pieces of black cloth that had offered pitiful covering in the tank. It took me a full minute to unravel the gauze on my feet, and that joined the refuse, too. Surprisingly, my heels felt a lot better than they had last night, but I stayed on my tiptoes, anyway, to avoid unnecessary damage or infection from the rocky soil.

I paused long enough to copy the coordinates onto one of the receipts in Reyes' wallet—just in case my "bath" washed them off my arm—then started pumping.

The water came out ice cold, but the sun was hot enough to balance the temperature. I still flinched as the icy stream splashed across my lower legs, so I decided to wait until my skin adapted to the cold.

I didn't even recognize my body. Even after all these weeks, the shock was fresh. My stomach was concave, and my breasts were barely there. I could see every rib. My hip bones stuck out like broken bird wings. For the last sixteen hours, all I'd worried about was surviving. I'd operated on autopilot, too desperate to get the hell away from that place to give my destroyed looks more than a few moments' thought.

In the harsh light of day, as I scrubbed dirt from my joints, I couldn't ignore it anymore. My gaze lingered and blurred with tears.

I rubbed Carl's manly-scented shampoo onto my shaved head and mourned my hair. My crowning glory—a thick mass of healthy waves that had fallen well past my shoulders. Now, there were only downy tufts where it was trying to grow back in patches around the raw suction-sensor bruises and the big, scabbed bed sore that had taken root during days spent strapped to hospital beds. I carefully massaged soap around the tender spots and cried for who I was before.

Before the flash bombs.

Before I fell in the pool.

Before I was kidnapped.

Before the experiments.

Before the tank and the oxygen mask.

Before I had to run.

I knelt in the growing mud puddle to duck my head beneath the stream of water. My hips and legs protested, and those bed sores stretched uncomfortably.

The sores on my hips and lower back were raw from constantly hitching up the guard's pants. I carefully scooped cold water over the wounds, then cleaned them with soap, hissing in pain the whole time. The cold helped ease the ache a little, and I thought of the ointment Jackson had used on my feet last night. It had numbed the pain enough for me to breathe. Once I was washed up, I should slather it on the rest of my sores.

After I rinsed off all the soap, I stepped clear of the sudsy mud puddle and carefully rinsed my feet. Nurse Violet had managed to keep my nails clipped during my incarceration, so at least I didn't have bear claws. Though, I didn't think her decision to manicure me had anything to do with worrying about my vanity. Lacking a towel, I sat on the stump and turned my face up to the sky, letting the sunshine dry my skin and warm my insides. KitKat left the remnants of her meal and moved beneath my feet where she fell asleep, while I listened to the birds chirping and the wind blowing.

It was peaceful. Probably the most peace I would have for a while.

I sat long enough for the water to evaporate. Long enough to feel fortified by the sunshine.

Long enough to rediscover hope. If the sun could shine and the birds could sing, I could get out of this mess.

Even if Vin didn't come. I'd go to him.

Once I was dressed in my ridiculous alien wear, I found Jackson sitting in an old lawn chair with an open pack of chips in one hand as he stared off into the distance. The back side of the trailer faced a vast prairie of desert brush that backed up to mountains a couple miles away. The single-wide may not have been a rich man's dream, but the view was pretty nice.

KitKat stretched out on the sparse grass, while I eased into a second chair beside Jackson.

"You still have that ointment? The numbing stuff?"

"Yeah." His gaze swept over the t-shirt, shorts, and my bare feet. "You want me to rebandage you?"

"No, my feet are fine for now. But the sores on—" I cut off, flushing with shame. "I was restrained on my back for a long time before you came."

Jackson's lips tightened. "I know. I saw when I pulled you from the water."

I glanced away, too embarrassed to look at him. To relive that moment. He had to think I was the most disgusting thing he'd ever seen. "It all just *hurts*. I'm hoping the ointment will help. It did my feet."

Jackson reached into his backpack, open beside his chair, and pulled out the white duffel bag that held the first aid kit. He set his chips aside, then angled his chair toward me. "Give me your back."

I blinked at him. "I can do it."

He tilted his head and gave me a look. "You can't even see your back."

"I can feel it!"

"Ellis," he said quietly as he unzipped the first aid kit. "Let me do this for you."

"I..." I didn't want to admit to him that I was ashamed of the way I looked. That seemed so stupid right now, after what I'd survived. Like I should reconsider my priorities. Stop being so shallow.

But it didn't change how I felt.

My heart hammered in my throat as I stood and turned my back to him.

Clenching my teeth and closing my eyes, I pulled my t-shirt up inch by inch, until I could feel the warm air brushing along my skin. I tugged the hem tight around my belly to expose the sores along my back and bent forward.

I felt naked, even though I wasn't. I knew he could see every single nodule in my spine. Every rib. Every festering wound.

I was so lost in feeling sorry for myself that when Jackson's fingers touched my skin, I jumped.

He didn't mention it.

He swiped the antibiotic ointment above the patch of sores, then carefully began working it down to where everything hurt. "I wanted to be a nurse."

My eyes shot open. "What?"

"When I was a kid," Jackson added, his fingers soft. "I was obsessed with the human body, with diseases, with medicine, the whole nine yards."

I saw what he was doing. Distracting me from the pain.

I hated how much I appreciated it.

"You didn't want to be a doctor?" I asked, then gasped as his fingers hit a sore spot.

Jackson paused, lifting his hand to give me a moment to breathe through the pain. Then he continued his story and his rubbing. "I couldn't afford that kind of education."

"So, why didn't you become a nurse?"

"I couldn't afford that kind of education, either."

His fingers dipped lower, toward my hip. I placed all my focus on his words so I wouldn't think about what he was seeing. How he was seeing me.

"Surely you could have gotten student loans," I said.

Jackson laughed, a short, sharp sound. "Not a lot of options for student loans when you don't have a family. No financial aid. No assistance. The government will feed you and find someone's shithole house for you to sleep in, shuffle you from house to house when you're no longer wanted, but college? Nah."

"Oh," I said, my heart aching for him. "You were a foster kid?"

"All my life." His fingers stalled out on my skin, warm and soft. "I need to get the sores under your shorts."

My breath hitched in my throat. "Um. Okay."

He left his fingers where they were and used his other hand to peel the elastic waistband away.

I closed my eyes and swallowed, my skin tingling where he touched me. His hand moved down, beneath my waistband, and my body caught fire.

"So, you became a soldier instead," I said, a little breathlessly.

"Free education. A home, a paycheck, even medical training. Next best option for a guy like me." He let out a soft half-laugh. "My interest in medicine is how Violet and I became friends in basic training. I found out she was training to be a medic and pestered her with non-stop questions. I'm surprised she didn't tell me to take a hike. Vi just let a motormouth kid trail behind her all day and read her training manuals, for some reason."

Friends. Just friends? I wanted to press a little, ask more about their relationship, ask what he meant by "kid". How old had he been? But his fingers swiped lower toward the curve of my butt, and I froze. The way the waistband pushed his hand in, I could feel heat from his palm, as if he were touching me. Palming such a private part of me.

If my face gets any redder, I'm going to spontaneously combust.

I needed something—literally anything—to keep me from focusing on his touch.

My roving eyes found the plastic shopping bag that held the rest of the snacks. Right on top was the bag of candy he'd picked up at the Little A'Le'Inn.

"Candied ginger?" I asked.

Ginger. Sugar. I could taste his lips again—sweetness cut with a spicy bite. I had no way of telling if the warm ginger tang on his mouth had been from candy or an innate flavor of *him.*

"My one sweet tooth," Jackson replied. "Picked up the habit from the only foster parent to ever give a damn about me. You know how some things just taste like home?"

Oh, did I. His ginger taste had brought memories of my sister and gingerbread cookies. A knot of homesickness clenched inside me.

My mouth felt dry. I licked my lips and swallowed. "Sure."

The waistband snapped gently back into place, and his fingers disappeared only to reappear on my head. He rubbed ointment into the wounds in my scalp, his fingers achingly tender.

"It didn't last long, but I had a real home with Henrietta. She was a good woman. Probably the only reason I didn't go down a darker road, to be honest." He paused, still rubbing, still gentle. "I never miss a chance to pick up a bag of those candies, to relive that time."

"If Henrietta was so wonderful, why couldn't you just stay with her?"

Jackson's fingers stopped moving on my scalp. "She died."

I straightened and turned enough to see his face, his hand falling to his side. I knew a little something about losing people you loved.

"I'm sorry," I said.

Jackson held my gaze for a long, silent moment. "Thanks." He cleared his throat. "It wasn't all bad. Dr. Craig helped me after that, got me into basic early and put me on the fast track through the military, so I wasn't alone."

"Early?"

"Yeah. He recruited me out of ROTC junior year." Jackson shrugged. "He said I had unusual talents. The tracking and other things." He dropped his gaze. "He wanted me for his program, as part of the security force. But his program is military, so I went through basic like everyone else. I was just younger than them."

"How old are you now?"

"Twenty-one."

I knew he looked young to be working special forces.

"You?" he asked.

"Just turned eighteen." I tried to smile, but it felt wrong on my face. "In the lab."

He flinched like I'd smacked him. "That's terrible."

I shrugged, at a loss for what to say to that.

"Happy birthday," he said with such serious conviction you'd think he was presenting me a medal of honor.

"Thanks," I said through a light chuckle.

He sucked in a loud breath. "Why don't you turn around, and I'll rebandage your feet?"

Letting my shirt fall over my ointment-covered sores, I plopped back into the chair and griped, "Do I have to? I felt like a mummy."

Jackson grinned and picked my leg up by the ankle, giving me a quick, graceful tug that slid me down the chair back. "But a mummy that isn't going to get an infection."

I slouched in the chair, my foot cradled in his lap. Beneath my calf, I felt solid muscle and body heat, and his hand on my shin was a lot more exciting than it should have been.

I'd missed human touch. Nurse Violet had been the closest thing I'd had to kindness in that place, and even she had handled me more like a piece of property than a person. Jackson's hand was decadent on my body, no matter where he touched me.

Even if it was a practical, medicinal touch. Nothing intimate about it.

As he set to work on my feet, he said, "So you know my sordid backstory. What about you?"

"What about me?" I hedged.

"Where are you from?"

I instinctively clammed up, breath hitching. But he'd opened up to me. I needed to give him something. Something true, even if it was partial.

I shrugged. "Nowhere in particular. We moved a lot, with Uncle Alec. Before that, way back, my parents had a nice house in the suburbs. I don't remember it much. I was pretty young. Then we moved to a farmhouse. We didn't stay long because… well, we lost our parents and our two baby sisters. And Uncle Alec took us in."

"I'm sorry," he said, eyes crinkling, sympathetic. "That's rough. To lose that many people."

I swallowed down the tightness forming in my throat and just nodded.

Jackson patted my ankle and offered me a tired smile. "All done. Stay off it for a few hours."

I was grateful he didn't press about what had happened to my family. I wasn't even sure, but the half-formed, horrendous idea I did have wouldn't make sense to him.

"Where am I going to go?" I said wryly, waving vaguely around us.

"I still think we should cut out. Find somewhere else less… exposed. Until we find your cousin."

Shaking my head, I straightened in my chair. "No. We wait here. Vin's coming. I know he is. He has to know about the fire and the breakout by now." Even if he didn't orchestrate it, I added in my head. "He'll be here. We wait."

Jackson blew out a long breath but shrugged. "All right. Good thing I've got entertainment."

I glanced at him, perplexed. "Entertainment?"

He dug a small box of playing cards out of his pack. "How about a game of War?"

"I don't know how to play."

"I can teach you," he assured me, grabbing the rickety, plastic patio side table to situate it between us.

We spent the afternoon playing cards. Mostly, it was Jackson teaching me how to play a game and then wiping the floor with me multiple times before I demanded a different challenge. In between hands and good-natured ribbing, we chatted about unimportant things. Favorite foods, favorite shows, bonding over the things we had in common and making fun of each other when our likes didn't mesh. I learned he hated broccoli, while I loved it; I nearly fell out of my chair when he said he also loved *Farraway Heights*, but he couldn't stand reality TV, while I'd binged on those shows (considering my own hermit-like reality had been so boring compared to them); he drove a Jeep Cherokee, but I didn't even have a license, which blew his mind.

I enjoyed every moment, even going so far as to forget why we were here.

Before the sun set, and when reality returned, I begged to go back to the Little A'Le'Inn so I could call Vin again, but Jackson refused. No amount of pleading could change his mind, not after the bartender's weird obsession with us. Of the two of us, I was the one most likely to be remembered. Jackson ultimately had me write down Vin's number, and he left me alone with KitKat to walk to the Inn. Soldiers, at least, weren't out of place in Rachel.

He returned a while later to tell me there'd been no answer. Again.

I moped on my lawn chair with my toes buried in KitKat's fur as I stared out over the dark desert. While he'd been at the store, the stars had come out and a half moon cast shades of gray over the valley, giving the landscape an otherworldly quality.

"We might as well get some sleep," Jackson said. "Get some rest, regroup tomorrow."

"Yeah," I said morosely.

"Your cousin's probably been traveling all day," Jackson assured me. "Maybe that's why he hasn't answered."

"Could be."

But I didn't really believe it. As I'd watched the sun sink over the mountains, a pit had yawned open inside me.

Maybe Vin wasn't coming.

How the hell was I going to get to Colorado?

I couldn't ask Jackson to help me.

I studied his profile in the moonlight. "Don't you need to get back to the base?"

"Probably," he agreed. "I'm not worried about it."

"Are you going to lose your job if you don't?"

Jackson's jaw tightened almost imperceptibly, but he shrugged. "I wouldn't be opposed to a transfer at this point."

"I'm sorry. I'm sorry I pulled you into this."

"I'm not. Come on," Jackson said, shoving against the arms of his chair to stand and stretch. "We'll be safer inside the trailer for the night."

We gathered our things, shoving excess belongings into our bags. I stood, carrying the boots in one hand and my sling bag in the other, but Jackson shook his head and pointed to the boots.

"Shoes on. In case we need to run."

A pang of fear tore through me. "Do you think we will?"

He smiled reassuringly. "No. I'm trained to prepare for the worst-case scenario. I think we'll rest, then go to the Inn as soon as they open tomorrow. Bet your cousin even answers."

"Yeah," I agreed, though it felt like a lie on my lips.

"I'll go air out the room. Get your boots on, then come inside."

"Okay." I watched him disappear around the edge of the trailer.

With a sigh, I sat to complete the painful task. At least the boots would hide the alien socks, with their lime green UFOs ringing the ankle. The shorts and shirt were bad enough.

I carefully slid my feet into the boots. Then I nudged KitKat with my toe. "Come on, girl."

Jackson stood over the bed in the back room, smoothing the blankets with precision. The single window in the bedroom was open, and a cool breeze fluttered the curtains.

"You can have the bed," he told me. "I'll sleep on the floor."

"What about the couch?"

He shook his head, and his dark eyes glittered in the ambient light. "If someone shows up, I want reaction time between them stepping foot in the trailer and reaching us."

I shuddered. "Then we can share the bed."

Jackson held up both hands. "No, ma'am. You take the bed. I'm used to sleeping anywhere I can."

"We're both grown adults," I pointed out. "I think we're mature enough to share a bed without any funny business."

"If you're sure."

I nodded and sat on the edge of the bed. I kicked up my boots onto the comforter. They were too big and bulky for my legs to lay properly, forcing me into an awkward position on my side. Jackson climbed in with more grace. My flopping and squirming, trying to get comfortable, stilled as he crawled in on hands and knees with the lithe motions of a panther. Braced on an elbow, he flipped up the covers to tuck in his legs, and my eyes traveled his dark, sculpted arms, exposed by his soft T-shirt. I startled when he looked over and caught me staring. Flushing, I buried my face deeper into the pillow, but he wiggled the blanket and said, "You should get under, too. Need to stay warm. There's no heating system in here."

My embarrassment's keeping me plenty warm, thank you very much. But I wriggled under anyway, avoiding his patient stare as he held the covers aloft for me. When I settled, he tucked them up to my shoulders.

"Thank you, nurse," I said, delighted when he burst out laughing—a velvety roar that came from his gut.

He retreated, still chuckling, and snuggled down on his side, one gorgeous forearm tucked beneath the pillow. "Goodnight, Ellis." Orangey yellow flecks gleamed bright in his eyes, as if stoked to life by his laugh, and a sensation like the brush of butterfly wings ran along my skin.

"Goodnight, Jackson," I murmured.

He let out a soft hum as he shut his lids.

We each lay on the absolute edges of the mattress. The bed

yawned between us, a larger space than I expected, given how very close I felt to him.

I could have reached out and touched him.

I wanted to.

But I didn't.

Instead, I fell asleep.

An indefinite time later, I awoke groggy and disoriented.

The room was still dark, which was the first strange thing. Then I realized I'd rolled toward the center of the bed, and a man's shoulder was beneath my head.

My heart skipped a beat as Jackson's comforting cinnamon sugar scent met my nose. I was curled into his side while he lay on his back, his arm around me and his fingers resting lightly on my waist in his sleep. I could feel KitKat's weight curled into the circle of my knees, and the room was hushed.

But something had awakened me.

I lay still for several long moments, listening. Waiting.

Then I heard it again.

The brush outside the bedroom window was rustling.

Careful not to wake Jackson, I slipped away from his arm and sat up, nudging KitKat awake. Her big black eyes blinked away sleep, then her hackles rose.

She heard it, too. Her paw pads hit the floor without sound as she followed me off the bed.

I tiptoed to the window and pressed against the wall to peek around the frame.

The moon hung higher in the sky now, illuminating the yard like a streetlamp.

There were shadows moving through the brush. Four of them.

Whether by the Summum Malum's thugs or the government, I'd been found.

12
RUN

A SCREAM ROSE UNBIDDEN IN MY THROAT.

No.

This can't be happening.

I clapped a hand to my mouth before I could utter a sound, backing away from the window so quickly I tripped over my oversized boots. My arms windmilled, desperately seeking anything to break my fall. If the soldiers or Summum Malum thugs heard me… KitKat's front paws slammed my backside, righting me. Steady on my feet, I glanced down at the cat in shock. What *was* this little miracle? A guardian sent by the Priestesses or my ancestors in the next plane?

No time to worry about that now. How did they find us? Who were they?

With my heart hammering painfully, I circled the mattress to Jackson's side. I shook his shoulder to wake him, and as his eyes shot open, I put my finger to my lips.

He sat up, movements jerky, and blinked away grogginess.

Outside, I mouthed, pointing to the window.

The bed creaked under Jackson's weight as he put his boots to the ground and stood.

I froze, unable to hear anything over the pounding of my heart.

What if they'd heard the bedsprings?

Jackson moved to the window with ninja-like silence. He was nothing but a shadow, fluid as air. I'd seen hints of this side of him, but this was the full soldier version—alert, watchful, calculating. Terrifying. An annihilator.

But four on one seemed like devastating odds. As far as I knew, there could be more than four.

Jackson pressed his back to the wall as I had done. For a single beat, he glanced outside, then he was on the move.

He crossed the floor in three steps, snatching up both our bags before he grabbed my elbow and hauled me through the trailer with KitKat at our heels. The accordion door to the bathroom stood open, and he shoved me through, then nudged KitKat in behind me before wedging himself into the too-small space. He slid the door shut carefully, then whirled on me.

I cringed when his arm raised. It was automatic. A fear response ingrained in me from my time at the lab, carried back on an adrenaline rush. Touch brought pain.

Jackson froze, his arm hovering in the air. He stared at me like I was a skittish deer, waiting to see if I would bolt. Then he slowly reached past me to the tiny window over the toilet.

It was small and square with no screen, and the frame slid up with surprising silence. Jackson leaned across me to peer outside. He ducked back in quickly and looked down at KitKat.

Out, he mouthed, pointing at the window.

KitKat huffed and glanced at me.

I nodded. *Go.*

The bobcat bounced onto the toilet seat, then the basin, and sailed through the window. I heard her paws thump the dry ground, then silence.

I started to climb onto the toilet, but Jackson grabbed my shirt.

He shook his head and lifted a single finger. *Wait.*

A man gasped outside the bathroom window. "What was that? It didn't look human." A gun cocked with a *click-click.*

Oh god. KitKat. I squeezed Jackson's arm as the trespasser continued, "On your six."

Beside me, Jackson's hand drifted to his dog tags, like he'd just remembered those men were his comrades.

"It's over there," the same man whined.

"Just a bobcat," another man said, voice hushed.

"Get it together, princess," the second man chided. "It's gone now."

My shoulders sagged in relief as I listened to their footsteps shuffle through the crispy grass and vanish around the edge of the trailer.

They sounded like armed soldiers, and they'd nearly gotten me.

The knowledge heightened my fear to panic. I leaned against the wall and took several deep breaths, careful to be silent.

Then the front door creaked open.

Jackson gave me a shove. That single gesture conveyed more urgency than I'd have thought possible, and I sighed in relief. Jackson was still with me, not them.

Without a second thought, I hurtled onto the toilet basin and vaulted through the window.

I was going for speed, not grace, so I hit the ground on my side and rolled with the blow. My head bounced off the dry, cracked soil with an explosion of blinding stars across my vision. I came to rest on a patch of scruffy crabgrass and scrambled to my knees, head whirling.

KitKat appeared from the trees ahead and huffed at me, her expression as panicked as a bobcat's could be, ears and tail twitching. I scanned the immediate area and saw the shadowed bulk of a Humvee in the sparse lawn, but no movement, no silhouettes.

I didn't wait for Jackson. I stumbled to my feet and took off to join KitKat, trusting that she had found a safe place to hide.

Every step I took sounded like an atomic bomb detonating. I just *knew* they would hear my bumbling boots. Any minute now, shouts would ring out behind me. Maybe even gunfire. They could hurt Jackson. Hurt KitKat.

Take me back to the dark, to the tank, to Hurst.

I crashed into the scrubby trees and slid into a crouch next to

KitKat. Still woozy, I had to drape an arm over her to hold myself on my knees.

Jackson was only half a step behind me, still clutching both our bags in one hand.

He'd drawn his gun in the other.

The safety was off, and that was enough to drive the real danger of this situation home.

When he caught my look, he whispered, "Just a precaution. I really don't want to hurt anyone."

He handed me my sling bag then threw his backpack over his shoulders before he crouched to peer through the trees at the trailer.

I tugged on his shirt and pointed to the vast prairie behind the trailer. When I spoke, my voice came out quiet as a breath. "Can't we run?"

Jackson shook his head. "We'd be seen." He let his gun point toward the ground and put his hand on my shoulder. In this thicket, he looked formed of shadows. "Do you trust me?"

I nodded.

"Then wait. We'll get out of here. I promise." He palmed the butt of his gun and held it out ahead of him, keeping a close watch on the trailer.

The sounds drifting into the trees told me they were searching the single wide. Banging. Yelling. Things being tossed around.

I kept sneaking looks at Jackson, wondering what was going on in his head. He had that calculating look on his face again.

These men were his co-workers. Maybe even his friends.

As far as I was concerned, they were the enemy, and he was one of them. So why was it so easy to trust him? How did I know he wasn't about to turn me over? That he wouldn't renege on his promise?

Because, when nobody else had been listening, as I'd lain underwater, Jackson had stood up for me and cared about my wellbeing. When everything hit the fan, he'd come back for me.

He'd saved me.

The measure of a man was what they did when no one was looking.

A dark figure approached the trailer and wrapped the door with a knuckle. "They were here," the soldier told those inside. "Found Charlie's, uh…" He lifted a wad of something. "Unmentionables? In a bush."

Oh god. My tank clothes scraps.

"Search the area," another voice commanded from inside. "They're close. The bed's been slept in."

Several shadows walked out of the trailer and into the night.

Jackson watched intently for a few seconds more, then motioned for me to follow him.

We took off through the copse of trees and burst through at the side of the road beneath the moonlight. Another Humvee crouched on the median, dark and silent like a monster lying in wait. Jackson circled the rear of the truck and started to lead me across the road.

As I cleared the bumper of the Humvee, a hulking shadow stepped between me and Jackson. The barrel of an automatic weapon pressed against my belly and stopped me short.

The soldier was huge. Not only tall, but twice the size of Jackson—built like the Titanic or King Kong. Army Kong smiled around the cherry-red pinpoint of a burning cigarette. "Look what we have here. The bitch of the hour. And I thought watch duty would be boring."

Fear rooted me to the asphalt. I opened my mouth, trying to find my voice and call out for Jackson. He was already halfway across the road. He thought I was behind him.

Oh god, I'm going back. I won't escape again. I'm going to die.

KitKat snarled—a terrifying, dog-like rumble in her chest—as she rounded the car and launched herself at Army Kong's arm, claws popping free. She savaged his wrist and knocked the gun away, sending it skittering over the concrete several yards. The moment her paws hit asphalt, she whirled and snapped at his groin.

He screamed like a little girl and flung himself back like she was a mountain lion going for his throat. Army Kong tripped over his own feet and landed hard on his back. KitKat capitalized on his fear, chasing after him to deliver a few well-placed bites on his extremities. He crab-walked away from her, making small, terrified sounds under his breath. His hands and pants were bloody when he finally managed to scramble to his feet and run.

While I'd been watching the comedy unfurl, Jackson had returned to my side. He touched my shoulder. "Come on. They'll have heard that. Time to run."

As I turned to follow him, a new figure popped out from behind the truck. The newcomer tossed a relentless punch, cracking Jackson across the jaw.

Time slowed as I watched Jackson fall to the ground. He landed on his back, catching his fall on his arm to save his head. Blood dripped from his nose.

"What kind of amateur-hour bullshit is this, A.J.?" the soldier snarled down at him.

The voice alone was enough to make me grit my teeth. Reyes.

"This bitch is government property, Hunter, and you're helping her escape?"

KitKat growled, crouching for another spring attack, but the soldier whipped his gun up and aimed it at her.

"No!" I cried, leaping in between the bobcat and the gun.

In the split second that Reyes' eyes shifted to me, Jackson kicked him in the same knee I'd popped out of the socket not two days ago. Reyes' scream split the night. He landed awkwardly, as if taking a knee, and his gun lowered.

Then Jackson hooked a leg around Reyes' stable knee, swiping him onto his back.

His plush head of hair bounced along with his skull as he struck the concrete, and he deflated like a basketball, coming to lie still.

Jackson rolled to his knees, tapped a finger to his bleeding nose, then stared down at the blood, disgusted. "He *hit* me. Asshole."

"Is he dead?" I asked, horrified.

"God, I hope not." Jackson pressed his clean fingers to Reyes' neck, then shook his head. "Unconscious."

From the direction of the trailer, someone called out, "Everything okay, Reyes?"

Jackson hopped to his feet and swiped his sleeve over his upper lip. "Run, Ellis. Don't look back."

I sprinted off down the road, ignoring the pain in my heels. Jackson and KitKat flanked me, all of us making a mad dash for cover before more soldiers showed up.

But we had nowhere to hide. There was nothing on this stretch of road beyond the trees and Carl Simmons' trailer. The moment the Psy-Ops guards reached the street, they were going to see us.

Bullets would extend their reach exponentially.

I noticed from the corner of my eye that Jackson was digging in his backpack as he ran. When he finally let the pack fall back against his shoulder, he had something small and cylindrical in his hand. He came to an abrupt stop, whirled around, and threw the object. I glanced over my shoulder to see a cluster of three bodies rounding the bulk of the Humvee.

My ears rang with an almighty *bang,* and the night exploded with white light.

I screamed, quickly turning away from the searing light, a high whine in my eardrums dulling the sound of my own breathing. I slowed and shoved a finger in my ear, wiggling it like I could pop free an obstruction.

Jackson grabbed my arm and tugged. "Run, Ellis!"

It sounded like I was hearing him through a conch shell.

"What the hell did you do?" I gasped the words out in between breaths as we raced away from the shouts and groans of those far closer to the blast. Little white dots popped in and out of existence on the pavement in front of me, remnants of the flash.

Jackson shot me a grin. "Threw a flashbang. Caused a diversion."

"You were carrying a *flashbang* in your backpack?" I screeched, floored. "We could have been permanently blinded!"

"That's not how stun grenades work," Jackson said wryly. "You'd have to have your face inches from it for that. I have good aim. Everyone will be fine."

The man wasn't even out of breath.

"And," he added with a sidelong glance, "I'm carrying more than one."

The darkened Little A'Le'Inn emerged from the moonlight up ahead. Jackson angled toward the shop, leaving the street for the patch of dried, dead grass surrounding the Inn.

"Where are you going?" I hissed, stopping in the middle of the road to stare after him.

"We need a car," he shot back and sprinted around the silent motel toward the RV park in the back.

I followed, trying not to think too hard about what he'd meant by "we need a car."

The only way we were gonna get one was by committing a felony. Just add it to my list of crimes.

Four RVs were parked behind the Little A'Le'Inn, all of them dark, though one had the faint, flashing blue glow of a television playing behind the curtains. Three cars were parked nearby—a red Honda and two black SUVs. Whether they belonged to the RV travelers or the people who operated the motel, I had no way of knowing.

Jackson edged up to the first SUV and tried the driver's side door handle. When it didn't open, he tried the second car.

The door opened.

He slithered into the floorboard beneath the wheel and started digging around.

"Oh my god," I hissed at KitKat. "He is *literally* about to steal a car."

She sat at my feet with a rumbling purr and watched, clearly less concerned about it than I was.

After several moments of banging and quiet cussing, the car rumbled to life.

Jackson popped back out and motioned for me to get in.

"Forget the facility. Now we're going to prison," I muttered as I hurried around to the passenger side of the SUV. I flung the back door open and paused to hold it wide for KitKat, muttering to her, "But I guess that would be better accommodations, huh."

She swished her tail.

Jackson looked over his shoulder and gawked at me from the driver's seat. Blood had turned tacky on the skin beneath his nose. "Are you serious? We can't take a bobcat with us."

"We aren't leaving without KitKat," I said with an "are you nuts?" snort as the big cat leaped into the backseat. She turned a circle and laid down, and I slammed the door before climbing into the front. I turned in my seat to give Jackson an amused smile. "You're stealing a car, but the thing you're worried about is taking a bobcat out of the desert?"

"She's a wild animal."

"She's our wild animal now." I calmly buckled my seatbelt. This was nonnegotiable. I'd get out of the car right now.

A light popped on in the closest RV.

"Shit." Jackson threw the car into reverse and backed out of the lot all the way to the road, tires squealing.

I clung to the handle above my head as the whole world pitched backward.

We came out facing the direction of Carl's trailer. Three men in riot gear were rolling in the road or leaning against the parked Humvee, still hurting from the flashbang. They were silhouetted by headlights from the second Humvee, now driving down the dirt path from Carl's trailer.

"I take it back," I said breathlessly. "Stealing a car is a good idea." Hell, I was already on the run from a place where I had no rights. What was one felony?

Jackson shifted gears, turned us around, and we shot off down the highway, leaving the distant light of the Humvee behind us.

13
DRIVE

WE DROVE IN SILENCE FOR THIRTY MINUTES AS THE SUN rose over the mountains and daylight fell over the desert wilderness. The moment the Humvees and the searchlights of the soldiers faded to blips on the flat horizon line, Jackson had gunned it, trying to put plenty of space between us and them before they clued in that we'd escaped by vehicle.

There was nothing out here on the so-called Extraterrestrial Highway. Vast empty fields of brush and bushes, earth tones, tumbleweeds, rocks, and distant mountains. The way we were cut off from civilization might have bothered me in my previous life, but civilization hadn't been kind to me lately.

Our getaway car could roll unhindered through the miles of Nevada nothingness and take us farther and farther from the experimental laboratory that had almost killed me.

When my adrenaline finally wore off, I was left with aches and pains, some of them old, like my bed sores, and some of them new. My head felt ten sizes too big from the blow I'd taken falling out of the trailer window. A fat knot above my right ear ached when I probed it. On the bright side, I wasn't nauseous, and Jackson assured me that both my pupils were the proper size and responsive. No concussion.

I'd take the small victories.

The sense of dread that had taken up residence in the pit of my stomach from the moment I left Uncle Alec back at the base seemed to be ever-growing, though. Especially after being ambushed.

A horrible thought struck me, sinking my stomach with guilt and, above all, unease. Was I safe in this car?

When I couldn't stand the silence any longer, I asked, "What happened back there?"

Jackson jolted and glanced at me, handsome face enigmatic. "Which part?"

"How'd they find us? Those soldiers. They shouldn't have known where to find us. In the trailer. They weren't searching. They were sure." My emotions got the best of me, and my voice cracked on the last word.

Kit Kat appeared between the seats and snuffled at my ear.

I had to force myself to ask, to put my horrible thought out into the universe. "Did you tell them?"

"*What?*" Jackson looked over at me so quickly the wheel jerked in his hand, and he had to correct the SUV before we flew off the road.

When we were steady again, I said, "When you went to the Little A'Le'Inn to call Vin, did you call the base? A friend?"

"Ellis, I told you I wouldn't turn you over to them." There was a note of something in his tone that I couldn't quite read, but I thought it might have been hurt. "If I had, don't you think I would have just let them take you?"

"But maybe you didn't mean for them to find us. Maybe it wasn't on purpose. You just checked in or something?"

Jackson shook his head, his jaw clenching and releasing twice before he spoke again. "I didn't call anybody but your cousin at the shop."

"I believe you." I deflated against my seat. Hearing it spoken gave me permission to accept it somehow, allowed me to see his actions plainly, as I wanted to see them, without a cloud of suspicion. He had attacked those men, after all, even after Reyes identified him. If he'd called them there, why would he do that? "So how did they find us?"

Jackson blew out a breath. "My guess? The Little A'Le'Inn bartender. I don't know how or why, but it's the only theory that tracks."

"You said we'd be okay," I accused, crossing my arms over my Area 51 shirt. "You said they didn't trust soldiers."

"I was wrong," he conceded. "But I *did* try to get you to leave Rachel."

"Yeah. You did." I sighed and stared out my window, watching the dull brown desert pass. "I should have listened. Now I've ruined your life."

Jackson's hands tightened on the steering wheel. "You didn't ruin my life."

"You don't have to lie to make me feel better."

"You didn't ruin my life, Ellis," Jackson said sharply, maintaining that white-knuckled grip. "You opened my eyes." He glanced at me. "No more blindly following orders."

Tension turned his broad shoulders into a solid wall. His words touched me. Helped me deal. At least something good had come of all this. I didn't know what to say. How to thank him.

Especially after I'd just accused him of betraying me.

Great job, Ellis. Way to show your appreciation. He's only saved you three times now. Sheesh.

He sighed heavily, one hand drifting to free his dog tags that had snagged on his shirt. "The only thing that bothers me is that those guys back there—those guys I had to hurt and turn my back on—can't see what's going on yet." He rubbed the tags with a thumb. "They're just doing what they think is right."

I dug around in my satchel for the remaining bottle of water and offered it to him.

He glanced at it like he didn't understand what it was, then loosened his grip on his tags and took it. "Thanks."

"There's still blood on your face," I said. "Around your mouth."

"There are wet wipes in the first aid kit."

While he gulped back some of the water, I unzipped his back-pack, hoping I wouldn't have to see grenades of any sort. The idea of him carting around explosives made me feel faint, even if it had gotten us out of Rachel mostly unscathed.

Luckily, the white duffel kit lay on top of all Jackson's assorted belongings and weapons.

I unzipped the duffel. "You came prepared."

"Side effect of military training."

When I handed him the little square wet wipe package, he offered me the water bottle.

I shook my head.

"I haven't seen you drink anything since… Well, since I found you in the desert," he added with a trace of confusion. "You have to hydrate."

"I'm fine."

Jackson raised an eyebrow and shoved the bottle against my chest. "Drink something. For me."

I glared down at the unassuming clear liquid, knowing that the minute it touched my tongue, I'd want to vomit. But getting into that conversation felt way too heavy on the heels of what had happened in Rachel. With my luck, he'd pull over and boot me from the car if he found out I'd basically become a leech.

So, I put the bottle to my lips.

It took all my willpower to let the water rest against my mouth long enough to pretend I was drinking. A trickle slithered past my clenched lips, and my gut reacted violently. KitKat purred in my ear and pressed her cold nose to my cheek, giving me something to focus on until I could put the cap back on the bottle and drop it in the center console. I swallowed three or four times, ingesting those few drops of water and fighting against the urge to expel them. Abnormal as my eating habits had always been, I'd never had any issues with water. It was supposed to be my element. I'd worn the blue guidestone, bonded to it. This was all wrong.

I *was* thirsty. Just not for water.

Jackson wadded the bloody wet wipe and tossed it in his backpack, still open at my knees. I found myself staring at it, my stomach knotting, hungry. I wanted to pick it up, but the thought of Jackson watching me casually suck on a bloody wipe like I was getting the last bit of cheese off a hamburger wrapper overrode my hunger with shame.

I imagined myself hunched over like Dracula, eating in darkness, face covered in crimson. What if my guidestone didn't balance me out like I hoped? Would I be like a vampire, driven to stealing blood bags, afraid of losing control and hurting somebody? *Hunting* somebody? No. It wasn't like that. This was a new exaggeration of my old differences, which Uncle Alec insisted had to do with some latent ability or tie to my element. I was bound to water, one of nature's most powerful life-giving substances. I fed off that nutrition. I stayed equally healthy with smaller portions than my sisters needed. My guidestone would cure me. I'd just been parted from it too long.

"Was that Reyes guy your friend once?" I asked, forcing my gaze from the blood.

Jackson snorted. "No. Dex Reyes and I were never friends."

"He called you A.J. Like a nickname or something."

"Yeah, that stupid nickname." Jackson shook his head. "It's just another way to mock me, not anything buddy-buddy. He's not very fond of me. The feeling's mutual."

"He does seem like a total ass. But you're both agents, and you're both pretty young for the position, so I thought maybe." I finished with a shrug.

Jackson smirked. "Yeah, he's the young hot shot at that lab. Hurst's little protege. He didn't like someone younger showing up with the new specialist. He *really* didn't like when Dr. Craig told him to defer to me on surveillance and security matters. He started calling me Amateur-Hour Jackson." He rolled his eyes. "A.J. for short."

"Ah," I said. "So, what do your real friends call you?"

"Jax, mostly."

"Jax." I tested it out, delighted when he encouraged me with a smile. After a comfortable silence, I added, "I'm guessing that harboring a fugitive and then breaking your coworker's leg is frowned upon by the military."

He grunted, lips tugging up in a wry smile.

"Is it safe to assume you no longer have a job?"

"Maybe. Maybe it just means I have a new job." He cleared his throat and let his head rest against the headrest wearily as he asked, "Where are we going?"

"That depends how far you want to take me."

He rolled his head on the seat to smirk at me. "Might as well go all the way now."

A double entendre, even if he didn't mean for it to be. Or maybe I watched too many smut shows like *Degrassi* and *Riverdale*. Regardless, heat rose in my neck and cheeks, and I looked away to hide it. "My family has a safehouse in Colorado."

"Okay. Got an address?"

"I have coordinates."

"Even better," Jackson replied. "We'll stop in the next big city and get some supplies. A cellphone, for sure, so we have GPS and a way to call your cousin. Some clothes. Food. I need to change into something a little less identifiable, anyway."

I glanced down at my own outfit and made a face. "I'd like clothes that didn't make me feel like I should be on an Ancient Aliens panel at Aliencon."

Jackson laughed. The heavy atmosphere in the car dissipated with the smooth, caramel sound.

We'd be okay if he just kept laughing at my jokes.

We had to be.

Unfortunately, the "empty nothing" of this corner of Nevada continued right on to the Utah state line. We passed through a couple of small towns that Jackson deemed too unsafe for us to stop in, though he never clarified what that meant. Too unsafe because we were still too close to the base? Too unsafe because the SUV we'd stolen had definitely been reported by now and Nevada highway patrol was most certainly on the lookout?

Whatever it was, he decided we wouldn't stop until we reached a place big enough to disappear in.

That place ended up being Cedar City, Utah. We rolled into town by early morning, right as rush hour was reaching its peak. Jackson started following signs to a Walmart, and I bit my lip most of the way there until finally working up the courage to say, "Hey, Jax? Could we go to a mall?"

I almost added, "I've never been," but I didn't want him to start asking questions.

He shot me a surprised smile but shook his head. "Sorry. No can do. Not right now. Something tells me you wouldn't want to leave, and we need to be quick. We also need to be cheap."

"Yeah, duh. Sorry," I said with a lackluster laugh.

He studied me like I was a tough puzzle. "How about a mall in Colorado? When we're near your safehouse."

My smile spread all over my face. "Deal."

"Deal. But for now, good ol' Wally World," he said, pulling into the lot, "where we can nab all our needs in one go."

Yeah, all our needs. Clothes, cellphone, snacks for Jackson and KitKat. Too bad they didn't carry blood, too. My hunger had become immense since choking down that miniscule amount of water. If only I could figure out a way to let KitKat go hunting for me without Jackson's knowledge.

As Jackson backed into a spot, I counted the money I had left in Reyes' wallet. "I only have $68 dollars. Not exactly shopping spree material, huh?" I flushed, still feeling stupid about my mall idea.

Jackson put the car into park and shrugged. "That'll get a prepaid phone. A cheap one."

"What about clothes?"

He grimaced. "I want to suggest we use my card, but I know we shouldn't."

"Not just *shouldn't*. We can't. They know you're with me now."

He nodded, his gaze sweeping the bright blue facade of the superstore. "I think I have fifty bucks cash."

I opened the glove compartment and rooted around inside, checking for hidden money. Unfortunately, the car's owners were annoyingly clean, and both the glove compartment and center console were empty.

"We stole a car," I pointed out. "Couldn't we steal some cheap clothes? I've heard this place works product loss into the budget. They'd be doing a public service."

Jackson laughed and then slouched further into his seat, banging his head lightly on the headrest. "Henrietta would whoop my ass if she could see me now."

"So would your unit commander, I imagine."

He turned an unamused glare on me.

I grinned. "Come on, Clyde." I shoved his arm and gave him my best attempt at a feisty starlet look. "Live a little. If we can't laugh about it, we'll fall apart."

Shoving open my door, I stepped out into the cold morning. We'd left the desert far behind us and ventured into higher elevations. With our change of state had come snow-covered peaks and a chill in the air that reminded me summer was long past.

Not to mention, the girl I was this summer was long gone.

Jackson stored his gun in the glove compartment, then left the windows cracked for KitKat on the assumption that anyone dumb enough to try to rob a car with a bobcat in it deserved to be bitten. He accepted Reyes' stolen wallet from me, sliding it into the cargo pocket of his camos since my dinky alien shorts didn't have pockets.

Once inside the store, Jackson split off to handle the phone situation in the electronics department, while I headed for the women's clothing section.

I hadn't ever really shopped in a place like this in my life. On the rare occasion Uncle Alec let us out into civilization, I'd discovered the clothes in superstores weren't my style—loose, flowing cotton and elastic waists. The kind of stuff women used to cover up, which hadn't ever been my thing. I'd liked to feel flirty, daring, show some skin even if there weren't any guys to look at me. I'd dreamed about going to school, for guys to look at me.

Though now, of course, there wasn't much of my body worth looking at.

The reminder stung.

I picked out a couple pairs of cute leggings and two long sweaters to match, trying to be stylish while also avoiding the dressing rooms where cameras might remember my face. Then I grabbed a plain, hooded sweatshirt for good measure—practical and capable of hiding my bald head. In the shoe section, I chose a pair of slip-on boots and some comfortable socks, then stopped by the intimates department. A packet of underwear and a three-pack of sports bras rounded out my purchases, because no way did I want to keep flying commando.

I left the intimates on my way to track down Jackson, but as I passed by the accessories, I caught sight of my face in a tiny mirror on a rack of sunglasses.

Oh god.

I stepped closer to my reflection, my fingers curling into the clothes in my arms. My breaths came quicker, and panic rose in my chest.

I didn't even recognize myself in the fluorescents. My eyes were sunken, and my cheeks were hollow above colorless, chapped lips. My skin was so sallow that I looked freshly released from a long stint at the hospital. With my hair gone, my head looked too large on my too-thin body, and my jaw looked overly masculine.

I immediately redirected to the cosmetics aisle.

That was where Jackson found me a few minutes later with tears on my cheeks and my arms weighed down by everything I'd need to make myself feel pretty again. Like Ellis again.

"You okay?" he asked, one eyebrow arched as he took the boots off my overloaded hands.

Hunching away, I swiped my wet cheeks on one of the sweaters I'd chosen and shrugged. "Fine. Did you get the phone?"

Jackson nodded and held out his arm. He had a shopping basket dangling from his elbow that held a few items of clothing and a stapled bag that I assumed covered our new phone, already paid for back in the electronics department.

I dumped my stuff into the basket with his, then laughed as I got a better look at his shopping choices. "Is that a full rotisserie chicken?"

"I'm hungry," Jackson said defensively. "I'm going to share it with the cat."

I held up my hands. "No judgment. But how are we going to—"

Jackson put a finger to his lips. "I have a plan," he said under his breath. "Just follow my lead."

We sidled into the self-checkout area. Jackson chose a machine and stepped ahead of me, handing me the basket to hold while surreptitiously angling my back to the clerk.

He picked up a plastic pack of tank top undershirts, then slid it over the scanner. The machine beeped, registering the sale price of $7.99. I raised an eyebrow at him. He knew we couldn't use his credit card. What was he doing?

Ignoring me, Jackson picked up a folded pair of jeans and swiped them across the scanner, before shoving them in the bag with the tank tops.

Except it didn't beep. Other shoppers all around us in the busy scanning bay were beeping in an annoying, overlapping symphony, but our silent machine's screen still only registered the t-shirts.

Nobody noticed. The clerk was helping someone at her register, and the people on either side of us were too busy with their own stuff.

Jackson did it again, wrapping the price tag up inside one of my shirts before he swiped it across the scanner. In the bag it went.

By the time he'd rung up all our items, the grand total only read just over thirty dollars.

My heart raced as he slid two twenties in the appropriate slot. Then the scanner dispensed our change, we grabbed our bags, and we left.

I was in the SUV before I finally breathed again.

"Where'd you learn to do that?" I asked as Jackson climbed into the driver's seat beside me. "That shoplifting trick?"

Jackson groaned. "Please, let's not mention shoplifting. I'm trying to feel better about it knowing that I paid *something*."

KitKat nudged the bag in my lap that held the chicken, and I pulled the black plastic case out, passing it to Jackson.

He opened it with one three-fingered hand and began tearing pieces off onto the lid for himself. After a moment of silence, he finally answered my question. "I went hungry a lot when I was younger. So, I learned ways to make sure I didn't starve. I'd find change in the couch cushions in the foster house of the month, then use it to pay for a pack of gum and come out with real food."

My heart hurt for him. I lightly touched his leg, to let him know I cared without being overbearing about it. Our eyes met and held for a long moment.

Jackson had obviously crawled out of his past with both hands and achieved an impressive career title at a young age to boot.

Here I was, turning him into a criminal.

When he finally looked back down at the chicken, he said, "You want any? There's plenty."

"I'm vegetarian," I lied.

He looked at me, surprised. "You ate rabbit last night."

"Well, I mean, I thought I was going to die," I said carefully. This newfound ability to lie off the cuff was coming in handy, even if I hated adding more deceptions between us. "But I'm not going to die now, so I'd rather skip the meat."

"You should have said something. I could have grabbed you some fruit."

"I promise, I'm fine. Let's just get back on the road. When we get to my family's safehouse, I'll have what I need."

Jackson nodded. "If you say so."

He finished divvying up the chicken, then slipped the bucket onto the back seat for KitKat before he perched the lid with all his pieces on the cup holder where he could reach it while driving.

We got back on the highway, and while Jackson ate his chicken, I called Vin's cellphone twice more. He didn't pick up, and his mailbox was still full.

That heavy dread inside me yawned wider. Why wasn't he answering?

I plugged the safehouse's coordinates into the phone's GPS. We had nine hours of car ride ahead of us. "We should stop at a rest stop to change," I told Jackson as I settled the phone in the cupholder. "Just in case. You need to get out of the army gear."

Jackson nodded, but whatever he was going to say vanished when he glanced in the rearview mirror. Instead, he hissed, "Shit."

"What?" I asked, looking for myself.

"Cop car," Jackson said, his voice hushed.

I swallowed down rising panic. "I'm sure he'll just pass us."

"He's not," Jackson said grimly.

I whipped around in my seat just in time to see the cop's red-and-blues light up behind us.

14
DESPERATE TIMES

A TENSION HEADACHE SETTLED BEHIND MY EYES AS I watched the distinctive lights flash through the tinted back window. The cop rode our back bumper and made his siren chirp to get Jackson's attention.

"We could keep going," I whispered. "Try to outrun him."

"He's in a Dodge Charger. Outrunning isn't an option." Jackson flipped the right turn signal and started to ease over into the emergency lane.

My heart stuttered. I grabbed his arm. "What are you doing? He's going to arrest us both! We're in a stolen car!"

"Exactly." Jackson shook my hand off. He looked way too calm and composed. I was about to self-destruct. "We're in a stolen car. We run, they chase, people could get hurt. *You* could get hurt."

"And if he arrests us, I will eventually end up back in that laboratory," I snapped. "Where being hurt is the least of my damn worries."

The SUV rolled to a stop, and Jackson put it in park. "We'll figure a way out of it. Trust me."

As the cop car pulled in behind us, I ducked down to look back at KitKat. "Hide. In the trunk. Quick."

The bobcat didn't hesitate. She slithered over the backseat into the open trunk area of the SUV, vanishing from sight.

"That cat isn't normal," Jackson muttered.

My hands were shaking in my lap, so I clasped them together. "Yeah. I know."

Silence fell between us as we waited for the officer to leave his squad car. Jackson kept his hands on the wheel, knuckles paling. I focused on my breaths, counting in for four, out for eight, so the panic wouldn't make me pass out. It was bad enough to be in a stolen car, even worse for the stolen car to have an unconscious girl and a bobcat in it.

The cop sidled up to Jackson's window and made a motion for him to roll it down.

Jackson depressed the electric button, plastering a polite smile on his face. "Good morning, officer."

State trooper, I realized. Early thirties, bronze skin, thick muscles, fairly intimidating. His dark brown uniform was clean and pressed, and a broad-brimmed hat sat atop his head, cocked forward over his eyes. A shiny metal badge on his shirt declared him as *D. Stanley.*

Stanley tipped his hat to us both, catching Jackson's eyes first, then mine, before he said, "Good morning, folks." His gaze raked over Jackson's military fatigues. "Sorry to bother you, sir. Stationed nearby?"

"Groom Lake," Jackson replied.

How could he sound so normal? My nerves were so hotwired I was two seconds away from vibrating off the planet. Jackson might as well have been greeting an old friend over drinks.

Stanley grinned, and the effect made him look almost boyish. "Area 51. Nice. You're a long way from base."

"On leave," Jackson said. He reached out and patted my bare knee. "Driving my girlfriend back to school in Salt Lake."

His hand returned to the steering wheel, leaving warm tingles on my skin. Such a simple touch, yet it implied an intimacy far beyond the scarce platonic gestures of the men in my life before him. Obviously, the implication was a lie, but it *felt* true. Like it *could be* true. I treasured it. Stored it away.

"I see," Stanley said, smiling indulgently at me. His gaze trailed back over Jackson's hands, and he noted the missing fingers with a small arch of his eyebrows. "Well, go ahead and give me your license and registration so we can get you back on the road."

"My wallet is in my back pocket," Jackson said. "I'll need to reach behind me to get it."

Stanley rested his hand on the gun at his hip. "Go ahead."

Jackson lifted his hips from the seat and, moving very slowly, pulled his wallet out, then extracted his driver's license to pass through the window. "Unfortunately, the registration isn't available. Had some water damage a while back, got destroyed."

Stanley nodded, but the lines around his eyes hardened. "I'll be able to look it up."

"Officer—"

"Sergeant," Stanley corrected.

Jackson inclined his head. "Apologies. Sergeant Stanley. May I ask why you pulled us over?"

Stanley motioned toward the back of the car. "Registration's expired."

"Oh. Well." Jackson let out a little laugh. "That's what I get for losing the paper."

"Indeed," Stanley said under his breath. "Hang tight, folks. I'll be right back with you."

As Stanley walked back to his cruiser with Jackson's license, Jackson watched the side mirror intently.

"He knows," I said softly.

"Yeah," Jackson agreed. "The registration isn't expired. I checked it when we stopped for gas in Crystal Lake."

"We could still run."

"He has my license."

I tapped the glove compartment. "We could shoot him."

Jackson rounded on me with abject horror. "We are not killing an officer of the law."

"I didn't say *kill him*," I said, exasperated. "You're a soldier. Don't you know how to incapacitate someone without killing them?"

"We aren't shooting a police officer. Get it out of your head." He glanced in the side mirror again. "He's in his car on the MDT. We've got less than a minute before he gets confirmation this car is stolen."

"Then you go to jail, and I go back to my glamorous life as a lab rat," I said hotly. "We have to do *something*."

"Give me a minute," he growled. "I'm thinking."

Curling my hands into fists, I laid my head back against the seat.

I could still feel Jackson's palm on my leg. I savored the sensation, figuring it was the last time those gentle hands would ever trace my skin, tend my wounds, or offer warmth. If we played by the rules of Jackson's moral compass, we would be separated.

He had looked at me like I was crazy, violent. But if we were arrested, he'd get due process, bail, and a broken form of his everyday life back. I'd be strapped back to a table, my alt blood rendering me subhuman to Hurst and his cronies, who'd hurt me again and again for the sake of harnessing powers they didn't understand. I wondered vaguely what they thought I was. A mutant? An anomaly? What did they call me? Did they really know about alts, or had they just stumbled across a few?

Didn't matter. I wasn't going to help them learn more. I wasn't going back.

"We could run," I suggested, glancing off the side of the highway. "Hide in the trees."

"I don't feel like getting tased today," Jackson muttered. "Or shot."

I looked at him, horrified. "*Shot*? You think he'd shoot us in the back if we're unarmed?"

Jackson sighed. "You don't watch the news much, do you?"

"No, not really," I muttered. The news was for people who actually lived in the regular world and left their house. I liked TV that took me other places.

"We don't know how much he knows or what orders the base

will give him," Jackson said, his gaze still on the side mirror. He straightened. "He's coming back."

"Any closer to a plan?" I hissed.

Jackson didn't reply. His lips were set in a hard, thin line I didn't like.

What if he's going to let the cop take me?

Stanley sidled up to the open window, his hand resting on his holstered gun and his face expressionless. "I'm going to need you to step out of the car for me, Agent Hunter."

My heart seized.

Stanley's gaze moved from Jackson to me. "Ma'am, if you could just remain in the car for a moment, I'd appreciate it."

I nodded and swallowed the knot of fear in my throat as Jackson caught my gaze. Then he opened his door and joined Stanley on the pavement.

I rotated in my seat to watch the trooper guide Jackson to the back of the truck, where he started questioning him. Jackson stood with his back to the trunk, while Stanley faced the car, his expression suddenly grave.

Shit.

KitKat poked her head around the back seat.

"He's not going to do anything to help us," I told her softly. "He has too high a moral code."

KitKat snuffled to let me know she agreed.

I watched another few seconds as Jackson spoke, his hands gesturing emphatically.

"He's also not going to be able to talk us out of this one," I murmured. "I can't let them take me again, KitKat."

The bobcat growled.

Moving slowly so I wouldn't draw attention through the tinted windows, I reached between my legs for my alien bag. I had a choice between the taser and the baton. The taser was potentially more powerful, but the baton offered better reach. It would be a miracle if I could sneak up on a trooper at all, much less get close enough to jab a taser in his neck.

I opted for the baton.

I hefted the cold, solid metal in my left hand. My heartbeat thudded in my ears as I slid my other hand to the door handle.

A wave of traffic passed by in humming bursts, drowning out Stanley and Jackson's voices. I used the sound to my advantage. Painfully slow, I pulled the handle until the door opened with a tiny *pop*. I slithered through the smallest crack possible, which was fairly thin considering how skinny I'd become. My boots hit the asphalt, and I levered my insubstantial weight with my knees to muffle the sound.

Judging from where I'd last seen Stanley, I knew if I approached from this side, the cop would see me before I had a chance to hit him. But if I approached from the driver's side, dozens of passing cars might see me and honk to alert him.

I needed a distraction.

Craning my head back inside the cracked open door, I hissed, "KitKat. Draw his attention away. Toward the road."

The bobcat let out a sharp, chirp-like meow, and the car shifted beneath her weight. I didn't wait for her to do her thing. I crept quickly toward the back of the SUV, trying to ignore the pain in my chest from my overly excited heartbeat. With agonizing caution, I pulled the baton out as far as it was made to go.

Right as I reached the trunk, KitKat made her move. The SUV jerked and something heavy thudded against the back window.

Stanley yelped and danced backward a couple steps, reaching for his gun. "What the hell, man? Is that a cougar?"

His surprise knocked him right into my path. I couldn't have planned it better if I were fate itself.

Putting every ounce of my weight behind the blow, I lunged. Metal connected with the back of Stanley's head right beneath his campaign hat. He pitched forward, and all two-hundred-eighty pounds of muscle hit the asphalt like a falling tree. Lucky for him, his substantial muscles took the brunt of the fall so his head didn't. His dislodged hat skidded toward the embankment.

Then he lay still.

Jackson's eyes went comically wide, staring down at the fallen trooper with cartoonish terror.

I pointed the baton at Jackson and barked, "Get in the car!"

"You just assaulted a police officer!" he said incredulously, a hand flying to his dangling dog tags. "That's a felony!"

I collapsed the baton back into itself with more force than necessary. "Do you want to go to jail for kidnapping government property?"

"What?" His gaze lifted from Stanley to me, shocked. He rubbed a thumb over his name engraved on the metal tags, as if he could wipe them and himself clean of this whole situation. "I didn't kidnap you."

"You think the facts matter to those people?" I shouted, my heart in my throat. "They bombed my house, Jackson. They took me from my family and turned me into a lab rat. Look at me!" I waved my free hand over my wasted body, my sores, my sallow skin. "I didn't do this to myself."

"I know," he said, and his low, sad tone was almost lost in the whoosh of a passing car.

"Then get in the truck, and let's get out of here before he wakes up."

Jackson hesitated, but finally let go of his dog tags. I left him standing over Stanley's unconscious form and got back in the passenger seat.

After all the ruckus, the interior of the car felt too quiet. I tossed the baton on the floorboard. Dammit. My hands were shaking. I hadn't wanted to hurt Stanley; I didn't want to hurt anybody. I just wanted to be back with Uncle Alec and Vin and my sisters where I belonged. I gulped down a sob as I reminded myself, *I'm the only sister left.* Cyn was out there somewhere, maybe. Little Aurora and baby Persephone, too, all grown up now without us, if Vin and Uncle

Alec's "hunches" were right. But they weren't coming to save me or waiting at the safehouse. And with each passing year they were gone, the more likely they were dead, like Mom and Dad, like poor, gentle Alanna murdered in the street. Lana had seen all of us die, over and over, in her visions—a blessing and a curse of her connection to the Aether relic. I shuddered, remembering sneaking through her room and snatching up her diary. I'd thought I would find some silly poetry to tease her about, but instead, I'd read her nightmarish premonitions. On those pages, Cyn, Vin, Uncle Alec, and I died at the hands of Summum Malum cult members in a plethora of horrific fashions. Strung up. Bled out. Eviscerated. Burned alive. And sweet, quiet Alanna had agonized over each one and what small choices we could make to change the future. All in silence. She hadn't wanted us to know, hadn't wanted to burden us with those fears. So, I had kept her secret. Never told anyone about her death visions. But she'd been the one to end up dead.

KitKat appeared between the seats as I buckled my seatbelt. She rested her fluffy paws on the center console and leaned into me, snuffling at my cheek with a low whine.

I dug my fingers into her fur and buried my face in the softest patch near her neck.

The driver's side door opened. A breeze gusted through the car, and the SUV bounced as Jackson's weight settled behind the wheel. The engine started, and we rolled away.

Hot tears pricked the edges of my eyes.

And just like that we were driving back to freedom.

We ditched our hot car in the next town. Jackson backed it into the furthest spot in a supermarket parking lot, then we walked several miles away into a suburban neighborhood where he tested car handles for one that was unlocked.

It was broad daylight but also a weekday, which meant most people weren't home. We found an unlocked older model Nissan with rust on the bumper parked on a landscaped driveway behind a line of tall evergreens that blocked us from the house. It had damage on the driver's door, and the passenger floorboard was covered in gum wrappers and Monster energy drink cans. Not the nicest car, but the beige color would ensure we faded into the background on the road.

The only downfall was no tinted windows, so KitKat would make a stir in the backseat if she didn't keep her head down.

We got back on the highway, and all signs of civilization began to fall behind us. Traffic thinned out as we entered more rural areas. The way the mountains cupped the road made me feel safer. More hidden.

An hour into the drive, we passed our first cop car running radar on the side of the road. I tensed and watched the rearview mirror, waiting out the terror. Had this vehicle already been reported stolen?

The cop didn't move, and I breathed a little easier.

When we took the exit ramp to I-70, and a big sign pointed our way to Denver, I really started to breathe again. We still had a ways to go, but we were making progress.

Jackson hadn't spoken since we'd left Stanley asleep on the pavement in front of his cruiser. Not a word. Not even when we stole the new car.

I didn't press him, but I didn't like his stoic silence, either. I knew he was bothered by the violence against a police officer, but I also knew he wasn't naive enough to think we had any other option.

But the silence had stretched on too long and become accusatory. I felt like a criminal, and I hated it.

I glanced at him. "Are you going to talk to me?"

He shot me a look, though his expression didn't change. "I'm processing."

"You've been processing for the last two hours."

"I'm accessory to the felony assault of a cop," Jackson shot back. "It takes time to process something like that."

The flint in his tone hurt. I looked out the window, the pit in my stomach yawning wider. Jackson was my only ally. At least, my only *human* ally. Without him, I would have been caught already. I didn't want to alienate my only companionship. At least, not before I found Vin.

And most definitely not after discovering how much I liked Jackson Hunter.

"I'm sorry," I said, my voice thick.

"I'm not mad at you," Jackson replied without skipping a beat.

I didn't believe him.

At midday, we pulled off into a moderately-sized town for Jackson to get some food and caffeine. He parked in a grocery lot and instructed me to stay in the car—like my alien wear was any more conspicuous than his fatigues. We still needed to change, but we needed distance between us and Stanley first.

The moment Jackson disappeared down the parking lane, I whipped around in my seat and looked at KitKat. "I'm hungry. But I need blood," I croaked through a knot of repulsion and guilt. "Can you help?"

The bobcat trilled.

I reached through the seat to open the back door. "Quickly," I told her, and she flicked her tail before bounding from the car.

She moved like the wind, darting into the trees next to the grocery store. I glanced around the lot, hoping no one noticed the wild animal sprinting across the grass, but the few visible customers were busy stowing their groceries.

KitKat returned a few moments later with a squirrel dangling from her fluffy muzzle and proudly dropped it in my lap.

The moment the squirrel's blood touched my lips, I only felt contentment. He hadn't had a chance to be afraid like the bunny from the desert. He'd been eating and never even saw the wily bobcat approach from behind to swiftly snap his neck. As the tangy blood slipped down my throat, fortifying me, I cycled through his emotions: Satiation. Sleepiness. Levity. A carefree sense of freedom and comfort.

I closed my eyes and let the sensations wash over me like a cleansing rain. They chased away the strain of the day and the tension in my shoulders. The worry over Jackson's silent treatment vanished. I eased back into the seat, going limp and boneless as I finished off what little blood there was in such a tiny creature.

"Do you want the rest?" I asked KitKat, offering her the squirrel.

Her deep purr broke the silence of the car, and she stuck her nose playfully into my ear before she snatched the squirrel from my hand and curled up in the floorboard to eat it.

"You're the best, KitKat," I murmured, then lay my head back and fell asleep.

Just before nightfall, I woke as we pulled off in a place called Cisco, not far from the state line, and did another car switch in an attempt to stay one step ahead of the criminal justice system. We picked up a nondescript Ford Ranger that was probably older than me and got back on the road.

But less than an hour later, we rolled into Grand Junction, Colorado, and Jackson signaled to exit the interstate.

"What are you doing?" I asked.

"I'm exhausted," he replied shortly. "We still have five hours' drive, at least. I need to rest."

"I can drive while you nap."

He finally looked at me, raising one dark eyebrow. "You don't even have a driver's license."

"But I *can* drive," I huffed. Uncle Alec made sure I had the skills of a getaway driver; he just didn't want my sisters and I registered with the DMV.

"You need rest, too. More than just a nap in the car," he added before I could argue. "Food. Showers. Sleep. For both of us."

I glared at him, but he just studied the road ahead. The light at the end of the off-ramp turned green, and he turned right onto a busy strip of road that cut through a downtown area. The buildings on either side were quaint boutiques and local restaurants, mostly red brick and attached in long rows. We kept driving and bypassed several nice hotels, then pulled into the dark lot of a small motel and cut the engine.

"How do you intend to pay for it?" I asked as the engine ticked in the silence.

"I have a plan." He unbuckled his seatbelt. "Trust me."

"You say that a lot."

His eyes met mine in the ambient glow from the registration lobby. "Have I let you down yet?"

"No," I hedged, though if it weren't for me and my stolen baton, we would have been arrested back in Utah.

"Stay in the car with the cat until I get back." He shoved his door open and jogged to the lobby, then disappeared inside.

KitKat popped over the top of the bench seat. She hardly fit in the small area behind me, even with both jump seats folded up.

"He has a plan," I muttered.

KitKat huffed. She wasn't amused, either.

Jackson returned less than five minutes later and hopped back into the cab. "Got the room at the very end so there's less chance the bobcat will be seen."

We relocated to the very last parking spot, and KitKat followed me out of the car, pressing close to my legs in the darkness as Jackson unlocked the door. The room wasn't anything to write home about. Four walls, two beds, a small bathroom, and a flatscreen television. The carpet looked like it had seen a few more years than the health department might like, and the covers were industrial-strength scratchy, but it was clean, at least. Run-down, but not overrun with cockroaches.

Jackson placed his backpack on the table next to the TV. "You can take the shower first."

Now that I was in a warm room with the promise of being clean and getting some honest-to-goodness sleep, I didn't even argue. I grabbed my bag of new clothes and shut myself in the tiny white cellar of a bathroom.

I didn't know how long the hot water would hold out, so despite how good the warmth felt, I made quick work of washing up. Jackson deserved a nice shower too. He hadn't even had the chance to use Carl's well pump.

God, was that only a day ago? It felt like a week had passed.

When I came out of the bathroom in my brand-new leggings and sweater, Jackson was nowhere to be found. Hmmm. I walked to the window and peeked through the curtains, thinking maybe he'd stepped outside, but the sidewalk was empty.

I dropped the curtain back into place and set my dirty clothes on the table next to my alien bag. The cell phone was gone.

My heart skipped a beat. I raked my gaze over the room, praying that he'd just moved it. To the bedside stand. To the TV stand. Anywhere.

But no.

I shoved my feet into my new ankle boots and opened the door. It was colder here, and I braced myself against the rush of cool air as I eased out onto the sidewalk and looked around for Jackson. I tilted my head toward the low rumble of his voice down the walkway and edged to the corner of the motel's stone building.

"I know it's traceable, but it was an emergency," Jackson was saying.

I stopped and pressed my back against the freezing stones, suspicion heavy in my heart.

"Hurst knows I'm rogue now anyway. Me using company money doesn't necessarily mean it was on your orders, sir. They can't remove you from—" Jackson cut off and sighed.

The suspicion turned sour in my stomach. I had a strong inkling who he was talking to, but I had to be absolutely sure. I gripped the edge of the building, then peered around the corner.

Jackson leaned against the wall, the cell to his ear and his other hand kneading at the skin between his eyebrows. "No, sir. There was already blood everywhere when we arrived. Did Hurst overhear our call and—?" His hand fell away from his brow, and he listened a long moment, while I forgot how to breathe. "Ah, I see." Pause. "Uh-huh. I was afraid of that."

The trailer. He'd told someone about the trailer. Had Hurst killed Carl? Had Jackson led him there?

He turned his face skyward and closed his eyes, banging his head gently against the stones. "I know, sir. Trust me, I know." He only called one person sir that I knew of.

Dr. Craig.

Shock froze me to the ground, colder than any mountain breeze. There was no denying it.

Jackson was betraying me.

15
SHADOWS

I WAS WAITING CROSS-LEGGED ON THE BED NEXT TO KITKAT when Jackson returned.

He smiled at me as the door shut behind him. Crisp, cold air wafted in, the spice of evergreen mingling with his usual sweet cinnamon. The heady combination harkened more vivid memories of Christmas with my sisters. I longed for home, for my family—such as it was—and I wished that Jackson didn't make me feel such sacred things.

Because he was the enemy. No family of mine would ever put me in danger the way he just had.

"Feel better after your shower?" He set the cellphone on the table inside the door.

I shrugged. "Feel better after turning me in to your boss?"

KitKat punctuated the accusation with a furious growl, crescendoing it into a feral scream.

Jackson's shoulders tensed, and he countered with a hooded stare. "Were you spying on me?"

Irritation prickled across my skin. "If by 'spying,' you mean I got out of the shower and went looking for you because I was worried when I found you gone, then sure. But maybe you don't really understand the purpose of a friendship. You know. Worrying about a friend's well-being."

Jackson's jaw hardened. "That's not fair."

I dropped my cheap boots to the ground and stood, my hands shaking as I balled them into fists at my sides. "No, what's not fair is that you called Dr. Craig and turned me in."

"I called Dr. Craig," Jackson said shortly, "but I did *not* turn you in. We needed a place to stay. We need access to money for basic survival. I have a business credit card in Dr. Craig's name, and I used it. So I had to call and give him an update."

Cold horror washed over me. "You used his credit card."

"I needed to pay for the mot—"

"No," I cut him off, shaking my head vehemently. "No, you could have let me drive. We've been breaking laws left and right since the minute we met up in the desert, and you draw the line at handing an unlicensed driver the wheel?" My voice had steadily risen and now verged on hysteria. Fear made my heartbeat a dull, hollow thud against my ribcage. I sank to the edge of the bed when I realized my knees wouldn't support me anymore. "They know where we are. They're going to come for me."

"They're not going—"

Frustrated by Jackson's inability to see past his own biases, I surged back to my feet and crossed the space between us to jab my finger in his hard chest. "You really think your precious Dr. Craig didn't *immediately* run to his superiors and tell them where we are?"

"He didn't. You don't know him."

"Neither do you. He's just your boss."

"He's not just my boss," Jackson said, some of the hardness seeping from his voice. "He's my mentor. He's… If it weren't for him, I'd be fresh out of jail with a mountain of debt in legal fees. You don't know him."

I let my finger fall from his chest but didn't move away. I wanted him to feel the full force of my anger. Burn under the fire of my glare. "I don't need to know him, Jackson. I know he's part of an organization that hurt me. I was a monkey in his zoo. You saw what they did to me. But you trust him?"

"He's not one of them."

"As far as I'm concerned, he is. And no matter how great you think he is, he has superiors to report to, just like you, and—"

"If he was going to turn us in, he would have done it when I called him from the desert," Jackson yelled over me, then instantly cringed.

I staggered back from the force of his words. "You… you what?"

Jackson made fists at his sides and shook his head at the floor. "I couldn't just disappear. Not on Dr. Craig. You don't understand. He deserved to know why I abandoned him, embarrassed him. I called that next morning, before we went to the trailer, on a satellite phone, just to explain why I couldn't be a party to this anymore, to what they were doing to you. He agreed."

I thought of that morning in that little alcove, him saying he had to "take care of some business."

"You said you didn't have a phone," I said through clenched teeth, but I couldn't put any real bite in the words. They barely came out a whisper.

"I didn't want you to get scared and run off."

"Oh, and why shouldn't I be scared of you?" I snapped. "You've been lying this whole time. You're still one of them."

Jackson turned his cheek like the words had slapped him. He sucked his bottom lip into his mouth and chewed on it. Head still hung, he slowly raised his eyes to meet mine, like a beggar coming before a queen, afraid to stare too long at her while he pled his case.

"Ellis, please. I don't want you to ever be afraid that…" He sighed, and his eyes shimmered. Welling with tears? "I'm so sorry I lost your trust. But please, hear me out."

He sucked in a breath.

"Dr. Craig understood. I told him I just wanted to get you away from the lab. He said he'd keep it a secret, that Hurst's experiments with you were total failures anyway, and there was no need to put you through any more. He told me to do what I thought was right.. He kept our secret. And he'll keep it now."

"Our secret?" I said, swallowing tears of my own. I wouldn't be weak right now. Not when I owed it to the voice of Cyndra in my head (who'd warned me from the start) to set this right. "It's my secret, and I never should have let you be a part of it. Of my family's world. I've already told you way too much, let you into their lives as well as mine. The safehouse? Ugh! I can't believe I'm so dumb." This time, when I gritted my teeth, the words came out a snarl. "You told Craig about Carl, didn't you? A friend of my family. And he's probably dead now, and probably on your precious Dr. Craig's orders."

"That's not true."

I scoffed.

"If you were listening to that phone call, you should know I talked to him about it," Jackson said. "He doesn't know what happened to Carl. He asked me about it, asked me if I'd done something stupid. Hurst doesn't know either, but he's the one who sent those guys to the trailer."

"How'd they know where—"

"The bartender, from the Little A'Le'Inn," Jackson said. "You were right. There was a bulletin sent out to the locals, and he did report us."

For a long moment, we stared at one another, neither of us moving or speaking. Then Jackson sighed and reached out, entwining his fingers with mine. "I need you to trust me."

"I need you to trust *me*," I countered, slipping my hand free. Even with my disappointment weighing down my shoulders, his fingertips left a tingly warmth on my skin. I didn't want to feel that way about him. He'd *lied* to me.

He'd promised me safety, then did the exact opposite. He might trust Craig explicitly, but I didn't. Even if he had expressed more concern about me than Hurst ever had.

But before I could move away, he reached tentatively for my wrist, and I let him take it. "Ellis." His free hand cupped my face. "Listen to me."

His nearness was all-consuming. I drowned in cinnamon sugar and the memory of his candied ginger kiss, the wild honey sweetness of his blood, the blood that made me feel stronger than I'd felt in years. The way his emotions filled me, chasing away all the shadows of my time in the lab and replacing them with something much purer.

Jackson. I knew he was a good person. I knew it before I ever saw his face.

The water helped me know.

Why were things so much more convoluted outside the tank?

His thumb brushed gently over my cheek as he held my gaze and said, "I promised you I'd get you to your safehouse, and I intend to follow through. I'm not double-crossing you. Dr. Craig won't hurt you. He doesn't even work for Psy-Ops. He's a specialist acting on his own. He won't report this to Hurst. On my honor."

Hot tears pricked my eyes. I leaned into his palm. "I'm scared."

Jackson sucked in a breath and then curled me into a hug. He was so tall, my head fit neatly under his chin. Warm. Protected.

But was I really?

"Please don't hurt me like they did," I whispered.

"I would never," he whispered back.

His heart beat steadily beneath my cheek. His arms were tight enough to hold me on my feet but loose enough that I knew if I wanted him to let go, he would.

I didn't, though.

I wanted to trust him. I wanted to believe him. I wanted him to be the guy I knew him to be—the good guy who'd done the right thing when nobody else was watching. When he had no idea I could hear his every word, every step, and every intention from my watery coffin.

That was the Jackson Hunter I needed him to be.

I was curled around KitKat atop the covers when Jackson emerged from his shower dressed in his new clothes.

I startled, my stomach doing acrobatics. I'd gotten used to him in his military fatigues, in drab, olive green. If not for the outline of his dog tags beneath his soft, gray, Henley shirt, he could have walked right out of the school halls of one of my teen dramas. He'd left three buttons at the collar undone, and the dark-wash denim jeans hugged his hips and thighs.

If I'd thought him gorgeous in his fatigues, I just hadn't seen the real thing yet.

"There's a little pub across the street," Jackson said softly. He'd adopted those "speaking to a skittish deer" mannerisms again. "I'm going to go grab us some food."

"I'm not hungry." I scratched KitKat along her scruff.

"You need to eat," he urged. "You've been through a lot in the last few days. You need your strength."

I couldn't very well tell him I'd had KitKat bring me a squirrel to suck on earlier, so I just shrugged. "Okay."

He pocketed his wallet and the room card key, but very obviously left the cellphone behind in some silent bid for apology. Then he left.

Maybe it was my paranoia. Maybe I didn't actually know whether or not I could trust him. All I knew was I intended to follow him.

I jammed my feet back into my boots and slipped a second card key into the waistband of my leggings.

KitKat tried to follow me out, but I shooed her back inside. "No, you stay here. We're in a city. If someone sees you, they might shoot first, ask questions later. I can't let anything to happen to you."

KitKat huffed and sat on her haunches, her stumpy tail flicking across the motel carpet as she glared at me. I could almost read her expression—*I don't want anything to happen to you, either.*

"I'll be *fine*," I said, exasperated that a freaking wild animal was trying to mother me.

KitKat huffed again, then turned and paced back to the bed, her tail still flicking irritably.

The walkway outside the motel was deserted, even though

there were several cars in the lot. I could hear tinny, canned laughter from a television playing in a nearby room, and somewhere beyond that, two voices raised in an argument. Just a slice of the small-town America I'd only ever seen in movies.

Jackson had gotten enough of a head start that he was already jogging across the street while traffic idled at the red light. I remained hidden in the shadows of the overhang, watching as he moved through the intermittent streetlights, up the short gravel drive, and into the restaurant called the Stiff Pig. Didn't sound very appetizing to me.

Once he was out of sight, I followed. I shoved my hands into the wide pockets of my sweater and hurried through the motel lot, angling for the crosswalk. The sun had sunk below the horizon, dropping the temperature. I shivered in a cold, mountain breeze as I waited for the light to change. Then I picked up the pace and passed through bright headlights on my way to the pub.

The Stiff Pig sat on its own plot of land with an overgrown gravel parking lot filled with unruly partiers holding half-drank pints. A small group of burly, bearded men in biking leathers had already downed half a dozen rounds, based on the empty pitchers and the posturing. I'd be steering *way* clear of them.

I ignored their ranting and laughing as I crossed the lot. How could I get inside and spy on Jackson without him noticing me? *Serves him right*, I thought, kicking rocks with a low grumble. He'd accused me of spying, so now, I'd make it true. One less lie out of his mouth.

Even as I thought it, my guilty conscious whispered that I'd told plenty of lies myself since meeting him, and I knew that leaving the phone had been a gesture of trust and genuine apology.

But I still didn't trust him.

Not like I had before.

"Hey!"

The voice cut through my thoughts, though I didn't acknowledge it. It was background noise; a reminder that a bunch of drunks were partying it up in the parking lot. All the more reason to keep my head down and get inside quickly.

"Hey! Baldy!"

Heat flushed up my neck. Without even realizing I was doing it, I ran my palm over the feather-soft down growing at the top of my head.

"Yeah, you! Lookin' like a damn holocaust bitch."

While I gasped in disgusted disbelief, his friends rewarded him with a chorus of raucous laughter.

The flush in my neck fanned outward to my cheeks and shoulders, more fury than embarrassment now. I turned and planted my hands on my hips, seeking out the offensive asshole.

A tall, rotund man in black leather stood next to his motorcycle with his meaty fist wrapped around a mostly empty pint glass. Broken shards from the last few victims of his revels glinted on the gravel at his feet.

He leered at me—a crooked gash of a grin shrouded beneath a bushy brown beard. "Where's your hair, bitch? Look like a boy, don'tcha."

A sour tang hit the back of my tongue—coppery terror and bitter anger. "At least I'm a prettier boy than you," I retorted, clenching my hands into fists to keep them from trembling. *God, why'd I say that?*

Because he'd hit me right where it hurt.

His cronies let out a small, petering round of laughter, cut off by his warning glance.

His scar-like grin slid away from his face, and he narrowed his bloodshot eyes. "What you say to me? Bitch?"

I rolled my eyes, trying to channel my offence into indifference. "Does it make you feel like a man to talk down to me like that?"

He took two wobbly steps forward. "T'you say to me?"

"Your vocabulary leaves much to be desired," I said dismissively, not looking directly at him, then turned away toward the restaurant door. It was all bluster. I kept my voice calm, my expression unbothered, but inside, my heart raced. I'd been raised to protect myself because of who I was and what I was capable of, but I was still small and weak compared to this man.

And his six other pals. I tried my best to avoid eye contact, focused on the entrance and what I hoped was relative safety. Jackson was in there, at least.

Before I could get very far, a short, thin man in leather chaps and a vest open over his bare belly stepped in front of me.

I halted before I ran into his hairy chest. As I tried to sidestep him, I looked up, and all the air left my lungs. My atrophied muscles turned soupy and useless. A darkness deeper than the night sky hovered over the man's shoulder, punctuated by two eye-like holes that showed the neon-lit building behind him. A Shadow.

"You're an ugly bitch," the skinny man said through the fog in my head, his voice like stone against stone. "But a bitch, just the same. Bettin' you'd be good enough for a night. How much you charge?"

The rest of the cronies roared with laughter, and I turned my head through a fog of panic. Shadows. Five of them. Hovering at their backs. Clawed hands cupped around the men's ears, crooked necks twisted inward. Whispering. Dark calling to dark. Calling the blackest bits of these men's souls to the surface where they could be fanned into flames.

God, how could I be so stupid? Of course Shadows would congregate around a seedy place like this, and I'd walked right into their path.

I backed away, putting space between my face and Skinny's open vest, and tried to scoot around him, only to find Asshole Number One blocking my escape route. He had a Shadow, too. It clung to his back, so melded to his black leather jacket, so naturally attached to his psyche, that I hadn't been able to tell them apart before.

"My boy's got a point, baldy," he said with a sneer. "Don't care what you look like, long as you're warm."

Bile rose in my throat, but I swallowed it back and commanded myself to stand tall. The Shadows couldn't touch me. I had to act just tough enough to remove myself from this situation before the Shadows' whispers dug deeper and urged these wicked souls into action.

My advantage? They were drunk. They could be startled into dumbfounded inaction, their brains too slow to catch up.

I'd deal with how to sneak away without any Shadows following *after* I'd found Jackson.

"Back off," I snapped, moving to charge past the fat man.

My shoulder smacked against his bicep, but instead of shifting aside, he snatched my right wrist and twisted my arm painfully.

I cried out as something popped uncomfortably in my wrist, and his Shadow rippled, like its inky half-form was bobbing with laughter. Fear and fury mingled inside me, a caustic cocktail. I braced myself against his grip and kneed him in the balls.

Fat man went down like a sack of potatoes, leaving his Shadow hovering like a dark mist. He rolled on his back, moaning an octave too high.

Freed from his grasp, I steeled myself and stepped right through the hovering Shadow only to come up against Skinny again.

"Excuse me," I ground out, then tried to shove past him.

The biker fisted my sweater in one hand and hauled me off my feet like I was weightless. My heart stuttered in my chest as he slammed me against the seat of a nearby bike, bending me uncomfortably backward over the leather. His fist—still wrapped around my shirt—pressed against my throat, closing my windpipe.

"It's real cute you think you can just walk away from me, baldy," he growled.

I couldn't breathe. I was in the tank again, that shadowy figure's hand ripping off my mask. The water was rushing in. That same aching gnaw returned, the desperate plea of my lungs for air. The two traumas blended—the fist around my throat and the weight of the water in the lab—turning my limbs to ice. I kicked out, bucking off the leather seat like a bronco, but it only made Skinny and his friends howl with laughter. Their Shadows rippled, sucking up the glow of the neon Open sign.

Skinny's Shadow bent its head to his ear, and his eyes glossed and shimmered. A wild, oversized smile stretched his face, and he breathed too hard as he said, "We know what you are, relic holder."

Fear doused me in ice water. They knew me. Not just that I was alt, which they always sensed, but that I was connected to a relic. How? Had they followed me here? *Oh God, the desert.* I'd thought I saw a Shadow, right before Jackson found me.

"There's no running from the Malum," Skinny crooned. "You're gonna burn."

The biker shoved me harder, until I was angled over the seat, my legs dangling and my hands brushing the ground. My fingers scraped the gravel as I searched for something, anything to use against him. I gasped, trying to get a breath around his fist. Why had I left the motel? What had made me think I could handle myself in a parking lot of drunk bikers? Why hadn't I paid attention, seen the Shadows? Now I was going to die by fire, like so many alt women and girls before me—my spirit obliterated before it could reach the next plane. Gone forever.

Skinny popped open the fuel tank on the bike with his free hand and pulled a lighter from his jeans. He flicked it and watched the dancing flame. It reflected in his eyes but not in those of his Shadow. It twisted its crooked neck to whisper again, stroking Skinny's cheek with a claw made of night. Its desires mingled with the biker's, their thoughts and threats merging.

"Don't worry, baldy. It won't hurt long. We'll let you off easier than your cousin. Pretty as a girl, wasn't he? Wish you looked a little more like him, huh?"

Vin? Was he talking about Vin? *Please, no.* My heart cantered, and tears sprung unbidden to coat my lashes. My fingertips scraped over something sharp and cool. I scooped it up, testing its edges with the pads of my fingers.

Glass. A broken bottle neck.

I didn't hesitate. I slashed the four-inch shard up and across my chest, going for his face.

Glass sliced through skin like a knife through butter, and hot blood spurted over me in a waterfall. It gushed over my face and neck and spattered my lips. Skinny's hand released me, drifting to his neck as he sank to the gravel.

Hot blood made the glass too slippery to hold. I lost it as I tried to steady myself on the bike. I watched in horror as blood pooled beneath Skinny, and his twitching body went still. *I hit the jugular. Oh shit, oh shit, I hit the jugular.*

I licked my lips, breathing hard, adrenaline racing over my skin like static. The man's blood was sour. I could taste the yeast and a stomach-churning, spoiled oatmeal remnant of the beer in his system. As it touched my tongue, I got a rush of terrifying emotions.

Anger. Control. The sensation of sadistic urges and screams of pain in a dark room. His fury was all consuming, his foulest tendencies called forth by the Shadow to fuel him. It tore through me like a shot of electricity to my heart. Suddenly, I felt stronger. Wilder. Meaner.

And really, *really* pissed off that these men had threatened me, that they'd dared even imply Vin's name, and that with or without the Shadows, they would have accosted me and any other woman who mistakenly crossed their path.

The surrounding group had gone stone still and silent as they watched their comrade bleed out on the gravel, those drunken cortexes working at half speed. But as I straightened, using the leather pack on the motorcycle to right myself, half a dozen menacing gazes turned to me. Half a dozen Shadows hovered, their orders given, ready to watch the show. I'd never heard of them breaking the same plane together in such numbers before.

For a heartbeat, I considered running.

The smart thing would have been to run.

But I was still licking the biker's blood off my lips. His anger pumped through me and morphed into righteous rage that men like this existed.

As three of them advanced, I searched the ground for my bloody shard. Instead, a glowing orb of light, like I'd thought I hallucinated in the desert, redirected my eye. *What the…?* It bobbed and hummed at me, like a singer warming up their vocal cords, and flared its soft luminescence over a fancy holster hanging from a leather jacket draped off the bike.

A knife.

Right as I jerked it from the holster, a man's ham-hock fist slammed into my jaw, ripping my cheek open on my teeth.

I lurched sideways, fireworks obscuring my vision. I hit the ground hard on my hands and knees, the knife hilt biting into my palm and gravel digging into the sensitive skin at my knees. Sharp, tangy blood filled my mouth—my own this time. Not sustenance the way someone else's could be, but a boost nonetheless.

I opened my eyes, trying to swallow back the deluge of blood from the cut. I felt the blow straight to my bones when I straightened, sitting up on my knees. I blinked away darkening edges in my vision, thinking *No, no, no, don't pass out.*

If I did, I might not wake up.

Throat and jaw swollen, cheek gushing, I found it difficult to swallow, so I spit out the blood instead.

The red-tinted wad landed on the knife blade.

Great aim, I thought, utterly exasperated at how useless I'd become. All Uncle Alec's training, all those muscles and battle reflexes gained, had turned to dust at the bottom of the laboratory pool. I sat back on my heels to flick the blade clean.

"I'll take that back now," my attacker, a beefy Rambo-type, snarled, pointing to the knife.

His punch had thrown me aside, putting space between us. And in the time it took him to take those few steps, something came over me. Something I didn't quite understand, couldn't quite define. It wasn't training instinct. It didn't come from memory or habit.

When I looked at the knife, it spawned in my core, a fresh life, an untouched thought.

Remnants of my blood and saliva still oozed down the blade, and the sight sang to me. It told me I wasn't as powerless as I thought.

I stood, still a little unsteady and with an ugly throbbing in my head. Then I held the knife out toward the advancing biker. "You want it back? Sure." I cocked it back, gripped lightly but balanced in my fingertips. "Go ahead and have it."

I threw it.

Uncle Alec hadn't been just a self-defense, martial arts guy; he'd taught us basic hand to hand and weapons' combat, too. I'd worked with knives before, but I was never proficient.

This knife, however, sailed with expert precision and sank hilt deep into Rambo's stomach.

I watched, wide-eyed with shock, as he keeled over.

Then all hell broke loose.

16
UNREQUITED CONFESSION

FOUR REMAINING MEN RUSHED ME, SHOUTING AT THE TOP OF their lungs. Elsewhere in the parking lot, answering cries began, and a crowd gathered as I dodged swinging fists and grasping hands. I caught glimpses of the Shadows, swirling and diving in a frenzy, watching their handiwork, egging on the violence. Most kept to the darkest corners. Others softened their forms and moved in time with the bikers. No bystanders would take note or think them odd.

My heart choked me, settling somewhere in my throat. I charged across the parking lot, gravel slipping and sliding beneath my boots and reminding me that my sores still hadn't healed. I shoved away the pain; no time for it.

I needed the knife out of Rambo's gut. Without it, I had nothing to protect me.

He was less than fifteen yards away but reaching him seemed impossible. I ducked one man's bear hug, but another nailed me in the shoulder with his fist. Pitching into a tailspin, I caught myself on my knee and rolled away from a third man's grasp. But now I was dizzy from Rambo's blow to my head and all the spinning.

As soon as I got back on my feet and charged the last few feet toward the dead biker, the fourth man's wiry leg snapped out and tripped me. I fell in what felt like slow motion, right on top of the dead man. My forehead smacked his. The knife I'd thrown into his belly hit my hip and shifted. As I rolled off him, vision vignetting, the knife fell out of his gut on a spurt of blood that splashed my forearm. It glistened in the neon, dribbling down his shirt and forming a tiny pool in the gravel.

I needed it.

My breath was shallow. My head was aching, my vision blurring. My bones hurt.

I needed it.

I dipped two fingers in, scooping, coating them, and then stuck the warm liquid in my mouth. I lifted my arm and started licking up the trails of dripping spatter from elbow to wrist. Copper hit my tongue first, sharp with a salty tang, but underneath, water. Fresh and satisfying as drinking from the hose in early summer.

Time slowed.

Fury.

Murderous rage.

The desire to squeeze the life out of the little bald girl.

"Ellis!"

Jackson's shout was the most welcome sound in the entire universe.

My tongue lapped up the last smeared line on my wrist, and I turned to him with a smile, only to see him staring at me like I was a wild animal, his nose crinkling in a subconscious signal of disgust. I looked between his face and the pink smears of saliva-wetted blood on my arm, the rich iron still fresh on my taste buds.

Nausea and shame rolled in my stomach, but I swallowed them back and let the blood do its thing. Strength flooded my limbs, making it so that I no longer felt the fresh bruises and scratches or the sores on my feet, now split open like overripe fruit. My aching head cleared, vision sharpening.

I snatched the knife off the gravel and slashed at the closest goon, who jerked back. Beyond him, Jackson barreled from the restaurant. He must have been driven out by the sounds of the fight. Thank God for his soldierly instincts.

The goon who'd tripped me grabbed my sweater and hauled me up until I dangled uselessly from his hands. I slashed again, but he was tall and long-limbed, and I only nicked his cleft chin. His friends closed in around him.

Jackson lunged into my field of view, his fist cracking across the biker's jaw.

The biker pitched sideways, his grip on me going limp. I fell awkwardly, landing on my butt and then my elbows, gravel digging painfully. But I held tight to my knife. *That's it, Ell,* the Cyn in my head praised. *Now get up and use it.*

The biker slumped to the ground beside me, out cold from one well-aimed punch. Some lingering fury from Rambo's blood sent a thrill through me, begging me to sink the knife in this man, end his wretched existence.

Horrified, I almost tossed the knife away.

Jackson offered me a hand. "You okay?"

He came for me. Despite seeing me dine on blood, he came for me. I couldn't stop the smile that tugged my lips.

I raised an eyebrow and jerked my chin to the snoozing biker. "Do you have Hulk hands or something?"

He let out a short, sharp laugh, then spun in a gorgeous, grace-ful roundhouse kick that took a charging biker out of commission with a military-issued boot to the head.

Jackson met the guy's buddy with raised fists, and I took the chance to stand and get a more comfortable grip on my knife. The crowd had grown, and by the amount of grumbling and glaring I could see, I had the distinct feeling that the men I'd killed were popular, and the more friends who arrived, the more likely I was to join the dead.

Jackson and I were outnumbered, no matter what we did.

Fat Guy came back for round two with me, but thanks to the blood's boost, my training came back. The rage was gone, but the adrenaline stayed. When he swung, I juked backward, then slashed, pretending to go for his throat. When he flailed in a clumsy dodge and threw up his hands, I delivered two rapid punches to the liver, using the handle of the knife to put extra force behind my right hook. He'd feel that tomorrow.

I danced away from his wild, retaliatory punch.

Stay on your toes, Uncle Alec's voice commanded. *Strike and retreat. Wear them out.*

The glowing orb returned with a hum, its soft yellow flare drawing my eye to an approaching dark form, and I spun, slashing a leather vest and leaving a gaping rip in a dingy T-shirt with my knife. The high yell assured me of my sneak-attacker's retreat, so I turned back to the Fat Guy, only to get jabbed in my diaphragm. I doubled forward, all the breath leaving my lungs, but I brought the knife down on his retreating forearm, earning myself time. I spun and tried to run, but I could only hobble, hugging my stomach. I stumbled over the gravel, keeping my eyes on my feet so I wouldn't trip.

I could breathe again; it just hurt.

God, it hurt.

"Ellis!"

At Jackson's cry, I looked up and skidded to a stop in a blood trail. Rambo wasn't dead. He'd pulled himself half up on his motorcycle, one hand clutching the wound in his belly, the other holding a gun. He sank to his rump in the gravel, the gun held steady as he leaned against the bike.

I stared down the barrel of the gun. After all I'd faced, after all I'd seen, after all the pain inflicted on my body, that cold steel and the dark mouth of that barrel still sparked a primal fear that seized me by the throat and squeezed mercilessly. My mind was a blank. No muscle control. No options.

The Harley tilted, crushing Rambo beneath its weight, and the gun fired, but the bullet flew wide and chipped off the thick concrete blocks of the pub.

I stared at him, splayed beneath his bike, grunting and pushing but not getting very far. He'd lost too much blood to summon the necessary strength. The weird thing was, he'd been close enough to pull the motorcycle over on himself but… he hadn't.

That bike had fallen over on its own.

I turned to look at Jackson. He was grappling with another biker. He shoved the man away, where he slammed into the side of the restaurant. Jackson glanced around wildly, then locked his gaze on the drainage pipe over the man's head.

The pipe disconnected from the building and slammed into the biker's skull.

By itself.

A prickle of unease worked up my spine. Had Jackson done that?

No. Definitely not. That was crazy.

His eyes found mine, and he ran for me, a hand extended.

"Come on," he said as I grabbed his arm. "We gotta get out of here before the cops show up."

I nodded but when I went to take a step, my legs crumpled.

Jackson let out a groan of frustration, then tossed me over his shoulder like I weighed nothing, and sprinted away from the chaos outside the pub. I heard shattering and crashing, but I couldn't pinpoint the source. My borrowed strength was waning, my injuries piling up, overcrowding my senses. I'd taken too many punches.

I searched the darkness at the edges of the lot, wanting to warn Jackson, tell him not to let the Shadows follow.

The night moved, deeper blotches shifting in the ink, swirling together. From the void, a black wing fanned out into the artificial light of the street, ready to take flight.

Before I could point it out or make my mouth work, I passed out, lost to my own darkness, praying that Jackson would run like death was on his tail.

17
CONFESSIONS OF A TEENAGE VAMPIRE

CONSCIOUSNESS CAME BACK IN PIECES.

First, I felt a warm weight stretched out beside me, vibrating like a massage chair.

Then I realized the world was moving. A small dip shook me out of sleep, and another jerked me to total awareness. I could hear the rush of the tires beneath me, feel the vibration of KitKat's purrs. Warm air filtered over me from the heating vent, which someone had so kindly pointed at my sleeping body.

That someone being Jackson.

I lay across the bench seat, my upper body draped over KitKat's belly and my feet resting on Jackson's lap. Our bags were stowed in the floorboard beside me, and it was pitch dark out the window. Passing headlights illuminated Jackson's face. He looked haunted.

"Where are we?" I asked groggily.

He didn't look at me. He swiped his finger on the cellphone screen and read the details, then replied, "About an hour from the safehouse coordinates."

I extracted my feet from his lap and sat up. KitKat didn't bother to move. Her bulk against the passenger side door scooched me close to Jackson, our legs almost touching. I studied that carefully maintained space, wondering what harm it could do just to allow my leg to relax and tip sideways. What would it hurt to lean in, rest my arm against his?

I had almost convinced myself to do it when I caught sight of my blood-drenched fingers. Grimacing, I held out my hands. The liquid had turned tacky between my fingers, and my nails looked stained with rust. "Did you sleep?"

"No," Jackson replied, glancing at my hands. "I threw you in the truck, got KitKat and our bags, then hightailed it out of town."

"Smart," I said as nonchalantly as I could manage, while surreptitiously searching the car's interior for any unnatural dark shapes. Nothing. Had we really gotten away clean?

Jackson reached into the compartment on his door and held out a bottle of hand sanitizer. "It's all I have right now."

I accepted the bottle, then unzipped my backpack, rifling through my meager belongings until I found my Area 51 t-shirt.

"So, no one's following?" I asked, peering through the rear windshield for the scattered, single headlights of motorcycles.

"No."

No one we could see anyway. The Shadows could be flying over the dark ground on the side of the highway, watching. That wing I'd seen… I pressed my forehead to the glass in a futile attempt to study the dark sky, expecting to see a flock of birds cross the moon. According to Uncle Alec's most recent intel, the Shadows had taken a liking to that shape when they traveled, now that they'd begun to swarm in bigger numbers. No one questioned the faint shadow of a bird passing far overhead.

But why abandon their tough biker pals? Without people to influence, they were just watchers.

Maybe they already knew where I was headed, like they'd known about Vin.

No, I assured myself. *The safehouse has to be a secret.*

After all, I'd never spoken the coordinates aloud, even if they were listening in the desert. I should have taken what I'd seen in the desert more seriously. It made sense the Shadows might have learned about alts being collected in one place and come to investigate. I was just so tired then.

But Shadows weren't all I'd seen back in the desert. That orb thing had made two appearances now. It felt… friendly. But what was it? I couldn't chalk it up to a sleep-deprived hallucination anymore, but I had no better explanations. Luckily, it seemed the least of my worries.

I had to soak and scrub my hands three times, drying them off in between, to get the majority of the blood off my skin. I fought the urge to suck them clean; I'd acted freakish enough for one night already. Even in the moment, I'd known it was wrong. Downright vile. But I'd needed it. Craved it, even. I shuddered. *You don't need it now. Control yourself.*

When I was done, I tossed the shirt on the floorboard and let my head fall back against the seat. Clean-up had taken a lot out of me—more than it should have.

I felt his stare before I heard the sharp sigh. I tensed, watching his hands strangle the wheel. The knuckles of all six fingers were battered and bloody.

"What the hell was that back there?" His voice was clipped.

My cheeks flushed. I looked out the passenger window, afraid I might find disgust or fear in his eyes. I shifted my whole body, using my back as a shield against the shame.

"Those assholes took one look at me and decided I was easy pickings," I said carefully, wondering if he had seen the Shadows, too, or just my pick-me-up snack.

"That's not what I'm talking about."

Now it was my turn to sigh. "Yeah, I know."

I hunched my shoulders and kept my eyes on the blurry road. I remembered how he'd looked at me in the lot. I didn't need to see it again.

"It's not what you think," I mumbled.

"Ellis, I have no idea what I think. I'm not even sure I saw what I saw."

I shut my eyes against tears, imagining what he'd seen—a ghoulish, skeletal girl lying beside a dying man, slurping up his blood like it was melted chocolate straight from a fondue fountain. An image straight from a demonic horror flick.

"I can't eat normal food." I bit my tongue when the tremor of a caged sob crept into my voice.

Jackson shifted in his seat, his thigh brushing my low back. "Excuse me?"

"I can't eat normal food anymore," I repeated, a little firmer this time. "That's why I'm so thin."

As if he hadn't noticed I was wasting away. If my guidestone didn't correct this mess, I'd disappear entirely. Next time the Summum Malum sent thugs after me, would I be strong enough to fight them off?

"If I eat real food, I throw it right back up."

"I thought that was a trauma response, from being strapped to a hospital bed and stuck in isolation." His voice was thick with a sympathy I didn't want. I didn't want to be the poor little lab rat. I wanted to be pursued by him, not pitied. *Fat chance, bloodsucker.*

"It's still happening?" he pressed.

I nodded, meeting his eyes for an instant. They were crinkled at the edges, troubled. I bit my lip and stared back out the window. "You probably saved my life back there. Again."

"Don't change the subject, Ellis," he said sharply.

KitKat rumbled and lifted her head, glaring at Jackson. I wasn't sure if she was irritated that he woke her, or if she was ready to clap his head between her claws for raising his voice at me. Either seemed likely.

"You mean you haven't eaten anything this whole time except...?"

"Blood." I trailed my fingers through KitKat's fur to calm her. "I can only eat blood."

The truck swerved—so slightly I might not have noticed if KitKat hadn't leapt to her feet and looked around like someone had attacked us. I slowly faced him and saw him work his jaw with the slightest shake of his head, like he was giving himself an internal pep talk, assuring himself that the crazy girl wasn't about to rip out his throat.

"Blood," he clarified, his dark eyes darting toward me. He cleared this throat. "Like a vampire."

"No, not like a vampire. That's ridiculous," I said, while glancing at the very hands I'd considered licking clean moments ago.

"What's ridiculous is you sitting there telling me you can only stomach blood. Like a vampire," he repeated.

"I can keep water down, too," I snapped, curling into myself at his obvious judgment, "but not well unless it's mixed with a little blood. Blood *tastes* more like water to me now."

He ran a hand over his short hair. "What the hell, Ellis? Was that guy the first?"

"The first human, you mean?"

He nodded, and I saw his chest still. He was holding his breath.

"Yes," I lied, not daring to even think too long about that moment in the lab. "KitKat's been bringing me squirrels and things." I scrambled to explain myself. "But, in the fight, I needed energy. I was just trying to survive. And his blood was there, and I needed it, and I thought he was already dead."

I cringed and snapped my mouth shut, realizing how insane I sounded. He was going to leave me now. Probably pull right over and kick me and KitKat out on the side of the highway. At least I was close to the safehouse. Maybe I could convince him to let me take the burner phone so I could find my way there by foot.

But Jackson let out a long, slow breath and said, "How did you not think this was important for me to know? Is it a medical condition? Should you be on medication?"

Startled, I peeked at him from the corner of my eyes. He didn't look mad or disgusted or weirded out. He looked worried.

Worried about my health.

"Um, no, not a medical condition," I said, wondering how much to tell him. I felt like the farther I dunked him into my world, the less likely he'd breach the surface intact. How far could I dive into my story and still give him the room to leave after we made it to Vin?

Vin. Oh God, Vin. Worry ensnared my chest, and I dug my nails into my thigh. Please, please don't let it be true. The Shadows were just trying to hurt me more, scare me into submission. Right?

"And you're not a vampire," Jackson said with skepticism, forcing me to address the present issue.

I snorted. "Vampires aren't *real*." I paused, struck by the idea. By all intents, I wasn't normal. I was *para*normal—abnormal. Out of the realm of normal human possibility. "I mean, of course not. They're not real, right?"

He must have heard the half-hysterical, half-plaintive edge in my voice. "No, of course not," he assured me, patting my knee. He left his hand there for a few seconds before returning it to the wheel. Five seconds to be exact. I counted every one. "Okay, so you can only eat blood. And you don't know why, I'm guessing?"

That, at least, was mostly true. "I'm not exactly sure, no. I've always had a hard time keeping large amounts of real food down, even when I was a kid. The blood thing, though, that's new. I didn't know that until…"

I trailed off.

I didn't know it until we kissed.

Jackson raised an eyebrow in my direction. "Until?"

"Until recently," I amended, too shy to bring up the kiss. Would it weird him out that I'd ingested his blood? Would the reminder of my wild kiss and half-crazed bite make him question whether helping me was worth the risk? To him and to society?

I needed—no, I *wanted*—Jackson on my side *at least* until we reached the safehouse and I knew for sure if Vin was okay.

All those voicemails. Had he still not cleared his inbox? Would he ever?

"Okay." Jackson let my lackluster explanation fly. "Well, you took some major hits back there, so when we reach the safehouse, I think KitKat should find you something to eat. Sound good?"

"Sounds good." I sagged a bit on the seat.

The farther we drove, the higher the elevation. My ears popped incessantly during the last thirty minutes of the journey, and KitKat spent the entire time growling and fidgeting in discomfort.

I marveled that we'd gotten away from those murderous thugs with only a few scrapes and bruises. But the Shadows were the more pressing matter. Had they really been following me since the desert? More importantly, how did they know who I was?

That part was troubling. A creeping dread crawled over my skin, realizing it was a question that I couldn't answer but would have to deal with all the same. But Shadows were always around. Always a threat. Nothing I hadn't seen. Though that was a lot of them in one place back there.

What I'd never seen before was a bike falling over on its own or a drainpipe disconnecting at a precise, strategic moment.

Had Jackson done that with his *freaking mind*?

Don't be stupid, Ellis.

Still…

"Anything you want to tell me?" I asked as he pulled off the main highway onto a narrow, winding road.

Jackson glanced at me. "What do you mean?"

"Any idea how that bike fell over on the man with the gun?" I asked evenly.

He shrugged. "Luck, I guess."

"And the drainage pipe that miraculously detached itself from the roof to brain that other guy?"

Jackson chuckled. "He hit the building. That place wasn't up to code. That drain was already hanging on for dear life."

I narrowed my eyes at his silhouette. I couldn't read him anymore since we'd lost passing headlights to illuminate his face. The blue glow of the dashboard was barely enough to glint off his pupils. "How'd we get out of there without getting caught?"

"I ran. Fast," he added, turning a pointed look on me.

Fine. He wanted to play dumb, I wasn't about to make a stink over it.

Even though I had shared my blood thing with him. Jerk. If I could confess that, he could at least admit—as I suspected—that he was more like me than he let on.

Still, running as fast as a cheetah wouldn't ditch a Shadow. You had to take evasive maneuvers. Maybe even hire a Cloaker. My palms started sweating, and my eyes jumped around the car again.

"Are you sure we weren't followed by something else?" I tried to make out any odd movement in the dark.

"Huh? Like what?"

Everything about my upbringing demanded I stay quiet and let it drop. But if Shadows were following us, I'd never shake them if I couldn't keep Jackson informed. And maybe, if he was what I thought he was, he already knew and was afraid to tell me.

"You didn't see anything weird hanging around those bikers?"

"No, I was kind of distracted by all the weapons and blood. 'Weird' how?"

"Like shadows that weren't theirs."

He scrunched one side of his face. "What?"

"You didn't see big, weird shadows moving on their own?"

"Like in *Peter Pan*?"

I huffed. "No, not like in *Peter Pan*." I clearly wasn't getting through. Either my theory was entirely wrong, or he didn't even know what he was. He'd been raised in foster homes, I remembered. If he was part of my world, he'd had no one to guide him through it.

I shifted to face him in my seat. "Listen, this might sound crazy, but we're already past the vampire thing, so maybe not that crazy."

"I'm listening."

"You might have noticed my family isn't normal."

He smirked slightly but stayed quiet.

I struggled through my next words, not sure if I should try to make it more palatable or tell the full truth. "Well, ever since I was little, we've been followed by these things. These malicious spirits, I guess you'd say."

"Your family is haunted?" He kept a straight face, but I heard the suppressed laugh in his voice.

I scowled at him, then faced the front, arms crossed. "Look, it's not like that exactly. And you don't have to believe me. But we call them Shadows, and they've been killing women and girls like me for a long time. So, I'm going to take them seriously." I looked over to find him studying me with genuine concern, all traces of brewing jokes wiped from his face. "If you hear me say there's a Shadow around, promise me you'll indulge me and do what I say needs to be done."

There was a long pause, and I dug my nails into my crossed forearms, waiting for him to laugh or call me insane.

Then he said, "Okay. Deal."

"Thank you." I tried to sound curt and huffy, but a warm feeling spread in my chest and softened my words.

The narrow, one-lane road wound further up the mountain, precarious in some places and potentially disastrous should we encounter an oncoming vehicle. Jackson drove slow, his full attention on the small halo of lights ahead. Mailboxes passed intermittently in the darkness, marked with numbers I could hardly make out. The dash clock said it was just past three a.m., and the GPS on the phone said we had ten minutes until we reached our destination.

Ten minutes to the safehouse.

Ten minutes to the truth about Vin.

I kept my fingers in KitKat's fur and sat stiff, anxiety making my spine rigid, unable to relax. Vin couldn't be gone. He was too smart. His ability helped him easily ward off Shadow-influenced goons. Vin was fine.

I'll let you off easier than your cousin. Pretty as a girl, wasn't he?

The phone announced we'd arrived, making me jump. Jackson turned onto a small, sloping driveway. We made two shallow curves, one right, one left, and then the trees opened up to reveal a rustic log cabin beneath a pale moon.

The cabin was dark.

Jackson pulled up in front but didn't cut the engine, so the headlights pointed right at the front door. "Doesn't look like anybody's home. No car in the drive. No lights."

"He's probably sleeping." I forced a smile to try and subconsciously lift my mood as I unbuckled my seat belt.

Jackson tossed me a look, but he didn't reply.

I didn't miss the fact he reached beneath the driver's seat for his gun, though.

I hurried to the front porch, telling myself I was home, that I was okay now, that Vin was alive and well and going to take care of me.

"Vin!" I didn't bother being quiet, my feet pounding raucously on the creaky wooden floorboards as I cried for Vin twice more. Then I was at the door, my heart in my throat, and my fist slamming into the wood.

Jackson joined me half a second later, his gun in one hand, angled away from me as he crept closer. "Ellis."

I stopped knocking long enough to snarl, "What?"

We were so close.

So close.

"Cobwebs." Jackson pointed at the top of the door.

"So," I scoffed. "Cobwebs can pop up literally overnight."

He pursed his lips but didn't say anything else.

I knocked until my knuckles swelled, praying for a response that never came. But Vin could be a crazy hard sleeper. He needed literal beauty sleep to maintain that perfect, slow-aging physique that enhanced his race's abilities. I didn't have to worry. It wasn't true. He was in there. I wasn't worried. Not really. Maybe a little, but… no. *I didn't come this far only to sleep on the doormat.*

After letting me go wild on the door for several long minutes, Jackson put out a hand and gently pushed me away. Then he tested the knob—locked. Taking a giant step back, he lashed out with his heavy boot and kicked the door open.

I shoved past him and barged into the cabin, searching blindly for a light switch on the wall. When my fingertips grazed the cool plastic, I flicked it up, only for nothing to happen.

"What the…" I trailed off, testing the switch a couple more times. "The light won't come on."

Jackson stalked past me, still holding his gun. "Here," he muttered, shoving the phone at me. "Turn the flashlight on."

I did as he said and swept the tiny beam over a very dusty living room. Jackson disappeared into the dusky recesses of the cabin, while I walked slowly into the sitting area, my throat tightening with every step.

The flashlight beam illuminated a bright square on the coffee table, and I froze, darting the beam back to the object.

A note.

Relief flooded me instantly, and I lunged forward, my hand slapping down on it. Vin had just gone out for a minute; he'd left a note.

My smile fell. The paper was covered in a thick layer of dust, too. It was only two words: *Narcissus. Νερό.*

I knew its meaning instantly, but I held the letter a long moment, not wanting to let it go. Vin had written it. How long ago?

Narcissus, the subject of the Greek myth about the dangers of vanity. Uncle Alec had ensured we knew everything possible about The Priestesses' homeland, where the relics were created.

I tucked the note in my pocket with care, then moved to the silver mirror hung in the hall, visible through the entryway. Narcissus had wasted away staring at his reflection. I hardly glanced at mine.

Νερό, the Greek word for water. My element. I knew what I would find inside the safe tucked behind the mirror, and I hurried to set the heavy silver frame on the floor. I spun the combination lock, putting in the numerical equivalents for the letters in Νερό. The lock disengaged with a soft click. A sigh of happy relief gushed from my lips at the sight of that blue oval nestled in coils of silver. I snatched up my guidestone and clutched it to my chest like a comforting blanket. After a long inhale, I let the delicate chain dangle over the back of my hand and smiled at the pendant against my palm. I ran a thumb over the transparent stone, composed of swirling aquamarine, lapis, teal, and sapphire. Through its glass-like surface, I read the slightly distorted etching in the wide, flat silver setting, murmuring to myself, "Wait for the wisest of all counselors, time." A silver laurel pattern surrounding the embedded guidestone completed the piece. My own little reflecting pool in the palm of my hand. In it, I could see myself growing strong again, feasting on veggie stir-fries and vanilla ice cream and banana-raspberry-hemp smoothies. Instead of a sallow vampire, I'd be a mermaid, sitting by the pool with my dark waves down my back. Maybe I'd even put in some blue streaks. Maybe—

"No running water," Jackson said, moving stealthily through the sitting area to join me. He stared curiously at the safe and the stone in my fist. "The beds look like they haven't been slept in in months. Maybe longer."

I abandoned the empty safe and sank to the couch, numbness spiraling into my stomach.

My guidestone was here.

But Vin wasn't. The Shadows hadn't lied.

Grief smothered me, snuffed out emotion, all feeling.

I stared down the harsh reality I'd been denying since I left Uncle Alec alone at the base.

No one was coming to save me.

18
BLOOD COFFEE

I WOKE THE NEXT MORNING TO THE SMELL OF FRESH COFFEE. Rather than making my stomach gurgle uncomfortably, like most food aromas, it reminded me of home. Uncle Alec would be down in the kitchen reading the news on his tablet with a cup of black coffee.

Home. I wasn't sure I even had one of those anymore.

Restless sleep had tangled the soft blankets around my legs like restraints. Morning sunlight beamed through the window over the twin bed, chasing away the shadows from the night before. I checked the corners, making sure other sorts of Shadows weren't spying.

Vin isn't here.

Vin hasn't been here.

That wasn't true. Not really. He had brought my guidestone and left that note for me. Whatever plans he and Uncle Alec set in motion had been going fine, minus the fact Vin hadn't shown up. Anywhere.

Kicking free of the blankets, I glanced at the analog clock on the nightstand.

Not quite eight.

I'd had hardly four hours of sleep.

For the first time in days, I'd been afforded a comfortable bed and the opportunity to fully rest. And I had passed out so thoroughly I didn't even remember anything but a mumbled goodnight to Jackson as he shut the door behind him. But in those dreamless hours, my body had given up the ghost. Now, every joint ached like I'd done eight hours of cardio daily for a week. Even my scalp hurt, though a tentative touch to the back of my head assured me the sores were healing.

I watched the second hand tick and considered going back to sleep. In sleep, I could forget my screwed-up situation, my loneliness, my impossible responsibility as a relic match, and how terrible I looked. For days, we'd raced from one obstacle to another, too busy trying to survive and avoid discovery to dwell on the other stuff. The inner stuff.

Now that things had slowed down, the harsh light of day scared me. I didn't want to face it.

But the coffee smelled delicious, even if I couldn't drink it. Maybe I could sit with Jackson and enjoy it vicariously through him.

I rolled out of bed and pulled my guidestone from beneath my pillow. I wasn't letting it out of my reach ever again. Maybe with its cool silver against my chest, I *could* have that cup of coffee. After pulling its chain over my head, I tossed my new hooded sweatshirt over my tank top and leggings, then stopped by the dresser. The stolen makeup lay scattered across the surface. I lined up the concealer, bronzer, and foundation, then cut the tape off the eyeshadow and blush lids. Then I set to work on the ghoul in the mirror.

Two stripes of concealer beneath my eyes hid the worst of the dark circles. I slathered on the foundation, smoothing it over skin that hadn't seen moisturizer in months. Base in place, I opened my new brushes and set to work with the bronzer, adding a bit of peach blush to my cheeks so I didn't look quite so much like a corpse. Black wings shaped my eyes—not as good as I used to do them, given how much my hands shook now, but adequate. I quelled the urge to do a blown-out smoky eye—as pale as I'd become, I'd probably look like a ghost in a horror movie—and did a brown, semi-nude look instead. Then I finished it all off with a peach lip gloss.

Understated. Elegant. The kind of makeup that used to make me feel beautiful.

But I saw past it to the mess beneath. Thick paint smeared over a misshapen canvas—my sharp bones high ridges, my sallow cheeks low valleys—distorting the image.

Blinking away tears, I tossed my hood over my bald head and walked away from the mirror before I gave up and went back to bed.

The cabin was modest and compact. Downstairs, a combination kitchen-slash-dining room fed into the living room, and a narrow staircase led to two bedrooms upstairs. The door to Jackson's room hung open. His bed was already made with military precision. His boots sat on the floor, aligned vertically to the nightstand. Unlike my room, where I'd already tossed clothes and makeup around in a hurricane, his space was spotless.

You can take the boy from the military, but…

I found him in the kitchen, standing over the stove while something sizzled in a skillet.

"I thought we didn't have electricity," I said, slipping onto a stool at the counter that separated the kitchen from the dining room.

"Gas stove," he said, glancing at me with his spatula hovering over the pan. He froze, his eyebrows raising toward his hairline as his gaze raked over my face. "How you feeling?"

"Like even my blood vessels are bruised," I joked and grabbed the edges of my hood to hide the flush rising in my neck from his stare. "Where's KitKat?"

"Hunting so you'd have breakfast." He finally looked away without mentioning my attempt at a beauty routine, then scraped the spatula around the skillet for a moment before he added, "She should be back any minute."

My stomach growled at the thought, and I swallowed hard, heart plummeting. Dread crept into my guts, which still craved blood. But maybe they didn't know better yet.

"What are you making?"

He blew out a breath. "Um, well, there were some dried goods in the pantry. I found a box of instant potatoes, grabbed some water from the lake out back, and… we'll see how it goes."

"Delightful."

He laughed. "Beggars can't be choosers."

KitKat shoved the back door open, prancing into the kitchen with something furry and bloody dangling from her teeth. She chuffed happily at me in greeting, then dropped a dead gopher at Jackson's feet.

To his credit, he didn't even cringe. He moved his potatoes to a cold burner, put a big metal bowl in the sink, then picked up the animal and sliced it open in several different places. He held the creature over the bowl, and when the blood supply ran dry, he gave it a shake before tossing it in the second sink basin. Then, like a gourmet chef finishing off an unorthodox meal, he put the metal bowl over the flame and let it sit for a moment, giving it a few swirls.

He served it to me in a coffee mug, piping hot.

"Your breakfast, my vampire queen." He grinned and winked at me, then went to plate his potatoes.

KitKat clambered onto the stool beside me and nipped at my ear playfully. I wrapped my arms around her neck and squeezed. "Thanks for taking care of me."

Her resounding purr vibrated through my body.

But I looked to Jackson, pushing the mug away an inch. "Could I… try some of yours first?"

He blinked at me. "Sure."

Potatoes seemed like a safe bet. Mellow, not overly flavorful. I had to know.

He scooped me a tiny serving in a bowl and slid it across the counter with a spoon. Though he half turned back to serve himself, I felt his eye on me. KitKat watched openly, whiskers tickling my arm as she leaned in, watching the spoonful of white mush rise to my mouth. The smell alone made my intestines buck, but I stuck out my tongue and forced myself to lick the tiniest morsel off the tip of the spoon.

Nope. Salty slime, so strong and vile it made my jaw lock like I'd eaten a tablespoon of sodium.

I gagged, cheeks puffing. Luckily, nothing came up, but I had to wipe the potatoes off my tongue with my hoodie sleeve, unable to swallow. Face hot and eyes stinging, I pulled the mug of blood to me, avoiding everyone's gaze, even KitKat's. Neither of them commented. They let me mourn in private.

Maybe a therapist for eating disorders could help me. But what exactly would I tell them? Maybe I needed my relic. *Yeah. Maybe that's it*, I soothed myself. But for now. I needed my strength.

I hated to admit it, but the blood was easily the best I'd had so far—okay, minus Jackson's. I got a few flashes of the gopher's flight and fear, but it wasn't nearly as overwhelming as it had been before. I wondered if it had something to do with boiling it or if I was just getting used to it.

After Jackson joined me at the counter, standing opposite so we could face each other, he asked, "What's our plan?"

I raised an eyebrow. "What do you mean?"

"Well, your cousin isn't here," he pointed out, scooping up another spoonful of mucusy fake potatoes. "So, what's our next move?"

I squeezed the mug between both my hands, letting the warmth of its contents banish my chills. "We wait."

Jackson washed his potatoes down with a swig of coffee and avoided my gaze. "Ellis, I don't think your cousin is coming."

My heart skipped a beat, then picked up a death knell in my chest.

"He's coming. He has to." I said louder than I'd intended, even though I didn't really believe it.

Because if Vin didn't show up, it meant the Shadows probably weren't lying. He was dead. The boy who'd raced me in the pool, who'd read me bedtime stories, and did the world's best impression of an angry Cyndra was dead. He'd never call me "little mermaid" or "Ariel" again. He'd never give me another one-armed squeeze and tell me not to worry.

I was entirely alone.

Well, I had Jackson, for which I was eternally grateful, but I had no connection to my roots. No one who understood what it was to be an alt, and certainly no one who understood what it was to be a destined relic holder. Or did he?

He hadn't known about Shadows. That incredulity wasn't fake. But what I'd seen him do last night and the fact that he worked at that lab suggested he had to know something. Even if he didn't know all the right terms.

Were all the prisoners at the lab alts? Did everyone there know about us? Had they targeted us specifically?

Jackson caught my curious eye. "Two days. We'll give it two days. Then we need to have a plan to get you to safety. Could I take you home? To your real home?"

I shook my head. "That's where they… They took me from home." I didn't need to clarify who I meant. "They're probably already casing the house hoping I'll show up."

He pushed his potatoes into a neat pile, silent for a moment. "Do you think you could tell me now why they came for you? Why they had you in that… situation at the lab?"

I jolted, like he'd read my mind, violated my privacy. So, he didn't know? Or was he fishing for what I knew before he revealed his hand? Shivering, I picked up the mug and polished off the rest of the blood. The animal's fear joined my own, snaking down my spine and into the mass of nerves in my stomach.

I didn't want to lie to Jackson. But I wasn't ready to tell him everything. First, I had to do some fishing of my own.

"I'm not sure," I said, going for vague half-truths. "I'm not like my uncle. I have nothing to offer a Psy-Ops scientist."

"The mind control thing that Hurst raves about, you mean?"

"There are lots of *alternate* theories, but yeah." I watched him closely, searching for micro-expressions, some indication that the word meant something else to him. He had a good poker face. "My uncle has a gift," I ventured. "They thought I was a blood relative, which I guess is why they took me, too. But he's an adoptive uncle."

Jackson leaned an elbow on the table, pondering with his mouth scrunched up, letting out a soft "hmm." He drummed his fingers on the wood surface, then said, "Dr. Craig studies... gifts." He shrugged like it wasn't as odd as it sounded, but his eyes watched me carefully. Judging my reaction? "That's why they called him in. But then why did Hurst keep testing you when you clearly didn't meet their criteria?" he asked.

I shrugged but ducked his gaze. I knew why. At least, I had an idea, and it wasn't my would-be murderer, Hurst, who was responsible. Dr. Craig had built my tank. What had he said? *This is bigger than Psy-Ops.*

But I'd learned not to speak against Dr. Craig if I wanted Jackson to stay conversational. Maybe Dr. Craig had wanted to find my "gift." How much did he really tell Jackson?

KitKat leaned against me, nearly hanging off her stool, which was already too small for her fluffy butt. Her dark eyes seemed to know more than she let on. I might have guessed she was an alt, too—a Shifter—if I didn't know better. But Shifter alts spent most of their time as human. They carried the spirit of the animal inside always, but its full form was strenuous to maintain. And she'd had plenty of opportunities and reasons to shift back by now. No, KitKat was her own anomaly. Perhaps the descendant of a sphinx or a chimera. Like me, she had her own secrets. Also like me, she wasn't ready to reveal them yet.

Secrets were an alt's currency. We kept them, or we died. A rule drilled in since birth. The only way around it was to strike a bargain with those who'd decimated us, to ally with the Summum Malum in exchange for the alleged return of your loved ones when their leader reopened the planes of the afterlife and returned to our world. I'd always thought that was for the greedy and the stupid, but now, facing the possibility of living the rest of my miserable life without my family, I realized it was for the desperate. The terribly lonely. The people whose reasons for living had been carved right out of their chests, leaving a dark, bloody wound behind.

Jackson relinquished his thoughtful expression to shove the last of his potatoes in his mouth. He chewed, swallowed, and then postulated, "Something to do with the food thing, maybe?"

"Maybe," I agreed. I'd almost forgotten what he was pondering, lost in my own thoughts.

If he bore secrets similar to mine, he was better at hiding them. Or perhaps he was less desperate to let someone in than I was.

He shoved his plate aside and swiped a napkin over his lips. "Hey, there's a fire pit down by the lake. It's a nice day. I thought we could eat dinner out there this afternoon, before the sun goes down."

"That sounds great. Except you can't keep eating instant potatoes," I pointed out, grinning.

"I'll run out and find a grocery later."

My heart seized at the thought of being left alone. "Take me with you?"

With a soft smile, he reached across the counter to rest his fingertips on my arm.

"Always."

The acrid scent of woodsmoke filtered through the forest as my boots crunched over a layer of dead undergrowth. KitKat pranced around me, darting in figure eights around my legs and pouncing on any leaf that dared to move. A curving dirt path meandered from the back of the cabin down to the lake, where Jackson bent over the fire.

We'd gone grocery shopping around lunchtime, finding a small general store with our burner phone. Pickings had been slim, but Jackson apparently wasn't fussy, and he still had a few of his favorite ginger candies stowed in his pack to tide him over. Then we'd spent the afternoon playing card games and swapping stories—me about my sisters, and Jackson about his time in the military. I'd laughed through a retelling of the time Cyndra and Alanna flipped Vin into a wheelbarrow during training and dumped him into the duck pond. He'd ticked them off by stealing the last piece of baklava and eating it obnoxiously in front of them. Jackson had wheezed himself silly telling me about a time his whole parajumper drill group got themselves stuck in a huge sycamore tree and were chewed out by their sergeant on the ground while they dangled and spun in slow circles for fifteen minutes.

He looked beautiful on the backdrop of the lake and mountains as he carefully dropped tree limbs into the growing flames with his tongue pressed between his lips. His dark skin shone in the late afternoon sunlight, his facial tattoo like a swirling void or portal to his soul. In his jeans and the flannel jacket he'd borrowed from a closet in the cabin, he looked almost normal—minus the muscles and military bearing. When his gaze met mine, his irises looked caramel in the sunshine.

"The only thing we're missing is marshmallows," I joked, crouching to sit on the fallen log he'd dragged over to the fire site. "Not that I could eat them."

"The only thing fresh in the pantry are spiders," Jackson replied with a wry grin. "Somehow, I don't think toasted spiders would land the same."

KitKat suddenly stopped her scampering, frozen with one fat paw in the air. She dropped it in slow motion, growling deep in her chest, and sank into a crouch.

Jackson followed her gaze and scrunched his brow. "After a bird, kitty?"

A cluster of leaves rustled as a small, curious garden snake poked up its head and stuck out its forked tongue at KitKat. She growled at it, but it seemed unafraid, fixing her with friendly eyes— the pupil rounded rather than a slit. The bobcat shimmied her shoulders, sinking lower with another growl, but the snake slithered right for her. KitKat sailed through the air in a graceful bound and landed on her prey. She yanked it out of the leaves, shaking it furiously. The scaly body wiggled feebly in its death throws, then went limp in her jaws. KitKat dropped the dead snake and strutted back to us like nothing had happened.

"Wow, you really hate snakes, huh?" I asked as I tickled her under the chin. "But they seem to love you."

In answer, she sat regally at my feet and lent me her warmth. It wasn't frigid outside, but the chill cut a little harder than usual on my ragged body. I bent and rested my chin on her head and took a deep breath of the woodsmoke, letting it fill all the dark corners in my mind.

Jackson dropped a handful of dried leaves on the flames, then settled on the log beside me. His hotdog sat on the opposite log seat, as far from me as he could get it, already half-eaten and growing cold. I'd told him the scent of real food made me sick, and he'd taken it to heart.

"Look what I found inside." He reached behind him and drew an acoustic guitar into his lap. "It was in the coat closet. Is it your cousin's?"

"I don't think so. Uncle Alec, maybe? This is his cabin, technically, and he loved music. But he kept to himself a lot." It came out blunt. I didn't want Uncle Alec to sound anything like the fosters Jackson had before Henrietta. "He was a reserved, studious guy, but the best replacement parent I could've asked for."

Jackson grimaced. "He's the one still imprisoned at the lab?"

Despair lanced through me. I thought of my uncle, looking decrepit, tortured, and completely alone as I left him behind. "Yeah. He is."

Jackson strummed the guitar with his three fingers, and the rich sound filled the air. He began twisting the knobs at the top while testing the strings, talking over his tuning. "Do you want me to ask Dr. Craig about him?"

My immediate and visceral reaction was *no*. But logic overruled my emotions. I trusted Jackson. In the short time we'd been together, he'd helped me in innumerable ways, even at the risk of his own moral compass. I knew it had bothered him to hurt that cop, and I knew he harbored guilt over the man I'd killed outside the bar.

Even still, he'd stuck around.

If Jackson trusted Dr. Craig, I owed it to *him* to trust the doctor, on some level.

"Yeah, if you don't mind," I agreed. "Just… make sure he's okay. Oh, and the person who set the fire. It's possible they were there to free me." Dangerous, foolish hope flared in my gut, flushing my skin. "It could have been my cousin."

Maybe Vin wasn't dead.

"Can your cousin become a giant grizzly bear?" Jackson asked. He side-eyed me, but avoided my gaze, like he was worried. It took me a second to realize he thought I might think he was crazy. I almost laughed. If he only knew the level of crazy I was accustomed to.

But then realization hit.

"No," I said in a small voice. "He's not a Shifter. Remember, I told you he's like my uncle."

"Shifter? You have a word for it?"

I tensed. "That's kind of a common term for something like that. I thought you were a *Farraway Heights* fan?"

"But that's fiction."

"But you saw it happen. Didn't you?" I pressed, watching him squirm with interest. Why did this make him so uncomfortable if he worked with scientists who believed in things like mind control? Why did he find it so outlandish if he could make pipes fall with his mind, like I was pretty sure he could? Maybe he thought I'd fear him or laugh at him. Maybe, I thought, we should stop being so scared of freaking each other out at this point, after all we'd seen.

"Yeah, and I still can hardly believe it." He shook his head. "One minute I had a bear on the monitor, tearing a security bar out of a door, and the next, I had some body-builder-looking dude casually turning the handle and walking inside."

"But the bear isn't who set the fire, right? I heard somebody mention two people on the radio. Something about a big one and a firestarter. I guess the bear was the big one."

"I'll say. I never saw the other one, though. The one who was captured."

"Maybe that was my cousin." He really could be alive, just trapped! "Can you check on that person, too?"

Jackson plucked a few pure, beautiful notes, then smiled at me. "I'll call him first thing tomorrow when I know he's on base, with access to the most recent status reports."

He struck up a folksy tune, his foot tapping on the ground. A heavy, bass-like background of strumming was overlaid with a pretty plucking, like drops of rain in water. I closed my eyes to soak up the melody's welcome calm and swayed against KitKat's fur.

Then his voice rose over the guitar, and my eyes snapped open, warmth flooding me at the clear beauty of his low vocals.

The song didn't make much sense, but it painted pretty pictures and waxed poetic in its lyrics. Lines about sticking loneliness and a lover's lips into pockets. Leaving on a train on a Sunday. Thinking of a proverbial "you" when the singer's mind was troubled. The chorus was about taking "small change" from your pocket, repeating that idea over and over for reasons I couldn't puzzle out.

And for the smallest moment, the most miniscule moment, I felt like he was singing not just *for* me, but *to* me.

Which was crazy.

Jackson continued playing, speaking over the music. "In my late teens, I was in a foster home with a few other kids. One of them was a guitarist in a cover band."

"You play pretty good for not having all your fingers," I teased.

He laughed, adding a little ditty that didn't match the rest of the music. "It took a *lot* of practice. Dylan, my foster brother, he was really good and really patient. It also helps that I was born with just the three on each hand. You can't miss what you never had."

"Yeah," I said, but I didn't think it was entirely true. I'd never gone to a real school or experienced half the perks of a normal childhood, and yet I'd ached for them almost every day of my life. "I've never heard this song before." I'd thought I had eclectic tastes in music. Of course, I'd never heard *live* music before either, though I always had my speakers blasting at home. Especially when I painted.

"It's 'Two Coins', by Dispatch. An indie band from the late nineties. Dylan didn't really care for mainstream music, so most of what I learned isn't well known."

"It's nice," I told him, my cheeks warming. What I really wanted to say was *It's the most beautiful thing I've ever heard, and I could sit here forever listening to you sing.*

But I didn't.

I couldn't.

Jackson continued the song, his voice rising like the sun.

Leaning into KitKat, I swayed with her, enjoying the warmth and the purring while Jackson's music and voice filled me. The simple joy of it chased away all the hard stuff. It helped me forget what had happened—not just my recent flight from the lab, but those weeks and months before, when I'd wasted away, wishing for home and my family. Jackson's voice and KitKat's purrs made me feel like one day, things would be normal again. One day, I'd be back with the people I loved, safe, comfortable, happy. Maybe I could be strong and beautiful again.

Maybe Jackson could be there too. Singing and strumming and looking at me with those eyes. We'd make a strong, beautiful couple that everyone just knew would go the distance.

A pipe dream.

His voice lowered, and the strumming slowed to a low, bass-like thump. He opened his eyes and met my gaze as he stopped playing and sang the last line again a cappella.

As his voice trailed off into the peaceful silence of the mountains, I couldn't imagine how anything could be more perfect.

I didn't know if it was the raging inferno a few feet away making me so hot, or if my burgeoning desire for him had turned up the heat, but I peeled off my sweatshirt. The cold caressed my bare skin.

Jackson set his guitar aside. "Hot?"

I shrugged, clutching the sweatshirt to my chest to hide my unrecognizable body. "A little."

"Bonfires get hot fast." He stood and stripped off his jacket... followed by his t-shirt.

KitKat huffed, and I swear the sound was almost disgusted. She tossed herself to the leaves at my feet and closed her eyes.

"What are you doing?" I asked, blinking at him.

His torso looked cut from granite—the valleys and plains of his muscles sculpted by a Renaissance artist. I couldn't tear my gaze away from his trim waist, from the trail of muscles that vanished beneath his waistband.

He undid the button on his jeans, then held out a hand. "Come on."

"Come... where?" I said slowly, raising an eyebrow. The elastic band of his boxers poked above his opened pants.

Jackson's grin widened, and he glanced at the lake.

I held up both hands. "Oh no. No, no. Not happening."

"But you're hot," he said.

"So is hell, but you don't see demons taking a dip in a mountain lake at sixty degrees."

"We don't have running water in there." He gestured at the cabin. "A dip in the lake will wash you off and make you feel better."

I shook my head and hugged the sweatshirt tighter. How many times had I daydreamed of a moment like this? I'd put myself in my favorite heroine's shoes to have what normal girls called "wild experiences," like skinny dipping with the hottest guy in school. How many times in my head had I taken that offered hand and given a flirty "yes" in return? But now, with the moment coming to life before my eyes, I said, "I'm fine. You go." I didn't want this moment when I looked like this. When I wasn't myself. When I couldn't begin to compare to his beauty.

Jackson finished shucking off his jeans, startling me into

wide-eyed silence. His black boxer briefs hugged his hips and butt, leaving little to the imagination.

I swallowed.

"Come on, Ell," he said, wiggling his fingers. "For me?"

Maybe it was the adorable way he'd called me Ell. Maybe the sight of him in just his underwear had made all the blood leave my brain. Maybe it was a fierce need to let go, to forget everything that had happened and just be young for once. I didn't want to worry about the fate of the world, or my hidden relic, or the men or Shadows who were likely out there searching for me right this minute.

I just wanted to be… free.

So I took his hand.

19
BELOW THE SURFACE

EVEN AS I RELISHED THE GENTLE PRESSURE OF JACKSON'S hand holding mine, insecurity gripped me harder. At least my tank top was loose, hiding the worst of my protruding bones. But the moment the water soaked it, everything would be revealed. I was horrified of him seeing me like this, as a shadow of who I'd been a year ago, even though logically, I knew he'd already seen more of me than any man ever had.

He'd pulled me from that tank, half-naked. Half-living.

Now he pulled me off the log and led me to the water.

The water sloshed over my bare feet, and I squeaked as the icy chill traveled up my legs. My toes sank into the soft silt, rocks sliding around my soles.

"This is insane," I said, breathless after the cold snatched all the oxygen from my lungs.

"Every moment I've spent with you has been insane," Jackson said. "This is the least insane thing we've done."

I couldn't even argue.

I let him drag me further into the lake, water rising over my calves, then my knees. When the surface hit my hips, I sucked in a breath and halted.

"Nope. Nopity-nope." I yanked on his hand. "That's far enough."

But Jackson tightened his grip on my fingers, a mischievous glint in his eye.

I eyed him back. "What?"

Before I could react, he scooped me up in a bridal carry and took me under with a splash. The water closed over my head, and my guidestone floated into my vision a moment before sinking back to my chest. I might have been scared, cast back into those moments of drowning in the tank, but Jackson's arm remained around my back and legs, anchoring me. I curled my fingers around his shoulders, his skin satiny smooth, and clung to him. Putting my faith in him.

I could hear *everything*. The dull thud of deer hooves on the ground nearby. The thrush of critters burrowing and running, going about their day, unconcerned by the two crazy humans in the lake. The lake was alive with thrashing fish tails and paddling frogs and the musical rush of running water in the distance like the sound of cars on the highway. There was an entire world down here, and I could hear it all. And instead of puzzling over it, wondering why it had started and what it meant about me and my relic, I let myself relish it. I let the music of it wash over me, and suddenly, I wanted to paint, to unleash the beauty of life below the water onto a canvas.

Then Jackson pulled me to the surface.

I came up laughing. Real laughter. The kind I hadn't experienced since home, since before my life fell apart.

"See?" Jackson said, dropping my legs to brush his tattooed palm over his face and clear his eyes. "Not so bad."

"It's freezing!" I argued.

He curled his arm around my waist, and I realized he was close. So close. Nothing but the wet cotton of our clothes separated us. Water droplets glittered like gems on his skin in the early evening light.

I looked up at him, my hands resting on his chest.

His gaze dropped to my lips.

Doubt crept in like a thief, stealing the moment away from me. He could feel how ugly I'd become. My curves were gone— not that he'd ever known me before, when I'd had long, lush hair, glowing skin, and an hourglass shape. The eyeliner, blush, and lip gloss I'd put on when I woke up today weren't enough to cover up my sunken cheeks or my sallow complexion. They were probably smearing down my face.

The thumb of his free hand brushed over my jaw line.

"Better?" he asked.

The real answer was no, but he was talking about the cold, and his hand on my face and his arm holding my body so close to his made the glowing embers of desire in my stomach burn hotter.

"Yes," I said.

He didn't release me. His arm tightened, pulling me up onto my tiptoes as water rippled around our waists. My hands sought purchase, wrapping around to cradle the back of his neck, and the sight and sensation of his dark skin glossed with water droplets drove all thoughts of my own body from my mind. Drove *thought* from my mind, as his head bent closer.

Then the cellphone rang from the fire pit.

Jackson glanced at the bank, surprise crossing his features. "Sorry." He released me. "Dr. Craig is the only person who has the number. I need to get that."

"Right." I wrapped my arms around my chest, trying to hide myself. "Don't forget to ask him about Uncle Alec and the new prisoner."

Jackson nodded, squeezed my shoulder with an unreadable look on his face, and then sloshed out of the lake.

I followed him out of the water, trying not to think about what had just happened. Had he been about to kiss me? There was no way. There was no way a guy like Jackson could have any interest in me. I was broken. A tragic ghost of myself.

KitKat mewled at me before heading deeper into the forest, probably for a snack. I waved her off and left Jackson sitting on the log, still dripping wet and apparently unbothered by the chill while I headed back inside to warm up.

I found towels in the bathroom cabinet, bemoaning the fact that we didn't have warm, running water. After draping my wet leggings and tank top over the shower curtain rod to dry, I grabbed clean clothes from my backpack in my room, then pulled my sweatshirt back over everything. Then I cocooned myself in a blanket on the couch to wait for Jackson and KitKat.

He came inside a few minutes later, still wearing only his boxer briefs and carrying the rest of his clothes under his arm. "Good news." He set the phone on the coffee table. "Your uncle's okay."

All the tension eased from my body, and I collapsed against the cushions. "Oh, thank the Priestesses," I sighed out of habit. Jackson looked at me funny, probably wondering what weird religion I followed, but I just picked up the spare towel I'd brought downstairs and offered it to him. "Is he healthy? He was really injured when I saw him."

Jackson accepted the towel with a "thanks," then wrapped it around his waist before he sank into the chair opposite me. "Dr. Craig mentioned he was injured, but that at this time, he's in stable condition."

"I guess that's as much as I could hope for. What about the person who set the fire?"

"They're calling her Echo," Jackson said.

"Her?" I asked, sagging. It wasn't Vin.

Jackson nodded, using the edge of the towel to dry off his chest. I tried not to watch, but it was difficult. "Dr. Craig said she's not talking, so they don't know her real name or who she is."

"What's she look like?"

He shook his head. "Dr. Craig hasn't seen her yet. They've got her locked away under tight security."

"Why?" I asked, flabbergasted.

He grinned. "I imagine because she single-handedly set the base on fire, according to Dr. Craig."

"Did he tell you *anything* about her?"

"Yeah, he did tell me something, but it's… weird."

"Weirder than me having to eat blood to survive?"

"Good point." Jackson chuckled. "Apparently, every time they touch her, she gets burns on her skin and screams like they're killing her."

My blood ran cold. I slipped off the couch and caught myself on the coffee table.

"Ellis?" He was crouched beside me in a blink, a hand on my blanketed back.

I barely registered him.

The burning hadn't been that bad two years ago, but if time had made my own abilities stronger and more potent, I imagined it could do the same to Cyndra. She *was* alive. She hadn't abandoned me. She'd come for me.

Of course she did. She's Cyn, I thought, tears of love and relief stinging my eyes. *Cyn's alive!*

But for how long in that place?

"Ellis?" Jackson's hand made circles on my back.

"That's my sister," I said, my voice small.

Jackson's eyes widened, his hand retracting. "Oh man." He sat back, falling out of his crouch onto his butt on the floor. "Then I have bad news to give you."

A sharp pain lanced through my chest. "What?"

"They're preparing to move her to another facility," he said softly. "A secret facility out of Dr. Craig's reach."

"But if that happens, I'll never be able to find her!"

Jackson scooted forward and reached for me. "It's okay. We'll figure it out."

Tears prickled my eyes. "She's my sister, Jax. I can't let them take her from me."

"Maybe Dr. Craig can request to keep her longer, for his own research."

"I don't want her poked and prodded and tested," I hissed, jerking away from him. "Not even by your precious Dr. Craig."

He flinched, but I couldn't even feel sorry right then. I was remembering that cold, hard bed. The jabs of the needle. The shocks. The pain. The fear. The helplessness of staring at the ceiling with your body bound and malicious shapes moving at the edges of your vision, promising pain but not telling you when it would come. Craig wasn't Hurst, sure, but the tank had been his idea.

"I want her free." I hugged my knees. "I want her with me."

"Ell, I understand, but—"

"Do you?" I snapped.

He hung his head and sighed, and guilt crept in. I hadn't meant to remind him that he didn't have a family of his own to worry about. He was trying to help. He wasn't like the others. Wasn't really one of them. But, how long had he been a bystander? Had he been there when Kit Katana died? Had he stood by, following orders?

He looked up at me, his mouth set and eyes intense. "Ell, I swear to you, I will do what I can to keep Psy-Ops from sending her away, but you have to understand, even the chances of keeping her with Dr. Craig are slim. Getting her out? That's—"

Suddenly, a static discharge crackled through the air. I thought I was imagining it at first, too caught up in my emotions, in the idea of Cyndra being in danger.

Until white noise flickered on the air above the coffee table.

We both turned to look at the strange, dancing spots. Jackson leaped to his feet.

"Jackson?" Fear crept into my tone as I retreated back onto the couch.

"I don't know…" His voice trailed off.

Because the white noise and spots were reforming. The static grew in increments, and so did the image above the coffee table.

A person. A girl. With brown hair, familiar pinched features.

My sister, Alanna. My dead sister.

The truth of what was happening hit me like a wrecking ball.

She hadn't been burned. She existed in the next plane, and her spirit had come for a visit.

20

VIN

JACKSON HIKED HIS TOWEL HIGHER ON HIS HIPS AND MOVED to shield me. "What the hell is that?"

I ignored him and climbed to my feet, sidestepping him to reach one hand toward Alanna, though I stopped short of touching her. She wasn't solid, not in the same way as me or Jax. She was more like a photograph. Colorless and translucent like a piece of thin linen wet and hung to dry in the sunshine. She glowed from within, a muted, pale yellow, and those little staticky sparks darted around her, softening her edges.

In front of me at last, within touching distance, and yet, I still couldn't hug her.

We locked eyes. Her dark brown hair was pulled into an elegant chignon at the back of her head, and delicate curls swung loose around her face. She'd paired a midi sundress with a long cardigan sweater in a fair imitation of her earthly style. Her green irises were startling against the rest of her colorless body, as if the full force of her soul was channeled through them.

Eyes are the window to the soul, I reminded myself.

And Alanna, being dead, was technically just a soul.

I managed to get my emotions under control and crossed my arms over my sweatshirt.

"Haven't seen you in a hot minute."

Alanna's pinched, worried expression fell away, and she smiled wanly. "I've been busy."

"Busy in the afterlife? Shouldn't you just be, like, playing a harp and having tea with Jane Austen?"

Her smile cracked into a small laugh. "You haven't changed a bit, little sister."

Jackson clutched his towel tighter, his wide-eyed gaze whipping between the two of us. "Sister?"

Alanna eyed him, her gaze drifting down his naked torso before she turned back to me. "Aren't you a little young to be with a naked man?"

"He's not naked," I said, exasperated. "Aren't you a little young to be dead?"

Alanna sighed in a world-weary, "How did I end up with such trying sisters?" way. I knew it well. She'd used it on Cyndra daily, too. Her own twin.

"As much as I would love to continue exchanging affectionate jabs," Alanna said firmly, "I'm here on pressing business, and I don't have much time."

"Wait," Jackson cut in, pointing at Alanna and looking at me. "Dead," he clarified, a hysterical note pitching up his deep voice. "You're telling me this is a *ghost*? Ghosts aren't *real*."

I grabbed his hand and pushed it down, so he wasn't spearing Alanna with his finger, but I didn't let him go. Squeezing his fingers, I said, "Jax. I drink blood, remember? And you're drawing the line at ghosts?"

"Ellis," Alanna bit out like a curse. "I have a lot to say and little time to say it. Please."

Dropping Jackson's hand, I gave my sister my full attention. "What is it?"

Alanna took a shaky breath and brushed a curl away from her eyes. "Vin is no longer of this world," she said, and a sledgehammer struck my chest. "He's been on my side about three weeks now."

A sob hitched against a knot of grief clogging my throat. Though

I'd toyed with the possibility so many times in the last two days, the shock was still as stark and breathtaking as my earlier dip in the lake. "H-how? How did he die?" I choked on the words.

"Saving Cyndra's life." Alanna hung her head, her hands clenching and unclenching at her sides like she was still processing what happened.

"He saved her," I repeated numbly.

"Yes, and in his final moments, he sent her looking for you."

I cleared the grief from my throat and exchanged looks with Jackson. "That's how she ended up at the lab."

His flabbergasted, fish out of water look flickered, exchanged for a soft, sympathetic curve to his mouth and concerned creases in his forehead.

"And how I found you," said Alanna. At my puzzled look, she explained, "Cyndra wore a bracelet that belonged to a dear friend of mine here in limbo. It's a long story. But the bracelet is an anchor that makes crossing over at the right location with my Aether powers a little easier. I followed Cyn to the lab, and I waited. But you came out without her."

I studied that yellow glow in her chest, cheery and familiar. "You were the light in the desert?"

She nodded. "And at that horrible bar." She wrinkled her nose and shuddered. Alanna wouldn't have been caught dead at the Stuck Pig in life, but her spirit had gone there, showed me the knife that gave me the upper hand.

Tears pricked my eyes. "Thank you."

"Always." Her hand reached out toward the couch, two fingers extended, ready to curl around mine for a little squeeze like she used to, but when I reached back, my fingers passed through hers like air.

Alanna tugged at the hem of her sweater, her expression twisted with worry. "But I may not always have the strength to cross over so clearly or even appear as anything but a speck of light. Things are… troubled on this side. The Summum Malum is growing in power, and people with"—her emerald irises darted to Jackson—"people like us are in danger."

Alternates. I almost said it aloud, sick of hiding and telling half-truths to the one ally I currently had in this world. But hearing the Summum Malum mentioned out loud had strummed a chord of fear deep in my chest. My skin went clammy, and my tongue didn't want to work right. As much as I feared the soldiers and the doctors from the lab finding me, I feared the Summum Malum more.

I swallowed back the knot in my throat and gestured at Jackson. "He knows about the Shadows. You don't have to be so cryptic."

Alanna raised an eyebrow but didn't comment.

"Stronger how?" I asked.

"They are getting better at feeding off souls in limbo. Some have gained new abilities in the living world." Alanna still eyed Jackson warily.

"We saw Shadows last night, and they acted like they always do. But there were a lot of them," I conceded. "More than I've ever seen in one place."

Alanna nodded. "They are organizing, finding more of the thin spots in the planes where they can breach."

"Are you safe?" I shifted closer to her.

"For now. But that's subject to change. Vin, however… he's in trouble. I'm doing my best to save him."

"A Shadow mentioned Vin to me. He knew he was dead. Do they have him?"

"A piece of him, yes."

"A piece?" I asked horrified, thinking of severed limbs.

"It's not like *that*." Alanna waved it off. "But it is bad. A piece of his soul. They're feeding off it. They can absorb information from it, like his connection to us."

"If Vin's in trouble, why aren't you with him? Why are you *here*?" I tossed my hands in the air.

"Because," Alanna said impatiently, "you're sitting here wasting time. You have to proceed on your own. Take your guidestone and go. Find your relic, then save Cyndra. A war is coming, Ellis. We need to be ready."

I turned to cold, rigid stone. "Go alone?" My fingertips brushed the lump of my guidestone beneath my sweatshirt. "Literally one hundred percent on my own without backup?"

Alanna dipped her head in agreement. "We're counting on you."

A niggle of fear worked its way up my spine. I was never meant to do this alone. I should have had Vin or Uncle Alec or my sisters at my side.

But it was just me now.

I had to be my own hero. People said that all the time in movies. It sounded good, but I had no idea how to make it a reality.

"I'll go," I muttered, despite the petrifying sense of foreboding clawing up my throat.

A smile broke across her face. "Good. I'm proud of you. Stay strong. I'll catch up to you when I get the chance. I may only be a flash of light, but know I'm there with you, Ell, and I love you."

Alanna glanced one more time at Jackson with a wary look, then with a flash of yellow light, she disappeared.

I love you, too.

The silence that fell over us in her absence was potent. Jackson hadn't moved from his spot in front of the couch, still holding his towel around his hips with one hand. We stared at each other for too long, and I could feel the questions racing around in his head.

The door swung open, and KitKat pranced in, a dead rabbit hanging from her sharp incisors. I had no idea how the hell she'd opened the door without opposable thumbs, but like everything else lately, I just had to go with it.

She glanced between the two of us, then sat on her haunches and dropped the rabbit to the hardwood floor. She cocked her head as if to say, *What'd I miss?*

Jackson threw his hands in the air before he turned and stalked to the stairs.

As his footsteps marched toward the second level, I sank down to the edge of the couch, looked at KitKat, and said, "You don't even want to know."

I watched the clock over the television mark away the moments. Every *tick* of the second hand caused a twitch in my right eye that was driving me insane.

Twenty minutes had passed since Alanna had vanished back into the light to return to whatever big bad was brewing in the afterlife. But each minute had felt like a lifetime for me. A lifetime of grief for my dead sister. A lifetime of grief for Vin. A lifetime of worrying about Uncle Alec and Cyndra, both of them locked away in that base, and the revelation that if I didn't get to Cyn soon, I'd lose her again. Probably forever.

KitKat had curled into the armchair beside me, and her purrs harmonized with the clock. I absently petted her back and ignored the mug of warm blood that awaited me on the coffee table. I couldn't even think about eating right now.

Jackson sat on the opposite couch, leaning forward with his elbows on his knees and a Coca-Cola dangling from his hand. He'd swapped his towel and wet boxer briefs for a fresh pair of cargo pants, a plain black tee, and a hefty dose of skepticism.

He let out a breath slowly, then nodded. "Okay. Let's start with the something malice?"

"Summum Malum," I corrected, sinking deeper into the overstuffed chair cushions.

"Right. What's that?"

"A cult. At least, that's how it's been explained to me," I added. "I won't pretend to know everything. Nobody really does. It formed so long ago."

Jackson held up his free hand, palm out. "It's okay. Just tell me what you *do* know."

What did I know? Sometimes, I didn't feel like I knew anything at all. Uncle Alec had done his best to prepare us in his own way, but there'd always been holes in the narrative. That was just the way things were when the story stretched back beyond ancient Egyptian times.

"Magic was real once." I jumped right into the crazy stuff. He needed to know. Whether he was alt or not, he was part of my world now. He'd earned his place, earned my trust by staying by my side. "Like actual magic—elemental magic that draws on the powers inherent in the earth, the universe, and the planes beyond. Prophecies and miracles and gods who spoke to man, all that jazz. Everything the Egyptians and the Greeks worshipped, in their own ways. It was all real."

To his credit, Jackson's expression didn't change. "*Was?*"

I nodded. "Until the Summum Malum formed. They built out of a belief that if they could harness the natural energies of elemental magic, and strip it from the practitioners, they could become stronger and rule. They could overturn all natural laws and beat death."

"Become immortal," Jackson clarified.

"Sort of. More like 'take over other planes of existence, namely the afterlife, and all the power that exists there.'"

I swear I thought his eye twitched at the word *afterlife*, but I let it slide.

"Those Shadows I was talking about?"

He nodded.

"They are members of the Summum Malum cult. They once used magic to cross into the afterlife while still living and absorb the magic and resources there, but now, cult members sometimes kill themselves ritualistically to cross over."

"Your sister said they 'breach'?" Jackson asked. Bless him, he was trying, but his stiff posture and scrunched face screamed, "This is crazy!"

"Yes. Some have grown strong enough in the afterlife to cross back over, but they lack physical form now. So they manifest as Shadows. Corrupted spirits. You saw Alanna. She wasn't like them."

He flinched like the memory burned his brain, eating away at everything he thought was real and unreal.

"Her soul isn't tainted, so she looks like herself," I said. I almost told him Alanna's spirit form was special because of her connection to the Aether element—that most spirits couldn't take a corporeal shape—but I didn't want to confuse him more than necessary.

"Okay," he said slowly. "And where do you come in?"

I sat up and bit my lip. This was it—the moment of truth.

It had been easier to promise Alanna I'd seek my relic alone when I'd assumed I wouldn't actually be alone; Jackson would go with me. But really, he'd already made good on exactly what he promised me. To get me here to the safehouse in one piece. Once the truth was out—the most unbelievable piece of the puzzle I'd shared yet—I couldn't guarantee he'd want to stick around.

In that case, I needed to prepare to let him go.

Bracing myself, I launched into an explanation, barely pausing for a breath. "When the Summum Malum began absorbing power from the afterlife, they really screwed things up. Their meddling got them and everyone else stuck in a limbo, unable to move on. The Shadows can come back to the living world, but they can't cross over the other direction, to the final planes of existence. No soul can. Not even people tied to magic, like my family, who have 'gifts' as you called them—we call ourselves alternates. Alternate or non-alternate, you're trapped there with the Malum when you die." *If you're lucky enough not to get burned.*

Jackson sat back but held my gaze, listening respectfully.

"A long time ago, a sisterhood formed to stand up against the Summum Malum. Back then, the Summum Malum could cross between the living world and limbo in their physical forms, and they were using their growing magic to wreak havoc on the living. I'm talking toppling kingdoms and spreading plagues. But a sisterhood called the Priestesses discovered certain ancient stones that could trap and contain magic. They robbed the world of magic to rob the Summum Malum of power and keep them in limbo. Now they can only cross as Shadows, who can't touch our world, though they can influence people to do bad things."

He blinked, realization flashing across his features. "Like those bikers?"

"Yes. But the magic lives on in the stones, called relics, and the Priestesses hid them away so that one day, they could be wielded against the cult by alternates who could channel their powers and reverse the damage the cult did to the afterlife. I'm supposedly one of those relic holders. Me and my sisters."

"The relic Alanna told you to find," Jackson clarified. Of course his strategic military brain had catalogued every part of the conversation. "So you don't know where this relic is?"

I shook my head. "No. But my guidestone is supposed to help me locate it." I reached into the neckline of my sweatshirt and pulled out the stone on its chain. "It's connected to the relic, wherever it is in the world."

"In the *world*?"

"Yeah. It could be anywhere." I grimaced.

His long lashes blinked a couple times, and he sat back, resting one arm over the back of the couch. The pose stretched his t-shirt tight over his muscular chest, and I couldn't keep myself from peeking.

He was more beautiful than any landscape I'd ever painted—a plane of dark, rolling hills, composed with soft curves that hid unwavering strength.

"The blood thing," Jackson said. "Is that a special power you get from your connection to this relic?"

"It's not just the blood thing." My heart fluttered uneasily. I'd never spoken about my powers out loud to anyone but my family. "When I'm underwater, I have ultra-heightened senses. I can hear everything—even people talking outside of the water. I haven't really had a chance to test out what else I'm capable of when I'm below water. I could be stronger or see miles ahead or… I don't know. My sisters and I each had innate abilities tied to the human senses from our mom's family. Her alt clan had all five of their senses heightened equal to animals—you know, night vision, smelling another clan member a mile away, that kind of thing. The guidestones and relics seem to be entwining with the senses we inherited from her, enhancing one more than the others." Cyndra burned at a touch. Alanna saw through the planes, through time and space. I tasted every grain of salt in my food and, now, stole feelings when I consumed someone's blood. "This water stuff is a fairly new development. Just since I was put in that tank at the lab."

The clock on the wall seemed louder than ever when I stopped talking.

Jackson stared at me, looking like he'd been beat over the head.

I couldn't blame him. As if my weird need for blood wasn't enough, now I was telling him I had water-based superpowers. Not to mention I'd raved about an evil cult, other planes of existence, and magic.

I didn't want him to leave me here alone. Honestly, since racing out of that lab, I hadn't felt strong enough to do anything at all. Jackson's take-charge presence had kept me from falling apart.

But it wasn't my decision to make.

"You don't have to stay." I avoided his gaze. "I mean, if you want to go back home... I get it. I can take it from here."

For a split second, he didn't react. But then he sat up and set his nearly empty can on the coffee table before holding out a hand to me. "Hey. Come here."

I slipped out of my chair, and KitKat rolled inelegantly into the impression I'd made with my butt. Ignoring her tiny grumble of irritation, I crossed the two feet to Jackson's side and placed my hand in his.

He tugged me down to sit beside him. "Listen. This has all been... Well, I guess crazy, but I'm no stranger to crazy."

"Could have fooled me."

He grinned. "Okay, the ghost thing was weird. I needed a minute."

"You look like you still need a minute," I teased.

"You basically just told me you're some kind of badass warrior mermaid who's supposed to defeat an evil magic cult," he pointed out. "I probably do need a minute… or ten."

We shared a laugh, but my heart sank into my stomach.

He could still choose to leave me.

Then I really would be alone.

Jackson's fingers tightened around mine. He raised his other hand to my face, and his thumb brushed over my cheek. His dark, orange-flecked eyes swept over my features as if he were trying to commit them to memory. "I intend to do exactly what I promised you in the beginning." His jaw firmed. "I'm staying. I'll keep you safe, and we'll get your relic together. And then we'll try to figure out how to save your sister from the lab."

Tears stung the back of my throat, and I blinked away the blurriness in my eyes before they could brim over and give my emotions away.

"Really?"

His gaze traveled up to hover over the coffee table, where Alanna had appeared.

"I think your family has been through enough. You and… Cyndra?"

I nodded, not trusting my voice.

"You've lost enough. You should be together."

"Thank you." I barely got the words out, my throat clogged and tight from unshed tears.

"Nothing to thank me for. Now"—he picked up the mug from the coffee table and thrust it in my hand—"drink your dinner."

"Yes, Dad." I turned up the mug and closed my eyes against the rush of emotions from the poor dead rabbit, and my own barrage of emotions, too.

Jackson snatched up his can and leaned back, his arm draped over the back of the couch behind me. "Has the guidestone given you any indication of the relic's position?"

I paused with the mug halfway to my mouth, surprised by the question. "I… I guess I haven't even given that thought."

"If we're going to go after it, we should probably have a general idea."

Wrapping my left hand around the stone, I quieted my mind and tried to get some kind of sense from it. "I don't really know how it works. I mean, I do, but not well."

"I would say don't overthink it." Jackson eyed my hand. "Trust your initial gut feeling."

I closed my eyes and focused on the smooth stone against my palm. It hummed with innate energy that felt like an extension of myself. Something deep in my subconscious tickled my mind, calling on a buried memory that didn't feel like mine, like reverse déjà vu.

My eyes snapped open. "South. Somewhere hot and tropical."

"There are a lot of places like that," Jackson said, amused. "Got anything more specific?"

"No, but… I think maybe if we just head south, I'll be able to get a better idea."

He toasted me with his can. "All right. We're heading south, then."

Jackson tossed back what was left of his soda while I swirled and then sipped my "coffee." The room fell silent except for KitKat's sleepy huffs and that incessant ticking on the wall reminding me that time continued to march on. Every second that passed was one more second that could take Cyndra away from me.

Suddenly, a new sound rose over the rest.

The crunch of tires on gravel.

Jackson and I stared at one another for a split second of total shock.

Then he launched to his feet and crossed the living room in four long strides to swipe his gun off the kitchen table.

The harsh metallic clank of a bullet being chambered drowned out everything else, as the car came to a stop just outside the front door.

21
CORPSE MAKER

JACKSON LOOMED IN THE OPEN DOORWAY, HIS LOADED GUN pressed against his thigh and his body shielding me.

I peered around him at a boxy white sedan with tinted windows. The sun was an orange fingernail above the horizon line, rendering the occupant nothing more than a vague silhouette.

"Recognize the car?" Jackson asked in a hushed tone, almost inaudible.

"No."

The engine cut off. The headlights winked out, leaving shadows to rule the surrounding forest. The driver's side door creaked open.

Jackson whipped his gun up and sighted on the car.

A mountainous man unfolded himself from the low-slung seat. He had dark skin, a bald head, and hands the size of pan lids that he held up to show us he was unarmed. As he shuffled around the car, I stared at his fleshy face and broad body encased in denim overalls, trying to figure out if I knew him.

The man kept his hands up and slowly approached the porch. "I'm looking for Miss Ellis?"

"Stop right there," Jackson barked. His body vibrated with tension. "No closer. Who's asking?"

The man halted immediately. "My name's Carl Simmons. Alec sent me to help Ellis."

"That's not possible," Jackson said evenly. "Alec is indisposed."

Carl nodded. "Yes, I know. He tasked me with the job before being captured. I was meant to wait for Ellis at my trailer, but I was attacked in the middle of the night. Carted off to a lock-up somewhere. But I'm more resilient than these gray hairs let on." He tapped his head and gave an ornery grin. "Hard to keep the squeeze on me." He flexed his massive arms. "I bounce back."

When Jackson returned only a stony glare, Carl's eyes flicked to where I peeked around Jackson's arm.

He turned a suspicious look back on my gun-toting protector, saying, "Who are you? Let Miss Ellis speak for herself, if you please."

I placed my fingers on Jackson's arm as I stepped around him. "The story tracks from what I know," I told him softly, while giving Carl a reassuring glance. Carl was certainly an alt, judging by his "bounce back" comment, we probably didn't want to threaten him into an altercation. "Uncle Alec really did send me to Carl Simmons. We saw the trailer. The blood…"

Jackson nodded once, acknowledging my words, but then spoke to Carl again. "If you were attacked and locked away, how'd you get free?"

Carl chuckled and glanced down at himself. "Boy, I'm three hundred pounds and built like a tank. They sent chihuahuas to a pit bull fight."

I snorted. This good ol' country boy was a far cry from my polished and elegant uncle, but I had no doubt Uncle Alec found him amusing and charming.

"I've got a business card in my pocket here," Carl said, turning his thumb down toward his massive belly. "It might make you feel better."

Jackson tightened his grip on his gun. "Slowly."

Carl's right hand drifted carefully to the large pocket at the front of his overalls. He dipped two fingers inside, then gradually slid out a slender white card.

"Put it on the bottom step," Jackson ordered. "Then back away."

The old man obeyed without comment, appraising Jackson's flinty stare.

Jackson stooped to snatch up the business card, then held it out to me, the gun still leveled on Carl Simmons.

I turned over the thick matte cardstock, and my stomach constricted. It was Uncle Alec's business card. His name was spelled out in gold leaf, followed by his contact details and a PO box. Written at the bottom in pen was my name in my uncle's distinguished handwriting. Beneath that were the coordinates to the safehouse.

"He's telling the truth." Shock settled cold in my gut at the reminder of my genteel uncle now caged like a criminal. I glanced up and met Carl Simmons' eye. "He's here to help."

Finally, a piece of the plan that was coming together as it should. An alt ally, here to help me.

"Pack your bag, sweetheart," Carl called with a beatific smile that I matched. "We've got a relic to find."

I shoved my hodgepodge of makeup in the inside pocket of my alien bag, then turned to fold the shirts flung across the top of the dresser.

Behind me, Jackson and KitKat both sat on the mussed bed, watching me intently. We'd left Carl Simmons downstairs to freshen up from his long drive, but Jackson had locked my bedroom door and still held his gun in his lap.

"Are you sure about this?" Jackson rubbed the scruff on his jaw. "I don't like it."

"If my uncle intended this man to help me, then we can trust him." I shoved my folded shirts in my bag. "Carl obviously knows about the relics and probably even knows how to use my guidestone to get me where I need to go."

"What if he's lying?" Jackson pointed out. "Or what if when he was captured, he went turncoat?"

I laughed. "This isn't a Jason Bourne movie, Jax."

"Alanna," he said, like that explained everything. "Don't you think your sister would have mentioned if someone was coming to help you? She told you to keep going alone."

"My sister is dead, not omnipotent and all-knowing," I pointed out.

"I just think you shouldn't be so quick to trust him."

"I won't." I petted my bobcat friend. "KitKat is going with me. I've got back-up. And now," I added, a pang of sadness crawling up my throat, "you can go home. Back to your life."

"Wait, what? No. I'm coming with you."

My heart fluttered. I'd been hoping he would say that, even if I knew I couldn't allow it. Not now that I had an opportunity to reverse the damage I'd done.

"Jax, I can't ask you to do this anymore. I'll be safe now, and you don't have to abandon everything you've worked for in your life. Maybe you can make excuses, mend things with the military before your career is ruined. Ask for a reassignment, though? I'm sure Dr. Craig will help with all that."

The bed creaked, and Jackson's fingers closed around my upper arm. He turned me around to face him. "I don't give a damn about my career. I'm worried about *you*."

In the lamplight, he looked soft. Boyish. I stared up into his eyes, paralyzed by his nearness. My mind traveled to the lake, to that moment I'd allowed myself, for the briefest second, to believe he was about to kiss me.

"I'll be fine." I jerked my head away then back. "Uncle Alec would never have given someone the safehouse's coordinates if he didn't trust them with my life."

"Let me come with you," Jackson implored, gripping his dangling dog tags. "That's what I want. Not my career back."

I eyed the tags in his fist. "If you don't want your career back, why do you still wear those? Why do you treat them like a talisman?"

He appraised them on an open palm.

"These don't represent my career, Ellis. They represent an oath, and they represent a brotherhood. They represent what Dr. Craig did for me, giving me a position and a home where I truly belonged." He dropped them and sighed my direction, his breath caressing my arm he still held. "But that lab isn't my home. The lab doesn't represent what these tags stand for. I don't want to be a party to any more torture. With you, helping you find your relic thing, I can help and protect people. Like I swore to do as a soldier."

I gently pushed away his hand, my heart aching because all I wanted to do was say *yes*. I wanted to beg him to come with me, to stay with me for as long as he wanted. Not because I needed him to guide me—I had Carl Simmons for that now.

But because the thought of Jackson disappearing from my life, probably forever, hurt too much to bear.

We'd come so far together. We'd survived a whirlwind of dangerous adventure together.

Unfortunately, this was *my* dangerous and deadly life. Jackson deserved better. He deserved to get back to his real life where he wouldn't have to clean up my messes or drag around a weak, half-starved, scared shell of a girl.

But if he *really* wanted to come… how could I tell him no?

Sighing, I turned back to my bag and tightened the drawstring. "I'll ask Carl. I have to default to him now. He's the guide my uncle chose."

Jackson frowned but nodded. "All right. If that's what you want."

I smiled weakly at him and headed for the door.

KitKat bounded out of the bedroom ahead of me, while Jackson trailed silently behind me.

My heart prayed Carl would say, "The more the merrier," and I'd find myself riding in the back with Jackson on one side and KitKat on the other. But my head told me that wasn't fair. Jackson was free now, and I had to free him of any lingering sense of duty to me, not string him along.

Down in the living room, Carl sat on the couch with his head laid back on the cushions and his eyes closed. Maybe I should offer to drive. He looked exhausted.

I broke the silence by clearing my throat. Carl smiled at me, but it slipped when he spotted Jackson at my back.

"Um, Carl. Is it all right if Jackson comes along?"

Carl squinted—a look I knew well. An alternate's default modes were skepticism, cynicism, and distrust. Survival mechanisms.

My heart took over, muting my brain's pleas to let it drop now. "He's been a big help. Without him, I wouldn't have made it to this safehouse. I didn't expect him to, but he says he'd like to come, and I think he could be—"

Carl raised a hand to stop my babbling. He gave me a tight-lipped smile. "I'm sorry, Miss Ellis. I'm sure, if you vouch for him, he's a good man, but I have my instructions, and I gave my word. Your uncle specified that I escort you alone and trust no one, and I don't ever go back on my word."

"Oh, I see." I swallowed hard.

"Ellis." Jackson's fingers trailed down my arm to take my hand.

"I'm sorry, Jax, but this is how it has to be. If it's what my uncle wanted, then it has to be what I want."

He stiffened, mouth twitching, but then he sagged with a long breath. "All right," he said, nodding. "If that's really what you want."

I nodded, not trusting my "yes" to sound authentic.

I turned back to Carl. "I'm ready."

Carl sat up with a more genuine smile. "Great. Got your guidestone?"

I pulled it out of my hoodie. "Yep."

"Good. I'll go get the car started and give you a chance to say your goodbyes."

He lumbered out the front door into the dusky night. Jackson escorted me to the porch, where we turned to face one another. Even in the darkness, I knew his features. I could make out the wiggle between his brow that told me he was worried, and the tightness at the corner of his lips that told me he had a lot he wanted to say.

Honestly, I did, too. But those things would have to be left unsaid. No matter how much I cared for him, how much I wanted him in my life, Jackson Hunter deserved better than me and my baggage. Truth was, Carl Simmons finally showing up to whisk me off was a blessing.

For both of us.

"Well… thanks," I said, eyes downcast. "For everything. I never would have made it this far without you."

"Call me if anything goes wrong?" Jackson brushed my arm one last time.

I forced myself to take a step back. "Of course. But I'll check in as soon as I can. Keep the burner phone on you. I've got the number."

I rushed forward then, stepping into him, wrapping my arms around his waist. He hugged me back, his strong arms like iron against my back.

"We're both going to be fine," I mumbled into his shirt, squeezing my eyes shut. I soaked in the sensations of him pressed against me from head to toe, wishing I could keep him close like this forever. Wishing I had the courage to lean up and kiss him, taste the ginger on his breath. Instead, I breathed in his cinnamon scent.

His lips brushed my hairline in a small, chaste kiss.

His mouth on my skin was my undoing. Hot tears blurred my vision, and I pulled in a centering breath as I broke free of his arms.

"Come on, KitKat." I patted my leg. "We're on the move."

The bobcat bounded down the shallow front stairs to the white sedan, then turned circles like a dog while she waited for me to join her. She didn't look back at Jackson. And I didn't either—I couldn't.

If I did, I knew I'd fall apart.

My guidestone glittered on my chest, and at first, I thought it was a trick of my welled-up tears. Then I noted the soft yellow tone, and the rhythmic way the tiny light sitting atop my blue stone twinkled. *Hi, Lana.* I pressed the guidestone and her light close to my chest. Had she come to comfort me? She'd always been the best at that. I hoped she knew how much it meant that she'd push the limits of her strength to give me a sisterly nudge right now.

Strengthened by Lana's presence, I opened the back door and held it wide for KitKat to leap into the backseat, then I closed her in. I paused with the passenger door open. I realized I hadn't asked an important question.

"All set?" the old man asked.

I forced myself to hop in and snap my seat belt into place. "All set. But where are we going?"

Carl squinted over my head, appraising Jackson with that same alt-brand of deep-rooted suspicion. "I'll tell you when we're alone"—his pupils swept the forest framing the cabin, probably looking for Shadows—"away from any listening ears."

"All right," I said, sighing internally at the same paranoia that had kept me locked up in the Zephyrus mansion for years.

Gravel crunched and shifted beneath the sedan's tires as he circled out of the cul-de-sac.

I could feel Jackson's gaze on me, even through the tinted windows.

We remained silent all down the long driveway. Carl fiddled with the radio, asking me, "You like music?"

I agreed with an ambivalent shrug, but he couldn't pick up anything but static, so he switched it off.

A stifling silence fell over the car. Lana's light had vanished, but KitKat hovered over my right shoulder, nosing my neck every few moments as if to remind me she had my back. Her presence was much appreciated, but she wasn't Jax.

How had he gotten so deep under my skin, anyway? I hadn't known him long. A few days? Not even a week. But I felt bereft without him. Alone. Unformed and misshapen, like he had been the frame holding my broken body and soul together.

Which was exactly why I had to leave.

At the end of the drive, Carl turned right—the opposite way that Jackson and I had arrived. A sharp curve carried us down the mountain, heading north, then leveled us out next to the far side of the lake.

The lake where Jackson had almost kissed me.

Stars glinted off the glassy black water as if there were two parallel night skies.

I fiddled with my guidestone, wondering if I ought to be using it. When Carl had inquired about it, he'd failed to ask the expected follow-up question: "Is it giving you any idea of where to go?"

Now, his deep, husky voice punctured the peaceful quiet as he twisted the knob for the heating system. "This Colorado cold isn't something I'd ever get used to," he explained, sitting back to rest his wrist atop the steering wheel.

"Me neither," I agreed, just to agree. I had no idea how to talk to this man. Not like I could with Jackson.

Warm air streamed from the vents and began to circulate through the car. With it, a nauseating scent like rotten meat assaulted my senses. I wrinkled my nose and shot a surreptitious glance at Carl to see if he'd noticed it. But his eyes remained fixed on the road ahead, where the headlights arced over the dark road.

Over my shoulder, KitKat huffed, then snuffled at the air. A low, almost imperceptible growl vibrated through her.

I looked back at Carl, to see if he'd heard the bobcat's threat, and did a double take, muscles stiffening.

Carl's eyes weren't reflecting the headlights.

That seemed… wrong. Eyes, as a rule, were wet—otherwise they'd dry up, right? But somehow, his were entirely matte.

The rotten meat smell thickened, cloying and vile.

KitKat growled again, hackles rippling in a wave of spikes.

A sense of unease began to settle between my shoulder blades.

I tried to surreptitiously study Carl in the low light. His dark skin looked ashen, sapped of its rich color. As he angled the car around another curve of the lake and began to climb toward a bridge up ahead, I caught sight of an odd patch on the back of his overalls—crusted and dried now, but the unmistakable rust color of blood. I'd smelled blood earlier but thought it was from the rabbit I ate.

It wasn't.

My heartbeat quickened.

"So, what happened back at your trailer in Nevada?" I asked, keeping my tone light and conversational.

If Carl noticed anything amiss, he didn't acknowledge it. He simply shrugged and said, "They came for me."

"They who?"

"Oh, some influenced thugs. The usual sort the Shadows like best."

"You said they took you to a lock-up?"

"Uh-huh."

"Was it the military lab that I was in?"

"No. Wasn't any lab coats waitin' for me." He turned on a stiff neck and smiled at me, flashing pearly teeth in unusually black gums. His lips were cracked and blueish. "Just the Shadows. Wanted information, 'bout you. They were sick of waitin' around and whisperin'. Wanted the *inside* scoop."

He rumbled a laugh, though I didn't get the joke. A glitter at my chest helped steady my breath. As if she'd sensed my distress, Lana had returned, her spirit light a faded fleck sitting atop my guidestone.

"H-how'd you get out?" I asked.

"Took time," he grunted.

"Liar," a weak, weary voice whispered. Was that in my head?

"I'm a tough SOB, ya know," Carl rattled on, while my breath quickened, searching for the source of that other voice. "I can re-grow what they break. Stitch up what they cut."

"Oh. Your ability?"

He grunted again, nodding.

"B-but, how did you get out?"

He didn't reply, except to start humming, a light little ditty like something off a laundry detergent commercial. His dull, dry eyes stared ahead, and his thumbs tapped rhythmically on his steering wheel.

"Ell?" That thready whisper. The light on my guidestone

sparkled like a miniature firecracker. "Foe, Ellis." Lana, out of breath, exhausted. The glow fizzled and died.

Dread was a crushing hand on my windpipe. I swallowed hard, then croaked, "Where are we going?"

He glanced my way.

"Why are we heading north?"

He flashed another broad smile out the windshield. "We're meeting your cousin Vin."

Horror struck me in the gut, and in my mind, I saw the despair in Alanna's eyes.

Vin is no longer of this world.

No. No. No.

I'd made a terrible mistake.

Heading the wrong way. The rotten meat smell. The dried blood. The ashy pallor of his skin. His dry, dead eyes.

One of his front teeth fell out of his still-smiling mouth. He didn't seem to notice. His grin faded as he continued his humming. The sound of the wheels changed as we left solid ground for the long bridge crossing the river below.

He's dead, I realized. *Carl Simmons is dead.*

And his body was being puppeted by the Summum Malum. Alanna was right. They'd obtained new abilities beyond everything Uncle Alec had taught us.

That must be how they knew about me. The Shadow in the desert had heard me mention an ally in a trailer in Rachel, and they'd tortured the information out of Carl or stole it from his head when they took him over. They hadn't followed Jackson from that bar parking lot because they hadn't needed to. "Carl" already knew where we'd end up.

"KitKat," I whispered, the sound wavering.

She responded with one of those bark-like growls. She'd scented the problem before me.

Carl didn't flinch or react to the sound at all.

If I could reach the taser in my bag, would it even work on a dead man?

We were halfway across the bridge when KitKat attacked.

She was a blur of fur, fangs, and claws as she soared between the seats and latched onto Carl's throat with an iron jaw.

He didn't make a sound as she tore through his rotten flesh and dried-up jugular with tooth and nail, but his body jerked in surprise. The car swerved madly, and while KitKat gnawed and ripped viciously at Carl's exposed spine, I grabbed the wheel to try to correct us.

Too late. We flew into a tailspin and slammed into the low railing at the edge of the bridge. Time stood still as the car flipped over the barrier, and we hovered, weightless, an instant before plummeting into the dark waters below, nose first.

The impact crumpled the hood and dislodged my seat from the frame, throwing me against the dashboard. My head slammed into the windshield, and KitKat slammed into me. All the breath left my lungs.

Cold water poured into the car, shocking my dazed senses.

My vision was blurry, and pain radiated up my body. I was pinned between the seat and the dash. Blinking away dark spots in my vision, I wriggled to better see Carl. His body clutched the wheel, sitting in a growing pool of water, but his head sat on the dash, staring sightlessly at me. KitKat had torn it completely off.

I wretched twice, but nothing came up. KitKat scrambled onto the seat behind me, letting out a startled, fearful cry as water poured around us both. Shoving against the dashboard, I tried to pull myself free from the chair but realized the seatbelt had me.

In a matter of seconds, water had bubbled up around me, rising to my waist.

I looked to Carl's body, searching his overall pockets for any impressions that might be a pocketknife. A Southern man who lived alone in the desert had to have a knife on him, right?

"Filthy witch!"

I screamed, locating the source of the foul words. Carl's head. Despite the severed vocal cords, the mouth was moving, speaking. But it wasn't Carl's voice anymore. Whatever Shadow was puppeteering him used its own raspy, hissing voice.

KitKat clung to my seat with her claws, spitting and growling at the head.

"Have you any idea how long it took to obtain and perfect this vessel?" it snarled at me.

The water reached my neck and inched toward Carl's severed spine. In the back of my brain, I knew I should be postulating a way out, but I couldn't look away from the talking head.

"Go to hell," I snarled back.

"I'm already there." Carl's blue lips leered at me. "But you? When we end you and burn your flesh, you'll be gone forever. No hell, no limbo, no heaven, no beyond. Just gone." The Shadow's laugh was the scrape of sandpaper on wood. "We know who you are, who your family is. It's all in this head. We know where you're going. You can't escape. We are everywhere. We are waiting. We are—"

Water garbled the Shadow's next words as it breached both our chins. I gasped in a big, final breath and went under.

After that, we sank fast. The river wasn't very deep, because we hit the bottom on the nose, then the car flipped over on its top, leaving me dangling upside down and sending Carl's head floating to the roof.

Every atom in my body felt electrified with fear.

A plan. I need a plan.

I gave Carl's head another nervous glance. It didn't seem able to go anywhere, but the Shadow was still inside, making the eyes blink. Why hadn't it left? Could it not leave once it possessed someone? I didn't have time to guess at the answers.

I closed my eyes and let the water settle around me. Somewhere nearby, I heard wheels on the road. Deer leaping gracefully in the woods. KitKat's frantic kitty paddles. Footsteps that sounded a lot like *human* boots. I couldn't exactly scream for someone to save me.

First—I had to get KitKat out of here.

I hit the button to roll down the window, but it didn't work. The car had shut off upon impact, which included the electrical system. Bracing myself for more pain, I elbowed the glass near the bottom of the pane. Over and over, digging into that slim bit of energy and power the water afforded me. It seemed to move with me, rather than slowing my momentum. One last blow, stronger with the water's force behind it, shattered the glass, then I waved my hands around in the pieces, knocking them all away into the currents.

Then I grabbed KitKat and shoved her out the window.

She paddled furiously, trying to come back to me, but I shoved her face away.

Go! I mouthed, letting out the last of my held breath.

The bobcat stared at me for another second, yellow eyes visible even in the deep, dark depths. Then she darted toward the surface.

My lungs screamed for oxygen. I blindly groped beneath me for my bag. I had a knife in there. Not a big one, but one sharp enough to cut myself free from the seatbelt. But I couldn't manage to lean far enough down to snag the straps with my fingertips.

Falling against the dashboard, I rested my head on the windshield next to the hairline fracture where my skull had nicked the glass.

Jackson was right. I shouldn't have trusted Carl Simmons. I should have known better to trust *anyone* in a world where the Summum Malum wanted me for what I could give them.

My relic.

But Carl hadn't even seemed concerned with where it was. Like he already knew.

Hopefully, I was wrong, and it would lay in its resting place until five more sisters were born capable of wielding the magic. The idea hurt more than the gash in my forehead or the sharp pains in my legs.

I'd ruined everything. I'd let Alanna down. And Uncle Alec. Cyndra. Vin had died in vain.

I should have known better.

Bright spots burst in my vignetting vision from the lack of oxygen. I thought I'd be more terrified as death closed in around me. More scared of leaving it all behind for the unknown of limbo. But a strange, peaceful calm settled over me.

At least I'd be with Lana and Vin.

I couldn't stand the burning agony in my chest anymore.

I opened my mouth and let in the water.

22
JAWS OF LIFE

… And breathed.

Breathed *the water*.

The ache in my chest eased, and the pulsating darkness at the back of my eyelids vanished as oxygen inflated my lungs.

Why didn't I think of this before? Vin didn't call me Little Mermaid for nothing! I'd dreamed about breathing underwater since I was five.

My eyes snapped open to the murky river outside the car. Goosebumps raced across my skin.

I wasn't entirely sure I wasn't still drowning, but it didn't hurt. Either way, it bought me time.

I blew out an experimental breath, and bubbles slipped up around my head. They scattered across the windshield, then darted out the open window beside me.

Maybe I'd already died, and now I was hallucinating.

But I breathed again, and the cold, robust, earthy water rushed into me like air. Heavier and thicker than air, but with the same desired result.

Oxygen.

Suddenly, a dark shape loomed outside the open window.

I screamed, more bubbles flowing from my lips.

But a familiar, three-fingered hand appeared beside me, upside down from my vantage point and wielding a knife. He'd come to save me, just like he had in the tank.

Jackson cut through the seatbelt at my shoulder with efficiency, then reached into the car and grabbed the belt by my hip to yank the cut end through the clip. He grabbed me with both hands and yanked.

I didn't budge.

I'm stuck, I mouthed, motioning to my lower half.

Despair twisted his expression, and he reached inside to wiggle the broken seat. The whole thing shifted, and pain lanced through my body and up my spine. I screamed, the sound entirely too audible.

Jackson yanked his hands away. He eyed me as I gulped at the water like a fish, then his eyes widened. He touched his nose.

I nodded. *I can breathe.*

He hovered uncertainly outside the door, stunned disbelief on his face.

Go breathe and get help, I mouthed, gesturing to the surface. *I'm okay.*

He darted toward the surface without another word, leaving me with a surprising hollow loneliness. Like an idiot, I'd hoped he wouldn't listen to me. How stupid was that? The man needed to breathe, and I was here gulping water like a mermaid that had dragged him out of a ship to drown.

The dark and silence pressed in on me in his absence. I carefully avoided looking behind me at Carl Simmons' dismembered body. At least it seemed like KitKat had destroyed his viability as a Summum Malum puppet by detaching his head.

KitKat. I hoped she'd made it to the surface okay.

I focused on the gentle bubbles of nearby river life. Fish swam around the car, out of sight in the darkness though I could hear them like tiny instruments. The water flowing along their scales sounded like music in the inky black, and I closed my eyes to listen closer and avoid focusing on how much the river bottom felt like a tomb.

Strong hands closed around my throat.

I jerked up and opened my eyes to find Carl Simmons'

decapitated body hovering next to me. Strangling me. The Shadow had expected me to drown, but now it had to finish the job itself.

Carl's strong fingers cut off my airways, or waterways. I struggled against his grip, but the way I was pinned didn't offer enough room to maneuver for one of my practiced self-defense strikes. I latched on to his wrists with a Jiu Jitsu monkey grip and yanked, hoping the water would give me adequate strength to break his grasp, but he had an inhuman hold on my throat.

The water around me displaced, and out of the corner of my eye, I saw Jackson return to the window. He reached inside the car and grabbed Carl's arms, attempting to rip them off me. I gagged as the corpse's fingers tightened.

Jackson disappeared for a split second, then his entire upper body shoved through the window. He pressed his gun against Carl's torso and pulled the trigger.

An explosion of sound cracked across my heightened hearing. The corpse bucked from the force of the bullet, and its hands involuntarily slipped away from me. I sucked in a grateful breath, my hands going to my bruised skin, while Jackson backed out of the window.

We locked eyes. His brow pinched, and he almost looked apologetic, even slightly guilty.

Then suddenly, the seat beneath me began to move.

On its own.

The car yawned open around me, the broken chair shifting backward, the dashboard denting away from me like an invisible giant was crushing it, tearing it open like a tin can.

The release of pressure on my legs was euphoric. I fell away from the dashboard and immediately reached for the door frame to haul myself out of the car.

My legs shrieked with pain when I tried to kick at the water. I halted just outside the upside-down car, gasping at the sudden, intense cramping.

And a hand snatched my ankle.

I shrieked and kicked out wildly, trying to dislodge Carl's deathly cold grip. The headless body oozed out the window at my feet, his other hand clawing for my legs.

Jackson wrapped an arm around my waist, then leaned past me and shoved his gun against the mutilated torso. He shot five times in quick succession, and each time the body writhed, more skin exploding beneath the destroyed denim overalls until I could see right through to the other side.

The body sank fast, the torso filling with water. Jackson kicked off and swam for the surface, still holding me tight against his side.

We burst out into fresh air, bobbing atop the water. Jackson breathed in deep, and I let out my breath, spewing water. My first inhale of air choked me, and I gagged, spitting up another lungful of water. But the second breath came easier—a little shaky, but functional. Jackson anchored me against his body and guided me to shore, moving as fast as he could.

Likely just in case Zombie Carl hadn't been put down entirely.

KitKat waited for us on the shore, making fearful chirping sounds. She raced back and forth along the rocky beach as we reached shallow waters. When both of us stumbled and fell to the ground, she took turns grabbing our clothes in her teeth and trying to haul us away from the lapping waves. I pushed the ground with my arms to help.

I lay on my back and stared up at the twinkling stars, breathing through the strange feeling in my chest. Switching from the sensation of dense water in my lungs to airy oxygen was a strange thing, and my body felt ten times lighter with every inhale. The earthy, silty taste of the lake left, too, replaced by the crisp, fresh flavor of air.

Jackson scooted closer, his wet face appearing over me, blocking out the starlight. "Are you okay?"

I stared up at him, mesmerized by the way he breathed so hard, by the water dripping from his tattooed temple and his shorn hair, by the way the river had made his skin look like ebony in the rain.

A split in his upper lip beaded with blood.

The smell hit my nostrils, filling me with a mixture of desire and hunger.

Closing the space between us, I kissed him.

His lips were warm and wet and tasted like the river, with undercurrents of Coca-Cola and candied ginger from his breath. I expected him to pull away, but instead, his arm encircled my waist, and he tugged me against his body, deepening the kiss.

Blood trickled into my mouth, sweet as wild honey. His tongue dipped into me, tasting me like I was tasting him. Ecstasy.

Jackson's emotions slammed into me on the heels of his blood. Fear that he'd almost watched me die. Anger that he'd let me drive away with a stranger.

And lust. Desire.

For… me?

The feelings fanned heat through my cold body. I rolled into him, latching one leg over his hips as I nibbled at his split lip. We breathed together, breathing in each other, and it was the most decadent and delicious moment of my life.

Finally, Jackson yanked away, breaking the kiss so abruptly I let out a sad little moan.

"You can *breathe underwater*?" he said breathlessly, one hand cupping my face.

"Well, I'd had reason to suspect. But it's confirmed," I replied, also breathlessly… and now embarrassed by how I'd jumped him. My cheeks felt hot. I looked away, back at the river, and diverted the subject. "What we really need to talk about is how you got me out of that car. Because there were no tools involved, Jax."

We stared at each other in silence long enough that KitKat nudged between our faces and lapped at my cheek, then at his. She certainly liked him a lot now. Our laughter mingled, and my cheeks flamed hotter as Jackson moved away from me to sit up. Rocks and dead leaves covered the entire length of his body from rolling on the bank.

Rolling with me.

Had he *actually* kissed me back? Felt something for me? The pretty girl who was no longer pretty at all?

"Let's get back on the road," Jackson said, suddenly subdued. "And we'll talk."

We both rinsed off in the shallows, then climbed up the embankment back toward the bridge. The little black Ford pickup Jackson had stolen after the bar brawl sat at a hasty angle in the center of the bridge, headlights staring over the river. A misty rain had started to fall, reflecting like glitter in the light. His door still stood wide open, as if he'd launched out of the truck and over the broken railing without stopping to breathe.

I halted at the edge of the asphalt, glancing between him and the truck. "You jumped off the bridge?"

He touched his split lip and shrugged. "Not the worst fall I've taken. Child's play compared to jumping out of a chopper over the Atlantic."

I wrapped my arms around my soaked sweatshirt and fell into step beside him as we crossed the silent, empty bridge. I tried to imagine Jackson in full army gear, leaping from a helicopter into the ocean in some search and rescue combat exercise. Even though he really was a soldier through and through, it was hard for me to imagine his life.

When we reached the car, Jackson said, "You can wear my clothes," as he leaned inside the cab and withdrew his backpack.

I grimaced. Everything I currently owned now rested in a ruined sedan at the bottom of a river, including the taser, baton, and wallet I'd pilfered from Reyes. Well, almost everything. Thankfully, my guidestone was still safe around my neck.

Jackson dug around in his bag and emerged with a clean t-shirt and a pair of basketball shorts that were going to swallow me.

"Thanks." I took them from his hands and circled around the truck to dress.

I stripped out of my leggings and sodden hoodie, replacing them with the dry clothes. Even tying the drawstring as tight as possible on the shorts couldn't keep them on my hips, so I tucked the shirt in to give them more to hang on to. Not my best look, but it would have to hold me over until my clothes dried.

Jackson rounded the hood in his own fresh clothes, holding his dog tags in one hand, the chain dangling toward the ground. "I gave it some thought. I can keep my oaths and be who I want to be without their reminder."

"It's okay to hold onto things."

"You're my reminder now."

His words stole my breath, and I let the conversation be. He slipped the tags into a zipped pocket on his bag, held open the passenger door for KitKat to jump in behind the bench seat, then helped me into the cab. I tucked my arms inside my shirt and shivered, using the collar to wipe my face clean from the rain, as Jackson hopped in the driver's seat and got us back on the road.

We drove several miles, putting distance between us and the accident scene, before he finally spoke again. "That man was dead, wasn't he?"

I shivered, and KitKat leaned forward to rest her chin on my shoulder over the seat.

"What gave it away?" I tried for lighthearted sarcasm to lift the dread. "The lack of the head or… the lack of the head?"

He snorted. "You know what I mean." His grin faded. "Dead the whole time."

"Yeah." I hugged myself. "I think he died in the attack at his trailer, and then the Summum Malum used him to get to me. There was a Shadow inside him that said they knew all about me from what was in his head." I made a face as I remembered the stench of rotten meat, his lost tooth, and the severed head on the dash. "He was like a… a *zombie*. Like he'd barely held his body together at the cabin, and when we got on the road, he began to fall apart."

Jackson shook his head in disbelief. "We're trusting no one from now on." His jaw hardened in the low lights from the road ahead. "Regardless of their 'proof.'"

I averted my gaze out the window at the passing trees. Shame heated my neck and cheeks as I agreed, "Nobody."

He paused, then without preamble, admitted, "I can control objects with my mind."

Whipping my head back around, I stared at him, floored by the confession I'd tried pulling out of him half a dozen times. "Like telekinesis?"

"In a way." He swallowed visibly, then reached out to turn up the heat.

"You peeled the car open around me like a can opener."

He nodded, not looking at me.

"You're like the organic Jaws of Life."

Jackson glanced at me then, one eyebrow shooting toward his hairline, but he laughed. "Dr. Craig calls it 'matter manipulation.'" He gave a one-armed shrug.

"He knows?" I asked, startled.

"Of course." Jackson's expression softened. "Dr. Craig was the first person to understand me. My gifts were why he fast-tracked me through basic training and asked me to work with him."

"Gifts? Plural?"

He nodded. "Telekinesis and tracking. That's how I found you in the desert, and again today. When I pulled out of the driveway and saw the tire marks, I realized he was taking you north instead of south like your guidestone said, so I came after you. Trails jump out at me, even the smallest indicators. It's like they're lit from within or something. And even if I don't immediately find a trail, I always seem to know which direction to go when I really want to find something or someone." He shrugged. "It's hard to explain how it feels."

"Oh. Well, why didn't you tell me before?" I asked. "I told you about the blood drinking, then everything about my abilities and history, and you didn't say a word. You're an alternate, like me! We don't have to hide from each other, just everybody else."

Jackson licked his lips and reached for the heat adjustment

again, turning it back down. I had a feeling his fiddling had little to do with the temperature and more to do with his discomfort.

"I don't like to talk about it."

"Well, I guess if you haven't been around many alternates… other than in labs… I can see why you would be hesitant to—"

"I lost control once," he said. So quiet, but raw enough that it shut me up. "I hurt my closest friend. She lost her eye because of what I did."

Lost her eye.

"Nurse Violet."

Jackson grimaced.

"It happened during basic. She was honorably discharged after I… after the accident. I convinced Dr. Craig to give her a job to make up for it, I guess. Not that anything ever could."

"I'm sure she knows you didn't mean to hurt her."

"She's only said it a hundred times. But her forgiveness, as wonderful as it is, doesn't fix what I did. I don't deserve it."

"Jackson…"

Hearing my skepticism, he sucked in a breath. "She was trying to help me, Ell. I was seventeen—easy pickings on the base. I was always in fights. I didn't start them, but I didn't walk away nearly as often as Henrietta would have wanted either. I liked to finish them."

He chewed his lip and huffed at himself. "There was one asshole, an older bully I'd known from my second high school, actually, who made my misery his personal mission, picking up right where he'd left off when he'd graduated my sophomore year. You probably know the type—beefy, stupid, and overcompensating."

I just nodded, though he was watching the road, not wanting to break the spell of memory he was under.

"Well, he ambushed me, put me on my ass. I was sick of his shit but fighting him wasn't working. So, I tried walking away, like Henrietta would have wanted, but then…" He shook his head at the memory. "Then he brought her up. Henrietta. It was something childish. I can hardly remember now. Something like, 'That's right, why don't you drop out and run back to your fake mom? Oh wait, she's dead, isn't she?' But it wasn't what he chose to say. It was the fact that he dared speak about her at all, you know?"

I murmured a soft sound of assent.

"I stopped with my back to him and picked up a rock. I turned so fast. I threw it without even looking. I knew I didn't have to. My ability would help it find its mark." He stared in horror at the windshield, like it was a screen playing a film of this terrible moment in his past. "But it didn't. The rock flew straight, sure. And *fast*. But I saw Violet too late. She'd stepped in the middle. She had her arms out to each of us, like she was going to force us apart if she had to. She looked at me, worried for me, and I couldn't curve it in time." His voice thickened. "I redirected it a little, away from her temple, but it hit her right in the eye instead. I thought I'd killed her. She dropped so fast. Blood everywhere." He cleared his scratchy throat. "And then, that same day, her mom got into a car crash, rushing to the hospital to be with her. Her mom died, Ell. Violet tried to help me, and to repay her, I caused the worst day of her life."

"Jackson, it was an accident. A terrible one, yes, but an accident. And her mom? You can't blame yourself for that. That's just… the shitty universe."

"The shitty universe gave me a power, and I believed it was infallible. But it hurt a good person because I trusted it explicitly and used it blindly," he said, his tone lowering. "Powers like what we have… We can't control them. Not really. We don't know *anything* about them. So even if we have the best intentions, we can hurt people who don't deserve it."

"But you can save people, too," I pointed out gently. "I'd be dead if it weren't for you. Zombie Carl would have choked me at the bottom of the river while I was trapped in my seat."

"It doesn't matter. This power is dangerous. I'm dangerous."

"Am I dangerous?" My heart clenched.

He didn't look at me as he replied, "Your powers are dangerous."

"That's not what I asked." I turned to face him more fully. "My uncle raised me to appreciate any abilities I'm bestowed. They're special, not bad. It's how you use them that makes the difference. And you shouldn't let your guilt or anyone else tell you otherwise."

He stiffened and flexed his fingers on the wheel.

I scrunched my brow. "Did someone tell you otherwise?"

His lips turned down in a frown, but he just shrugged.

I wanted to press for more. Make him open up to me. Make him see how special his powers were. Ask how he'd ended up with them—if it ran in his bloodline or was gifted to him. I'd never met someone else with a force *so* powerful. His mind was a lethal weapon. And there were fewer and fewer alternates left now.

It also wouldn't hurt to ask him about Dr. Craig and the other scientists, fish for what they knew about my people. Our people.

But his expression remained closed off. Whatever he was internalizing wasn't sitting well with him, and I got the feeling if I pressed, I'd find myself feeling pretty terrible. Maybe even pushing him away, when that was the absolute last thing I wanted.

After a few more minutes, Jackson asked, "Where to?"

I shifted back in my seat and wrapped my fingers around the guidestone. It hummed beneath my palm like an old friend, much happier now. "South. I'll tell you when we get there."

23

BRUSHSTROKES

W E DROVE ALL NIGHT, LEAVING COLORADO BEHIND FOR New Mexico. By the time the sun rose on a new day, we stopped in Albuquerque for gas, then continued through the morning toward the Texas state line, and beyond that, El Paso. After a quick gas station meal, we drove around the city for an hour until Jackson found a place for us to snag some clothes—some ridiculously rich man's adobe mansion that had cameras that weren't plugged in and a pile of mail in the box that indicated the residents were on vacation.

Or rich enough that they had a home elsewhere.

I helped myself to a shower in the master bath, standing beneath the scalding water as long as I could stand the heat. The warmth sank into my bones, easing some of the ache left behind from my legs being almost crushed inside the submerged car.

In another bedroom, I found a closet full of clothes meant for a girl probably younger than me, but I was small enough to fit. I picked out a couple pairs of jean shorts, a cute pink and white polka-dotted sundress, and a few shirts, and helped myself to a satchel from the back of the huge walk-in closet. I dressed in a pair of comfy green linen shorts and a small, white, scooped-neck t-shirt. My boots were still soaking wet, so I also dug around until I found a pair of sandals that could fit my larger feet.

With my new bag flung over my shoulder, I headed down the

hall, intending to go downstairs to the kitchen, but I paused when I saw an easel through a half-open door.

I pushed the door the rest of the way and smiled. It was a little art studio. The floor was covered in a sheet, and beside the easel by the window was a low table laden with acrylics in orderly rows. I dropped my bag in the doorway, called to the paints and the stiff brushes waiting in a purple holder.

It had been so long since I'd held a brush.

I searched for a canvas and found one in a small closet. I set it on the easel and trailed my fingers over the paints. The color selection was phenomenal. I could paint any landscape in the world with these. But I already had one in mind. A waterscape.

I plucked out the blues, several greens, a brown or two, a few pops of yellows, and a palette knife and got to mixing.

With the prepared palette balanced on one hand, I selected my first brush and began swiping the pre-primed canvas with my base blue. I lost myself in the strokes, in the blending of tones, breathing easier than I had in a long time.

As the gradient of the sunlit lake water came to life, I thought of the first time I'd painted an underwater scene, at fourteen. A painting that dropped the viewer at the bottom of our pool, staring up through the wavering surface at a strong male figure, looking down from the water's edge. I hadn't known who he was, just what he represented. The romance I craved. The adventure. The average kind, like being whisked off to risk-taking couples' activities and candle-lit dinners on the water. A way to get out of the house, be admired, be wooed like a real romance heroine.

I'd been painting in front of the television, swooning over Shane Greenvale. My first ever binge of *Farraway Heights,* season one.

While I sat in the art studio's one wooden chair to wait for the paint to dry enough to add the details over the blues, I thought of that day.

Alanna was on the couch nearby my easel, but she was somehow ignoring the TV and reading a massive book.

Cyndra strutted through the French doors into the living room, already sweating through her workout clothes. She was in a tank top and shorts, something she wouldn't be able to wear later, after the burning started and she lost control of the visions.

"Time to train, Ell." She clapped her hands. "Chop, chop."

"I'm in the middle of something," I whined.

Cyn came to stand at my elbow and see the painting. "It's good, but I know you have to let that layer dry. So come on. This is important."

I huffed. "It's pointless is what it is. It's not like I'm running into thugs every day. We never leave the house. And I'm sick of the bruises." I flashed her my side and frowned at the green-blue mar on my golden, tanned skin, left by her foot last time.

Cyndra rolled her eyes. "Would you rather be bruised or dead, Ell? Now get outside."

"Why doesn't Lana have to train?" I tossed a thumb at her, and she finally glanced up from her book to scowl at me. "She's worse at sparring than me."

Cyndra crossed her arms. "Well, I was going to spar you both individually, but I have a better idea." Her auburn eyebrow raised in a mischievous look she usually flashed right before she knocked me on my ass in a sparring contest. "Why don't you two spar each other, since you're both allegedly so bad, and the winner doesn't have to do drills?"

"Deal," I said, flashing Alanna an ornery grin. "You ready to lose, bookworm?"

Alanna rose from the couch with the poise of an English noblewoman and began tying back her bushy brown hair. "Bring it, Barbie," she said in a voice too demure to have any bite.

Cyndra laughed. "That's what I like to hear."

When I drifted back from that peaceful morning stowed away in my heart, I touched the canvas. It wasn't an ideal level of dry, but I didn't have the patience to wait. The details were itching to come out. I let my hand do what it wanted, adding highlights and lowlights that made the water dance, alive. A dark, muscular torso took shape in the side of the canvas before I was fully aware of what I was doing.

My mystery man now had a name, a three-fingered hand, and he was in the water with me this time. Around him, I tried to capture the essence of the beautiful music of nature I'd heard in the lake, and the background became more abstract. I added my planned pops of yellow, but then purples and pinks joined.

I fell back into my memories and let the paint do as it pleased.

I didn't see Alanna's punch coming. She threw it before she even got into a proper fighting stance. Shy and quiet she might be, but she was sly like a fox. I staggered back, a hand going to my smarting jaw, and my foot came off the mat spread over the back lawn.

Technically, that was an automatic out, but Cyndra said, "Keep going. You just got started. Nice one, Alanna. Ellis, remember to bend your front knee so—"

"Ugh, I forfeit." I threw up my arms and walked off the mat entirely. "I'm out. Just get on with the drills. I'm sick of this crap."

"Oh, come on, Ellis." Alanna frowned apologetically. "I kind of cheated. I'm sorry. Let's have a fair fight."

I turned my back on her, pouting. I knew I was acting like a baby, but I didn't care… until I remembered Uncle Alec sitting in a lawn chair watching us. Last year, he'd turned over most of our physical training to Cyndra. Because she was the best. At everything. But he still watched most days, sometimes accompanied by an annoyingly bossy Vin, and gave pointers every now and then. My ears flushed when I saw him watching me, but I stood my ground. The embarrassment of losing yet another sparring contest—to Alanna, especially—outweighed the embarrassment of Uncle Alec seeing my tantrum.

"There's no such thing as a fair fight with you." I rounded back on Alanna. "With either of you." I glared Cyn's way. "You're both older than me. You're, like, automatically stronger."

"Bullshit." Cyndra stalked toward me. I flinched back when she stuck a finger in my face. "You need to start taking this seriously, Ellis. That's why you're not as strong. It's not because you're younger."

"Is too."

Cyndra sighed, but it was more like a scoff. I thought she was going to shout at me. I thought she was going to make me do fifty pushups. I thought she was going to tell me I wasn't good for anything but looking pretty. Or maybe that was just an echo of what my own head was always telling me.

But instead of any of that, she took me gently by the shoulders, careful not to touch my skin and invade my privacy with her ability, and smiled at me. "Ellis, you are gorgeous, and you are funny. You know that. But what you don't know is that you're capable. You're a relic holder. You can be as strong as you'll let yourself be. But that means it's up to you to decide how strong that is. And what's sad is you've already decided. You have to... redefine yourself. Get it?"

"Like a makeover?"

"Like a makeover," Cyndra said through a giggle. "Into the badass I know you can be."

Back then, in that moment, I'd thought, *I have to be like you, you mean.* I'd resented her for it, like I wasn't good enough, like she thought I could magically be perfect like her by snapping my fingers. But now, thinking back, I realized I was wrong. She'd really thought I could be strong in my own right. Somehow, I'd have to find a way to prove her right. Otherwise, I was going to let her down way more than I had that day. I could never match up to her, but maybe I could come close.

I looked at my bony arms and sighed. How was I ever going to do that now, though, like this?

"Wow," someone said behind me.

I jumped and squeaked.

Jackson chuckled, saying, "Sorry. I thought you heard me come in."

Cyndra would have heard you come in.

I turned to him with my hand over my chest. "No worries. Just a mild heart attack."

He was beaming at me, and I thought I really might have an arrhythmia. He came to my side and roved his eyes over the painting.

"It's incredible." He stared at. "Really, Ell. You're amazing. You just keep…" His eyes roved over me, minute pauses softly caressing my lips, my jaw, my hands. "…surprising me. You're limitless." His tongue stroked the *l* and *s* sounds in a way that sent tingles down my spine. Then he cleared his throat, breaking our joined gaze. "Your talents, I mean."

"Thanks." I blushed and tried to push hair that wasn't there behind my ear.

"How long have you been painting?"

"Ever since I was ten," I said. "I love it."

"I can see." One corner of his mouth curled in a sly grin, and he pointed to the ab-laden torso. "Who's the hunk?" He wiggled his eyebrows at me, and instead of dropping dead from embarrassment, like I expected, I laughed.

"Oh, just some dude."

He snorted. "Some dude?"

"He has great abs, though, huh?"

"Definitely." Jackson puffed his chest theatrically and rubbed a hand over his stomach. "Adonis-like, even."

Now I snorted, though it was true. "What's in the bag?"

Jackson held out the reusable grocery bag stuffed with supplies. I peeked inside to find snacks, bottled water, and a fat wad of bills.

"Money?" I asked.

"Found it in the office. Guy just keeps a couple thousand in his desk drawer apparently."

"Good for us, bad for him." I shrugged.

"Are we going further south?" Jackson eyed the blue stone on my chest.

I touched its smooth surface. "Yeah. I get the sense we're going somewhere tropical." When I rubbed the stone, I felt sensations of humid air, warm water around my ankles, and sunshine baking my shoulders. There was also a sixth sense feeling, a *knowing* that whispered "tropics" in my head.

"So not south Texas. More like Mexico?"

I shrugged. "Maybe? I can only tell in increments."

He blew out a breath and carried the bag to the table, sitting it down next to me. "That's a problem. I've got a passport. You don't."

"Unfortunately."

"We're going to have to sneak you into the country."

"How?"

Jackson bit at the inside of his cheek, his face thoughtful. His gaze swept over me, sending a rush of heat to my face even though there was nothing sexual about the glance. It was more calculating. Strategic. "I have an idea."

24
STOWAWAY

I FOLLOWED JACKSON THROUGH THE PARKING LOT FROM THE corner of my eye, but I was really watching three girls in miniskirts laughing their way through the automatic doors of the shopping mall. They glowed, hips and shiny hair sashaying. Princesses entering a castle.

I bumped into Jackson's back.

"Sorry."

He gave me a warm, knowing look. "You want to go in and look around for a minute while I find us the right car?"

"Really?" I gasped, then blushed at how childish I sounded.

He smiled. "Yeah. I promised you a mall stop, didn't I? And you're not exactly in stealth mode right now. Probably easier to nab the car myself."

"Yes, yes, a million times yes! I just want to look."

"Ah, screw that." He pulled out his wallet. "We have ten bucks to spare. I don't know if that will buy much, but maybe, like, some earrings or something?"

I laughed. "Earrings or something, huh?"

"I don't know." He gave a sheepish shrug that broadened my smile.

I took the offered ten and stuffed it in my pocket. "Thank you." I suppressed an urge to kiss his cheek. "I won't be long."

"Ten minutes. That's all I should need. And if you see any of those Shadow things, book it back out here. We'll find another lot."

"Aye, aye, captain."

I ran through the lot, then slowed at the sidewalk. I avoided my reflection in the glass doors so I could envision myself in full glam and a miniskirt. I walked in with head high, like I owned the place, like the party girls on TV.

Whoosh.

The doors emitted me.

First, I heard the crowd. A beautiful white noise of giggles and shouts to friends.

Second, I saw the bright purple and white sign of a Claire's and the mannequins of a giant clothing store.

Then I smelled the food court. A hundred rich, greasy scents all at once. My stomach flipped. *Please, no. Don't ruin this, please.*

I just wanted to walk in like a normal person. No barfing. No running out.

I braced myself on a pillar by a trash can, eyes closed.

As I took shallow breaths, one scent jumped out. Cinnamon. I focused on it, leaned into it like a hug. It was Jackson's scent. My stomach settled, and I opened my eyes on a Cinnabon.

I knew Cinnabon. That was a classic mall thing, right? Cinnabons and pretzels and Orange Julius drinks. Perfect food items to tote around while you shopped.

I knew I couldn't eat it, but God, it smelled like heaven, cutting through the sickening grease and soothing my roiling guts. Maybe Jackson would like it. Maybe, if I carried it around, the other food smells wouldn't bother me so much.

I got in line and ordered the classic one. The box was a warm talisman that I kept close to my chest, over the guidestone tucked in my shirt.

I only had a few minutes and a few dollars left, so when I saw the carousels of earrings in Claire's, I ducked inside. Soaking in the cinnamon sugar of my Cinnabon—so strong that I could practically taste it—I slowly spun the carousels, watching the sterling silver and cubic zirconium glitter and shine on those lavender holders. So many options at my fingertips. Yet I came back again and again to a pair of silver sea turtles with turquoise shells, hung beneath a clearance sign. My guidestone seemed to hum when I reached for them. I checked the back. Five bucks. Meant to be.

When the cashier handed over that glossy bag, I swung it at my side like a trophy all the way outside. It took a few minutes of surveillance to find Jackson. I hurried over to the black SUV he was stepping out of, the engine now purring. He unlocked the passenger side as I approached and smiled bright enough to melt me when I slipped inside and he saw my bag.

"Earrings?"

"Earrings."

"You bought a Cinnabon?" He pointed. "Getting your regular appetite back?"

"Sadly, no. But it smelled…" *Like you.* "… so good. I just had to." I held it out. "I thought you might like it."

"Thanks," he said eagerly. The second it was in his hand, he chomped a huge bite and nodded his appreciation.

Mouth still full, he pointed back at the trunk and said, "Found what we needed."

Cinnabon in one hand, he pulled out of the spot and onto the main road. I set to work easing the silver sea turtles into my partially closed piercings, then admired them in the mirror, turning my head side to side.

When we saw the sign for the border, he licked his three fingers clean and pulled off to the side of the road.

"Come on." He hopped out.

He popped the trunk and started rustling around while I came to join him. He heaved a spare tire out of the back, jutted his chin at the trunk, and said, "What do you think?

I scrutinized the tire-sized impression beneath the floorboard with eyebrows arched high enough to fly off my head. "You can't be serious."

Jackson rolled the spare tire into the bushes on the side of the road, then brushed off his hands with a sheepish grin. "It's the best plan we've got."

He'd ousted the spare tire from its hidden resting place in the thick, dirty floorboard to allegedly make room for me. While I appreciated his out-of-the-box thinking, there wasn't a chance in hell I'd get that floorboard closed over me.

"A toddler couldn't even fit in there!" I waved a hand at the hole. "It's the size of a Barbie doll hot tub!"

Jackson chuckled, reaching for his army shirt draped over the back of the seat. "You're small."

Once, I would have considered that a compliment. Now the thought rang hollow and made me hug myself, rubbing a hand along my bony arm. I'd give up compliments for the rest of my life to have my health and a natural shape back, no matter its size.

"It won't be comfortable," Jackson said, oblivious as he shrugged into his camo, "but I promise you, it will work. You have to trust me."

"I do trust you." I planted my hands on my hips. "It's me I don't trust. One wrong move, and I'll knock it open. I'll breathe wrong, and they'll realize I'm down there."

"No. They won't." Jackson held out a hand. "Come on. Get in."

Eyeing him warily, I used his hand to hoist myself into the back of the SUV. The metal was warm on my bare legs as I kneeled inside the depression and rearranged myself to lay on my side.

Much to my surprise… I fit. With room to spare.

God, I'm even thinner than I thought. Wasted away. I used to toss my hair and command a room when I entered, confident in my own presence. Now I could disappear in a tiny hole in a trunk. I needed to get healthy again, eat real food again. My relic was my last chance, and to get to it, I had to endure this one final (I hoped) indignity.

Jackson handed me my bag, and I shoved it in the small space between my stomach and knees. Then he hooked a finger through the loop on the underside of the floorboard. "I'm going to lower this. You need to have your hand close enough to this loop to latch on tight if they open the trunk. Hold it down so they can't figure out the floorboard comes up. Okay?"

I nodded, cringing as he let the floorboard down. It thunked into place, and all light vanished. Just like Dr. Hurst's tiny isolation room. Fear tightened my chest. An urge to claw my way out, to run, to scream grew like a tumor at the base of my throat. My legs already burned from the fetal position, but I managed to hook my finger through the loop and test my grip. The task helped refocus me, pull me out of that tiny room in my head.

Jackson propped the floorboard up a moment later, just enough to catch my eye. "You okay?"

"A little warm, a little uncomfortable, but I'll make it work." I glanced past him at KitKat, whose nose was poking over the edge of the trunk, sniffing at me. "What about KitKat?"

"She's going to have to go on foot." He glanced down at her. "Can you cross the border on foot? We'll pick you up on the other side."

Worry trickled in. "How is she going to keep up with us?"

"Bobcats can run thirty miles an hour." He grinned down at her. They were clearly friends now. "You think you can do this?"

KitKat sat up straighter and snuffed at his leg. Yup, definitely more enamored with Jackson after he'd saved us.

"We won't forget you," I promised her. "Keep up with us on the other side, okay?"

KitKat bobbed her head, *literally* nodding to me. She had to be the great-great-great- great-granddaughter of a sphinx. Something partially human.

She loped off into the bushes beyond the spare tire and disappeared.

"You ready for this?" Jackson paused with his hand on the floorboard.

"No, but let's do it anyway."

Jackson guided the floorboard down. I heard the *pop* as he removed the plastic hook on top that opened it from the outside.

The trunk door slammed shut, and I listened to the scuff of his boots on the asphalt. The car shifted under his weight as he climbed in the driver's side. The engine roared to life.

We were on the move.

I focused on my breathing—in for four, out for eight. Centering, expelling the excess anxiety. Jackson had assured me the seal to this tire well wasn't airtight, so I wouldn't run out of oxygen. Even still, claustrophobia loomed, ready to suffocate me.

I clutched my bag against my stomach, grounding myself in the faint leftover citrus scent of the house where I'd stolen the clothes. I could almost taste the lemon on my tongue. The outfit I'd worn out was roomy enough for me to roll up like a beetle, but the white shirt was going to be super dirty when all was said and done.

I listened intently to the sound of the wheels on the highway, so I knew when we began to approach the border. Jackson eased onto the brakes, slowing the car behind what I imagined was a line of people waiting to cross into Mexico.

Latching a finger through the metal hoop, I got my arm at the right angle to hold the floorboard down and waited.

Sweat dripped down my hairline. I almost couldn't breathe. My heart threatened to choke me each time we inched forward. The stop and go went on interminably, dragging out the choking tension and my worry that KitKat would get caught and shot by Border Patrol.

Finally, we eased up again, and I felt the jerk of Jackson putting on the parking brake.

This is it.

What would happen if I got caught? Would they arrest me? Send us back into the States?

What if they figured out who I was?

I can't go back to the lab.

The tension in my finger radiated up my arm. I clung to the tiny metal hoop, prayed to it, worshipped it, begged it to hold back the certain death circling outside.

Jackson's voice drifted to my ears, muffled by the floorboard and the purr of the engine echoing through the metal frame. I couldn't make out any words as he spoke with the Border Patrol agent, probably flashing his military badge.

Then a door opened. And another. I heard unfamiliar voices, and the sounds of items being moved around the backseat. The *drag-thump* of Jackson's heavy backpack. The rustle of the reusable grocery bag of food.

The whir of the airlock on the SUV's trunk.

I froze. Stopped breathing. Stopped fidgeting. I threw my entire weight behind the tiny metal hoop and waited.

The voices were closer now. A man asked, "Business in Mexico?"

"Vacation," Jackson replied. His tone was so easy-going. I could hear the smile.

How was he so damn calm?

I felt like my heart was going to shatter my rib cage and break free.

"I'm sure you deserve it," the agent replied. "I was Special Forces in my twenties. Blew out my knee in a basketball game, can you believe it? Honorably discharged. Never walked the same since."

The floorboard jerked against my grip.

My nerves were so raw, I almost screamed. But I'd been braced for this, and the floorboard didn't budge.

"All right, sergeant. You're good to go," the man said, fainter with each word. The trunk door slammed shut. The two men exchanged a few more words while I silently screamed at Jackson to get back in the car and get us out of this place.

Then the SUV lurched forward, and we crossed into Mexico.

A big grin crossed my face. I loosened my grip on the metal hoop, letting out a sigh of relief that turned into laughter. Lots of laughter, loud enough that Jackson could probably hear me as I released some of the pressure.

One more step closer to the goal.

Now we just had to find the relic and save the world.

After retrieving KitKat a half mile from the border, we drove for nearly two days through the Mexican countryside, following the subtle hints the guidestone offered me. We made our stops few and far between, while Jackson subsisted on warm bottled water, beef jerky, and chips. All restroom breaks were done in the empty wilderness rather than a roadside gas station—less likely to be noticed that way. KitKat hunted a couple times a day, keeping food in her belly and blood in mine.

Jackson and I talked constantly, leaping from one story to the next, discussing more of our favorite movies and TV shows, telling stories of our childhood, anything just to pass the time. I found myself telling him about Aurora—or Rori, as Cyn had nicknamed her—and what a little hellion she'd been at barely three. Charging through the house in nothing but her Pull-Ups, playing dragon and "burning" up all our things until someone conjured an imaginary sword to try and slay her (unsuccessfully). I told Jackson how she'd cannon-ball on Dad in his recliner whenever he found a spare moment to read and how she'd demand to cook with Mom by pushing her little stool against Mom's ankles. How she'd squeeze her chubby cheeks through the bars of Persephone's crib and make faces at her. I found I could speak Aurora's name, speak all their names—Mom, Dad, Rori, Penny—with a smile. With Jackson, I could speak of what I'd lost without feeling the grief of what had happened that October all over again.

In one breath, we spoke of our old wounds and sorrows, and in the next, we laughed and joked, but neither of us brought up the kiss.

Like it had never existed.

I was too embarrassed by how forward I'd been. Not to mention the nagging worry that Jackson regretted it—that if I mentioned the kiss, he'd tell me it was a mistake made in the heat of the moment.

We should just be friends. The death knell to a girl's self-esteem, when mine was already in critical condition.

So, I pretended it wasn't on my mind twenty-four-seven.

We took turns driving and sleeping so that we didn't have to stop. Even though we were moving as fast as possible, and Jackson had Dr. Craig in his ear promising that nothing had changed at the lab, I still worried about Cyndra. Even when we were deep in conversation, I watched the digital clock flip over, watched the sun set and rise and set again, all the while knowing that timer was running down for Cyn.

But what good would I be to her and Uncle Alec without the relic's powers? Alanna had told me to find my relic first, and Lana always had the right answer.

After sundown on our second day, I was sound asleep and dreaming of lounging in a bikini at the edge of Uncle Alec's pool—beautiful again with dark mermaid locks cascading over tanned, rocking curves—when a frigid sting on my chest shocked me awake.

I nearly leapt out of my seat, launching straight up and grabbing the door handle to steady myself. In the immediate moments between sleep and wakefulness, I felt a pang that the dream hadn't been real—that I hadn't been restored to my former self. I was still ruined, unrecognizable.

But then I realized the guidestone lay beneath my t-shirt, freezing cold and biting my skin like I'd had an icepack resting there too long.

I hissed and reached through my collar to yank it out. A crystal-clear blue glow lit the SUV.

A glow from inside the stone.

"That's new," Jackson said from the driver's seat.

KitKat nosed between our seats and shoved her snout in my ear as if to check on me.

"Where are we?" I croaked, voice thick with sleep.

"Somewhere in Guatemala," Jackson replied. "You okay?"

"We need to exit. Soon. The next chance we get." I let the necklace fall back against my t-shirt, where I could still feel the chill through the fabric. "The guidestone's fully awake. I think we're close."

I stayed on the edge of my seat for the next hour, focused entirely on the vague sensations I was getting from the stone. I directed Jackson to exit the highway, where we stayed on a side road for a while as the sun fully sank and gave way to the night's stars. We drove another couple hours, heading west, until we passed a street sign advertising Tecojate.

The word felt infinitely familiar, like it was burned into my subconscious.

The guidestone dropped several more degrees and pulsed, like a wave crashing into me.

"That's it," I gasped each word, jamming my finger to the glass as the sign flashed past the car. "Tecojate. We're going there."

It turned out to be a touristy town right on the beach. The Pacific stretched into a black horizon away from the lights lining the sand, and the guidestone urged us to head south, away from civilization. Once we left behind the dimly glowing lights of the city, we passed into total darkness beneath a moonless sky.

Until the guidestone led us to a dead end.

Jackson coasted to a stop on a small gravel lot and put the car into park. Dark forest stretched ahead of us, forming a barrier between the end of the road and the ocean. I couldn't see the Pacific out there, but I could *feel* it. The guidestone pulsed relentlessly, as if screaming at me to continue.

"We have to keep going on foot." I shoved open the passenger door. Thick, cloying humidity spilled into the car, turning my skin immediately hot and wet.

Jackson reached into the floorboard and grabbed his gun. "Wait for me," he called out as I opened the door to let KitKat out of the backseat. "We don't know what's out there."

We both grabbed our bags to the tune of ceaseless cricket chirps and the gentle rustle of leaves in a sluggish breeze. KitKat sniffed around the gravel but didn't seem on edge as we set off into the trees.

Jackson took point holding a long blade he'd pulled from his pack, chopping our way through the thick undergrowth. "You had it right when you said we were going somewhere tropical."

I swiped at the sweat already pouring down my face, now welcoming the guidestone's cooling touch on my chest. "I wish I'd been wrong."

All three of us fell silent for some time, too focused on not losing our footing in the pitch black to carry on a conversation. After a while, the sound of rushing water triggered a strange vibration in the guidestone that staggered me.

"A river," I said, feet planted. "It's a river."

Jackson looked over his shoulder. "Yeah, sounds like it."

"No, I mean I *know* it is," I corrected, touching the guidestone. "The stone is telling me it is. We have to go to the river. Rio Coyolate." The words spilled from my lips with a strange accent that didn't belong to me. Somehow, the guidestone had given me the river's name and taught me how to pronounce it without me even realizing. "Where Rio Coyolate meets the ocean, we'll find the relic being guarded by… by someone."

I couldn't quite make out what the stone was attempting to tell me about that last part.

Jackson nodded, though his gaze dropped to the guidestone with more than a little suspicion. I guess I couldn't really blame him. Inanimate objects didn't usually have a metaphysical consciousness.

He chopped out at the branches, angling toward the rush of water.

By the time the trees broke, I was covered in sweat and scratched all over by the brambles and bushes we'd climbed through. We came out on a short cliff overlooking the river, which swirled and eddied beneath the starlight on its way to the ocean.

Edging closer to the drop-off, I looked out to sea, heart pounding.

Dozens of tiny fires burned on the ground about half a mile away. Smoke curled like ghosts into the sky, and even from here, I could see the sprawled bodies in the amber glow.

Someone had beaten us here. They'd set the place aflame.

25

RIVER AND RUIN

SCORCHED EARTH CRUNCHED BENEATH MY BOOTS AS I walked into what I now saw was a camp built along the banks of the estuary.

A few log cabins remained standing, but the majority had been set on fire, left to burn to unrecognizable ash. We didn't have to walk far to find the first of the bodies—three of them burned so badly they were nothing but charred husks. Tears blinded me, and the overpowering burnt meat scent in the air clung to my tongue, bitter and acrid.

I gagged, and my dinner promptly vacated my stomach. Stumbling away from the bodies, I retched on a bare area of untouched grass. Regurgitated blood spattered the ground, and a gnawing ache yawned open in my stomach.

KitKat sat down beside me and pressed her warmth against my legs, whining.

Placing a hand on her head, I closed my eyes and waited for the nausea to pass.

Jackson crunched further into the village, past more bodies, his voice drifting back to me. "They're all armed."

I finally opened my eyes and swiped the back of my wrist over my mouth. He stood a few yards away, looking down at another set of bodies. Girding myself for the desecration, I released KitKat's fur and joined him beside another three dead.

Each held a fully intact spear about four feet long with a wicked arrowhead-shaped blade on either end. Fire hadn't taken them, though they had singed brows and soot-coated mouths. One had a savage, gory tear that had nearly taken one arm. The other two had an odd, dried green substance around their bloated, purpled faces and throats.

"They didn't burn the men," I said, heart seizing. My gaze wandered back to the charred bodies, realization weighing down my shoulders. Alt women, doused in gasoline like so many others. "The Summum Malum did this." Horror snaked up my throat and twisted into chills at the base of my neck.

Jackson squatted next to the nearest body and gently extricated the spear from bloodied fingers. "It's bone. Whale bone, I think, given how long it is."

"Who are they?" I rested a hand over my chest, glancing around the fire-lit camp. Uncle Alec had more alt connections than most, but he'd never spoken of a spear-wielding clan in Guatemala.

"I don't know." Jackson gave the body its spear back before he stood up. "But they were absolutely massacred. Are you getting anything from the guidestone?"

Confronted with the horror of what had happened here, I'd tuned out anything the stone had to tell me. Scolding myself, I wrapped my fingers around the cool necklace and opened my mind, listening for instructions. My body turned of its own accord, like a weathervane in the wind, until I faced the ocean.

"It's out there." I gestured toward the vastness in the dark.

Jackson let out a long whistle. "That's a whole lotta ocean."

My shoulders slumped and I released the necklace, drawing in a deep breath that smelled too much like destruction. While staring out over the gently rolling waves, I noticed movement from the corner of my eye.

"Jax!" I snatched at his arm.

He glanced at me, then followed my gaze down the long dirt path that wound through the village.

Several yards away, an arm raised from a clump of fabric, then sank wearily back to the ground.

We ran to the survivor, our boots pounding in time with my heart. I fell to my knees at his side and looked down into an aged, brown face with calm, gray eyes.

As Jackson approached his other side, the old man focused on me. His arm raised again, and he touched my face. *"Eres tú."*

I exchanged glances with Jackson, who shrugged.

"I don't know Spanish," I said helplessly.

The man grimaced, and his cold fingers fell away from my face. I peeled back his dark robe to find a massive wound in his stomach—three catastrophic slashes. It took every ounce of self-control I had not to vomit at the sight of his intestines.

Jackson hissed and grabbed an edge of the robe, pressing on the wound to stem the blood. "God. That's bad."

The old man waved his hand, slapping ineffectively at Jackson's arms. "Leave it be, child," he said in heavily accented English. "I do not fear death." His head rolled heavily toward me, and he gave me a pained smile. He wrapped his fingers around mine and pressed my hand to his heart. "It is you. The bearer of *la aguamagia.*"

"The what?" I asked.

"The water *reliquia,*" the old man said, then sucked in a painful breath that sounded entirely too wet. He leveled his gaze on me again. "We have been waiting for you. For so long, *mija. La agua gente,* the water folk, we were here waiting…"

All the air left me. I'd known from an early age that I was destined for this—one of five sisters fated to bear the Priestesses' relics. My sisters and I were the reason all alt women were burned at the Summum Malum's hands, and families with multiple daughters were hunted relentlessly.

But to hear the confirmation from this man… this man whose whole clan had guarded my relic and died for my destiny?

Tears burned the back of my throat. "I'm sorry I took so long."

"No, no, *mija,*" he croaked. "No apologies. All things come to pass in their own time, in their own way. But you must hurry now. This place is no longer sacred. No longer safe."

Jackson spoke up. "Who did this?"

The old man's pale eyelashes fluttered. "A bear and his army."

"A… bear," Jackson repeated, his tone leaving no room for interpretation as he scanned the beach. He thought the old man had already lost his mind in the throes of death. This wasn't exactly grizzly country.

"A human," the old man said, gasping at the air, "a human masquerading as a bear."

Jackson paled. But, no. It couldn't be the one from the lab. He'd been there with Cyn. He was an ally.

"Scarred by fire around his chest, up his neck, all the way to his snout…"

Jackson blinked and gave me an almost imperceptible head shake that loosened the knot in my stomach. It wasn't the same Shifter.

The old man's eyes fluttered closed.

For a hesitant moment, I thought we'd lost him.

Then he sucked in a breath, and his eyes popped open. He squeezed my hand, still clutched against his slowing heartbeat. "You know who the enemy is, *mija*. No matter who leads the army into battle, you know who commands."

"The Summum Malum," I whispered.

" *aguamagia* is safe." He closed his eyes again. "*Mis nietos*, my grandchildren, they fled the battle with the *reliquia*. You must find them. *Mi lanza*…" His other hand struggled to surface from the folds of his robe, and the edge of a whalebone spear slipped out. "Take my spear. They will know it."

I picked up the weapon and slid it onto my knees, nodding, too overwhelmed to say anything intelligent.

He nodded in return. "Yes. Good. Take up your mantle, *mija*. Keep the other races safe."

I watched, my throat constricted with unshed tears, as the old man took a last, shaky breath. Then his fingers loosened, and his arm slipped away, landing on the scorched ground.

Jackson pressed his fingers to the old man's neck, then shook his head. "He's gone."

My body went boneless, and my head swirled. I sank back and dropped to the ground, hoping the solid dirt beneath me would ground me. Digging my fingers into the earth, I stared down at the old man's whalebone spear, the painted colors blurring in my vision.

KitKat softly padded up beside me and nuzzled my cheek. I realized she must have stayed back so as not to alarm the dying man.

What a smart kitty. I nuzzled her with my forehead.

"If we'd gotten here sooner," I said thickly, leaning against her fluffy neck. Guilt was a sack of sharp stones in my stomach, ripping and stabbing at my insides. "We were too late by hours to save an entire race. *La agua gente.*"

"The water race," Jackson translated. "What does that even mean?"

I reached for the old man's spear and pulled it onto my lap. The pale bone shaft was covered in colorful pictographs—geometric symbols, curlicues, fish, and sea turtles.

"It means they're alternates. Their race is tied to their power. Shifters, Cloakers, Element Wielders like my sisters and I are supposed to be—things like that." I rubbed my face, exhausted. "Every relic has a guardian race, whose powers help them understand and protect it. These people were my relic's guardians, and I failed them."

"Ell…" He reached for me, but before he had a chance to finish, I stood and hefted the double-sided spear, pointing to the docks barely visible in the dusky night. "The boats are intact. It's time to go relic fishing."

The outboard motor puttered and slogged as the flat ferry boat sliced through the gently rolling waves. Once we left the smoldering village behind, the night turned inky as heavy cloud cover blew in off the ocean.

I sat at the prow on a stationary metal bench and clutched my guidestone, the salty spray stinging my eyelids. Jackson steered from the back, following nothing more than my half-hearted hand signals, while KitKat sat between us like a guardian cat.

My guidestone told me the relic—*la aguamagia*, as the old man had called it—was somewhere beneath the ocean. That tracked, knowing it was in the hands of a race suited to guarding the water relic. More than likely, the old man's grandkids had used their abilities to flee where the bear and his army couldn't follow.

I dreaded being the one to tell them their people were gone.

Not with this guilt choking me.

They were a reminder of how much I'd failed.

The guidestone flared with blue light, and I jumped to my feet, chest goosepimply from the stone's sudden chill. I waved madly at Jackson. "Stop the boat! It's here!"

He cut the engine, and the boat skidded several feet forward before coming to rest. The ensuing silence was deafening. Nothing moved this far from shore except for the waves lapping the side of the boat.

I stripped off my t-shirt and reached for the drawstring on my shorts.

Jackson stepped over the metal bench to come closer. "Are you sure about this? We could go back to Tecojate and find some scuba gear so I can go down with you. In the light."

"We don't have time," I said simply, shucking the linen shorts and kicking them off my already bare feet. "You heard the old man. The sacred ground isn't safe anymore. For all we know, some demon bear and his entourage are still out there waiting for the kids to come back. Cyndra's counting on me," I added. "Her time is running out."

Jackson sighed and sank to the edge of the bench. Now he was eye level with my chest, and I suddenly realized that I'd stripped to my borrowed undies right in front of him. Granted, the sports bra

I'd swiped from that El Paso house covered my diminished breasts well, and the boy shorts were a little less revealing than the bikinis I used to wear back when I had a butt.

Jackson slid his warm palms over my hips. He drew me closer, and my heart skipped a beat at the caress of his callused hands on my bare skin. It was odd to be so much taller than him, to look down at him from above. I felt a strange sense of power—like I was the one in charge for once.

"The first sign of trouble, you come back up and we find another way," he said.

"Okay," I agreed, knowing full well it was a lie. Once I sank beneath the surface, I wouldn't be coming back without the relic.

KitKat whined and rubbed against my legs. I stepped away from Jackson's hands and patted her head, then snatched the spear off the floor of the boat. "Wish me luck."

"Good luck," Jackson said dutifully, though I could hear his worry.

Clutching the spear in one hand, I stepped onto the back ledge of the ferry, took a deep breath to calm my nerves, and jumped into the void.

I slipped beneath the surface easily. The water closed over my head, warmer than the cold river that had nearly been my grave back in Colorado. It closed in on me, shutting out all noise, all sight, all sensation except for the silken water on my skin.

A part of me feared that my powers wouldn't transfer to breathing salty ocean water. I held my breath for a moment longer than necessary, scared to take that first gulp.

But as soon as I did, my lungs filled with a comforting, painless weight, though the taste left much to be desired—the decay of fish waste, the tang of copious salt, and hints of stale, sour blood. The emotions rushed in next, traces of hundreds of beings hitting my taste buds and muddying my sense of self for several chaotic moments.

As the sensations faded, I opened my eyes, blinking against the sharp sting, and waited for my vision to adjust. For a normal person, the underwater world at night would be too dark to navigate, but minutes later, I could see pretty well through the gloom, like walking the woods at dusk.

I began to descend.

A school of silver fish darted past me as I dove, kicking hard. Far below, I could see and hear the bottom dwellers going about their business—crabs scuttling across the sandy bottom, eels slithering through coral and rocks, and flat-bottomed fishes shuffling across the ground.

The guidestone pulsed, and I felt a nudge to level out and swim west.

Moving with the spear in hand proved a little difficult, so I ended up pausing to turn my sports bra into a makeshift back sheath. The spear was long enough so that I could angle the two sharp points to either side of my body, though the whale bone still wasn't exactly comfortable digging into my spine. With the maneuverability it afforded, I quickened my strokes, following the guidestone's silent directions.

I was so focused on the stone's pulses and subconscious whispers, I didn't notice the looming shadow in the murky depths until I tasted fresh blood on the water. I gasped bubbles and dove left. The giant shark lumbered past, one alien eye latched on me. I could taste the sharp terror of its recent prey on the water displaced by its tail.

Moving slowly, I reached over my shoulder and palmed the spear.

We stared at each other. The shark wiggled through the water like a snake, its attention pinned on me for far too long.

But it journeyed on, disappearing into the shadows from where I came.

I released the spear with a long, shaky breath, then swam away as fast as I could before it changed its mind.

Dive. The urge was a prod in my brainstem, demanding. I obeyed. The water shifted tones, but my sight stayed clear. Bulky silhouettes startled my heart into my throat, until I realized they were giant boulders. Mountainous, even, bisected by deep ravines that cut black scars into the bottom of the ocean.

I slowed my approach, trying to make sense of the guidestone's intentions. I swept past a smooth rock wall and rounded it over a deep canyon, then dipped into the darkness beneath the sand. The guidestone pulsed, excited this time, and I pushed myself faster. The canyon grew up around me, tall enough to block the light from the faraway surface. Rock pressed in all around me, but I ignored the spike of claustrophobia and clung to the guidestone, mouthing, *Close. So close.*

A cave entrance materialized in the cliffside. A dark mouth in the charcoal stone. I hovered in place outside the opening, staring into an abyss that felt like it stared back.

I thought of Jackson sitting on the boat, making me promise to come back if it got dangerous. And here I was, about to enter an underwater cave alone. I wasn't naive enough to think my heightened underwater vision would allow me to see where *no* ambient light could reach.

Cave creatures had no eyes because they didn't need them.

But I didn't have time to be scared. Not with an unknown enemy on the shores and my sister stuck being a lab rat in my place.

It was now or never.

I drew the spear and let it lead my way as I pressed forward.

The darkness swallowed me whole, blacking out the world as if I'd closed my eyes. The spear tip bumped a rock, and I slowed, adjusting, trailing the weapon along the unseen wall.

I had to rely only on my sense of touch and the guidestone's calm guidance. With my left hand out to my side and the spear in my right, I felt the walls squeezing in around me, and my old terrors arrived unannounced. In the black, it was too easy to convince myself I was bound and submerged in that tank, that my breaths came from a mask, my entire existence drilled down to the oxygen drying out my lips.

I shoved down the growing hysteria. I *had* to do this. I *had* to be strong, even if I didn't feel like I could, even if I didn't believe that I had strength enough to do anything at all in this world.

I had to do this for my family.

The guidestone pulled me toward the left wall, and I felt blindly for the entrance.

There!

A small crevice. A tight squeeze.

Taking a deep breath, I shoved the spear through and followed after.

The crevice went on for several feet. I propelled myself along it with my fingers, rocks scraping my bare thighs.

A sunspot blossomed in the upper corner of my vision.

Light?

I was so startled that I stopped entirely. It wasn't the murky blue glow of the ocean, but a warm firelight orange.

What the hell?

I gingerly continued forward until I met the end of the crevice and could wiggle my way free into open water.

The glow came from above. Waves flickered and shone overhead as if the sun awaited me on the surface. But that was impossible. What surface? I was deep in an underwater cave.

The guidestone urged me to surface.

Halfway to the strangely mesmerizing colors above, a large shape moved in the shadows of my periphery. Before I could flinch, it barreled through the water—right for me.

26
SALTWATER TEARS

BEFORE I COULD LIFT THE SPEAR, THE CREATURE SLAMMED into me. A sharp edge sliced into my side, firing red hot pain across my nerve endings, and I was knocked backward into a tailspin.

The murky, orange-tinted world tilted and twirled until I managed to toss my arms out and right myself in the water. Upside down, unfortunately. Wriggling like a discombobulated, hooked fish, I saw the dark shape dive from above.

In the spare seconds I had before impact, I glimpsed the creature's silhouette, backlit by the surface glow. Not a shark, too round.

It looked suspiciously like an oversized sea turtle.

A sea turtle torpedo.

I rotated out of its path and lashed out with the spear—not to injure, but to block. The giant turtle's beak slammed into the whalebone, and the impact shuddered up my arm. Blood poured from the slice in my abdomen, painting clouds on the water. I gritted my teeth to steady the shake in my arms, wondering how much this damn thing actually weighed.

The turtle bounced back and shook its head as if shaking off the blow. It was lovely, with flippers as long as my body and a shell big enough for me to ride like a rodeo cowgirl. Dark patches painted its forehead above knowing black eyes. It was sleek and streamlined—youthful.

Mis nietos, I thought. The old man had said his grandchildren were with the relic.

The guidestone's thrum in the mall came back to me, and my free hand reached for my earrings.

The water race… were sea turtles?

I held up both hands, loosening my grip on the spear in a gesture of peace. *Wham!* A blow to the backs of my knees sent me somersaulting.

The spear fell from my loose fingertips and sank rapidly. I spun out of control, trying to keep an eye on the weapon. It was my only tie to the old man; the only thing I had to prove myself to his grandchildren. Unless they thought I'd hurt him and stolen it. My heart leapt into my throat as the ivory shaft faded into the murky depths.

When the spinning slowed, I kicked my tingling legs, held my aching side, and dove.

Reaching, reaching, I expected two shadows to loom over me, to hear flippers by my ear, but when my fingers closed on the spear, I whirled around to see both turtles treading water high above. They eyed me suspiciously, confused by my lack of retaliation.

I held the spear over my head, careful not to point the blades at them.

The old man had spoken Spanish, so it stood to reason his grandchildren did too. I said the only thing I knew. "*La aguamagia.*" It was a jumbled moan on the water, but the turtles' flippers halted their rotation. They began to sink, turning their heads to stare meaningfully at each other. I swore one of their mouths dangled open in shock.

When they drew closer, I slowly pulled my guidestone necklace over my head and held it up to them in my other hand.

With another shared look, they both darted for the surface.

Lacking any other option, I followed.

I breached the water and, out of habit, attempted to suck in air. I hadn't exactly perfected the art of switching between water breathing and air breathing, so what transpired was a very long, very awkward bout of choking and gagging.

Strong hands took hold of my elbows. A girl spoke, sultry and comforting, with only the faintest hint of an accent. "Breathe, *hermosa*. Just breathe."

I clutched at her arms in the water and gulped air, expelling the rest of the fluid in my lungs with every exhalation. Finally, I managed to tread water on my own, breathing somewhat normally.

I lifted watering eyes and saw that the girl wore an unzipped wetsuit. She was gorgeous, even wet. Her long, inky hair trailed into the water around her bare shoulders, and her eyes shone like onyx in the low light. She had a long face and high cheekbones with thick, cherry red lips.

She was a reminder of everything I'd lost.

"Thanks," I said, releasing her arms. "I'm not used to"—I waved a hand vaguely around my head—"this yet."

"No problem," she replied with a shrug. "Come on. Let's get you out of the water."

She swam away, and I took my first look around.

We were in a cave of some sort. The rocky ceiling arched high overhead in a natural dome. The room was finite—three walls where the water lapped at the stone, and ahead, a rocky platform. Two torches wavered atop a pile of fallen stones. The source of the light.

A guy waited on shore, a wetsuit covering his lower half but pulled down to reveal his slender, tanned torso. Like the girl, he couldn't have been much older than me, if at all. He, too, had sculpted cheekbones, but his dark brown hair hung only to his ears, mussed on top of his head and hanging rakishly into his doe eyes.

The girl heaved herself out of the water, zipping up her wetsuit.

I tossed the spear on the rocks and followed her out, the gritty ground cold beneath my palms. She helped me stand, waiting patiently for me to find my land legs again. Her fingers probed the cut over my lower rib cage.

She winced and met my eye. "Sorry about that, *hermosa*. We thought you were another alt traitor."

"Not a very good one," the boy added in a light, half-teasing tone.

But I was still stuck on the fact that we were breathing air so deep beneath the ocean.

"How is this place even possible?" I asked, gazing stupidly around at the strange, underwater pocket of oxygen.

"A combination of physics and elemental magic," the girl explained. "Our people have known of this safe haven for many centuries."

Elemental magic. It was one thing to know it was once an everyday natural phenomenon and be told there will still pockets hidden away today, but quite another to see it in action.

The boy picked up the spear. He said something in Spanish to the girl, who only nodded.

He pinned me with a suspicious gaze. "Why do you have our *abuelito's* spear?"

Neither of them shared their grandfather's thick accent. I only heard it in some of their vowels, as if they'd grown up bilingual.

"He gave it to me—"

"Why?" the boy cut me off.

I swallowed. Neither of them looked particularly dangerous, but looks could be deceiving.

I hadn't thought Carl Simmons was dangerous, either.

"I'm the relic bearer," I said simply.

A beat of silence passed.

"You're not what I expected." The boy's doe eyes swept over me.

Heat flooded my clammy cheeks, and I wrapped my arms around my sports bra. "What did you expect?"

He flopped onto a long, low stone with a shrug. "I don't know. A warrior, maybe?"

"I can fight."

He arched a brow. "You didn't do too well down there, *amiga*."

"Matty," the girl admonished, giving his shoulder a shove. She walked forward and offered me her hand. "I'm Sofia. This is my brother, Mateo."

I shook her hand and looked between the two of them, guilt weighing heavily on my spirit. "I have… bad news."

Sofia's expression didn't change. "If you're going to tell us the rest of our tribe is dead, we know."

"We sensed it through *la tela*," Mateo added, head hung low.

"*La tela*?" I asked.

"It's what we call our ancestral web." Sofia tapped her heart, then her head, sinking onto the rock beside her brother. "A kind of metaphysical connection between our people. The fabric that connects us no matter where we are."

"I'm so sorry," I told them. "I'm sorry I wasn't in time to help."

Mateo jerked toward me, a movement of distress. "What could you have done? You'd be dead, too, and then where would we be? Our people didn't protect *la aguamagia* for centuries only to lose the bearer in the thirteenth hour."

"Is it here?" I asked. "The relic?"

Sofia eyed me. "It's close. It used to rest in the ocean right on the shores of our village. But when the battle…" She looked away, eyelashes catching unshed tears.

Mateo put an arm around his sister's shoulders, squeezing her tight to his side. "We have it safe. As we promised our *abuelito*."

"And we will *keep* it safe," Sofia said firmly, blinking away her tears to focus on me.

Startled, I stammered, "D-does that mean I can't… have it?"

"No." Sofia swiped at her damp eyelashes and squared her shoulders. "It means we're coming with you."

Slipping back into the pool and switching to water breathing was a little easier this time. Maybe one day, with some practice, I could leap between land and sea with ease.

I followed the two sea turtles deep into the water. We passed the crevice where I'd come into the interior pool and continued downward. The walls narrowed like a funnel into a gradual curve. We soon leveled out, swimming through a stone corridor.

My guidestone cooled to an icy sting the further I swam and began to emanate a low blue light that illuminated the cave walls. After several yards, a second azure light source filtered in ahead, spiraling in beams that made it feel like we were swimming at warp speed.

We spilled from the narrow passage into an underwater rotunda.

Below, on the cavern floor, an oblong object rested atop a flat stone.

The water relic.

I halted in mid-water, pummeled by a dozen emotions at once. Shock. Awe. Excitement. Happiness. Despair. Fear.

Tears heated the corners of my eyes, though they dissipated into the ocean.

Sofia and Mateo didn't wait for me. They swam in elegant circles around the relic, regarding it with obvious reverence.

I'd always thought when this moment came, my sisters would be beside me. Uncle Alec. Vin. I'd thought we'd retrieve my relic as a team.

But it was a childish, rose-tinted dream. Never meant to be. Nobody could have journeyed with me to the bottom of the sea. Uncle Alec's scuba gear couldn't have slipped through those narrow crevices.

It was always me.

It always had to be me.

I swam to the glowing orb, my heart beating in my throat and my stomach turning circles.

Mateo may have not expected me to be the relic bearer, but I hadn't known what to expect of the relic, either. It was long and cylindrical, oblong with tapered ends. At first glance, I thought it was a natural stone formation, but as I drew closer, I noted gouge-like tool marks on its surface. It was hard to tell what it had been originally. Like my guidestone, it glowed from the inside, though it was subdued. I expected a zap from my guidestone, a miraculous sign, a surge of power—something—when I reached it. But nada.

Mateo and Sofia backed away, their turtle faces glowing in the soft light.

The moment of truth.

I picked up the relic.

Nothing happened.

The surface felt smoother than I'd expected after seeing the pocked marks. It was roughly the length of my forearm, and I could hold it like a baby against my torso.

I guess I'd thought there would be a flash of light or an explosion of magic pouring out of my body. The relic rested benignly in my hands, even as the guidestone pulsed happily at its proximity.

I glanced up at the two water race Shifters and shook my head.

I don't understand, I mouthed.

The two of them exchanged that same intelligent glance, like a silent conversation transmitted between their pupils. Then the smaller of the two, Sofia, turned a gentle circle around me and pushed me back toward the exit.

Swimming back through the tunnel with the relic in hand turned out to be trickier than maneuvering with the spear. Not because the relic had any serious weight to it, but because its bulk forced me to push it ahead like a ball through the narrowest parts of the tunnel.

Finally, the walls widened, and we angled up toward the pale orange light of the cavern.

Sofia shifted back into her human form before I reached the surface, and I averted my eyes as she grabbed her wetsuit from the rocky platform. When I broke into the air, she paused zipping her suit to latch tight onto my arms as I struggled to transition.

"Slowly, *hermosa*," she soothed. "Don't rush it."

I hacked up the last of the water and sucked in a deep breath. "What is '*hermosa*'?"

"Beautiful," she replied. "Are you okay?"

I stared at her, warm tingles spreading through my body. She'd been calling me *beautiful*? Me? Like this?

"I'm... okay," I assured her, digging my fingers into the relic's hard exterior.

Hermosa.

Beautiful.

Sarcasm? Or a beautiful lie, maybe. But I spotted that same reverence in her face as when she'd circled the relic.

Sofia helped me swim to the edge of the pool, where she easily hopped up onto the rocks, her legs dangling into the water beside me.

I hefted the relic up next to her, surprised by how much heavier it was outside the water, then leaned on my elbows next to it, too exhausted to pull myself from the pool. "I don't understand. Nothing happened."

Sofia brushed her fingers over the relic, her dark brows furrowed. "It's been hidden beneath the ocean for ages, totally dormant, until today." She looked up at me. "Before those alt traitors attacked, it glowed and turned icy cold, like it knew someone was coming for it. But it only lasted an hour or two. Maybe it needs time?"

"For what? It's a water relic," Mateo argued, half in his wetsuit again. "It's literally been *in* the water."

"But, like, empty," Sofia snapped. "Away from anybody who could use it, like a toy forgotten in the back of the closet."

I cocked my head at her, processing what she'd said.

"Dead batteries," I murmured.

Sofia raised an eyebrow. "*Qué, hermosa?*"

"I think you're right." The idea took root.

The way I sensed things and breathed beneath the ocean was *slightly* different than the way I operated in fresh water. Every minute beneath the ocean, I was all too aware of the salt—the weight of it on my skin, the tang of it in my mouth. It left me almost… thirsty, even after just an hour or so.

"The saltwater," I said. "The saltwater has something to do with this. Maybe that's why your people always kept it down here. To force the relic into a kind of… a kind of stasis."

Mateo's face lighted up. "So that if someone other than the bearer came for it, they wouldn't have access to its powers. It's brilliant."

Sofia added, "All the more reason that our race was chosen as its protectors. We're saltwater creatures."

Excitement edged in, shoving away my initial despair. "So, it stands to reason maybe fresh water can activate it? The Rio Coyolate is fresh water, right?"

Mateo agreed. "Cleanest fresh water around."

"So, we go back," I said. "We go back and put the relic in the fresh water. It cleans it and reactivates it, then boom—powers."

"Is it even safe to return?" Mateo asked, exchanging glances with Sofia.

She chewed her cheek. "The enemy could still be near. Waiting."

I shrugged helplessly, pressing my fingertips to the cold, hard surface of the relic. "We don't really have much of an option, do we?"

27
SETBACK

THE RELIC PROVIDED LIGHT IN THE MURK. WHEN THE shadowy silhouette of the ferry loomed overhead, I bobbed up to the surface, and for the first time, released the water and took a shaky breath without choking.

Jackson sat on the back of the boat with his gaze trained on the sea. The moment I surfaced, he scrambled to his knees and reached for me with both hands, oblivious to the way he hung out over the abyss.

"Thank God," he said, somewhat breathless.

KitKat seemed to share the sentiment. She bounded wildly around the boat and chittered a reprimand for my lengthy absence.

I clutched the relic to my chest and took Jackson's hand, letting him haul me in. Braced on the plastic edge, I held up the relic. "Here, take this. Be careful."

"Is this it?" He took it gingerly and twisted to set it safely inside the boat.

"That's it," I agreed as I shifted sideways to the metal ladder. "And I brought some friends."

Jackson looked past me as Sofia and Mateo surfaced. As the two massive turtle heads breached the inky water, they began to change: snouts shrinking, stretched necks compacting, flippers becoming arms treading the waves. As they set to untying their wetsuits from the twine wrapped around their torsos, Jackson swallowed visibly, then stumbled back a step and plopped on the metal bench. "Did they…"

"Yes." I climbed out of the water. The ocean poured off me as I stepped over the top rung onto the back platform, then motioned for my new friends to join us. "Jackson, this is Sofia and Mateo. They were tasked with the safety of the relic, and according to them, that means they're sticking with us for the foreseeable future."

"We already have a bobcat. What's two hybrid turtle people?" he said with wry amusement and a hint of disbelief. I kept throwing him curve balls, but he kept swinging. His alt blood helped, I was sure.

Still, my entrance into his life had made him question *everything*. It was kind of exciting.

Sofia offered him a small, awkward wave. "Nice to meet you, Jackson. And…" She trailed off, catching sight of KitKat at his knees. "You weren't kidding. That is a bobcat. Is it tame?"

Jackson chuckled. "Sometimes, I think she's human."

Mateo's head popped over the lip of the boat. "A bobcat?" he said, climbing the ladder. "An actual bobcat?"

Sofia rolled her eyes. "My brother likes cats."

Mateo hopped out of the water, bypassing Jackson entirely to sit on the bench and address KitKat. "Hello, *preciosa*," he cooed softly, holding out his hand.

KitKat cocked her head and fixed him with an expression that seemed to say, *Boy, have you lost your mind?* But she nudged his fingers with her nose and sniffed him, before ducking under his hand for scratches.

Jackson nudged the relic with his bare foot. "Is it done then?"

I grimaced and tugged my shirt onto my clinging, wet skin. "Not… exactly." I gave him a brief rundown of what had happened beneath the waves and our conclusion that we needed fresh water.

"It's just a theory at this point," I finished.

"As good as any," Jackson agreed. "It makes sense. I'll get us back to shore."

As Jackson started the motor and put the boat in motion, Sofia took the bench next to me.

"What is her name?" she asked, motioning to the bobcat.

"KitKat," I said. "She showed up one day and never left."

KitKat huffed at me, then tossed herself between Mateo's legs, rubbing her face on his bare, wet stomach. He laughed and ran his hands through the downy fur on her chest, murmuring and cooing at her.

"We had a housecat back in California," Sofia explained, watching her brother with a loving smile. "At our boarding school. She had a special bond with Matty. He was so upset when we moved back home."

"Boarding school?" I asked, raising my voice as the motor whirred and the wind whipped around us. I clutched the railing behind me so I didn't fall overboard as we picked up speed.

Sofia nodded. "My father wasn't a fan of the rustic village life. He left years ago and made a name for himself in the US. He enrolled us in boarding school early. But when he died six months ago, *Abuelito* called us back home."

My eyes scrunched, and the fingers of one hand twitched toward her. "I'm sorry."

Sofia shrugged. "He wasn't really a great dad, to be honest."

"And your mom?"

"Died in childbirth," Sofia said softly. "I think it's one of the reasons Dad chose to leave."

I surveyed the dark shore ahead. A few fires still burned, but they were benign campfires compared to the infernos from earlier. "Did you hate to leave California?"

"No." She flashed a smile. "I like the slow life. And I love my *abuelito*." Her face darkened, and she glanced away. "*Loved* him. I loved him."

Mateo bit his lip, gaze flicking to his sister before he buried his face between KitKat's ears, nuzzling his forehead against the white markings on hers. Sofia held her chin high, but her jaw twitched and trembled, and she entwined her hands too tight in her lap. The moonlight caught the sheen of tears she didn't allow to spill.

I touched her shoulder in an awkward show of solidarity. I didn't know how to comfort her, ensnared in my own damn soap opera full of loss and danger and violence. But I could be there. Just a person on a bench, our knees touching, my hand attempting to convey that I knew her pain. I recognized it and wished I could do something to ease it, if only a little.

We rode the rest of the way in silence.

Jackson carefully navigated the ferry up to the pitch-black dock, where the fingers of light from the three dying fires couldn't reach. Mateo released his hold on KitKat to leap over and tie us off. He seemed to have good night vision, like I had underwater, and I assumed it had something to do with sea turtles' ability to live between land and sea.

As a group, we cautiously trekked back to solid ground. I carried the relic hugged against my chest, sticking close to Sofia, while KitKat hovered around Mateo's legs, ears alert. She and I knew seeing their village like this—the burned bodies, particularly—would be hard on our new companions.

Halfway up the central pathway, Sofia took hold of my bicep, leaning against me. "I-I'm sorry, Ellis. I just…"

Slipping my arm around her shoulders, I shook my head. "Don't apologize. Please."

Tears slipped over her long, dark lashes and painted trails down her cheeks as she surveyed the decimated village. "Do you know where my grandfather is?"

I glanced at Jackson.

"I remember," he said in a gentle tone, already turning to lead us to the old man's resting place.

Sofia and Mateo's *abuelito* still lay as we'd left him: on his back, his robes tucked around his body, his front soaked in blood. Mateo knelt beside the old man, a muscle knotted in his jaw as he peeled back the robe and peered at the grisly wounds.

"Bear claws," he said stiffly, letting the robe fall back into place.

"We should bury him." Sofia rested a hand on Mateo's shoulder. "In the manner befitting our people."

Mateo sat back on his heels and bowed his head. "Yeah. We should."

We stood there for some time over *Abuelito*'s still body. I pulled his spear from the back of my sports bra and passed it to Mateo, then stood at Sofia's side while she cried.

Though I knew the relic could dictate the fate of not just us but the world—avoiding a possible apocalyptic future, defeating the Summum Malum, freeing the souls of billions—its importance paled in the face of grief. Grief was immediate. The kind of emotion that could halt the breath in your lungs, that could root you to the ground, make basic functions foreign concepts, and scoop out your sense of self, leaving you hollow.

After a while, Sofia brushed her face clean and turned to me, her expression resolute. "Let's go to the river."

"Are you sure? If you need more time—"

"I'm sure, *hermosa*," she cut in with a small, sad shake of her head. "*Abuelito* is no longer here. But we are. And we are here to make sure you remain safe. It's what he would've wanted, before all else. Even his own farewell and burial rights."

Her words saddened me but at the same time buoyed my spirits. Having Jackson on my side—and even KitKat—had been wonderful, but now I had two allies with intimate knowledge of the relic. Maybe I really could do this.

Leaving behind *Abuelito*'s body, we headed straight for the river, but Mateo still carried his grandfather with him in the form of his whalebone spear.

The air had that crisp coolness reserved for the quiet hours before dawn, when even the tropical humidity slept. We left behind the devastation for the rocky bank of the Rio Coyolate, shimmering like a silver ribbon beneath a starry sky.

My feet sank into the shifting, rocky sands, and I tipped my face to the inky universe overhead. While I'd been in the ocean, the clouds had dissipated, letting the twinkling starlight immerge to remind me that life was so much bigger than me, bigger than this little plot of land in rural Guatemala, bigger than our enemies.

I splashed into the shallows.

I was already soaked, so I dropped to my knees in the water and dipped the relic below the surface, letting it rest against my thighs.

The river flowed around me, slow and steady. There was nothing wild about the river at this juncture, where the delta split to meet the ocean. It gurgled and brushed my hips in a passing, friendly greeting. It felt cooler than the ocean. Purer.

I watched it surge over the relic and held my breath.

Any minute.

I pictured the decades, maybe centuries, of saltwater washing away beneath the calm, clean waters of the Rio Coyolate. Once the salt dissipated, it would activate. Its captive powers would flow into me, fortifying my innate abilities, giving me the strength to keep going. To right the wrongs.

To save the world. To save the souls befouled and trapped by the greed and darkness of the Summum Malum. To find and free my sisters and locate their relics. To storm limbo together, like avenging Valkyrie.

But ten minutes passed uneventfully.

Mateo's voice nudged me from the edge of the water. "Maybe you need to go under?"

I didn't hate the idea. I could still taste salt on my tongue and crusted all over my body.

Standing, I waded deeper into the cool waters, holding the relic like a precious baby. The river rose over my knees, then past my thighs. It lapped at my hips and belly button, before tickling my armpits.

I dunked the relic first, then let the water close over my head with a silent suction. I exhaled the last of the oxygen in my lungs, then pulled in water, going slow. Going easy. I hardly noticed the difference now. I walked along the thick, silty bottom, headed for the deepest part of the river, where I sank to the ground and crossed my legs.

The peace down here was incredible. Dark. Cool. Quiet. Best of all, open and alive. Not like the tank.

Somewhere nearby, a school of freshwater fish darted past.

Sofia's voice broke through my thoughts. "It's crazy how she can breathe underwater in human form."

And Mateo laughed. "You jealous?"

I smiled at their banter.

But my smile didn't last long. It soon became clear that nothing was going to happen.

Dammit.

I'd been so sure this would work. I didn't have any theories left.

I slogged out of the water, dejected, battling a wild need to throw the relic as far as I could just on principle.

"Nothing?" Jackson asked as I got close enough to hear.

I shook my head and glared down at the relic. "I don't know what I'm doing wrong. I don't know *anything* about this thing. Do you?" I directed the question to Sofia and Mateo.

Mateo shook his head. "No, but we have one last resource."

Sofia gasped. "Matty, no. Outsiders aren't allowed."

I cocked an eyebrow at them both. "What is it?"

"A secret library," Mateo said over his sister's grunt of indignation. "It holds all the knowledge of the water race. Including a stone tablet that legend says belongs to the relic. Nobody of our tribe has ever been able to read it."

"But maybe I can." Excitement hitched my breath. "So where is this secret library?"

We packed a few satchels of meager supplies plucked from the charred wreckage and Sofia dug out her own whalebone spear from a collapsed dwelling. Mateo hovered around his grandfather, casting regretful looks at the body until Jackson clasped his shoulder and asked, "Are you sure you don't want to bury him now? The library will still be there."

Mateo looked to Sofia, and though his lips barely twitched, I could feel their unspoken conversation thickening the air—a "web" stretched between them.

"You're right," Mateo finally answered in a soft grumble to his sister. He turned to Jackson. "*Abuelito* would want us to help Ellis before anything else." His large eyes scanned the forest bordering the sand. "Yes, the library will still be there, but the bear and his friends could still be nearby, too."

Sofia gripped her spear tighter. "*Abuelito* died with honor, protecting the relic. We will respect his choice and put its protection first. Then, when Ellis has her power, we will tend to his body."

Jackson studied the sky. "We should probably try to get an hour or two of sleep before we go, then."

"No time for sleeping," Mateo said.

"Yeah, we need to keep moving." I brushed sand off my hands. "That bear Shifter and his army could come back to search for the relic again."

Jackson's brow scrunched with worry, but he shook his head. "It's either risk the possibility of the bear coming back, or head straight into a guaranteed accident, charging into the jungle at night. There's no native bears here, but I'm betting there's plenty of other nasty predators, and we won't be able to see them coming."

"He's right." Sofia shot down Mateo's protest before it could start.

"I'll take watch." Jackson turned, looking for an area to settle.

"For an hour." She shook a finger in front of his face. "Then I'll do it. You need rest, too."

Jackson raised an eyebrow. "There's no arguing with you, is there?"

"Never," Mateo said wearily.

So we curled up in the sand, using satchels for lumpy,

uncomfortable pillows. Jackson sat cross-legged nearby with his eyes on the jungle and a hand on a machete hilt. I thought I'd doze at most, but watching the rise and fall of his breaths, I dropped into a deep sleep. Until his warm hand on my shoulder stirred me awake.

"Is this okay?" he whispered as his arm started to cautiously curl around my waist. "Just want to keep hold of you tonight."

I half-opened bleary eyes, wrapped his arm around me tighter, and nestled against his side, heart ballooning in my chest.

I caught a glimpse of Sofia tossing her dark hair over her shoulder as she took over the watch, and then I drifted again.

Jackson woke me just after sunrise, and we set out.

The thick forest that lay south of the water race's village was more rainforest than woods. As soon as we passed beneath the overgrown canopy, the humidity clung to every inch of my bare skin like a wet rag. Within minutes, my already damp shorts and t-shirt were soaked. Sweat trickled in places on my body that had never perspired before. Thankfully, Jackson was lugging the relic in his pack, or I wouldn't have made it half a mile.

Not even a hint of a breeze passed through the low-hanging branches and draping vines. Mateo and Jackson took point, using machetes from the village to chop a path through the brush. With every swipe, a fresh swarm of bugs launched into the air so that I spent almost every minute batting little wings away from my face.

The forest floor began to pitch uphill, and our momentum slowed. Climbing over massive fallen trees and finding footing beneath bramble bushes overflowing with beetles and spiders became even more difficult at an angle. But worst of all were the boas and green tree snakes that kept dropping down in front of me and KitKat, dangling from perches in the branches. Every startled backpedal nearly sent me rolling down the incline, and KitKat's furious hisses and barking growls were likely to draw bigger, curious predators our way. Sofia seemed unaffected at first, swatting the snakes away as if scolding a house pet, but by the third one, she muttered something in Spanish that sounded like a curse.

"They're everywhere today." Sofia huffed. "Someone must smell good."

"Probably KitKat." I scrunched my face in an unspoken apology. "She seems to attract them."

"Well, I'll take care of them." She cast a sidelong glance at the bobcat by my feet.

After half an hour of intense exercise, my malnourished skeleton of a body began to feel the pressure. I paused, leaning heavily on my palm against a tree trunk, and focused on taking in air. My stomach let out an impatient growl, seizing with hunger I'd been ignoring since we set out. I didn't want to have to suck on a dead animal in front of Sofia and Mateo. Or anybody.

I just had to hold out until I activated the relic, and then I could have a taco instead. I hoped.

From up ahead, Mateo called, "We're almost there."

I waved him off. "I just need a minute." I gasped out each word with serious effort.

Sofia and KitKat backtracked to my side.

Sofia put a comforting hand on my shoulder and said, "It's okay, *hermosa*. Take your time. The library isn't going anywhere."

I gave her a grateful smile. There was something soothing about Sofia's presence—well, about both of them, really. The way taking a leisurely swim in cool, calm waters could lower blood pressure and release stress, being comforted by Sofia sent a wave of serenity through me. It was tangible, chartable—an ability, not a vague feeling. A power tied with their water race heritage, and I definitely wasn't mad at it.

KitKat didn't have the same strange, subconscious effect on me, but the strength of her pressing into my leg helped me ground myself.

My stomach growled again, long and gurgling. Sofia frowned. "We shouldn't have made you take this hike without food. I'm sorry."

She didn't say a word about my protruding bones, but I saw her worried eyes linger at my collarbone.

"It's not your fault. I'm a picky eater."

"Well, there's some berries that are to die for." She pointed to a low-hanging branch laden with fat clusters of the dark fruits. "And if you need something more filling, the roots of—"

"Thanks. Really." I cringed, touched by her kindness and extra embarrassed at what I had to say next. "But I can't eat any of that."

She gave me a "Mother knows best" kind of smile. "Ellis, I promise they're really good, especially when your stomach is talking like that."

I couldn't meet her eye, even as she touched my shoulder and that calming effect settled over me again. "I can only eat blood."

She startled but didn't withdraw her hand. She wasn't afraid to be near me. "Is it something to do with your alt race?"

I shrugged. "I wouldn't say that exactly, but I think it is tied to my elemental powers somehow. It started before my eighteenth birthday. My older sister's powers changed after she turned seventeen. They started to cause her pain."

Sofia nodded sagely. "Your powers are strong, but that means they can take a toll on you."

"But blood drinking, really?" I hugged myself. "I thought our connections to the relics were supposed to give us life-saving powers, not turn us into monsters."

"You're not a monster, *hermosa*. You are bound to the water relic, and blood is more than half water. Some have tried to corrupt that connection in the past."

"Tried," I repeated, uneasy. "But they didn't succeed, right?"

Sofia pursed her lips, pondering the canopy. "Not entirely, no. Though, I guess *la aquamagia* could have changed in some ways. For the worse. I can't really say; no other possible relic holder ever reached our lands before the schism."

"Schism?"

She made an affirming sound low in her throat. "Many centuries ago, *la agua gente* became part of a Mayan tribe and allowed the Mayan priests to use *la aguamagia* in blood sacrifices to their gods. My family's ancestors knew this was not as the Priestesses intended and feared that if such sacrifices continued, they could change the benevolent nature of the relic forever. So, they split from the main tribe, along with a few other families, and waited for their chance to liberate *la aguamagia*. The conquistadors gave them that chance. The Spanish tried to destroy the relic when they tore down the Mayan temples, but they failed, and our people returned the relic to its original purpose for good. You are meant to continue that noble purpose." She squeezed my shoulder. "You see, *hermosa*, water is nourishment, a bringer of life. Blood is a life force, and your elemental magic wants to draw you closer to the source of life. That doesn't make what it's done to your body right or fair. Maybe it has become confused, from the blood sacrifices?"

"Hmm." I placed a hand over one of hers. "I guess that makes sense. I wish it would get itself right, then."

She snorted. "I understand. Who knows? Maybe once you have the relic's full power, and the life force it holds, you won't need the blood anymore."

Knowing she thought that was possible might have reassured me if my relic's unintended use in blood sacrifices weren't still bouncing around in my head. "That's what I've been telling my-self." I straightened, breaking our connection as I pushed off the tree. "I think I'm okay now. Let's keep going."

We started back up the steep hill with Sofia sticking close, glancing back every so often to make sure I was okay.

Everyone clambered over a massive dead log in single file, grunting and wheezing. I planted my boot on top to crest over it last, following their footsteps, and the whole thing collapsed.

My leg fell through the dead, hollow interior, but my body tumbled backward, arms windmilling. The position was going to break my leg and send me careening back down the steep mountainside. I could see it as clearly as if it had already happened.

I closed my eyes and braced for impact.

28
ANCESTRY

SOFIA'S FINGERS SNATCHED MY T-SHIRT, HOLDING ME parallel to the ground, tipped back to stare at the sky. A wad of thin fabric was the only thing between me and bone-crushing death, and it tore with a sound like ripped paper.

I latched onto Sofia's wrists, and she hauled me back onto my feet, leaving a gaping hole in the shirt over my ribs.

I blew out a breath, still holding onto her as my heart beat wildly in my chest.

A sharp sting at my ankle made me jump. Then a second burning sting made me yelp. I jerked my foot out of the dead tree and danced away from it, stomping to dislodge whatever had bitten me.

"Ellis?" Sofia asked. "What is it?"

"Something got me." I bent down to study the area of skin around the tongue of my boot. I didn't see anything, and Sofia squatted for a look, too.

"No snake or scorpion wounds," she assured me. "Maybe fire ants. You'll be itchy, but it's not deadly."

"Thank the Priestesses for that." I shook out my leg as the sting subsided. "Let's get out of here."

Mateo hadn't been exaggerating. Less than ten yards ahead, the trees broke open on a breathtaking cliffside overlook. Below, the river wound to the glittering blue jewel of the Pacific to one side, and rolling mountains of green formed a vast ocean of their own on the other.

But the most magnificent part was the twin cliff across the river that rose like a pillar from the shallows and reached out over a forested plain, independent of any mountain. All four sides of the pillar were smooth, unscalable, cut rock. It didn't look real, or even physically possible from a natural erosion standpoint. Then again, breathing oxygen in a cave beneath the ocean hadn't seemed physically possible either.

Elemental magic.

Our mountain and the pillar were connected by a rope bridge that swayed in the breeze. A dark, yawning crevice in the side of the pillar aligned with the bridge, making it look like a long, wooden tongue protruding from a gaping mouth.

We circled up at the fat, wooden stakes that held the bridge onto our mountainside.

Jackson whistled. "That looks dangerous."

Mateo shook his head. "Our people have cared for this place for centuries. It's perfectly safe."

"Unless the wind makes one wrong move," Jackson pointed out wryly.

He had a point. The "railings" were more like suggestions that rose barely hip-high. The only way I wanted to cross the thing was on my belly, army crawling. Or not at all.

"You could get the tablet thingy and bring it back," I suggested to Sofia. "I'll wait here."

She snorted. "It's part of the cave wall, *hermosa.* You either cross the rickety bridge or you don't find out how to activate the relic."

I pulled a face. "Fine. But if I die, I'm coming back to haunt you."

Her laughter was like trickling water falling into a pool. "We could be friends forever."

Mateo stepped onto the swaying planks first. He moved with swift, sure steps, keeping his torso stick-straight and his arms stiff, held out evenly by his hips, fingertips trailing the rope rails. Not the first time he'd crossed the bridge of death, apparently.

Sofia motioned for Jackson to go next. "I'll cross with Ellis."

He questioned me with a glance.

I took her hand, trusting her completely. "I'll be okay. Keep the relic safe."

Jackson patted the backpack on his shoulders, then took on the bridge, mimicking Mateo's stance. Despite his usual grace, the bridge moved a lot more beneath his combat boots, forcing him to keep a slower pace.

KitKat sat back on her haunches and swished her stumpy tail through the underbrush as she assessed the drop. She chuffed, then glanced up at me, panting hard.

Apparently, my oddball bobcat was afraid of heights.

"You can stay here." I let go of Sophia and patted her head. "Keep an eye on things. We'll be back before you know it."

She chuffed again and lay on her belly, spreading her front paws and licking her black jowls as she yawned.

Sofia gave me a gentle push. "Come on, *hermosa*. Your boyfriend's on the other side."

My cheeks burned. "He's not my boyfriend."

Sofia hummed under her breath, her fingers still urging me toward the bridge. "But you want him to be. It's all over your face. He looks at you, and you melt."

"That's so not true." The goofy smile smeared over my face smoothed the sharp edges of my tone. The teasing and prodding didn't bother me. I'd grown up with sisters. But this was even better. Light ribbing between girlfriends. Banter straight from TV dialogue.

"Whatever you say, *hermosa*." Sofia patted my back.

I turned and scrunched my nose up at her.

I could protest all I wanted, but she was right. Even with Mateo and Sofia hovering nearby, I was always deeply attuned to everything Jackson did. Any move he made. Any change in his expression or even the sound of his breathing.

And yeah, maybe I was smitten. Lately, I couldn't seem to stop thinking about the riverbank. Despite all the fear, despite the chill and the horrors of what I'd just seen in Carl's car, what I remembered most was that I'd kissed Jackson. I could relive every second of it, every detail.

We were halfway across the bridge before I realized Sofia had used my crush to keep my mind off imminent death.

I let out a little "Eep!" and halted on the skinny planks.

"You were doing so well," Sofia chastised over my shoulder.

"You distracted me!"

"It worked, didn't it?"

In the middle of the sagging bridge, I felt weightless and out of control. I clutched the useless railings, as the icy terror of dangling over yards and yards of open air took hold.

"We're fine, *hermosa*," Sofia said softly. "Take a breath. I'm right here. We cross together."

I nodded, then immediately regretted the motion when the bridge swayed ever so slightly. Sofia's hands alighted on my shoulders, and I took that breath she'd suggested. As I let it out slowly, I felt that same calm trickle down my body like a warm shower. It reminded me of the serenity Uncle Alec's ability-charged smile caused, but my head remained clear, my thoughts my own.

I started to walk, heart steady but head still very aware of the danger.

"Your people couldn't have made an actual bridge?" I focused on the planks ahead of me. "Like a suspension bridge with metal and iron?"

Sofia laughed. "The library is sacred. We needed a bridge easily destroyed in the event of invasion."

"Easily destroyed," I repeated, a bead of sweat trailing down my cheek. "Yes. Good to know that it could be cut right out from beneath me."

"You'd fall into the water," Sofia said, her tone all matter of fact. "The river would protect you as the relic bearer."

"I don't think the river could stop me from splatting after a hundred-foot fall."

When I stepped off the rickety bridge onto solid ground, I had to quell the urge to sink to my knees and kiss the dirt. Instead, I crossed the rocky surface to join Jackson and Mateo at the mouth of the cave.

Mateo had a whalebone torch in one hand, taken from a makeshift holder on the wall, and Jackson held a lighter to its fuel-soaked cloth tip. It went up with a low *whoosh*.

"Ready to figure out your destiny?" Mateo bounced up on his toes, more excited than me.

I couldn't find the right words, so I just said, "Uh-huh," and gestured him ahead.

I was beyond excited. I'd been ready for ages.

Mateo's torch, as small as it was, fully illuminated the narrow passage into the cave. The path was only wide enough for one person, so we moved forward single file, breathing the acrid smoke.

The passage opened into a conical room much larger than I'd expected based on the slenderness of the pillar. Shadows of towering rock structures pressed in all around, and the torch struggled to fight through them as Mateo walked further inside. A cauldron-like basin loomed from the darkness, sitting on the floor, about hip height and full of kindling. Mateo touched the torch to the pile, and it shot up in flames.

I gasped.

The library consisted of shelves upon shelves built out of the rock and connected by a series of crude wooden ladders. Several tables dotted the floor, and one segment of the conical wall was covered in tapestries and artwork.

"The history of our people." Sofia ghosted her fingertips over one of the tapestries. "All in one place."

"Whoa," I replied lamely. I had no words sufficient for the cave's magnificence, but I itched to capture it in brushstrokes.

"The stone tablet is this way." Mateo picked his flaming torch back out of the kindling.

He led us to the wall of artwork. Up close and in the direct firelight, the colors were stunning—rich burgundies, earthy greens, abyssal blacks, and layered tones of gemstone blues. Most were pictographs depicting historical scenes, presumably from the water race. But we bypassed the huge tapestries and canvases for an unassuming stone tablet the size of a textbook.

And totally blank.

"Here it is," Mateo said, tapping the stone with his fingertip.

"It's empty."

He grinned. "Technically."

Sofia slapped his shoulder. "Legend states it has a message for the relic bearer. We always assumed the message wasn't physical. Maybe mental transference, like *la tela*."

"You mean I should touch it and see if it talks to me?"

Sofia shrugged with one shoulder, giving me a sheepish look. "Maybe?"

"This is crazy. I'm not even part of your 'ancestral web.'" I reached out anyway and placed my palm in the center of the tablet.

My guidestone cooled immediately, like a freezer burn against my skin. I yanked it out of my dirty t-shirt before it could give me frostbite. The blue glow fell over the tablet.

Instantaneously, knowledge swept into me like…

Rushing water. A maelstrom.

"We were right." I stared unfocused at the stone tablet as the message settled deep inside my mind. "The saltwater put the relic to sleep on purpose. But it isn't just freshwater it needs to recover. It needs deep and fast-flowing water. Faster than we'll find in a regular river." I dropped my hand, still trying to process the way the information was just kind of *there*. "Is there a waterfall close by?"

Mateo's boyish face grew serious. "I think there's one a few miles south."

Jackson shook his head. "That wouldn't be deep. A waterfall is fast flowing but only while falling."

"Good point," Mateo agreed.

Sofia caught her brother's eye. "*El torbellino*," she said as if she were invoking a deadly beast.

Mateo gawped at her like she'd lost her mind. "We want to activate the relic, not kill her."

"Ellis can breathe underwater," Sofia said, exasperated. "If anyone can survive *el torbellino*, she can."

Wanting a little more clarification on how I might meet my demise, I interrupted. "What's *el torbellino*?"

"It's a gate to the afterlife." Mateo's voice was laced with fearful reverence.

"It is *not*." Sofia rolled her eyes. "It's a whirlpool at the bottom of a nearby lake," she explained to me. "It's said to be a 'gate to the afterlife' because it's way too dangerous for people to swim there. Get too close to *el torbellino*, and it'll suck you in."

Mateo added, "And your family will be lucky if they ever find your body."

I fought the urge to gulp like a victim in a horror movie. "Is it deep?"

Sofia nodded solemnly. "Very."

"Then it sounds like my only option. Where is it?"

The two of them exchanged glances, and Sofia grimaced. "We aren't really sure. But I think there's a map in one of these books." She gestured to a shelf beside the stone tablet. "Just give us a minute and we'll find it."

Jackson and I left them to do their research. Quite frankly, I was glad I couldn't read Spanish and get roped into helping, because the idea of sitting for even just a couple minutes sounded like nirvana.

I sank into an unsteady metal folding chair and slouched deep against the cold backrest with a weary sigh.

Jackson took the chair next to me, sitting his backpack carefully on the ground beside him. "Everything okay?"

I shook my head and glanced Mateo and Sofia's way. They stood over an open book, arguing in fast-paced Spanish. "I wish we'd been faster. They're all that's left of an entire race of people."

"There might be more of them out there," he assured me. "Like their dad, who left the tribe."

But was dead, I added silently. "Still. I feel terrible."

"You aren't responsible for everything bad that happens in this world."

I raised an eyebrow and poked him in the shin with one boot. "Look in the mirror, Mr. Telekinesis. Mistakes happen."

"Except I am responsible for what my own powers do." He massaged a thumb over the tattoo on his palm. "Keeping my abilities controlled at all times is necessary for the good of society." He tapped the tattoo at his temple. "That's what these are here to remind me."

I frowned before I could stop myself. Those beautiful swirling markings I'd admired suddenly looked like coiled chains.

I leaned forward to unzip his backpack. "You can't be ruled by your guilt forever," I told him, carefully extracting the water relic. "At some point, you have to realize that what you've been given is a gift." I set the relic on the tabletop and caressed the smooth surface. "You can literally save the world with something that powerful."

"You truly believe that," Jackson said as not a question, but more like a surprised observation.

"Of course. I was raised by people who not only preached it, but lived it." Letting my fingertips rest on the relic, I caught his eye. "Has nobody ever praised your abilities?"

Jackson leaned an elbow on the table next to the stone. "Nobody knows. Nobody but you, Violet, and Dr. Craig."

The fact that he'd avoided the real question didn't escape me.

Careful to keep a rough edge out of my voice, I asked, "And did Dr. Craig tell you that you were a threat to society?"

"No. He didn't have to," Jackson said darkly. "He knew my past, my problems in the system, and why Violet got hurt. And after he fast-tracked me through basic, to learn to control my body, he trained me to control my mind, to only use my skills when absolutely necessary, and only for the good of others."

"But, I thought you said he calls the abilities he researches 'gifts.'"

"He does. It doesn't mean we get to use them like they're toys on Christmas." He picked at his dirty fingernails. "He's seen how dangerous they can be, just like I have. More so, probably. Part of his research is tracing the lineage of people with gifts."

Jackson's lips curled in a wistful smile, but my blood chilled. Dr. Craig was tracking alt groups? How many had he found? How many did the government have under surveillance?

"He unsealed my records and helped me find out who my mother was," Jackson said, and then I understood his smile.

"Was she telekinetic?"

He shook his head. "I think that must come from my dad. My mom and her tribe are where I get my tracking aptitude. My non-violent gift."

"Tribe?"

"Native American. A small tribe that split from the Apache and called themselves the Kanohali."

Small tribe of alts, I corrected in my head. *People on the fringes of their society who shared a secret.* Alts always split off eventually, once they found enough people like them.

"Some of their ancient oral histories were written down in recent years, and Dr. Craig discovered they all had my ability to find a trail on instinct, before any physical signs like footprints. It's like a little compass inside, pointing us in the right direction. But my mother was one of the last."

"I'm sorry," I said. "Do you know what happened?"

"Not really. Dr. Craig said she died in a…" He paled. "A fire."

I reached for his hand and confirmed the suspicion in his eyes. "Summum Malum. They've taken so many of us. That's why my sisters and I have to use our 'gifts' to stop them. There are always two sides to a coin."

His smile was more like a twitch. "Dr. Craig gave me all his research, and a photo he found of her." He rubbed the tattoo on his palm again. "The Kanohali used to paint markings like these on themselves before a battle. That's why I chose them. To honor my heritage and mark my weapons of war—the hand that fires the gun and the mind that guides the bullet—to remind myself they must be used wisely."

"Using them wisely and fearing them aren't the same," I said softly, leaning on my elbow next to him, putting us face to face over the relic. "Sounds to me like you need to expand your support system. Find people who understand what it's like to have an ability, not just people who study them from the outside."

Our gazes locked. Silence fell between us, despite the mumble of Sofia and Mateo bickering and the scuffle of their feet across the rocky floor.

I wanted to kiss him again. Right here, right now, leaning over the water relic I'd been preparing for my entire life. I'd found my place, reached my destiny, and he was here with me. It couldn't be coincidence.

A sharp pain lanced up my right leg.

"Ow," I grunted, breaking eye contact to study my throbbing ankle.

Two red dots rose from my pale skin, a couple inches apart. They looked like small, inflamed pimples, but a strange purple blister sat right in the center, while a circle of red rash radiated from them.

Jackson lifted my leg onto his knee for a better look. The warmth of his hands on my skin chased away all lingering pain. "Spider bites, maybe?"

Mateo appeared next to me and dropped a book on the table. "We found it."

I slipped my leg off Jackson's lap, dropping my boot back to the floor, sad to lose his touch. Leaning over the book, I eyed the hand-drawn map. "What am I looking at?"

"Here's where we are," Mateo said, jabbing a finger at the pillar in the river. He swooped his finger up two curves in the river, headed inland, then paused. "At this cliff right here, we go south for a half mile through the jungle. Can't miss it. The only lake around that's so turquoise it doesn't look real."

I opened my mouth to ask if we could take the book with us, but a strange sound pierced through our conversation.

It was… horrifying. A croaking scream, like a cross between an injured raptor and a banshee. The sound pulsed four times, then five, then six.

"What *is* that?" I breathed, clutching the relic to my chest.

Mateo shook his head, unsheathing his grandfather's spear from the holster on his back. "I've never heard anything like it."

"It's almost inhuman," Sofia said, lifting her fingers over her shoulder to her own spear.

Jackson tensed beside me, muscles like taut, vibrating rubber bands. "It's a bobcat scream."

Dread flooded my veins. "KitKat!"

29

EL TORBELLINO

I WAS THE FIRST OUT, CHARGING INTO THE SUNLIGHT WITH THE water relic tucked under my arm like a football. Nothing mattered more to me than reaching KitKat. Not the relic. Not the trouble of *el torbellino*. Not even the burden of guilt I carried for the water tribe's demise.

Just KitKat. If something had happened to her because we'd left her alone, I'd never forgive myself.

Except… she was fine. She bounced around, agitated, turning messy circles like she'd lapped up a few too many beers, but she was alone and seemingly unharmed. I met her gaze across the divide, and she scented the air. Those horrific, panicked sounds came out of her mouth again.

Jackson slid to a halt beside me and pointed at the riverbanks far below.

A winding, precariously narrow path wove up the cliff face toward where KitKat waited.

I followed Jackson's finger to the figures marching up the path. Led by a bear.

"She was warning us," Jackson said grimly.

Sofia gasped behind me. "It's them. It's the enemy who destroyed our people."

My heart stuttered, then galloped. We were outnumbered ten to four. Five, with KitKat. Some of them were human, but several were in various states of animal transmogrification. Shifters. Were more lying in wait in the forest?

"What do we do?" I asked, embarrassed by the tremor in my voice.

This wasn't drunk assholes in a bar parking lot.

This was a full-blown alt battle, and I wasn't ready for it. I didn't have my powers. Breathing underwater wasn't going to put that bear down.

Mateo glanced back at the cave, his jaw set and his onyx eyes flinty. "We must protect the library at all costs," he said with none of his usual lighthearted flippancy. He looked at his sister. "You guys go. I'll cut the bridge."

Sofia shook her head. "Not a chance. How will you get down?"

He shrugged and motioned at the river below. "I'll jump."

"There's no guarantee you would survive that fall," she snapped. "Not happening. We all cross, and we'll cut the bridge on the other side."

"You know that's not how the bridge was made," Mateo admonished. His voice was so calm, so soothing. I could tell it was intentional on his part. It eased my fears. "It's indestructible from that side. In the event of an attack, a guard remained here for as long as it took to declare safety again."

"We don't have time for that!" Sofia snarled.

I cut in. "I'll do it. Give me a knife. I'll cut the bridge and jump."

All three of them turned to me in varying states of surprise.

"Hell no. You don't like heights," Sofia argued.

At the same time, Jackson said, "Over my dead body. I'll do it."

"Shut up, both of you," I snapped, whipping the relic up between us and shaking it at them like a weapon. "I can breathe water. If anyone can make that jump, it's me. We're getting out of here as a team, all in one piece."

Sofia hesitated, her gaze darting down the silver ribbon of the river. I could almost see the wheels turning in her head as she raised a hand. "Wait—it's a good idea. You can jump and swim for *el torbellino.* Two curves in the river, then head south by land parallel to the next cliffs. You'll be stronger once the relic's activated."

"I'm not leaving you guys—"

"Ellis," Jackson cut in. His expression turned grave. "You do what you need to do. I'll do my best to hold them off until you get back."

Fear and worry wrapped like twin snakes around my spine. Not just at the idea of going ahead *alone,* but over what could happen to him—to any of them—while I was gone. I didn't think I was some all-powerful savior, but if something happened to my friends and I wasn't with them, I couldn't live with that.

I stepped into him, resting my hand on his arm. "Jax, I could be gone an hour. Maybe more. I don't know. I'm not leaving you to deal with them." They'd killed an entire tribe.

He cupped my face in his hands, anchoring me with those brilliant caramel eyes that caught the sun.

"Yes. You are," he said firmly. "We'll be okay."

I clutched his wrists, a turmoil of adoration, despair, and crushing concern making my heart ache and my stomach clench. What if they all died? More deaths on my hands because we didn't get here in time, because I waited around like a stupid damsel in distress, thinking Vin was coming to save me.

Because I didn't know how to activate my relic.

Jackson released me. "No questioning it. Just do it." Then he nodded at Sofia and Mateo, turned on his heel, and took off across the bridge.

Mateo gave me an encouraging smile and hefted his spear in one hand, offering me his machete with his other. "Go get 'em, *amiga.* Be the superhero you were born to be."

"I don't know about that," I said wanly, though I shifted the relic under my arm to take his weapon.

As he paced after Jackson across the swaying bridge, Sofia wrapped me in a tight hug that smelled like saltwater and smoke.

Between the machete and the relic, I could hardly hug her back, but I leaned into her anyway.

"Please be careful." I pressed my forehead into her hair.

"We'll hold the line." She stepped back and squeezed my shoulders. "Activate your powers, *hermosa*. Come back as soon as you can."

Sofia flew over the bridge, and the thing barely swung beneath her light-footed steps. As soon as she leapt off onto solid ground on the other side, she whipped around and gave me a thumbs up.

I didn't hesitate. Maybe I couldn't save the dozens who had already died, but I could preserve the sanctity of their culture.

I swung the machete with all my might into the right support rope.

The rope split easily, and the bridge listed sideways. As I lifted the machete to cut the left rope, a massive crash echoed over the river. I glanced at my friends.

Jackson stood at the head of the group, his jaw tight and his eyes on a tree that had uprooted and crashed in front of the climbing bear. His gaze shifted to a cluster of vines hanging from the fallen tree's neighbor, and he crinkled his brow. The vines reared like cobras and struck at a large man behind the bear. The vines looped around his legs and hauled him off his feet. He swung upside down, yelling to his buddies and flailing his arms.

Jackson had unleashed his powers.

The bear roared his irritation as he lumbered over the fallen tree. Another tree bucked out of the ground and tipped on top of him, pinning him against the slender path. He thrashed wildly, and his strange minions gathered around to help.

If Jackson could delay the small army from reaching the top, he and the others would have a chance to flee through the woods.

"God, I adore that brilliant man," I muttered, then let the machete swing.

The bridge fluttered away from the cliffside like a leaf in the wind. I stepped up to the edge, my heart beating a rapid staccato in my throat as I watched pebbles fall away into the water below.

Far, far below.

I had no way of knowing how deep the river was here, but I didn't exactly have another option. Honestly, it felt like the last couple weeks had been one "only option" obstacle after another. I threw the machete into the water, hoping I'd be able to find it before the river swallowed it. Then I held my guidestone for good luck, and before I could second-guess myself, I leapt.

My stomach pirouetted as I began to free fall, clinging desperately to the relic. Wind whipped past me, and the shimmering surface of the river rose to meet me.

Too quickly.

Much too quickly.

Please protect me, I thought, squeezing my eyes shut and clawing at the relic. *Please.*

I sliced into the river feet first, parting the waters with little resistance. The water swallowed me whole, closing around me with an almost preternatural ease. I sank several feet without obstacle and slowed in the gentle current.

I didn't know if any of the bad guys had seen my jump, but I wasn't sticking around to find out. Thanks to Jackson's tree pileup, the bear and his minions were closer to the riverbanks than they were to my friends.

So, I sucked in water and opened my eyes.

The river stretched around me, glowing a beautiful orange-blue beneath the early morning sun. It was deeper than I expected, and the shining surface looked miles away as I gently touched down on the bottom. Mateo's machete had fallen blade first into the silt—a lucky break. I ripped it from the sand.

Holding the blade and the relic, swimming wasn't an option. But I felt in tune with the water. Like I'd become a part of it. Like it was an extension of me.

I pushed off from the ground and sailed forward like an astronaut walking on the moon. My big, bouncing steps moved me upstream faster than seemed possible. Where had this power been all my life? I'd always loved the water, but now it felt like it was danc-ing with me, lifting me high in a twirling hug, like it was overjoyed to see me. If this was a taste of what the relic's power could do, I was ready for it all.

Being underwater made it a bit harder to watch the curves of the river, such as my generic directions were. I kept my eyes on the sloping shallows so I could piece together a picture of the banks above without having to surface. After what I assumed to be two turns in the river's path, I started up the southern bank.

I emerged from the water and emptied my lungs before taking a deep breath of fresh air. Shoving the machete under my arm with the relic, I swiped a hand over my face to clear my eyes, then brushed a palm over the dark fluff on top of my head. My feet slogged in the shallows, the soft riverbed shifting erratically beneath my steps.

Thick jungle stretched before me. I glanced back at the other side of the river and found the cliff Sofia had told me to look for several yards down, so I turned and headed in that direction. If I entered the woods too soon, I could miss the lake, surrounded by that thick undergrowth.

As I reached the ideal spot on the bank parallel to the cliffs and turned to enter the woods, I heard a splash behind me.

My breath caught, and I twirled with the machete raised.

The river was calm and silent.

A fish? The handful of fish I'd seen on my trip weren't big enough to make a splash like that.

I waited another few seconds, but time wasn't exactly on my side. Not now, not ever.

I darted into the trees.

And ran.

The machete was an awesome tool. A few good thwacks as I ran, and I had a workable path. Small furry things skittered clear of my sprint, and birds took flight from the canopy.

I hadn't gone very far before I heard crashing footsteps be-hind me.

Shit.

They had noticed my exit.

And they'd sent someone to find me.

I gritted my teeth and put on a burst of speed, ignoring the branches whipping my face and limbs. I hadn't made it this far to only make it this far.

The tree line ended so abruptly that I tripped over my own feet in surprise. I landed hard on my hands and knees, the relic rolling away into shallow water and the machete skittering through the rocks.

Lifting my head, I stared over a lake too pristine and too flawlessly turquoise to seem real.

Thin, wispy fog hung over the surface as if it were smoking, and the thick jungle hugged its sides so tight that drooping branches and hanging vines kissed the crystalline surface.

I scrambled to my feet, stunned by the hidden beauty.

This had to be the place.

Something large trampled the underbrush behind me.

I turned just in time to see a hulking, malformed man leap from the forest, his meaty fists bigger than my head.

Even through pure, unadulterated terror, Uncle Alec's training kicked in. Muscle memory. *Learn the right moves under pressure,* he'd promised, *and you'll fall back on them time and again.*

I lunged, ducking the man's raised arm. My smaller size and speed allowed me to spin around him, while he stumbled forward without anywhere for his fists to land.

He looked unfinished. Like all his skin had melted and then hardened out of place. Beneath his plain white t-shirt, his bulky muscles were lumpy and misshapen.

He stomped around with an irritated roar, seeking me with a singular eye in the center of his forehead. In place of a nose was a sunken socket bisected by a gnarly bundle of red, raw scar tissue.

He roared again and grabbed for me.

I ducked his deadly hug and swiped the machete off the ground. No way I could take on this gargantuan beast without a weapon.

He swung a tree-trunk arm, and I juked sideways, just out of reach. His size made him awkward and slow.

Adrenaline put a maniacal grin on my face. Time to do Uncle Alec proud.

I arced the machete, catching the cyclops in his shoulder with the tip. Blood blossomed on his sliced t-shirt, but not enough to stop his rampage.

He grunted, then rounded on me with another punch.

This time, when I tried to dodge, he faked me out.

He backhanded the side of my head, hard as a brick to the face.

I fell sideways, barely managing to keep a hold on the machete as I hit the rocky beach. A warbling cry was forced from my lungs as my shoulder hit stone.

Then the cyclops was there, bearing down on me.

I didn't have time to stop and think or calculate a plan.

I just swung the machete in a wide, forceful slash.

The blade dug into the man's head with a gross, meaty thwack.

Surprise made his eye go wide.

Hot blood spurted down on me, and I released the machete to roll out of the way as he keeled over.

I clambered to my feet and inched toward him on wobbly knees. Breathing hard, I moved to check that he was dead, but I made the mistake of licking my lips. Spatters of his blood teased my growling stomach. Beneath the buzzing adrenaline of his final moments, I tasted sadness, salty as tears, and had to pause, choking on a sorrow that wasn't mine. But I recognized the sense of alienation, of otherness, and had to hug myself as I inched closer to him.

The machete was buried in his skull like a knife left in a shoulder of ham. Blood pooled around his lumpy head, and he stared out over the turquoise lake with a glassy, unblinking eye. I heaved a sad sigh for him, made empathetic by my brief glimpse into his head. He'd chosen the wrong side in hopes of finding a new tribe after the Summum Malum decimated the female population of his clan. He wanted a place where he fit, where his appearance wouldn't ostracize him.

I couldn't fault him that, but I could fault him for his choice of friends. And some of them might be on their way to me now.

Sparing him one last glance, I murmured, "May you find family again in limbo."

Stepping away from the cyclops' body, I listened to the surrounding forest, trying to make out any sounds that didn't belong. The birds still sang, and the bugs still chirped. Wind rustled the leaves. But I didn't hear any sign of another pursuer.

The others must be occupied by my friends. By the looks of things when I'd left, Jackson had plenty of creative ideas for detaining them.

Leaving the machete, I picked up the relic and tucked it into the curve of my arm.

Then I dove into the lake.

Piercing cold water took my breath away. I gasped at the intense difference in temperature and barely managed to not choke as I switched from air to liquid. The throbbing pain in my head from the dead man's backhand vanished immediately as my skin prickled with cold.

It was just as brilliant blue beneath the water. I could see far into the clear depths of the lake. No fish. No plants. No creatures of any kind.

Only the faintest swirling at the very bottom, dead center.

El torbellino.

Shoving aside my rising fear, I began to swim.

Down.

Down.

Down.

Like sinking to the bottom of our pool, my head ringing from flash grenades. But I was in control now. Or so I hoped.

The weight of the water pressed in on all sides the farther I descended. Eventually, I had to slow. My breaths became shallow, harder to drag into my lungs, as if I'd left the breathable atmosphere for the thin layer of nothing before the edge of the universe.

I struggled to get enough oxygen. The relic became much heavier in my arms, as if it had taken on the weight of the passing depths. Refusing to let it go, I shoved it against my belly with both arms and let it drag me down.

This is what I came for. No stopping now.

The water began to swirl around me like a brisk wind. It caught me broadside and sent me flipping head over heels, my entire body wrapped around the increasingly heavy relic.

Squeezing my eyes closed, I let the edges of the whirlpool grab me and yank me into its dizzying pattern.

My flailing guidestone burned like dry ice when the frigid water pressed it against my chest on my next dizzying turn. As if in response, the relic pulsed, letting out an invisible wave of sheer, supercharged energy that shook me to my core. A single wave, as if it were a car that didn't want to start on a cold morning.

I let out my breath and sank further into the whirlpool. My steady rotation kicked up a notch, and the water rushed past me so quickly I couldn't catch my breath. I had to close my eyes because I was moving too fast to focus on anything.

It was so heavy.

So cold.

So fast.

Can't breathe.

Oh God, they didn't plan on a half-starved girl doing this. I'm going to die before this thing activates.

I felt like I was spiraling down a massive drain, clinging to a rock instead of a flotation device. Faster and faster, I spun until I was nauseous. There was no way to breathe here, and black edges crept into my vision.

Wake up! I screamed at the relic. It dug into the skin of my belly, and my fingers gripped it so tightly I could feel my brittle nails shattering on the surface.

The relic pulsed again. Then twice more.

A low hum powered through it and entered my body.

Please, please, please.

I thought I felt static at my fingertips, but it could have been the oxygen depleting from my blood. Tingles. Dying nerve endings. Bile rose in my throat, jostled by the turbulence.

I sucked uselessly at the water.

It couldn't end like this. Didn't the relic want to be free? To be alive again? To inhabit its true match?

It had to help me.

I heaved it to my lips and let them brush its sides as I whispered, "Please, help me."

The relic shuddered, startling my eyes open. The blue stone began to swirl, like a cerulean fog was trapped inside. Then I tasted it. Icy refreshment over my tongue, with a slight mineral complexity. I gulped it like water in the desert. But though it drove away the bile and the nausea and sparked a bit of hope in my chest, it didn't help me breath. It didn't chase away the vignette around my vision.

Please, please, pl—

And I knew nothing more.

30
WITH GREAT POWER

POINTS OF LIGHT HOVERED ABOVE MY NOSE.

Smaller flecks drifted in the distance.

The shining dots spread, flickering out, into the surrounding blackness.

Brightening. Dimming.

Twinkling.

Like stars.

A sky full of stars.

Wait…

I've been here before.

I've done this already.

No. This is different. I am more than alive.

I floated on my back, exactly as I'd awakened in the lab tank, but I wasn't restrained. I waved my arms like wings, gliding through cold water that almost felt like static against my skin. There was no heavy haze over my senses, no drugged feeling. I stretched my body like a starfish, and every inch of me—every sinew, every bone, every muscle, every square inch of my skin felt powerful.

My heartbeat was strong in my ears, like the boisterous ticking of an antique clock. In the background, a gentle, steady *whoosh* summoned an unwanted memory.

Heavy.

Sodden.

Trapped.

No. I shook off the reminder of the night I met Jackson, the night I fled for my life and everything changed. Then and now merged in my head in an awkward dance, making it hard for me to separate the two.

I'd been lost in a total wall of darkness then. The lights—the *stars*—I'd seen had merely been my vision reacting to total sensory deprivation.

Slowly, my vision returned completely. The lights of the present rearranged themselves, and I realized they weren't twinkling stars, but the sparkle of sunlight glinting off the surface of the lake. The brilliant, breathtaking turquoise water shone as if set aflame.

Light.

Strong.

Absolute freedom.

I'd never be trapped again.

I pinwheeled my arms to right myself in the water and took a look around through eyes incredibly attuned to the underwater world. Everything was crisp, the colors vibrant. The whirlpool still raged around me like an underwater tornado, but my body had become the eye of the storm, untouched in a calm bubble at the heart of the spiraling death trap.

Had I done that?

No way.

The relic may have activated and flooded me with my new powers, but I didn't know how to use any of them.

The relic.

The reminder sent me scrambling to find the stone. I'd lost it in the chaos of nearly drowning inside an underwater hurricane.

My darting eyes found the relic resting benignly on the bottom of the lake. I dove for it and picked it up, surprised to find it was featherlight. As I brought it up, the whirlpool bowed out around me, wherever the relic moved too close.

The relic had parted the whirlpool with whatever conscious-ness or grain of power it had kept stored inside itself.

I held it ahead of me, laughing as the whirlpool's bubbles split open around its secret forcefield. Keeping it aloft in one hand, I swam forward. The vortex split open like a curtain around my body, a few stray bubbles tickling my feet and legs. I realized then that I'd lost my boots in the whirlpool, too.

At least I still had my clothes and my guidestone.

I left *el torbellino* behind, swimming faster with one arm than I'd ever been able to swim with two. The lake felt like an extension of my body, or my soul, or maybe both. My previous abilities beneath the water were nothing compared to this new sixth sense. I was one with the water in a way that I didn't fully understand.

I breached the surface into the sunlight and took a breath of air without any kind of transition. On the shore, I could see the strange, melty cyclops' lumpy form still lying where I left him, ma-chete sticking out of his skull like a flower growing through a crack in the sidewalk.

When I swam for the bank, I did so with astonishing grace. My body sliced through the water so easily, it felt as if I floated on air.

I was a dolphin, a shark, a predator.

Nothing could stop me.

Well… except the fact that I had no clue how to use any of my new powers. I didn't even know the extent of them. But if the bear Shifter and his buddies got in my way, I'd jump at the opportunity to test them out.

I retrieved the machete from the dead man, then quickly re-traced my steps through the forest. I was worried I'd get lost and be unable to find the river, but after a couple yards, I realized I could smell the river. I zeroed in on the trail like a drug-sniffing hound.

Water doesn't even have *a scent*, I thought, shaking my head as I followed the trail through the woods. But it did for me. The river smelled like algae, sharp minerals, and fresh fish. From half a mile away, I could smell it so intensely that I tasted the robust flavors on my tongue.

I reached the river without incident and splashed into the shallows, still toting my machete and the relic. The river welcomed me like an old friend, the sloped bank falling away between my bare feet, mud and silt squeezing between my toes. Again, I swam double-time, even with a one-armed stroke. And I realized that if I swam just beneath the surface, instead of trying to keep my head above, I moved even *faster*. If I kept this up, the enemy alts might not ever see me coming. I could get all my friends on a boat, use my powers to somehow increase our sailing speed, make sure they couldn't catch us. The water was mine. In it, we'd all be safe. But I had to find my little crew first.

The terrain around the library pillar was deserted. The collapsed bridge dangled against the cliff wall, and Jackson's pile of trees on the cliffside path had turned into a falling hazard. Tree trunks were piled high in a blockade, but several had slipped right over the edge and plummeted to the rocky bank below.

I could only guess that my companions had taken off into the woods to head back toward the village, where they'd have more weapons, more opportunity to fight back, and boats at their disposal. I assumed the bear and his minions had lost track of me and backtracked the way they came, given that Jackson's barrier was still intact.

Good. That meant my friends had time to put distance between them.

Instead of finding a way up the cliff and into the trees, I just kept swimming and cut the trip in half.

I smelled the first hints of smoke before I caught sight of the village. Under the morning sunlight, the devastation looked stark and haunting. I hated to see the bodies still lying where they fell, especially knowing that Sofia and Mateo had delayed laying them to rest because of me and the relic.

If only the chips had fallen differently.

At first look, I didn't see anybody moving—friend or foe. Until I scanned the docks. A giant brown bear stood on hind legs, his beady gaze trained on the sea. From this distance, I could see the scars the water clan leader had mentioned. An angry red stripe of bare skin circled his barrel torso and ran up his neck to his snout. A football-sized stone rested by his massive paws; the surface was smooth, colored with a marbled mix of red and orange.

I knew that stone.

I knew it intimately.

My sister Cyndra wore an identical, miniaturized piece around her neck as her guidestone.

It was the fire relic.

Cold shock doused my chest, freezing me on the water. I ducked beneath to study him, leaving only the top of my head and my eyes above the surface.

How was this possible? Cyn had obviously obtained her relic powers. She'd set the lab on fire singlehanded. So why did this guy have it? What had he done to my sister to get it?

Maybe it was how he'd beaten me here. Had he used it in some way to find the water relic's location? I knew he hadn't followed me.

Carl! The Shadow inside him hadn't seemed concerned about me leading him to the relic. He hadn't asked a single question about it. Because they had another way to find it... A damn demon bear with my sister's empty relic.

The scarred bear was framed by several boats, all of them on fire, billowing dark smoke. Fresh fires. The boats hadn't started collapsing just yet.

Then I knew. Even in the short time I'd known Jackson, I'd come to understand how his brain operated. He'd taken our friends out on a boat and destroyed all the others to keep the enemy from following. His strategic mind constantly impressed me.

Could bears swim? He stood stock-still on the dock, his fur dry, but he was totally alone.

Which meant his minions had probably gone into the water.

Sinking out of sight, I put on an extra burst of speed, heading for the delta where the river met the ocean. If I concentrated, I could sense the chugging boat motor ahead. I rerouted for it, whispering a plea to the Priestesses, to my guardian angel Lana in the afterlife, to anyone in planes beyond who could hear me to keep my friends safe.

The underside of the boat came into sight, and a split second later, I realized I'd been right—I wasn't alone in the water.

Several yards away, between me and the vessel, half a dozen bodies swam on a clear trajectory for the motorboat.

I surfaced to yell out a warning, but it wasn't necessary. Jackson stood at the prow, one foot braced on the railing as he pulled the pin on a grenade. He hauled his arm back and let the grenade fly right into the enemy's ranks.

Shit.

I didn't know what kind of damage a grenade could do underwater, but I didn't really want to find out.

I dove as deep and as fast as possible.

The grenade exploded with a strangely quiet *pop*. A compression wave flowed past me, shoving me a few yards deeper into the ocean. Though it felt like someone had slammed me against a wall, I came out of it unscathed—except I'd dropped the relic and the machete. Unfortunately, they couldn't be my priority right now.

My friends were still in danger.

Rolling to my back, I searched the waves for the forest of enemy arms and legs with my perfect, almost telescopic underwater vision. I could see *everything*.

One body floated listlessly down into the murky depths. Another cyclops. Two more unidentifiable foes were a bloody mess too akin to raw meat to stare at for long.

But three had escaped, not only unscathed, but not even slowed. They were almost to the hull of the boat.

They were... odd. Clearly humanoid, with two arms, two legs, and a normal-sized head. But their hands weren't quite right. They had four spindly fingers on each hand, each finger tipped by a flat disc. I couldn't quite place what they reminded me of.

I glanced down at the relic. It had already disappeared into the deep.

It would have to wait.

I swam full speed, angling up, hoping against hope that I could beat those alt traitors to the boat. Did Jackson know the grenade hadn't killed them all?

The creatures latched onto the underside of the boat and began to climb with their fingers like they were sticky suction cups.

I swam so hard my limbs burned.

I didn't breathe.

I couldn't.

The three creatures surfaced, only their legs visible now.

My heart hammered against my rib cage, and I sucked in a desperate breath as I broke through the surface and screamed, "Watch out!"

Water poured down my face and into my eyes. I swiped it away, just in time to see one of the alts reach over the railing and grab Sofia from behind. He shoved against the hull and hauled her overboard, their bodies splashing into the water together.

A gunshot rang out over the water, and another of the spindly-fingered monsters splashed back into the water. Almost simultaneously, Mateo skewered a second one with his *abuelito's* whalebone spear, yelling his sister's name.

I ducked below and swam for all I was worth. A splash bubbled up from the back of the boat, and Mateo dove with me, his spear in one hand as he looked around wildly for Sofia. We caught sight of her at the same time—limbs splayed, face down, sinking rapidly.

The alt that had yanked her into the water was nowhere to be found.

Please be okay, I prayed, clawing at the water in a desperate need to reach her. *Please be okay.*

Mateo reached her first and looped an arm around her waist,

dragging her to the surface as I caught up. We breached together, and I reached for Sofia, brushing her hair away from her face.

She was nearly unrecognizable. Her skin had turned red and bubbled as if she'd been burned. Something greenish, like mucous, clung to her eyelashes. I touched it with my fingertip and hissed when it sizzled my flesh like acid.

Frantic, I splashed water over the goo to no avail, then gathered a thick lock of her hair to use as a makeshift towel to wipe it away.

As I desperately tried to rub off the foul acid, Mateo jammed his fingers against Sofia's neck.

An interminable moment passed before his face crumpled.

"She's gone," he moaned. "She's dead."

31
BOILING POINT

RAGE FLOODED THROUGH ME LIKE A TIDAL WAVE. I GRITTED my teeth against stinging tears of fury.

Sofia's beautiful, ravaged face could not even look upon the stars as the ocean lapped at her hair. Her swollen eyes were closed forever. The playful, friendly way she'd called me *hermosa—beautiful*—had boosted my spirits. She'd buoyed my sagging self-confidence. Sofia was one of the good ones. The kind of girl who lifted up everyone around her because it brought her joy.

Now she was dead.

Because of me.

Because of the relic.

The water around me began to boil.

Actually boil, as if my body were a flame around a boiling pot.

Mateo hissed through his teeth and clutched Sofia to his chest, kicking away from the epicenter of the heat.

"Ellis?" he said worriedly, his voice still thick with tears. They glimmered like diamonds on his long dark eyelashes. He looked so much like his sister.

My heart cracked in two.

"Get her on the boat, Matty." I didn't recognize the low rasp in my voice. I flexed my fingers, and the bubbles expanded, bursting and spitting heat with loud, hissing pops. "Now."

His dark eyes widened, but he obeyed. He swam backward

with his one free arm, headed for the back of the boat where Jackson waited.

I tried to restrain the boiling bubbles, keep them close, but they were already loose, fueled by my fury. Beside the boat, Mateo glanced back at the bubble's widening ring as he fought to tread water with Sofia's dead weight in his shaking arms.

"Hurry!" I said, as Jackson pulled Sofia's limp body onto the vinyl.

KitKat put her paws on the stern by the motor and mewled urgently at Mateo. He grabbed the ladder and began to climb, KitKat tugging at his wetsuit with her mouth. But the racing bubbles were faster. Mateo flopped to the deck with a cry, holding his red, scalded foot.

Jackson looked between Mateo, me, and the water, eyes wide and almost desperate. He held out a hand to me over the boiling sea. "Come on, Ell. Let's get out of here."

I heard the begging note. I saw fear pull his concerned frown into a sour shape. I saw Mateo wincing at his burns and felt a twinge of guilt. But I also saw Sofia's body laid on the bench.

"No." The word bubbled over my lips like water in a pot.

KitKat put her front paws on the railing again and gave me a scared little whine that almost broke through my fury. I could stop this before it went too far. Take Jackson's hand, crawl onto the boat to hug KitKat, and drive away from this awful place forever.

But I wouldn't.

I turned away from them both. They'd saved me too many times already. I wasn't helpless anymore, and I wasn't going to let those alt traitors get away with this.

I closed my eyes and sank below the water.

It closed over my head, momentarily enhancing the gentle rumble of the boat's motor to a roar. With a little concentration, I banished it—totally in control of my enhanced hearing. Finally, in control. The water was mine. Those alt traitors had perverted it, killed Sofia, one of the ocean's daughters. The water was supposed to protect her. *I* was supposed to protect her. In that, I'd failed, but I owned this sea, and if I couldn't use it to save, I could use it to avenge.

Spreading my arms, I hovered on the water, breathing in and out, letting the ocean fill me. Fill my lungs. Fill my nose. Fill all the dark crevices and cracks I'd earned since the day the government tore me from my uncle's home.

There were five presences in the water near me, fleeing the edges of my boiling ring, never turning back.

Two of them were marine life. My new sixth sense said they "belonged."

Three of them did not belong.

Three of them had hunted down my friends.

Three of them were complicit in the murder of an entire race.

Oh God. Matty's the only one left now.

Don't get distracted.

I breathed deep.

And I screamed. Screamed for the atrocities committed here. Screamed for Sofia. Screamed for all Mateo had lost.

The vibrations became three spirals of hot water, whipping like corkscrews toward the alien presences. The whirlpools acted like hands and shoved my enemies, throwing them above the surface of the ocean.

I kicked for the surface and broke through, treading water as I admired the waterspouts that held the bear's evil henchmen.

The distant boiling spouts loomed twelve feet over the surface, spiraling like mini tornadoes wrapping watery tendrils around the evil bastards who'd hurt my friends. I had no idea how I'd manifested them, outside of my obvious anger. If there was a craft to it, I was ignorant. I'd done it automatically, reactionary, and it felt damn good.

I swam a little closer, hoping to let the monsters see me, but I didn't want to leave the boat unguarded. I couldn't see their eyes, just thrashing limbs, but I could hear the screams and imagined their faces puffing and blistering like Sofia's.

Then, with a downward thrust of my fists, I dragged them to the bottom of the ocean.

And held them there until the amplified sounds of their thrashing went silent.

I don't know how long I treaded water, letting their bodies grow cold as the bubbles dissipated around me. After a time, I heard a splash in the lukewarm water, and I sensed KitKat paddling behind me. Her furry nose snuffled at my neck, and then her teeth latched on to my t-shirt and began to pull.

Releasing the cooled waterspouts, I turned to the bobcat and her adorable efforts to pull me to the boat. "What are you doing?" I tickled her under the chin.

She cocked her head and gave me a look that said, *Get out of the ocean, dummy.*

Resigned, I fell into pace with her and returned to the boat.

What else was there left to do?

It was Mateo who met us at the ladder. His eyes were bloodshot, and tears had joined the salty tracks of ocean water on his face. His hands were strong and sure as he guided me onto the boat. I climbed onto the slippery deck, where I crawled onto a bench and collapsed against the railing.

Tired.

So tired now.

Jackson stood at the front of the boat, binoculars pressed to his face.

"The bear's gone." He lowered the binoculars to glance back at us. "Ran when things got hot."

Neither of us replied. Mateo was cross-legged on the deck, holding Sofia's hand while KitKat gave him a cowlick with her kisses. I stared at them, my stomach in knots.

We won.

I should be glad we won.

Instead, I felt empty.

Jackson spoke again. "What happened out there? Where did you send the rest of them?"

"They're dead," I said, voice hollow as I met Jackson's gaze. "I drowned them. It was better than they deserved."

Something flashed in Jackson's eyes.

Something I didn't want to dwell on. So, I averted my gaze, choosing instead to stare at Sofia so that I would never forget what they did to her.

What the Summum Malum did to her.

What they did to Carl. What they tried to do to me. What they did to Mateo's tribe. All for my relic.

It was always the Summum Malum.

Everything led back to them.

The motor kicked into gear, and Jackson silently steered us back to shore.

Mateo brushed Sofia's wet hair away from her red, mutilated face. I felt achingly empty inside. I'd accomplished what we came here to do: I got my relic, which I still needed to retrieve from the bottom of the ocean. Got my powers. Got the confidence to use them. But at what cost?

I *knew* I wasn't the catalyst for the bear Shifter's attack of the water race. Maybe my guilt over being too late to save them was exaggerated or misplaced. Maybe I was carrying the guilt out of some hero complex I hadn't even realized I'd internalized after all the years of Uncle Alec teaching me and my sisters that we were special, chosen to one day save the world.

My guilt for Sofia, though? That wasn't misplaced.

I wasn't in time to save her.

Me.

I lost her.

"I'm sorry about your foot," I croaked to Mateo around the knot in my throat. It wasn't all I was sorry for, but it was a start, and it was all I could manage to get out.

"Don't be. Just as long as you burned them worse," he said, but any malice he'd intended was missing. He only sounded weary.

He pulled the afflicted foot into his lap, resting across his left thigh, and tested the fattest blister with a delicate poke.

"You need to bandage it." Jackson's voice was clipped.

He didn't look at either of us as he pulled his first aid kit from his pack and tossed the burn cream and some gauze to Mateo.

"You're lucky," Jackson said. "You could have died, too."

I balked. "I wouldn't have let that—"

"Oh, yeah?" His head snapped my way for the first time. "Did you 'let' it burn his foot then?"

"No," I grumbled, at the same moment he said, "No, you lost control, all because you got angry. He's lucky."

I swallowed bile. Swallowed my pride. He wasn't wrong, but I couldn't help but think, *You threw a grenade in the water with me. I'm lucky, too.*

But that wasn't worth arguing over. He hadn't known I was there. What I was really upset about was that I'd probably lost him, too. Not to death, but to his moral compass. To his fear. Right as I'd thought I'd started breaking through his fear of his abilities. Right as I let myself hope that my world could become our world, and we might get a shot at traversing it together as something more, turning whatever it was that we had into something more substantial.

I glanced at him standing at the wheel, stiff and awkward. I cared for him. He was probably the first person outside my family I'd ever cared for. Just a smile from him could make my heart skip a beat. The sound of his voice sent shivers up my spine, and the way he called me Ell could warm the coldest corners of my heart.

But the way he'd looked at me just now…

He was scared of me. Or maybe just what I was capable of. Or maybe my tendency to cross his invisible lines. Hitting cops in the back of the head. Drowning fleeing adversaries that had already fled a fight. Even if they'd started it.

The same morality that had urged Jackson to follow me into the desert had now turned against me. But did he have the right? He'd freed me from the injustices of that prison, but he'd also acted as a warden. He wasn't perfect, either. He rejected his ties to my world, hadn't lived in it, so how could he have any final say on how justice was dealt out among alts? If I was honest, I wasn't sure I had any claim to that authority either. But what was done was done, and I hadn't acted without cause. He had to see that.

But he feared my strength. Women weren't meant to single-handedly drown three grown men without touching them.

He'd never seemed to care that I was no longer the "pretty one," but he didn't want a warrior woman, either. Didn't want an alt. Hell, he didn't even want to *be* an alt.

If I was strong, if I struck back at my enemies, I'd never be good enough for him.

I'd just be the broken girl he dragged from a tank of water in a secret underground military facility who ruined his life the moment she got stronger and tasted independence.

The ruined, corrupted girl with powers he didn't understand—powers he hated as much as he hated his own.

Hate and shunning came with the territory of being an alt, but we never stopped fighting for our clan. I hoped Jackson would come around, that he'd join my new hodgepodge group, but if he didn't, well, I still had a war to win.

It felt wrong to walk around in a pair of shoes taken from one of the dozens of dead we couldn't bury. But I didn't have a choice. There wasn't time, and we had no way of knowing if the bear would circle back with more of his buddies.

But Mateo couldn't leave without giving his *abuelito* and Sofia the sendoff they deserved. I understood—I'd never have been able to leave my family lying alone, either.

Jackson and I helped him salvage what he called "palm coffins" from a storage shed with minimal fire damage. Mostly, the boat-like structures made of giant palm leaves were still intact, though a dark sheen of wispy smoke marks covered their sides.

They resembled giant baskets with several handles looped into the woven leaves. *Abuelito* went into one, wrapped carefully in his blood-soaked cloak, while Sofia went into another, still in her wetsuit.

Mateo climbed a palm tree at the edge of the water and cut down several leaves to lay over their bodies.

"The *bruja*, our priestess," he explained, "would wrap them better. Like a blanket of palm leaves. And she had a special tincture to smooth their transition to the afterlife." He reached between the leaves and brushed his fingers over his grandfather's eyes. "I'm not trained in that." His voice cracked as he shifted away from that palm coffin and carefully tucked more leaves around Sofia.

I put a hand on his shoulder, but I couldn't find the right words to say. The water race's culture was abstract to me. Did Matty believe that without the tincture, his sister and grandfather wouldn't make it to the afterlife? What could I possible say to help ease his pain if that were the case?

Using the handles, we carried *Abuelito* and Sofia onto the boat. Mateo took the wheel, stone-faced with grief. KitKat stayed glued to his side, rumbling a chorus of comforting purrs as she wound herself in loops around his legs. Jackson and I sat across from each other on opposite sides of the boat, the bodies between us.

It was a silent ride.

Once out in the open water, Mateo and Jackson carefully heaved the palm coffins over the side and set them on the water.

"They're made to sink," Mateo told us. "In death, we return to the water."

Water trickled into the open-top coffins, surrounding the bodies in a gentle hug. Bringing them home.

Mateo began to sing in Spanish.

He had a smooth, beautiful tenor. I didn't understand the words, but I could sense the emotions behind them. His voice rose and fell, as musical as water rushing over stone.

Still singing, he looked back at me and offered me his hand.

I laced my fingers with his and stepped up to join him at the boat's edge. He serenaded Sofia and *Abuelito* as we watched them sink into the ocean.

When Mateo's song trailed off, he broke down.

I caught him as he collapsed, and the two of us crumpled neatly to the deck of the boat where I held him as he cried, anguish pouring from the crack in his broken heart.

He squeezed my arm too tight, but I didn't flinch until his doe eyes looked through me and he said in a ragged whisper, "I can't feel *la tela*, Ellis. I can't feel them. I can't hear them anymore."

I hugged him tight in trembling arms and bit down hard on my tongue, but the silent tears came anyway, spilling into his thick hair. He shook and gasped for air, no matter how I held on. And then KitKat licked my shoulder and nudged me with her head. It was time for me to step aside. It was her turn to try.

She wiggled into the loop of his embrace, climbing into his lap to press her entire furry form to his torso. With fat paws on his shoulders, she licked his tears away and purred to him as his fingers made waves in her fur. He finally began to calm, cooing to her as he rubbed his forehead against hers. Some of what crossed his lips was nonsense love language, and some was Spanish, but I thought I caught something like, "*La tela* lives on in the sea." Then they locked eyes, bobcat and boy, and Mateo sucked in a breath, eyes widening. "And in you?"

KitKat cocked her head, and Mateo cracked the smallest of smiles.

I left them in their quiet, sweet moment, with a silent, enigmatic Jackson at the helm, and dove into the water to look for the relic.

I found it easily, even in the dark. It called to me, broadcasting its location through the water. We were connected, and I could sense it wasn't entirely empty, but had given as much of itself to me as it could.

Mateo's grandfather's spear stuck in the thick sand only a few feet away. I pried them both from their nests in the ocean floor.

Back up top, Mateo accepted the spear from me with a subdued, "Thanks," then sank back onto the bench beside KitKat. Jackson drove us back to shore.

There was no pomp and circumstance for Mateo when it came to leaving his home. He packed a few of his belongings from his undisturbed tent, and some of his sister's things as well, and then the four of us trekked back through the woods to the stolen SUV.

Even though I was smaller than Mateo, he insisted on riding in the back with KitKat, where he promptly fell asleep with her on his lap.

I passed out not long after we pulled out onto the road and slept hard, and thankfully with no dreams. When I awoke, the sun was starting to set, and the rural areas had started to give way to more populated places with restaurants and grocery stores lit by electric signs.

I rubbed my eyes and straightened in the seat, twisting my neck to try to stretch out the crick from sleeping hunched against the window.

"Where are we?" I asked Jackson.

"Guatemala City." He tapped his phone screen. "Almost to the hotel."

"A hotel?" I perked up. "With beds? And a shower?"

He gave me a wry smile that didn't quite meet his eyes. "Presumably."

The Colonial Maya was housed in a large stone building in the downtown area that looked more like a government facility than a hotel. But the place was cheap for a private room, even if it was small for housing two beds. We were able to smuggle KitKat in through a side door, and then each of us—minus the bobcat—took turns washing off in the shared bathroom.

Taking my turn last, I stood in the small shower under flaming hot water for a long time. My joints ached, and the car ride had left me feeling nauseous. I'd hoped that a shower might make me feel better and ease the burn in my muscles from all the traveling and surviving I'd been doing lately. But by the time my skin and hair were scrubbed clean, I still felt like crap.

Worst of all, I was still hungry.

Jackson and Mateo were both missing when I got back to the room, but KitKat was curled up on the twin bed. The only clean clothes I had left was the pink and white polka-dotted sundress, so I yanked it over my head. It hung halfway to my knees, and the thin material clung to my shoulders and waist, then flared out around my hips. Stomach rumbling, I swished the skirt a few times in a futile attempt to feel "pretty," but it didn't work. At least the hand-woven slip-on shoes I'd taken from the village would look cute with the dress.

My heart beat like a rabbit's as I grabbed one of the complimentary snack bars out of a small basket by the coffee machine. I peeled back the wrapper, and the moment I smelled that mix of peanuts, sugar, and dried fruit, revulsion turned my stomach.

Trying to convince myself it was a Pavlovian response, I cracked open my mouth and inched the bar through my teeth, holding my breath. I nibbled off the corner, and the salt of the peanut smacked my taste buds first—intense as eating straight out of the shaker. I raked my tongue against the roof of my mouth, and the cloying sweetness of the chocolate punched me next. I felt the grit of sugar crystals between my teeth.

It had been too long. That was it. My brain just wasn't used to processing strong flavors.

I'd already pulverized the bite, so I tried to force it down my throat and gagged instead. Stumbling along the wall into the bathroom, I tossed the bar in the trash can and then hugged the toilet, where the bite plunked into the water, along with half my stomach acid.

Still the vampire life for me. Those Mayans had corrupted the relic (and therefore me) forever.

I flushed the toilet with a sigh, biting my lip to keep it from trembling. Then I collapsed on the bed beside KitKat, burying my face in the pillow. A sharp pain lanced up my leg, and I gasped, bolting upright.

The bite wound. I'd completely forgotten about it.

It looked bad. The two red pimples had turned into two small ulcers. The darkened sores in their centers had grown three times as big, and the edges seeped watery blood.

"What the…" I poked around at the painful lesions. "That can't be good."

KitKat huffed her agreement.

"I'll ask Jackson about it when he gets back," I promised her as I lifted the sheets to let her crawl in with me. I curled up beside her and relished the feel of the pillow under my head.

I never even heard Jackson and Mateo return.

The next time I opened my eyes, sunlight was filtering through the small window over my bed. I could hear the hustle and bustle of the city outside through the glass. I blinked away the vestiges of sleep and reached out for KitKat, but she was gone.

"She went with Mateo," Jackson said quietly.

I rolled over to find him sitting at the edge of the other mattress, fully dressed in his army fatigues. Watching me.

"He's driving her to a rural area to hunt," Jackson added. "I asked him to."

"Oh. Good." I stretched beneath the fuchsia blanket, surprised to find that even a good night's sleep hadn't made my aches go away. My joints felt like they'd grown five times their normal size. Eyeing him again, I asked, "Why are you wearing your army clothes and your dog tags?"

Someone pounded on the door.

"Agent Hunter?" a voice called. "Special Forces. We're here for the girl."

32
CUFFED

I SHOT UP IN A TANGLE OF BLANKETS.

The military had found me, and there was no back exit.

Could I jump out the window? We were on the second floor, so the fall couldn't be worse than the hundred-foot drop I'd taken into the river yesterday. Right?

Knees on the pillow, I tugged open the curtains, ready to break the glass with my elbow if I had to.

No good.

The window was barred.

"How can we get out of here?" I hissed to Jackson, turning to entreat his strategic brain.

I couldn't go back to that awful place. It was run or die trying. No way I was letting those soldiers lock me up again.

The soldiers… who'd used Jackson's name.

He saw the revelation hit my expression, and he just looked back, the skin between his brows pinched tight.

The truth rammed through my chest like a sword, and I sagged on the blade, my head swimming, nausea tearing through me until I doubled over.

I'd seen the look on his face yesterday after I killed those alts.

I'd heard the disapproval in his silence after the fight.

But I never thought it would mean this. Never thought it would drive him back into his fatigues, ready to go back to work.

"You did this." My blood ran cold. I bunched my fingers in the blankets to steady myself as the bed seemed to rock beneath me. "You called them."

Jackson reached the bed's edge in three strides. "I'm sorry, Ell."

"Don't call me that." My hand tightened into a fist on the comforter.

His hand drifted toward mine. "This is for the best. You'll be safer."

"Safer?" I swatted his fingers away, hiding my agony with anger. "Safer in the place that *almost killed me?*"

The soldier on the other side of the door pounded this time, shaking the wood in the frame. "Agent Hunter. Open the door."

"You have no idea how to control your powers." Jackson tossed a worried glance at the jiggling handle. "Dr. Craig said he'll help you."

"Oh, Dr. Craig said?" I snapped, throwing the covers aside so I could slide out of bed. "Your precious mentor said he'd take care of me, keep me 'safe,' and you just blindly trust him?"

Jackson stood, too, his mouth a hard line. "Of course I do. He's never lied to me."

"He put me in the *tank*, Jackson!" I shrieked so loud spit flew out my mouth. The venom in my tone surprised even me. "I heard him, when I was underwater, with my ability. The tank was his idea. He failed to tell you that, didn't he?"

Jackson shook himself like a dog that'd had its nose smacked. "What? No. No, you misunderstood something."

"Oh! Yeah, sure. I'm the liar here. *I'm* the idiot." I scoffed and jabbed my finger at his chest. "I kept my mouth shut because I know he's like a father to you and I wanted to believe you when you said he wasn't the enemy. But you know the truth, Jackson. I'm just another experiment to Dr. Craig, just like I am to the rest of them! You know they'll strap me down and treat me like an animal. And you're offering me back up to them on a silver platter. Why? Because you're scared of me?"

Jackson sighed and raked a hand over his face. "I'm not scared of you, Ellis."

"No, you're scared of things you don't understand." I was seething now, unconcerned with getting him back on my side. Furious tears burned my eyes. "You're afraid of yourself and your 'evil' abilities, and you're putting your bullshit on me."

"That's not true."

"It is," I said simply.

Bam. Bam. Bam.

"Agent Hunter! Open the door or we'll break it down!"

"I won't go without a fight." I assumed a boxer's stance. "If they kill me, it's on you."

"They're not going to kill you," Jackson said, exasperated.

"Right. Sure. Not like someone tried drowning me in there already." Sick of the anticipation, I slipped my feet into the flats I'd taken from the water race village, straightened my ridiculously girly sundress, then stalked to the door.

I threw it wide and punched the soldier in the face.

He was eight feet tall and built like the Titanic. Army Kong! He had a bandage on his wrist. *I needed KitKat!* But she wasn't here, and after one punch, my knuckles had taken a beating on his craggy face. Thanks to Uncle Alec's technique and the element of surprise, however, I managed to knock the gargantuan green beret back several steps.

I darted around him as he stumbled. I took off down the hall, not daring to look back. Jackson yelled my name amid a chorus of surprised shouts, but I ignored him, putting on a burst of speed.

I didn't make it far. Army Kong hadn't come alone, and I wasn't as fast on land as by sea.

Another soldier slammed into me from behind, tackling me like a *Friday Night Lights* linebacker. I slammed into the thin industrial carpet on my front, and my arms twisted painfully beneath me, absorbing most of the blow. My forehead bounced off the floor. Stars burst in my vision, rendering me virtually blind for several seconds.

Handcuffs clicked into place, viciously tight, and panic crawled up my throat. Captured again. They'd put me back in the tank. In the dark. *Please, not the dark.* The soldier hauled me to my feet, and my aching head did a loop-de-loop. My shallow, frightened breaths worsened the nausea, and without my captor's grip on my arm, I would have toppled backward.

There was an odd shuffling sound behind me and a creak or two, then the soldier holding me greeted someone with a crisp, "Sir."

Suddenly that someone's breath was hot on my cheek, and I flinched, unable to run or fight. "Don't have your Professor X uncle here this time, do you, bitch?" I knew the owner of that voice. Reyes. He'd made it here, regardless of his broken knee, now fitted with a brace. He probably had a vendetta for that, but I had one of my own, and I wasn't about to let him see my fear.

I couldn't retort through the lingering fog. My arms tingled from the fall. My knuckles hurt like a mother. I worried Army Kong's face had broken them.

As I stood there breathing hard, squinting against the sudden intense headache, I realized my restraints weren't normal hand-cuffs. Instead of thin, sharp circlets, these enclosed nearly half of my forearm.

And they were hot.

Heating up, actually.

By the time I mustered the energy to stand on my own, and pull away from the soldier I didn't recognize, I was sweating.

"What the hell did you put on me?" I snapped, focusing on Reyes' perversely handsome face.

"The doc's latest toy." Reyes had a glint in his eye that made me shiver. He glanced at the other solider and said, "I'll take care of her now." He adjusted a crutch under one arm and gripped my arm.

Army Kong sauntered over, with Jackson like a distressed puppy at his heels.

"You've got quite the punch," Army Kong told me in a deep baritone, no trace of the high pitch he'd used when KitKat had snapped at his groin. He gingerly prodded the skin beneath his right eye. "Tae kwon do?"

"A scrappy uncle," I replied, pulling against the cuffs' unyielding restraint.

"Yes, quite the family you have," said a soft, fatherly voice.

Army Kong and Jackson parted like the Red Sea to let the prophetic Dr. Craig through. He smiled genially at me, like we were passing each other in the breakroom.

"What did you guys put on me? I'm burning up."

"Thermal cuffs." Dr. Craig gave a little clap. "Experimental, at this point, but it does come in handy for little mermaids."

I startled. He knew about my powers?

I gritted my teeth. Of course. Jackson had his little satellite phone. How many reports had he given on me? How long had this been the plan?

The idea that he'd meant to betray me all along was a knife twisting in my gut.

Searching for the truth in Jackson's face, I caught him inspecting the sweat rolling down my hairline. "Is it going to hurt her?"

"No, no, Jackson. Of course not," Dr. Craig tutted. "They'll simply make her sweat. Dry up her natural water reserves, so she can't unleash any geysers on us."

Tears pricked my eyes, but I twisted up my face to hold them back. "How much did you tell him?" I asked Jackson. "Did you tell him about my whole family? About Matty's family? Did you tell him about that day at the lake and all the things you promised me?" I swallowed hard, but my voice still cracked when I asked, "Was it all an act?"

He avoided my gaze, ignored my questions.

"You'll take them off as soon as she's in the lab?" he asked Dr. Craig.

"Yes, son. I intend to keep my word to you. No harm will come to her. No more deprivation experiments or bed restraints." Dr. Craig smiled my way again. "Now that her true gifts have come out, she falls under my area of expertise, not Hurst's. I'll treat her well and help her." He reached out a hand, like he intended to caress my cheek, and addressed me directly. "I hope to help you understand and control your gifts, Ellis, not treat you like a lab rat. I hope soon you'll come to believe that."

I glared and jerked my head away from his hand, pulling against Reyes' painful grip on my arm. But Dr. Craig wasn't going for my face. His stumpy fingers curled around my guidestone. I snapped my teeth at his wrinkly knuckles, making him jump back. Reyes punished me with a vicious twist of my arm that made my shoulder scream.

"Stop it," Jackson hissed.

At Dr. Craig's nod, Reyes eased up.

Dr. Craig gave me a pitying *tut-tut* then clapped his hands again, grinning wide at Jackson.

"So, where is that marvelous stone you mentioned. Her 'relic,' was it?"

My heart plummeted.

Jackson's lips parted in surprise. "I-I'm not sure, actually. If it's not in the room, then the Guatemalan boy has it. It's sacred to him. He doesn't like leaving it unattended."

I smirked, relaxing my fists. Matty had the relic. I knew it, as surely as I'd known where to retrieve the empty stone from the ocean floor after Sofia's death.

Of course Matty had it. He wasn't an idiot like me, blindly trusting outsiders he just met.

"You just let him go? Let him take it?" Dr. Craig asked.

"I didn't think it was important." Jackson took a startled step back. "Ellis already obtained its power... or energy, or whatever it is."

"Didn't think it was important?" Dr. Craig asked with an incredulous scoff, shaking his head. He snapped his fingers at Army Kong and a female solider who'd appeared behind him. "Turn the room upside down. Search every cupboard and under every piece of furniture," he snipped. Then, when the soldiers turned to obey, he shook his head at Jackson. "That is possibly the single greatest scientific discovery of my career, and you possibly let it waltz out the door because you didn't think it was important?"

Jackson stood at attention. "I'm sorry, sir. I wasn't thinking clearly. This assignment has been… strenuous."

"I should say so. You didn't think clearly enough to call me before you crossed the border, either." Dr. Craig huffed and massaged the bridge of his nose like a haggard father.

Scraping sounds and bangs issued from the hotel room, drawing the doctor's attention.

"I don't think he's having much luck in there, doc." I gave a Cheshire cat grin.

"Reyes, Burman, secure her in the second vehicle, please." Dr. Craig waved a dismissive hand.

Reyes yanked on my cuffs, and I had no choice but to follow, though he soon handed me over to Burman so he could shuffle along with his busted knee. We left the hotel for a black SUV out front, where I was shoved into the very back between two massive armed men, while Reyes carefully maneuvered into the front seat.

Dr. Craig, Jackson, and Army Kong joined us ten minutes later, empty handed, and crammed themselves into the center aisle. The good doctor was sulky during the whole winding ride through the city as we dodged pedestrians and bicyclists. He'd left two soldiers behind to await Mateo's return, but I had to believe Mateo could evade capture, especially with KitKat by his side. I watched through the windshield, the insufferable heat momentarily distracting me from the fact that Jackson's betrayal had ripped my heart to irreparable pieces.

I panted, leaning awkwardly against the soldier beside me so I didn't crush my own hands. In my misery, I cursed Dr. Craig's name in every language I knew how, for his sweat-sapping cuffs.

Sweat?

A lightbulb flickered in my head. Dr. Craig worried that I could use my powers out of the water. And maybe he was right. Maybe I could use something as simple as sweat. I'd never tried.

Maybe this time in the lab would be different. Maybe I could get free on my own.

Black spots began to dance in my vision as the driver turned into a small drive closed off by a tall chain link fence with barbed wire. A figure in military fatigues opened the gate, waving the first vehicle and us through.

Nausea turned my stomach as our SUV made a semi-circle on a runway in front of a small plane. My eyelids fluttered closed, and I struggled to open them. To stay conscious.

But I couldn't.

Maybe I didn't even want to.

At least in the darkness of sleep, I could forget how terribly Jackson had hurt me.

Something sharp pinched my hand. It tore through my dreams where I was twirling through underwater whirlpools, and I crashed back into reality with a gasp.

After a few tries, I fluttered my heavy lids open. Slowly. Painfully.

A slight woman in sapphire scrubs and a blue surgical mask leaned over my hand, taping an IV in place. The room behind her was nondescript—four white walls, an inset fluorescent light high overhead, and no furniture beyond the uncomfortable, sweat-soaked bed beneath me. But I knew these itchy blankets. I knew those cameras, bolted beside a wall-length two-way mirror. Welcome back to the lab, Charlie.

Biting back a high, frantic scream, I thrashed my limbs in time with my racing heart. I still wore the thermal cuffs, but now they were connected to the metal rods of the bed instead of each other. At the clanking my fruitless fight created, the nurse looked my way, a manicured brow cocked.

"Thirsty," I rasped.

"Sorry, no can do," the nurse replied, ripping off the last bandage strip and pressing it into place. She straightened and leveled astonishingly blue eyes on me. "Doctor's orders."

"I'm *dying*," I argued.

The nurse *tsk*ed and reached for the blanket at my knees. "Your IV provides just enough fresh fluid." She tugged the blanket up over my sundress, then turned back to her rolling table of supplies.

I was in no shape to struggle. My stomach was in cramps (*When did I last have blood?*), and my joints ached so much that the overbearing heat almost felt good. My leg, where the spider bites marred my skin, felt like fire.

"I have… a wound," I rasped through my dry mouth. "My leg."

The nurse didn't acknowledge me. She jabbed a needle in a vial and filled a syringe with a clear liquid, then swapped out the needle before leaning over my IV.

"What's that?" I asked, hysteria raising my pitch. I yanked against the cuff, but I only hurt myself, digging the metal of the thermal cuff into the crook of my elbow. That prick of pain brought me back: Scalpels scraping off skin cell samples. Cold, rough fingers prodding my body without care for decorum or decency.

A whine that was meant to be a scream slipped through my lips.

"Something to help you sleep." She depressed the plunger, and the liquid slid smoothly into my hand.

"I don't need sleep," I said, attempting to yank away from her grasp again. "I want water. Real water. To drink."

Of course, I couldn't really drink it. But maybe with a glassful I could break the cuffs?

If she replied, I never heard her.

The drugs did their dirty work, and I drifted away.

When I awakened again, the room was in pitch darkness, and I was alone.

I felt like I'd fallen off a cliff. Everything hurt. My leg burned worse than the heat from the thermal cuffs, radiating up from the spider bite. I kicked off the blankets the nurse had pulled over me, praying for the air to be cold, but it wasn't. The room was hot, too. I heard a vent pumping air somewhere close by—warm air.

They were trying to kill me.

So much for Dr. Craig's promises. Or was this Hurst's doing? He was the one who'd tried to kill me before, or Reyes, as far as I could tell.

It didn't matter who was behind it. I just needed it to stop.

I felt so sick to my stomach that I started dry heaving. Luckily, I hadn't eaten in days, besides that hurled piece of snack bar, so there was nothing to come up. It wasn't like I could lean over the bed to vomit.

Heavy.

Dry.

Trapped.

Again.

All because Jackson had turned on me.

"You didn't think clearly enough to call me before you crossed the border, either." Dr. Craig's words came back, and I pondered them. What were Jackson's orders? How many of them had he disobeyed? Was everything between us a ruse, or had he really cared and really meant to help me? Until Guatemala. Everything changed in Guatemala.

Again. It didn't matter. No matter what his initial intentions, he'd betrayed me. Fresh heartache flooded me, sending a wash of tears to my eyes. I stared up into the darkness wishing I had a light of some kind for comfort.

He'd promised me safety. He'd promised to take care of me. To help me reach my goals.

Well, he'd done that, I guessed. Once I had my powers, he left me in the worst way possible.

At least Matty, KitKat, and the relic were safe. They had to be.

With that comforting thought, I slept again. Time passed. I dreamt of Sofia. She had wings on her feet and turtle scales on her neck, but her beautiful face was thankfully unmarred and blissful.

She smiled. Tried to speak to me. I couldn't hear her over the rushing of water.

The blue-eyed nurse woke me again while taking my vitals.

Her stethoscope felt soothingly cold against my bare skin. "Breathe in."

I obeyed, focusing on the security camera in the corner. "Breathe out."

I let my breath out and wished I was underwater.

"I'm thirsty," I said for what felt like the twelfth time. "Please."

"No can do," she said with a shake of her head. "No water. The cuffs stay on. That's the way it is, so you'd better get used to it."

The camera shook.

Huh?

She slid the stethoscope an inch over. "Breathe in."

The mirror rattled.

Nurse Blue-Eyes sucked in a little gasp and squinted at it. Biting her lip, she returned to her work, moving her stethoscope one more time before adding a fresh pump of that sleeping drug into my vein.

My vision went hazy. Was that why the whole mirror shook? A mirage?

My lids fluttered.

Boom!

I jerked to semi-consciousness and saw a large crack snaking up the white cell wall, stone and paint dust raining onto the floor. Clattering and thumps echoed from beyond the wall. Where was Nurse Blue-Eyes?

My lids were too heavy. Sounds faded away. The crack blurred, smearing to become just another part of the white nothingness…

I dreamt of Cyndra. She was on fire. Her hair was red flames like Hades in the Disney version of *Hercules*. There were embers in her eyes. I heard her voice, but it was so disjointed, like five voices layered atop one another in an echo chamber.

Time's running out.

Tick-tock.

Tick.

I woke up in the dark again with chills from the cold sweat coating my clammy skin.

I was burning like Cyn in my dream, but shivers chattered my teeth.

How the hell had I come full circle back to this place?

The water relic had given me phenomenal abilities, and even without any training, my emotions fed off the powers. Or the powers fed off my emotions. I doubted the two were really separate anymore.

So how had I let this happen?

I'd been so afraid for Jackson to see my true self. Knowing how much he hated his own powers, knowing that regular society didn't accept my family, and no one ever expected a "pretty girl" to be powerful or successful. Unless, of course, that pretty girl was squeezed into vinyl bodysuits, pushup bras, and other impractical ensembles in an action movie. I'd deferred to him every moment since he found me in the desert. I'd let him take the lead; hell, I'd begged him to take the lead. I'd given him the power, over and over, and for what?

For him to betray me.

If I wasn't so exhausted, so hot, so cold, so wracked with agony, my anger would have been legendary.

No more, I promised myself. *No more damsel in distress.*

You never were one, Ell, the Cyn in my head chimed in.

She was right, even in my imagination. I'd fought off those bikers before Jackson ever showed up. I'd bested a cyclops. I'd discovered how to activate my relic and braved *el torbellino* on my own.

No more pretending I'm not the baddest bitch out there.

You can be as strong as you'll let yourself be, the Cyn of my memories echoed, bringing back that day on the mat, when we were together and happy.

Time to be strong for me, and then for everyone else relying on me.

Redefine yourself, Cyn whispered.

Time to transform into the badass Cyn had always believed I could be. The badass I knew I could be.

If I made it out of this place alive, I vowed to do what was right one hundred percent of the time, no matter how it made me look or how people judged me.

No one else would die.

Not on my watch.

Unless I died first.

The door opened in the darkness—a loud, bracing click that made me jump.

A split second later, the fluorescent overhead flared to life while I was looking right at it.

I cried out and squeezed my eyes shut too late. Dancing dots rotated behind my eyelids, and I waited them out, listening to the creaky wheels of Nurse Blue-Eyes' supply cart.

But when I opened my eyes and focused on the woman, I realized it wasn't the blue-eyed nurse after all.

It was Nurse Violet.

She had a black patch over her empty socket, and a headband held her bobbed hair away from her face. Her scrubs were covered in tiny hearts—an off-the-wall choice for an army medic in a Black-Ops lab. She had on her gloves, but she'd forgone a surgical mask, giving me a full view of her heart-shaped face.

"Hey, Charlie." She gave a wry smile.

Clipped front and center on top of the cart was a fresh vial of the sleeping drugs.

"No!" I snapped, struggling against the cuffs. I'd break the damn things off me if it was the last thing I did.

Violet raised an eyebrow, then walked away from the bed, taking the cart with her.

I stopped struggling, startled.

Wasn't she going to drug me?

She wheeled the creaky cart over to the corner beneath the

security camera. With surprising grace, she climbed on top of the cart, picked up the small vial of drugs…

And used it to smash the camera lens.

I stared at her in shock as she brushed broken glass off her hands, then tossed the surprisingly sturdy vial aside.

She met my gaze. "I diverted the guards at the door, but we only have two minutes before reinforcements arrive." Violet dropped down from the cart to the concrete floor. She brandished a set of keys. "Let's get you out of those cuffs."

33

NO SHRINKING VIOLETS

As Violet leaned over my right hand, I stared at her, dumbfounded. "Um. What?"

"We don't have a lot of time." She adjusted her sliding headband. "Long story short, Jackson sent me." She jabbed a thumb at the wall, where I noticed a thick layer of calk stuffed into the white concrete. "He wasn't very happy with what he saw on the cameras."

I hadn't imaged the crack. Jackson had done it?

I scoffed. "He regained a conscience?"

"He knows what he did was wrong. Trust me, he got a dressing down from me." The thermal cuff on my right wrist fell open, and Violet circled the bed to my other hand as she continued, "But he let Hurst see his powers when he got angry. When he saw the video feed of you strapped to the bed, he tore the door to the observation room right off its hinges with his mind and barged in. That's when he heard they weren't giving you water—learned how they were really treating you. Sent chairs flying around like a damn poltergeist. If you hadn't been in here, he'd probably have collapsed the whole room." Her eyes flicked to the mirror. "They've got him locked away in a bare cell belowground. We have to get him out of there."

"I'm sure Dr. Craig will let out his favorite puppy," I said, bitterness lacing my tone. The left cuff fell away, and I pulled my arms in, gently massaging my stiff wrists.

Violet dropped the railing on the medical bed, then leaned in to put an arm around me and helped me scoot to the edge. "Dr. Craig's missing. Another reason Jackson asked for my help."

"You've seen him? Or he got you a message?" I asked, putting my bare feet to the floor. Even though they'd left me in my pol-ka-dotted sundress, they'd taken my shoes.

Violet lifted me to my feet, keeping her arm around my waist to steady me. She smelled like lavender and soap. A clean smell but not antiseptic, which helped calm my nerves. "I covered for the nurse who's administering his morphine."

"So that's what Nurse Blue-Eyes has been giving me." I took a ginger step away from Violet, but I made the mistake of doing it on my right leg. The spider bite leg. I collapsed with a sharp cry.

Violet caught me before I could fall and lifted me bodily back onto the bed. "Jane. She's a friend."

"She's a dick," I replied.

Violet laughed and lifted my leg to examine the wounds. Her smile vanished. "What happened here?"

"Spider bite. I think."

"This isn't anything I've ever seen," Violet forced through a tense jaw. "Not a widow or a recluse. Where did it happen?"

"Guatemala. We were in the jungle."

Violet's one eye flashed. "Wandering spider."

"Is that bad?"

"We need to get you antivenom. Right the hell now." She tossed the blanket over her shoulder, then slipped an arm back around me. "I saw a wheelchair outside. Let's go."

In the lingering morphine fog, it felt like I'd only blinked before Violet had me in the wheelchair with the blanket draped around me like a cloak. At some point, she'd procured a surgical mask and cov-ered her own face, as well. She appeared in my small porthole-sized line of sight and tucked the edges of the blanket around my head.

"Stay hidden," she whispered.

I sank back against the wheelchair.

"Oh," she said, reaching for a silver tray atop a spindly table.

"Your personal effects." She lifted the chain of my guidestone necklace on two fingers and offered it to me.

"Thank you." I slipped it over my head, relishing its comforting weight on my breastbone as she wheeled me out.

The hallway was blissfully cold compared to my heated dungeon. Even through the blanket, I could feel the cool air pouring from the vents overhead. Violet picked up a brisk pace, and the breeze cooled my cheeks. The overwhelming heat began to fade, and even though I still hurt, some of the symptoms eased.

"No alarm yet." Violet's voice was close to my ear, slightly muffled by the blanket. "But it won't be long."

We took several turns down hallways lined with shiny white floors, passing only a couple of white-robed individuals who Violet greeted with a polite, "Good afternoon, sir." Neither of the passing men seemed bothered to see a nurse transporting a patient wrapped tight like a mummy.

Not that I should have been surprised, given what I knew about the place. Brain experiments probably left lots of people—alt or not—incapacitated in wheelchairs.

I searched for familiar landmarks from my previous excursion to Uncle Alec's cell, but I didn't recognize this wing of the facility. Was Cyndra in that same hallway, in a dark, heavily guarded containment room?

Violet stopped outside a metal door, and something beeped, followed by the clack of a door lock releasing. Then she wheeled me into a dim room.

"Medical supply." She slid me next to a pristine steel table in the middle of the room and locked the brakes on the chair. "It's a military base. We've got all the antivenoms possible. Honestly, it's a damn miracle you aren't dead." Violet's voice grew fainter as she walked deeper into the room. I heard the tell-tale sound of a refrigerator opening. "The wandering spider is one of the most venomous in the world. Its venom attacks your nervous system. Any normal person would have fallen into convulsions within an hour of being bitten."

I gulped, rubbing my fingertips nervously over clammy palms. "I'm not a normal person." I felt the truth of it more strongly than ever. But how long did I have, if an average person only had an hour?

"No. You definitely aren't normal." Violet's footsteps padded back across the floor, and she set a handful of supplies on the table. She tugged the blanket off me, draping it on a nearby chair, before she dragged over a rolling stool. Her single eye roamed over me as she pulled on a pair of surgical gloves. "I like your dress."

"Thanks. I stole it."

Violet laughed and picked up a syringe. "I can see why he likes you."

"Who?"

She turned up a vial to draw out the medication, and her eyebrows arched toward her hairline. "Jackson. You goober."

"He doesn't like me." I studied my toes as she twisted my hand around to expose the IV still taped to my veins.

Violet scoffed. "Ha. Yeah, right. I've known him a while, you know. I've never seen him light up the way he does when he talks about you. I only got five minutes with him in that cell, and he might as well have declared his undying love for you. How brave. Funny. Fierce. Loyal. He went on and on."

"He can take his compliments and shove 'em," I snapped. "If he knows who I really am, then why'd he get me caged in here like a monster?"

Violet puckered her mouth in concentration and poked the needle into my IV. "This might sting."

I braced myself, using my other hand to clutch the wheelchair arm for support. I could feel the antivenom sliding into my veins, and it made me lightheaded. It wasn't too painful. More uncomfortable.

"I hate to break it to you, Charlie," Violet went on, "but the people you love the most are always going to be the ones who hurt you the worst. That's life for you."

Tears pricked my eyes. "Ellis. My name's Ellis."

"Ellis," Violet repeated. "Yes, of course. Jax called you Ell." She offered a soft, sisterly smile. "What he did, he did out of fear. You know about my eye?"

I nodded at the wall.

"He's denied his own abilities for so long. Long before he hurt me." There was a little tug at my hand as she removed the syringe. "My forgiveness was never enough for him. He associates his powers with fear—fear of being different, fear of losing control, fear of hurting someone he loves. So, you see, in his mind, he did what he did so you *wouldn't* get hurt. Because he feared losing you."

"Then he's an idiot."

"Honey, when it comes to emotions, most men are," Violet teased as she capped off the IV in my hand. "We'll need to keep the IV in. I'll have to give you a couple more injections over the next hour." She dropped the used syringe in an orange hazardous waste bin on the wall, then began to pile vials and syringes in a first aid kit. "And you're probably going to have side effects. Fatigue, itching, swelling, and hives are all normal reactions to antivenom. If you suddenly can't breathe, tell me immediately. We'll need to give you epinephrine."

"I'm starting to think the spider venom was the better option," I joked, curling my hands in my lap. "How am I supposed to help you with your plan if I'm falling apart?"

"The spider bites were unexpected," Violet agreed, rolling forward again to meet my eye. "But I don't think it'll keep you from doing what needs to be done to get Jackson out."

"I want my family out, too. Is my sister still here?"

Violet fidgeted. "Yes, but she and the older man—your uncle? They're more heavily guarded."

"Are they near Jackson's cell?"

"Your Uncle is just a door down from him, in the newest reinforced containment cells. Or he was yesterday. They keep moving him for testing of some kind. I'm not sure about your sister," she said with an apologetic cringe. "They've kept her more hush-hush."

"Do we have anyone else who can help us?"

"I've got one of Jackson's buddies on standby to help, but you're the only one with the power to pull this off." Violet rested her hand atop mine.

"I don't feel very powerful at the moment," I said wryly. "I feel like I have the flu. Aching joints, chills, burning in my leg—"

"All attributable to the spider bite."

So, what would I even be capable of doing in this prison break?

Why even try? Did Jackson even deserve it? Maybe I should let him find out what it felt like to be strapped to a bed and experimented on. Let him feel what he condemned me to because he *cared* so much. That crack in the wall said maybe he knew he'd made a mistake, but part of me wanted to let him stew in that realization a while.

"What exactly is my part in this plan?" I asked.

A small smile crossed Violet's face. "The cell where Jackson is being kept is on the floor below, directly below the water tank. *Your* water tank."

Just the reminder of that horrible place sent chills racing over my skin.

"According to Jackson, you can do some pretty deadly things with water," Violet went on. "Like break down walls, maybe?"

I clutched the wheelchair arms, summoning my resolve. If I was going to use every last iota of strength to bust down a wall, it was going to be for Cyndra and Uncle Alec. Then, if I happened to have anything left, I'd decide whether or not I'd get to Jackson. But Violet didn't need to know that yet. Best to have her take me in the right direction first.

I nodded at Violet. "Let's go."

<h1 style="text-align:center">34</h1>

POCKET CHANGE

I F I'D THOUGHT BEING BACK AT THE MERCY OF MY TORMENTORS was bad, standing over the water tank where I'd nearly died was even worse.

The lid to the tank stood open. Remnants of the wires and netting that had held me down on the awful, bolted-down medical chair now drifted near the bottom. Nothing about the warehouse had changed. Same domed ceiling; same stacks of crates and boxes filled with God knows what weapons.

I stood on the metal platform where Jackson had dragged me from the water, where I'd kissed him and tasted his blood, reliving the nightmare as if I'd just crawled dripping from the tank. I clenched my hands into fists to stop the trembling in my hands, but then my knees knocked together. I wanted to blame it on the antivenom working its way through my body, but it was pure, genuine fear of this place. The trauma I'd sustained at the hands of these monsters had taken root in my subconscious. It weakened me.

Reminded me that I was small.

I wasn't good enough.

Wasn't strong enough.

Especially not without blood, my seizing stomach reminded me. In the fog of the drugs and the terrifying revelation of the spider bite, I hadn't thought to ask Violet if she could rummage up some blood bags for me. Another stupid mistake. I still wasn't used to my new powers and their limitations. I frequently forgot how to care for this new version of myself. How was I supposed to free Cyndra and Uncle Alec when this place had once again reduced me to a starving ruin?

Violet's voice broke through my inner turmoil. "The walls are plastic, but the bottom sits right on the concrete floor," she told me, capping the syringe she'd used to administer my second round of antivenom. "Jackson's cell is directly beneath us. My guess is if you can use the water to break through the floor, we can drag him out while the guards are dealing with the sudden deluge."

"I don't even know how to use my powers," I protested.

Violet raised an eyebrow and peeled off her gloves into the first aid kit. "Jackson told me you killed three enemy soldiers with just water."

Enemy soldiers. What a funny way of saying *supernatural henchmen.*

"Where exactly am I aiming?" I asked. If I knew precisely where Jackson's cell sat, I could better guess where Uncle Alec's was.

Violet pulled a folded schematic from her pocket and strolled the length of the platform as she examined it.

"Okay, it's a pretty big target." She walked a large square. She waved her arms to indicate the area within the outline she'd traced with her footsteps. "Anywhere here should be good." She pointed to the leftmost edge of the platform, drawing a line with her nail. "The closest neighboring cell starts there. That will be a solid concrete divider wall, so avoid that. You won't make more than a dent from up here."

Uncle Alec. I eyed the tank. I couldn't be sure it held enough water to bust down two walls. Uncle Alec had to come first. I'd aim farther left than Violet had pointed, past that divider wall, and bust through his ceiling. Then his ability could get us to Cyn, wherever the hell she was. Once we had her, I'd decide whether to come back for Jackson, based on how crazy things got around here.

Down on the surface level, a faint, rhythmic knock echoed up to us from the door in the corner. Clearly some kind of coded password, because Violet simply said, "Ah. Reinforcements."

I swallowed and glanced over the railing as the door opened. A man wearing military fatigues entered carrying a rifle on a strap across his back.

"Reinforcement, singular, I suppose," Violet said with a shrug. "Allies are few and far between here."

"Can we trust him?"

"Scott? Absolutely. He's one of us—he sees the way things are broken here." Violet leaned over and waved at the newcomer. "Up here."

One of us. Violet and Jackson had freed me from this place, freed me from the injustices they saw. And yet, Jackson had put me right back in here. When his own traumas were triggered, he'd come back to what he knew, convinced it would be different somehow. Coming back to what he considered home, who he considered home, despite all the broken promises. But when he'd realized he was wearing rose-colored glasses… he'd come back for me. He'd broken his own golden rule. He'd let anger rule his powers. He'd almost busted down the wall to my room. He'd sent his friends to retrieve me.

I shook off my sympathy. He didn't deserve to be caged, but neither had I. Whether I busted him out or not, I wasn't going to risk my heart another time.

Scott climbed the metal ladder to join us. He was older than Jackson, but not by much. He had bleached blond hair, shaved close at the sides but long on top, and the dark, swarthy tan of an outdoorsy type—which was interesting since I recalled he worked on tech, but he was a *military* techie. His eyes were a pale gray, and they twinkled as he offered me a hand.

"Special Agent Scott Keegan, head of tech and surveillance," he said. As we shook hands, his gaze raked over me, and he added, "You look better than the last time I saw you on the cameras. Nice to see you out of those beds, Charlie."

Heat flashed up my neck and into my cheeks. I smoothed my

palms over my sundress and looked down at my bare toes. "Um. Thanks. You can call me Ellis, though."

"You're damn right I can. Never liked that alphabet bull. It's nice to finally meet you, Ellis." Scott's gray gaze swung to Violet, and that twinkle intensified. "So what's the plan, gorgeous? Do we need explosives?"

Violet rolled her eye at Scott, but her lips twitched upward. "Always wanting to get your hands dirty. When you think it's safe. Shoulda gone a different path after basic." Violet turned to me. "We don't need explosives. We've already got one."

My flush got hotter.

Me. I was the explosive.

"Sounds good," Scott offered, but rubbed his chin with a confused expression.

I ignored his presence and stripped to my underwear and bra, draping my dress over the railing. For the first time in a while, I didn't care about my protruding bones or the fact a good-looking guy was watching me. I still wore Sofia's *hermosa* title like a mantle, layered with Violet's offhand, "I like your dress." They helped me feel like me again, even as the tank tried to steal my sense of self.

Sitting on the metal edge, I carefully lowered my legs into the water—unfiltered and unheated now—and fought the visceral terror it provoked.

The darkness. The absolute emptiness. I'd been stripped of everything that made me human in this tank. Listening to the sounds of life with that heightened hearing had been everything I had to live for.

Jackson had pulled me from this tank without a thought for himself. All he'd known was that the base was on fire and Charlie was in trouble. It was that moral compass and caring heart that had brought us together and torn us apart. Because he applied it to everyone. Everyone got the same chance, the same benefit of the doubt, the same mercy with Jackson.

Was it right for me to admire that trait only when it suited me and condemn him for it now?

Right now, Jackson was the one in trouble. Was I really going to let him be an afterthought? Was I really going to trick his friends—who were risking not just their jobs but their freedom, and possibly their lives, for me—and use them to free my family but not Jackson?

Who was I, if I did that? Who was I to claim I should have the final say in whether someone stayed locked in a cage? I'd be no better than Jackson, operating under a misguided sense of my own unquestionable morality.

A squeak startled me, and I looked over my shoulder to find Violet twisting a valve on the side of the tank.

"So you can take what's in the pipes, too," she explained at my questioning look.

I slipped into the water wracked with uncertainty, but the relief was *immediate.* All the heat from the spider bite and the thermal cuffs' torture vanished the instant the water swallowed me whole. I took my first breath, filling my lungs with cold, refreshing liquid that strengthened me from the inside out, and I could have wept for how beautiful it felt.

But I didn't have time to bask in the feeling.

I dove to the bottom of the tank.

Keeping a wide berth between me and the artificial webbing, I sank all the way to the smooth plastic covering the concrete.

Now what?

I rested my palms flush to the plastic and gently kicked at the water to hold myself in place.

How had I used those waterspouts back in Guatemala? With anger, mostly. My fury had built them, extensions of myself and my emotions. Like new hands I'd just automatically known how to use.

I had plenty of anger, but right now, I couldn't channel it at a single source. All my emotions were overshadowed by moral conflict, the ticking clock hanging over all our heads—especially Cyndra's—and unadulterated terror.

Focus.

I closed my eyes and centered myself.

Violet's flats paced on the metal platform overhead. "Something's up. Dr. Craig's still not answering his cell."

Scott grunted. "Yeah, I agree. Hurst knows Ellis' and Jackson's abilities fall under Craig's jurisdiction, not his, so he's gotten him out of the way somehow. He's hated him and Jackson both from day one, for butting in on his little kingdom."

"But how far would Hurst actually go?" Violet asked.

Scott made a noncommittal sound that I imagined went with a shrug.

"It's suspicious they haven't raised an alarm about her going missing," he said after a pause. "Even without the security footage I wiped, they should realize she's not where she's supposed to be."

"Jane's covering for me," Violet explained. "But she can't do it forever. Once Ellis breaks the ceiling…"

Scott chuckled. "All hell will break loose."

"Right," Violet agreed. "We'll figure it out from there."

"Is she okay down there?" To his credit, he actually did sound worried for my well-being.

"She can breathe underwater."

I braced myself for his response.

"Oh. That's pretty badass," Scott replied.

That stupid blush came back.

They continued talking in low voices up above, but I tuned them out and widened my reach, searching for signs of my family—the familiar rhythm of Cyndra's pacing, Uncle Alec's absent-minded whistling. But what I found instead constricted my heart and stole my breath.

Jackson's voice.

Singing that song. The one he'd sang to me on the shores of the lake at the cabin about carrying loneliness and lips and the "coins" of someone's eyes in your pocket. This time without the guitar to accompany his voice. Just *him* and the gorgeous, solemn tenor of his singing about reaching into his pocket for small change when his mind was troubled. Riddles and metaphors that finally unraveled into their true shapes as I listened for the second time.

It's a love song. It had seemed so nonsensical before, but now, really listening to him, I heard what he was saying.

We, as living, breathing people, carried parts of each other with us all the time. Whether we were together or apart, whether we were happy, sad, or lonely, those bits of the people we cared about—those lips and eyes, those memories—helped us keep moving. The world could fall apart around us, and those people we loved could hurt us, but we could always cash in on those memories to help us keep going.

After being torn from my sheltered, isolated life, surrounded only by family, I'd made another lifetime's worth of memories with Jackson over our short time together. Good memories, bad memories, memories I would cling to forever.

I had Jackson in my pocket. All the time.

And I didn't want to just throw out those pieces of him and the moments we'd shared. Even now, after all that had happened. Each painful memory came with a dozen uplifting ones. To extract them, to sever him from me, would be to lose all those new experiences, to lose all I loved about him along with his one mistake. I couldn't do that.

He deserved a second chance. What he did with it was up to him, and there wouldn't be a third, but I wouldn't deny myself another shot at happiness either. I could forgive him.

Because the way he sang—the sweet, longing cadence, with sorrow and passion entwined—told me he wasn't passing time by singing that song at random, either.

He was thinking about me.

Me!

The water began to churn. Apparently anger wasn't the only emotion that could harness my powers.

Happiness. Happiness made the magic flow through me like life-giving blood.

Who knew?

I took several deep breaths, releasing them slowly, and with each one, the water rotated faster. Energy roared through me, and my guidestone glowed blue as if to assure me I was on the right track. The power settled deep within, a core of electricity ready to arc out and destroy like lightning.

I knew exactly where to aim it.

Jackson and I were better together.

Together, we stood a chance of getting Cyn and Uncle Alec free, too.

I gathered my power and released it.

Water barreled from me like a torpedo. The plastic floor exploded beneath my palms, and I pulled back as the water grenade slammed into the concrete.

Then I was falling.

I slipped right through the hole I'd made, riding a waterfall. The water caught me, but I sank inside and hit concrete with a grunt. Then the flow picked me up and tossed me into metal bars in a dizzying flash. One arm shot through the metal rods, sticking at the shoulder, and the other slapped across a warm body.

Jackson.

Despite the onslaught of water pouring through the ceiling and pinning us to the bars, he turned his head and his mouth dropped open in elated shock. He choked on the water spraying around his neck and jaw.

"Ell?" he sputtered. "You came."

"Violet didn't give me a choice," I joked.

"Thank God for that." His brief smile flickered, and he swallowed hard. "I am so sorry, Ell," he said, voice ragged at the edges. "You were right. I put my own hang ups on you. I saw myself and all I've done wrong, and I couldn't see you anymore. I did what was comfortable, and I chose to turn a blind eye on everything you'd showed me. I chose to believe things could change around here, without any proof that they would, when you've given me proof again and again that you're… God, you're magnificent, Ell. And I put you in a cage." A glossy sheen of tears coated his dark eyes, and my heart squeezed. "I know I sent Violet, but I don't deserve to have you save me."

I took a shaky breath and said, "You don't deserve a cage either, Jax. No one does. That's why I came."

He put a hand over mine, still pressed against his chest by the water. "Thank you." He brought my fingers to his lips, and when I made no move to pull back, kissed them. "What I did, it was a momentary lapse in judgment. But the worst possible one. I betrayed all the faith you put in me. I hope you'll give me a chance to make it up to you."

He looked so earnest. In the dim cell, his curly black tattoo on his wet temple shone like polished stone. His striking, angular features begged to be touched.

"I forgive you." I traced my fingertips up his jaw to his cheek, my heart fluttering in my throat, but they came away bloody. I stilled, salivating at the sight of the shiny crimson liquid.

"Banged my face on the bars when you came busting in," he said, watching me as he gripped the metal enclosure with one hand and drew me closer with another. "They're reinforced somehow. I couldn't use them to break free." He gently tilted up my chin, the question already in his eyes before he said, "Are you all right? When was the last time you ate?"

I sagged in his arms just thinking about how hungry I was. "Not sure," I croaked.

"Ell…" He tilted back his head, exposing the shallow gash along his jaw, where it met his neck. "Take it."

I braced myself on his shoulder with one hand and let the other wrap in his hair at the back of his head. His long lashes fluttered, and his eyes closed as he leaned into my touch.

"You're sure?"

He nodded. "Take it."

My stomach jumped on the invitation. I pressed my mouth to the soft, delicate crevice and ran my tongue over his cut.

He let out a soft gasp that made my stomach somersault.

A honeyed sweetness mellowed the coppery tang exploding across my taste buds, and sparks fired a brilliant kaleidoscope of emotions through my brain. I felt his regret first, like a fist twisting my diaphragm in a knot, mixed with anguish over what he'd seen on those cameras—a knife to the heart. But love came next, in a glorious rush that washed everything else away, calling to feelings I'd shoved away the moment that knock came on the hotel door. Both our passions collided in an explosive starburst, and I saw myself as he saw me, and it brought tears to my eyes. A shining beacon lighting up the dark. A warrior goddess swathed in a cloak of ocean spray. A beautiful, tranquil Madonna, arms and hands stained with bright paints.

When I'd had my fill—just a few swallows—I pulled back reluctantly. My next breath filled lungs stretched to a new capacity. My muscles felt powerful. My head was clear and singing an angel's chorus.

"You love me," I said on an exhale.

He blinked, and then that gorgeous face lit with a shimmering smile that put even sunlit water to shame. "Yes." He pulled me against him, warm and solid and safe. "I know I didn't act like it yesterday, but I love you, Ell."

I moved in, drawn by his eyes, and he kissed me. He tilted my head back, his lips opening mine to him, and I melted into his arms as his tongue swept into my mouth.

I didn't have to taste his blood to feel what he did.

Elation. Affection. Awe.

He broke the kiss and pressed his forehead against mine.

Could this really be a thing?

Us?

"My life is messy," I told him, still holding tight. "And weird." I kissed his cut and licked a transferred drop of blood off my lips to prove my point. "I can't change who I am for you. I won't."

"I know. I'd never ask you to."

"So, you have to be okay with this. With all of this," I added, waving both arms at the river flowing through the bars. The raging current had slowed somewhat, the water level falling around our waists. Somewhere down the hallway, voices were raised in surprise, but I knew the flow of the water against the door was still too strong for them to get through just yet. We had time. But not much.

"I'd rather have all of this than not have you," he said. "And, just to be clear. You're more important to me than anything. They took my dog tags away, but even if they hadn't, I'd never need them again. You're what I want to hold onto. What I want to remind me of who I want to be."

"You're everything I want to hold onto too." I looked at him through lowered lashes. "Don't break my heart again. Please."

"I swear to God and your Priestesses that I won't."

He pulled me close, his wet lips crashing into mine.

I lost myself in his hands and his lips. The taste. This had to be paradise—the pinnacle of my life. Everything I'd been through had led me to this man, to this moment, to these feelings of strength and belonging. Intoxicating. What I felt from him was *real*.

Suddenly, Scott's voice tore through our little glow. "Hate to break this up, but we need to get a move on before the men with guns arrive."

Jackson pulled away from the kiss with obvious reluctance, arms still around me. We both glanced up at the hole in the ceiling where Violet and Scott were smirking.

Jackson glanced back at me, heat in his eyes. "I need you to put clothes on, anyway."

An instinctual pang of shame and hurt hit my chest, and I pulled back in shock, the fingertips of one hand tracing my sharp collarbone.

"Ell." He brushed his lips against mine. "I know what you're thinking, but you're wrong." His palm spread over my bare side. "If we don't get out of here and get you dressed, I'm not going to be responsible for my actions."

Oh. *Oh.*

He meant...

Heat unfurled in my belly and crawled along my skin.

Jackson desired me.

The thrill of it quickened my breath.

He didn't care how I looked.

He still wanted me.

"Besides, we don't have time. And I know you have people to save." The flowing water had reduced to a trickle and the stagnant pool swayed around our hips.

"Uncle Alec is next door. I have to break a hole in that wall." I threw a thumb over my shoulder at the left-hand side of the cell.

"The old man, you mean?" Scott called from above. "Delta?"

"Yes." I strained my neck up. "You've seen him on the cameras? He's okay?"

"Well, relatively. But he's not in that cell. They moved him to D-wing to get him closer to the med bay. Complications from his injuries."

I clenched my fists. "Complications?"

"Infection, I think. I don't work in that department."

The raised voices at the end of the hall were growing louder.

"Come on. We'll regroup up there." Jackson gripped both sides of my waist.

He picked me up without further comment and lifted me easily toward the hole, where I latched onto Scott's waiting hands. He pulled me into the empty tank.

Violet grabbed my hand and made a small noise of distress. "Your IV came out. We still need to do another dose."

I wiggled my fingers. "No, I don't think we do. I feel... good. Like maybe using my powers helped speed the antivenom through my body?" My gaze drifted down to Jackson, the memory of his blood on my tongue. Maybe the strength he'd offered up had helped heal me too.

She eyed me suspiciously with a squint, skin bunching around her eye patch. "Okay, but if you feel weird at all, you tell me."

"I promise."

Scott hauled Jackson through the ceiling, then the four of us hurried up the metal ladder built into the side of the tank. Back on the metal platform, I yanked my dress over my wet body, and we made quick work of climbing back down to the floor.

At the door, Scott held out a hand and turned up his radio. He listened to the chatter for a moment, finally sliding it back into a carrier attached to his belt. "They're still focused on the underground."

Jackson glanced back at the tank. "We don't have much time before they come up here. I'd say we need to get to the nearest exit and get out of here"—he fixed me with a soft expression—"but I know you're loyal to a fault."

"Yup." I stepped in front of him, loving he knew me. Loving that he loved who I was.

He took both my hands in his. "We aren't any good to your sister or your uncle if we get caught and locked away, but—"

"They're my family."

"Yeah. I know." He squeezed my fingers. "I always wanted a family like yours."

"I'll share mine with you, but you have to help me save them first."

"Absolutely."

I looked to Scott. "What about Cyndra? Is she in the same wing?"

"We've got a few female detainees." Scott pondered my question. "Do you know her code name?"

"Maybe Echo? The one who set the base on fire."

Scott blanched. "Yeah. Echo. She's…"

I swallowed against the fear rising in my throat. "Where is she?"

"She's in an outpost building. They wanted her away from the main facility. She was a bit of a hellraiser. She's in underground solitary now. Max security." Scott glanced at Jackson with an almost apologetic expression. "Last I heard, they're shipping her out at 1700 hours. Less than three hours from now."

My head whirled. I latched on to Jackson's arm, breathing through my panic. Violet, who'd remained silent and watchful through the exchange, reached out to clasp my shoulder, lending me her support.

Out in the hallway, the high alert alarm began to wail.

They were onto us.

Tick tock.

Time's up.

35
DEADLY COCKTAIL

THE TUNNELS BENEATH THE BASE'S MAIN UNDERGROUND levels felt like something out of a horror movie.

Dim, flickering fluorescents lined the curve of the ceiling with a sickly green light. I felt like we were walking through a dried-up sewer, and I could easily imagine a swamp monster trudging through these tunnels looking for a victim. Or orange-clad prisoners trying to escape a maximum-security prison. The muffled alarm on the floor above helped bring that last image to life. At any minute, the thud of pursuing boots could join the din.

The reality was a little funnier. *A telekinetic, a techie, a one-eyed nurse, and a water wielder walk into a government lab to bust out their mind-controlling buddy,* I thought with a soft snort.

We'd entered the tunnels through a concealed hatch in the floor close to the warehouse that held my old tank. Scott explained that these secret, stuffy passages were meant for emergency evacuations, so they weren't frequented often, and the base cut their budget by foregoing security cameras down here.

"We never had problems before the Psy-Ops program decided to extract mind control capabilities *from* people, instead of testing mind control on regular convicts," he explained. He and Jackson had taken the lead through the corridors, setting a fast pace that Violet's long legs easily matched, while I had to jog in my bare feet at the rear. "Each detainee has been a worse pain in the ass than the one before."

I snorted. "Maybe that should have been a sign not to kidnap people with special abilities."

Scott flashed me a grin. "You'd think."

He led us around six or seven corners before we halted at the bottom of a metal ladder leading up to a hatch in the ceiling. *D WING* was emblazoned on the wall beneath the door in white stencil next to a medical red cross.

Scott grabbed a rung and reached for his belt holster with his other hand. "I'll go first. I've got the weapon."

"No. No weapons," Jackson said. "Nobody dies today unless absolutely necessary. Most of the guys stationed here are regular soldiers on security detail."

"There are two guards up there," Scott argued. "We aren't going to just waltz in and make off with Delta without a little bit of gunfire."

"No," Jackson repeated. "No gunfire. I'll go first. Just trust me."

As Jackson climbed the ladder, Violet and I exchanged glances.

Was Jackson going to use his telekinetic powers?

On purpose?

He'd done it back in Guatemala under duress from the bear and his minions, but that was a "no other option" situation—something the two of us had landed in frequently of late.

Jackson turned the lever on the hatch and shoved it open, popping his head through the hole.

I heard a shout and then a loud crash in the hall above.

Jackson poked his head back into the tunnel. "Come on. Before help arrives."

The hall above was blisteringly white and sterile, but empty—except for the two uniformed soldiers taking a snooze beneath a pile of debris from the drop ceiling. Broken wires and pipes hung from the shadows behind the demolished particle board.

Violet climbed up beside me, those heart-dotted scrubs adding to the absurdity as she murmured, "Instead of gunfire… *ceiling* fire."

I choked on a giggle that was slightly hysterical. The familiar guard uniforms and whitewashed hallways reminded me I'd just walked right back into the danger zone. One of their blinking digital wrist watches then reminded me we only had ninety minutes left to save Cyn.

There were several doors leading off the hall, most of them marked only by a number. We took the first right, and then an immediate left that spilled us into a gloomy medical area.

Curtains sectioned off a dozen "rooms" in the expansive facility, each equipped with a hospital bed, a table and chair, and other medical supplies like IV racks and blood pressure cuffs. Most of the curtains were open, revealing empty beds, but a handful were closed.

Violet put a finger to her lips, indicating I should be silent.

We crept through the room on high alert. My bare feet made no sound, and Violet tiptoed in soft-soled flats, but the guys' boots squeaked on the shining, clean linoleum. Even so, nothing moved in the room, and I started to think nobody was in residence.

As I was passing by one of the closed curtains, it swished open, metal rings clacking on the rod. I jerked, surprised, but didn't leap away fast enough. An arm snaked around my neck and yanked me off my feet. I hitched against a wall of muscle covered in a layer of fat—a man who'd once been fit and gone to seed.

"Jax!" I shrieked.

The man's arm tightened on my neck. Something sharp pricked my shoulder.

Jackson and Scott both whirled on their heels. Scott lifted his gun in a practiced movement and leveled the barrel on my attacker.

I didn't like being on this end of a rifle. The barrel's dark hole was a hypnotic eye demanding my attention, upon pain of death.

"Hurst," Jackson spat.

My nails dug into the lab coat sleeve around my neck. Hurst! Ready to finish the job he started in the tank.

"Hunter," the man returned, too close to my ear as he inched us back behind the "room" curtains. "Unlucky for you that Delta is my patient."

I heard a metallic clatter, and then the doctor jerked me out of the way as the curtains fell.

"Shoddy pieces of shit," Dr. Hurst swore, jamming the needle back into my shoulder.

He'd thought the curtains fell on their own.

I knew better.

"Drop your weapon, Keegan!" Dr. Hurst snarled, his elbow crease jamming so hard into my throat that I gagged. "You're an idiot, throwing your lot in with this violent AWOL. And Nurse Bodin—you're fired."

"That's fine, I already quit," Violet returned with venom. I knew she'd needed this job because of her father's bills, and my heart ached that she'd given it up for me. For my family.

"Let her go," Jackson said, deadly calm. Danger seethed below still waters.

Jackson hadn't wanted anybody to die, but that was about to change.

Dr. Hurst barked a laugh. "This syringe is loaded with a potent cocktail that will stop this little troublemaker's heart within seconds."

"If you had that, why'd you bother trying to drown me, asshole?" I choked out with false bravado.

"What?" Hurst spat.

Jackson advanced a step.

"Don't believe me? Try me," he challenged Jackson, panting hot breath on my neck. "Give it up, Hunter. You won't risk her life. You've lost."

A second jangling noise behind us made Hurst partially turn. In my peripherals, a rod whistled through the air like a home-runner swing, right at Dr. Hurst's head.

He absorbed the blow to his face without loosening his grip. His entire body jolted, and there was a crack of bones or cartilage, but he only hauled me tighter against his chest and shoved the needle further into my arm.

Sharp pain made me cry out, though the sound was strangled.

Worry and indecision warred in Jackson's expression. Logistically, neither he nor Scott could guarantee a good shot on the doctor with me acting as a shield, and Jackson was reining in his ability's full power, probably unsure how much he could get away with before Hurst depressed the plunger. I could struggle all I wanted, but I was quickly running out of breath in Hurst's grip.

At the clink of metal rings, I braced for another impact, but the white curtains in my peripheral vision swished open with the help of a hand.

Someone shuffled into the main aisle a few cubicles away. I couldn't turn my head for a better look, but none of my companions reacted as if the newcomer were a threat.

A familiar, accented voice rang out, echoing off the high ceilings with authority. "Release the girl."

Uncle Alec!

Relief slammed into me.

He was okay, and he sounded stronger than when I'd left him, though his words were slightly slurred.

Hurst's arm loosened around my neck but didn't release. Proof that Uncle Alec still wasn't at his best.

"I gave you enough morphine to knock out a horse!" Dr. Hurst's snarl couldn't mask his fear.

"I am no horse. Weakened as you've left me, I am still alternate. But you will never truly understand what that means." Uncle Alec took another shuffling step toward us, dragging his cast along. "Move the syringe away from her."

"This is impossible," Dr. Hurst roared, inching closer to hysteria. The syringe moved away from my shoulder. "You were in a medically induced coma!"

Uncle Alec hadn't properly rested. All his bruises had faded in the time I'd been gone, but the wrinkles on his face were still too deep, and the scruffy hair growing back on his shaved head had gone gray. He still wore a bandage over his right ear, and he hunched like his body ached just from walking.

His eyes, though—they held the old fire I recognized as he narrowed them at Dr. Hurst, a smile lifting his sallow cheeks. "Now, inject that poison into your own arm."

Dr. Hurst let out a short, sharp cry of alarm. "No! *No!*"

The doctor fought his own hand, arm jerking and trembling as his fist pulled back, inching out the needle in agonizing spurts. It began a twitchy trajectory toward Hurst's forearm, and the doctor broke out in a torrential sweat. He still hadn't fully released me, so I could only watch raptly as the needle inched toward a bulging vein in the crook of his elbow.

"Inject yourself," Uncle Alec commanded, his stiff grin broadening to flash all his teeth.

"Wait!" Hurst shrieked. "It's not me. It wasn't—" The needle pierced the skin, drawing a whimper to Hurst's lips.

Huh? What wasn't him?

His thumb moved into position. "He led us to you!" They were his final words. The plunger depressed, and he let me go, already convulsing.

I danced away as his body crumpled to the floor. He foamed at the mouth, gagging and flopping his limbs. Until finally, he went still.

Silence fell over the room.

Jackson stepped over Dr. Hurst's still form and gently took my arm. He eyed the puncture wound and the thin blood trail down my bicep. "Are you okay?"

I nodded. "I don't think he got any of it in me."

Uncle Alec crumpled, and I gasped, ready to race to his side. Violet beat me there and wrapped her arm around his waist, anchoring him to her side.

"Thank you, nurse," he said, breathless. "I overextended myself."

I reached for his hand. "I'm so happy to see you."

"The feeling's mutual." He squeezed my fingers, allowing a single twitch of his lips to serve as a smile. "You got your relic?"

"Yes, uncle."

"Vin helped?"

I choked like he'd punched me in the throat. He didn't know. How could I forget he didn't know?

The tears that sprang to my eyes told him too much too quickly. His hand clutched the dingy scrubs above his chest. There was a long moment of silence where he held so still I wasn't sure he'd taken a breath. Then a single, gasping sob ripped from his throat. He doubled over on himself, staggering a step, and I rushed to his side to steady him.

He lifted his head, holding my hand on his arm, and searched my face. "He's dead?" The question held a silent plea: *Say it's not true.*

"Lana told me. He's with her," I said through a tear-strained throat. I omitted the part where she'd said he was in trouble.

"Alanna?" he asked, dazed. Tears tracked down his face and wet his collar, and he made no effort to wipe them away.

Thank the Priestesses for Violet. Without her, we both might have tumbled to the ground as I tucked myself into the circle of Uncle Alec's arms for only the second time in my life. The first was when they found Alanna in that alley.

"He saved Cyn, Uncle Alec. He died for Cyn." I nestled my head under his chin, so he wouldn't have to fear influencing me, so he could hopefully take comfort in the rare display of affection. "He's a hero."

His chin dug into my hair as he nodded. "Let him not be unsung," he said through a shuddering breath. Hearing him wax poetic gave me assurance he was going to be all right, in time.

I squeezed him as tight as I dared, and he rubbed my back in stuttering, hesitant circles.

"We won't let his sacrifice go to waste either," I said into his shoulder. "Cyndra is here. She was the one who came to rescue us and set the base on fire."

"I suspected as much." Uncle Alec pulled back, hands drifting to my shoulders. "From what Vin told me in our last communication, I thought she'd be capable. But I feared if I told you my suspicions, you'd prove more difficult to compel, and I had to get you out." He hung his head. "I hope you can forgive me for that. I vowed never to influence any of you, but under the circumstances—"

"Already forgiven."

His eyes shot to mine, twinkling with the smile he didn't dare show.

Scott cleared his throat. "I'm so sorry," he said, brow knitted with sympathy, "but we need to get outta here before backup arrives. Hurst was a narcissist, but he wasn't stupid. Reinforcements are coming."

Jackson nodded once. "You're right," he agreed, eyeing Uncle Alec. "But we're going to need wheels."

Scott rubbed his chin. "Four UTVs are always parked outside the decoy level. We could jack one and take off into the desert. Assuming they actually have gas."

"Decoy level?" I asked.

"The part of the facility that's above ground," said Scott. "It's mostly for show and for storing office supplies. Unless you've pissed off the late Dr. Hurst. Then you get shoved in the smallest office space with a bunch of empty file cabinets, like Dr. Craig."

"Can we actually get up there from here?" asked Violet, pushing a wheelchair over to Uncle Alec. "I thought the only exits were the tunnels."

"There's a ladder entrance hidden in a dummy supply closet. I've watched Dr. Craig use it every day on the cameras," said Scott.

"Okay, but what about Cyndra?" I squeezed my uncle's hand as he sank into the wheelchair with an appreciative sigh. "We're not leaving without her."

Jackson brushed his fingers over my cheek. "We're going to get her. I promise. But we have to get out of here first."

"Onward and upward." Scott turned and strode toward the door.

He led the dash out of D Wing's medical bay, making sure he always rounded the corners first, before waving the all-clear back to us. The emergency alarm still rang, and the white halls were washed in red, flashing light. So if someone was in the hallway, Scott hailed them with an urgent, "Which way?" and then let them race on by after temporarily pretending to join their group. He only had to do so twice, but Uncle Alec was always waiting in the wings, ready for Violet to wheel him and his powerful smile into view if things went south.

Scott groaned out a "Finally," as he came to a halt outside a closet marked *Supply*. He started to reel back for a kick, but Jackson stopped him with a hand across his chest. He frowned at the lock, and it twisted on its own.

"Nice," Scott said with a boyish grin.

Getting Uncle Alec up the ladder didn't prove as difficult as I'd thought—just slightly indignant for my poor, proper uncle, who had to cling to Jackson's back like a monkey. Jackson set him down next to the dull grey desk jammed into the tiny office, so he could lean against it. Scott hadn't been kidding. Most of the space was taken up by a line of locked file cabinets, but apparently Hurst hadn't given Dr. Craig the keys, because the desk was blanketed in stacks of papers and manila folders.

Scott hefted the one stiff metal chair and threw it at the window. Glass shattered, raining down inside and outside. He drew his hand into his sleeve and knocked away the excess before leaping through with little effort.

He turned back and motioned to Uncle Alec. "Come on, old man. You first."

Violet and Jackson closed in behind Alec, but he held up a finger. "Wait," he said, in a voice I knew well. It was his "don't disturb me while I'm in my study" voice.

He extracted a paper poking out of a manila folder and frowned at it.

"Summum Malum," he said.

"Huh?" I bolted to his side.

He handed me the paper and picked up its accompanying file, saying, "It's an interview. The detainee appears to have been influenced by a Shadow."

I scanned the typed record as Uncle Alec shuffled through more folders. The man being interviewed was dubbed *Mason Whittaker, a.k.a Ghost.* My breath caught when I saw a name in his answers.

Ghost: *Yeah, at the Stiff Pig. That's our spot.*

I knew that name. I'd seen it in the flashing neon of the Open sign while men in leather formed a threatening circle around me, Shadows hovering at their backs.

"No time. Come on." Scott snapped his fingers through the busted window.

"We need to take this." I slipped the paper back into the file.

"And these." Uncle Alec scooped up two more.

"Fine, just move it," Scott said.

How much time did we have left? Two hours? Tops?

Jackson and Violet boosted Uncle Alec over the tall sill, the folders tucked against his chest. Jackson gave Violet a little shove to indicate she should climb through next. Then he picked me up.

"No more wounds on your feet on my watch," he told me, glass crackling beneath his boots as he carried me to the window.

I couldn't help the smile on my face as he passed me through to Scott.

By the time Jackson vaulted over the windowsill and joined us on the dirt outside, Violet drove a UTV right up to us, tires skidding on the dry ground.

"Found a couple desert essentials in the storage box." Violet held a pair of men's boots out to me. "Might want to put them on. They're not too enormous."

"Thanks."

I took them from her as we all piled inside—Uncle Alec in the passenger seat, Scott hanging off the back, and me and Jackson in a tangle of limbs in the backseat. Violet put her foot down and got us the hell out of there.

I'd come full circle since the night Cyn set the place on fire, and I'd disappeared into the desert in a desperate bid to survive.

The five of us sat in the same narrow crevice where I'd slept cuddled between Jax and KitKat. I probably wouldn't have recognized it, but Jackson led us here on purpose to use it as a hideout while we planned our next move.

I sat between my uncle and Jackson, so happy to have them both beside me that I couldn't figure out who I wanted to fuss over more. I passed Uncle Alec a water bottle, being sure to loosen the cap first, and brushed ceiling dust off Jackson's shoulder. Now that we'd left the base behind, Uncle Alec seemed better—more alert, brighter eyed. He studied the file stolen from Dr. Craig's office with rapt attention. Maybe a few hours' nap in the desert could recoup some of his youthful vigor. Though we didn't have a few hours, as I'd told him. I didn't really know how his agelessness worked. It had clearly helped him digest Hurst's drugs faster, and he seemed healthier and stronger with each passing minute.

Scott and a very flushed Violet sat across from us, and the crevice was so small that our knees touched.

Scott dug a small notebook out of the inside pocket on his military shirt and flipped it open on his knee. He clicked a pen and began to scratch.

"I've only ever seen blueprints, not the actual interior of this particular building." He glanced at Jackson. "It was originally built as an off-site storage unit. Or so they say. Once we're in the building, there's the exterior door opened only by Level 1 clearance badges."

"Which we don't have," Violet pointed out.

Uncle Alec spoke up, though his gaze stayed on the interview transcripts. "I could obtain one, if put in close proximity to a person who carries this badge."

"Sure," Scott agreed, scratching another ninety-degree angle on the notebook. "But this door is a fingerprint sensor. And the guys guarding it won't have access. Too easy."

"Which means we need the finger of someone with the right clearance." Jackson sighed.

It was a little gross, but… "Dr. Hurst?" I asked.

Jackson shook his head. "They'll have found him by now and taken his body to the morgue."

"So, we need to find a way to get the high-clearance soldiers to the containment cell without anybody being the wiser." I shrugged.

Scott continued his sketching, adding a third level of security. "This third door is supposedly bomb-proof, but there are two armed guards protecting it."

"Which means it's possible to make them unlock that one," I said.

"Maybe," Scott agreed. "If we catch them off guard."

"So, the problem is the fingerprint door, right?" I asked. "We have a radio. We could just call for help. Someone who has the finger we need is bound to come."

"That might sound a little suspicious," Scott replied.

"What if we lob a grenade at the door?" Violet asked. "We don't need it to break. Just someone to come."

"That would definitely bring backup," Jackson agreed.

"I'd love to do that. But…" Scott shook his head. "Maybe a little more than we're prepared to deal with on our own. There's only five of us."

Alec raised his head. "Might I borrow someone's cell phone? I know of someone who could help us in that aspect."

Scott unhooked his phone from the holster at his hip and

handed it over. Uncle Alec typed a text with expert speed and then returned to his documents with a curt, "He'll call when he sees Vin's name in my message. Just a few minutes, I'm sure."

An unhappy thought struck me. "Um, you don't mean Carl, do you?"

Uncle Alec turned with a frown. "Not who I had in mind, but why?"

I squeezed his forearm. "Summum Malum got him. Before I reached him." He didn't need to know the grisly details, especially not the same day I'd told him his son died.

Uncle Alec let out a strangled grunt. "Oh, Carl." He shut his eyes. "May you find peace in limbo until we are able to open the beyond."

Giving Uncle Alec an awkward, one-armed hug in the cramped space, I looked to Jackson. "What about Mateo and KitKat? Where are they?"

"Hopefully close." He leaned over to check the time on Violet's cell. "When I realized what an ass I'd been, and lost control of my powers, Hurst ordered me detained. He was scared of me." He shot me a sheepish look. "I ran and went looking for Dr. Craig, but he was just... gone. He didn't answer his phone either. I don't know what Hurst did, but he obviously got Dr. Craig out of the way somehow, so he could experiment like he wanted to, without supervision." He shook his head, jaw tight. "Anyway, I had Reyes and another guy on my tail, so I didn't have much time, but I made a call to Mateo. I really only managed to shout some coordinates, but he's smart. I'm sure he'll figure it out."

"Call him again now. Get him out here, away from the base," I said. "The more allies with abilities we have, the better. We aren't leaving this place without my sister. No matter what it takes."

"This Dr. Craig, does he know about alternates?" Uncle Alec cut in.

"Sort of," Jackson said. "He calls alternates 'gifted.' He studies abilities. It's his life's work. But he doesn't know the half of it. He just thinks some people are flukes of evolution. He doesn't realize how many communities there are or know anything about your histories. Until I opened my mouth, he didn't know about your relics."

"I think he knows more than you think, young man." Uncle Alec extracted a paper and handed it to me. "Look there." He tapped a handwritten notation in the margin. "These bikers that attacked you at this… Stiff Pig—he recognized the signs of Shadow influence on them."

I read the note, scrawled next to a biker's account of hearing voices in his head the moment he caught sight of me outside the pub.

Summum Malum legends true?

I showed it to Jackson, too stunned to speak. Just how deep had Dr. Craig dug into the alt world? And when?

Jackson frowned at the note, then shrugged. "He calls it a legend. He probably found mentions of them in his studies, when he stumbled on other alternates like my mother's tribe."

"Yes. Perhaps," Uncle Alec said slowly.

"He believes in hard science. He'd be reluctant to believe something like that," Jackson pressed, desperate to prove his point—to Uncle Alec or himself, I couldn't be sure. "He only began publishing his discoveries on alternates when he discovered reports of DNA discrepancies. People with extra chromosomes. He tested his 'gifted' subjects, me included, and linked the abilities to the extra chromosomes."

"DNA reports?" Uncle Alec went so pale I almost asked Violet to check his vitals. He scrambled for another folder and yanked it open on his lap, spilling papers. "No, it can't be." His hands swished through the fallen papers, printed with charts and readouts of some kind. He plucked one out and stared at it in dumbfounded horror.

"What is it, uncle?"

"These were supposed to be confidential." He pressed a hand to his mouth.

"What was?"

Uncle Alec swallowed. "A few years ago, I had a hunch that alternate DNA might carry specific identifiable markers, like extra chromosomes. I knew an alternate man who worked in a lab, so I sent him blood samples from me and Vin to test in secret. I received these same results back a week later, but… someone must have copied them, or they were stored in the database by accident."

I rubbed his shoulder, though my hands were cold with shock.

He reached up to put his hand over mine. "Ellis, what if these reports are why they came for us? How they found us? Why you were taken?" He turned to me with a look of such sorrow and shame that it hit me like a physical slap. "I am sorry, Ellis. So sorry. I only meant good to come of this. I thought…" His voice broke, and he had to try again. "I thought we could find others in need. I thought perhaps we could find other girls who could bond with the relics, somehow, now that Alanna is gone from this world, and Aurora and Persephone and all their guidestones are missing. I've failed in everything. Especially in keeping you safe."

I took both his hands in mine and squeezed, meeting his teary gaze. "Uncle Alec, you have nothing to be sorry for. You haven't failed. I promise you that. You are not responsible for the wickedness of others. And look at me and Cyn, we've made it with your help." Though that last bit probably wasn't the best thing to say, given how many hardships me and Cyn had dealt with recently, all possibly stemming from these tests. But Uncle Alec had to stop putting the fate of us and the rest of the world on his shoulders.

He studied his lap and wiped his expression into its usual stoic lines, but he nodded.

Jackson looked between us, chewing the inside of his cheek.

"I can't speak for what Dr. Craig knows about you guys, but he's still in the dark about the big picture. He's just following legends. He always says folklore are exaggerations that can lead you to real scientific discoveries. I told him entirely too much, and betrayed your confidence, but I didn't tell him about the Summum Malum or about the history behind your relic—its purpose for saving the afterlife and all that. I didn't tell him about the extent of the alternate community or about Mateo's tribe's abilities either. I swear."

"I believe you." I patted his knee.

And I did. But I was having a harder time believing Craig was fumbling blind in the dark. If he knew about the Summum Malum, one of the alt world's most closely guarded secrets, he could know anything. And where the hell was he?

36
BEARS

WE DIDN'T HAVE THE LUXURY OF WAITING FOR THE SUN TO go down for cover. Cyn's transfer deadline of 1700 hours was quickly approaching.

Nobody was taking one of my sisters from me again.

Mateo and KitKat showed up just as Uncle Alec got a call back from his mystery buddy. Jackson and I squeezed out of the alcove to greet them. KitKat pounced on me like we'd been separated for months. She knocked me to the ground and licked my face, snuffling happily at my neck and ears. I laughed and rolled around with her in my arms, feeling normal for the first time in ages.

Although a bobcat greeting me like a dog probably wasn't really "normal." Just my new version of it.

Mateo helped me up. "I'm glad you're all right, Ellis." He pulled me into a hug. "What happened back at the hotel?"

Jackson cringed and fiddled with a loose thread on his fatigues. "I—"

"Long story short," I cut him off, "Jackson made a mistake and his old buddies at this Psy-Ops lab found us."

Squeezing my shoulder, Jackson offered a grateful glance, and I leaned my head onto his shoulder.

"Psy-Ops lab?" Mateo asked, adjusting Jackson's backpack on his arm and flashing me a glimpse of my empty relic. "That's what that concrete building is?"

"Yeah. Well, underneath it. It's where Jackson and I met." I caught Jackson's eye and smiled. "He's helped me out of that pit of hell twice now."

"Well, I guess we can forgive you for screwing up then," Mateo told Jackson around a teasing grin.

"Thanks." Jackson rubbed the back of his neck with a sheepish look that said, *You don't know the half of it.* In my opinion, Mateo never needed to know; it was behind us now. Besides, I had a feeling if I told the story in front of KitKat, she'd give Jackson a scar to remember her by.

"Here's your bag back," said Matteo shirking it off his shoulder. "Sorry to take it without asking, but you'd stepped out, and I didn't want to leave *la aguamagia.*"

"I'm glad you did," said Jackson, taking the offered backpack, relic and all.

"What happened with you two? Are you all right?" I asked.

"Yeah, thanks to KitKat." He patted the bobcat's head. "She started sniffing around like she'd lost track of something, freaking out on our hunt. Made me run back to the hotel. But there were creepy soldier dudes hanging around. KitKat saw them first. Made sure I hid. She's the reason we got here so fast, too. She found some tire tracks and started hunting. We were halfway here when Jackson called with the coordinates."

Jackson crouched in front of KitKat and scratched behind her ear. "What *are* you?" he asked, shaking his head.

"She's super kitty," I said.

KitKat squinted at me and yowled her distaste for the moniker.

"She's crazy intelligent," Mateo said.

"Trust me, I know." I reached for her. "It's like she speaks English."

"No, I mean, her thoughts and feelings are clearer and more complex than most animals."

"You can communicate with her in your *mind*?" I asked, startled.

Mateo waved a hand. "Not as easily as I can with sea animals, but the more I get to know her, the easier it is."

"Lucky. I'm officially jealous," I said.

He dropped his hand and looked down. "She makes me feel… connected again. But I still feel like half a person."

I pulled him in for another hug, missing Sofia. She'd know the right thing to say. I had no doubt she would have become my first real girl friend. He looked so much like her it was like staring at a ghost.

Uncle Alec poked his head out of the crevice and wiggled Scott's phone. "Well, that worked out even better than I'd hoped," he said. "We have a meetup point." He inclined his head to Mateo. "You're the friend Jackson called?"

"Yes. Mateo of the water tribe. Nice to meet you." Mateo hurried forward to offer a hand. Uncle Alec took it but caught sight of KitKat bounding at Mateo's heels and did a doubletake.

"Your pet?" he asked.

"I think she might take offense to that." Mateo grinned down at her. "But if she's anyone's pet, she's Ellis's."

KitKat chuffed and swatted Mateo's leg with her fat paw.

"She's not exactly a normal bobcat," I said. "I think she might be tied to the old magic."

Uncle Alec's brows jumped. "Ah, fascinating." He did his best to bend down to KitKat's level without tipping over on his cast, and to my surprise, she stretched out her neck to meet his hand with her head. She purred when he scratched the white marks on her head.

Scott shimmied out of the alcove. "Are we ready to go?"

Following Uncle Alec's instructions, we drove the stolen UTV back through the desert and ditched it to walk the rest of the way, assuming six people on foot would be less noticeable than a rumbling engine and a tire-spun dust cloud. Jackson and Scott scouted ahead, choosing our route based on Scott's intel regarding the base's somewhat lax security. The only problem with the plan was Uncle Alec's broken leg and overall fatigue. Even with me and Violet supporting him from both sides, our arms linked at his back, it was slow going. But his powers, drained as they might be, were still up to getting us inside Cyndra's cell. Someone had to convince the last armed guard to unlock the door, and it sure wasn't going to be me.

When KitKat suddenly stopped between Mateo and me to growl out a low, vicious warning, Mateo unsheathed his spear, and I steadied Uncle Alec while Violet reached for the stun gun at her belt. Jackson and Scott were dark figures up ahead in the wavy heat, but KitKat stared off to the right.

Toward three hulking shadows.

Three bear-shaped shadows.

Terror chilled my veins, and I gasped. "Demon bear! He found us!"

Mateo snarled, hefting his spear higher. "I'll kill him."

Jackson heard the outburst and turned, head swiveling toward the bears. I heard a shout, and then he and Scott came flying back toward us, but Uncle Alec held up both hands. "No. Everyone relax. They're friends."

My heartrate didn't slow as the bears padded closer, but I saw that none of these bears had the same burn scars as the one from Guatemala. The oldest bear, with gray on his muzzle, was missing an eye, though, and the broadest bear bore a trail of long scars that slashed down the right side of his muzzle and chest. But those looked like weapon wounds, not traces of fire. He stepped ahead of the others and bobbed his massive head in a silent greeting to my uncle.

"Gabriel," Uncle Alec returned the greeting. "Nice to officially meet you. I'm not sure what my son told you about me, but he said you were a good man. A good friend." He wrapped an arm around my shoulders. "This is Ellis." He smiled between us. "Gabriel's a friend from the town where Cyndra's lived the last two years. He was a part of her attempts to free you and has been waiting nearby since she was detained."

"So you're the bear man," Jackson said, just as Scott said, "That was you? Man, that's cool."

I smiled, thinking of Jackson's story about the bear Shifter on the security cams.

"When we spoke on the phone," Uncle Alec continued, "he told me that since two of his family arrived as reinforcements, they've been mostly staying in bear form for defense."

"Um. Thank you," I said. "For everything." I wasn't sure what the bear equivalent of shaking hands was, so I kept mine at my side. The bear let out a low huff of acknowledgement with a look that projected, *No worries.*

Alec continued, "We need you and your family to be the muscle for us."

The bear nodded again, scraping his claws at the rocky ground as if to say, *I'm ready.* His smaller companion, who looked younger around the face, bounced around like a puppy, his fat, fluffy booty knocking into his elders. He bared his enormous teeth at me in an unsettling attempt at a smile, and KitKat raised her hackles in a warning to chill out. Gabriel actually rolled his eyes with a weary sigh.

"Cole, I presume?" Uncle Alec asked the little brown bear with a smile-free chuckle.

Cole grunted his affirmation.

"Bernard, then?" Uncle Alec inclined his head to the oldest bear, who nodded back.

"Nice to meet you all, but we should really keep moving," Jackson said, checking his phone clock. "We've got forty-five minutes, tops, to pull this off."

So we formed a new line, with the bears as the rear defense, and resumed our trek through the desert. But it wasn't long before Gabriel nudged my back and indicated, by lowering onto his belly and bobbing his head at Uncle Alec, that he wanted to let him ride. Violet and I hoisted Uncle Alec onto the bear's back, speeding up the last half of the journey, leaving us a measly twenty minutes to spare.

The small, nondescript building where they'd housed Cyndra sat beside a small outcropping of rock. It was made of thick, silver metal that caught the sunlight with blinding intensity, and there was no signage to indicate its purpose. A single lightbulb hung beside a solid black metal door, lit despite the afternoon hour.

We bypassed the building and circled around the outcropping. Jackson and Scott halted in an area of overgrown brush, where they started yanking bushes out of the ground until they exposed a hatch clamped shut with a large padlock.

"The tunnels," Jackson explained. "They stretch for miles."

"These, however, are out of commission and in disrepair." Scott toed the padlock, then looked to Jackson. "What do you think? Shoot it?" His gaze drifted to Gabriel. "Or go with bear power?"

Gabriel answered with a low grunt, volunteering himself. After a short show of force with tooth and claw, the screaming metal snapped free. Jackson raised the hatch.

Scott stepped over the lip, his boot seeking the first railing as he added, "It's probably messy down there. Stay close."

"What about the bears? And KitKat?" I eyed the tiny port-hole entrance.

"We'll let them in from the inside, through the door," Scott assured me as he began his descent, flashlight tucked into his pants.

When Scott's head vanished into the dark hole, Jackson glanced up at Uncle Alec. "You stay with the bears. We'll let you in through the door, too."

It was a testament to how weak my uncle still felt that he didn't even argue. He clutched Gabriel's fur in both fists as the bears circled back around the outcropping toward the building.

Scott was right—the tunnel below wasn't even illuminated, much less maintained. Stacks of crates and boxes covered in inches of dust lined the narrow corridor as if the place had served as a storage facility before being forgotten. As I dropped off the bottom rung of the ladder, something skittered across the floor nearby, and my heart leapt into my throat. I danced away, and Scott's flashlight swung over just in time to illuminate two beady eyes.

I jumped and gripped Jackson's shirt.

"Rats." Jackson slid an arm around me.

"Oh." I released his shirt. "Cool. Um, just no spiders. Or snakes. KitKat hates them."

"Yeah, sure. KitKat. Even though she's not here." Jackson gave me a playful squeeze.

He withdrew his arm and handed me a flashlight from his bag. He offered another to Violet. Then the four of us moved carefully into the shadows.

Patches of the tunnel walls had flaked away over time. Somewhere nearby, water dripped—a rare sound in the middle of the desert. I swallowed hard when I noticed a giant crack bisecting the ceiling and hoped like hell the tunnel was structurally sound. I didn't fancy dying in a cave-in so close to freedom.

Scott tilted his flashlight up like a spotlight that illuminated another hatch. He spoke so low I could barely hear him. "We should be directly under the lobby. It's the only tunnel entrance in the building."

Jackson set his backpack on the floor and unzipped it, sliding his flashlight back inside. He retrieved a grenade, double-checked the pin, then offered it to me.

It was heavier than I expected.

Jackson climbed the ladder, careful to make as little noise as possible on the hollow metal rods. At the top, he hunched to press his shoulder against the hatch and paused, listening. I knew the lobby above was supposed to be empty but given how close we were to Cyndra's transport time, it seemed safe to not assume.

Finally, Jackson lifted the overhead hatch and peered through into the hallway.

"Clear," he grunted, shoving the hatch aside. He held out his hand to me.

I stretched up to place the grenade in his palm. "Remember how I thought you were crazy for carrying around grenades? I no longer think that."

"It's the Marine Corps in him," Scott said. "They're fun, but nuts, the lot of 'em."

I had to disagree. Jackson was the calmest, most logical person I'd ever known. But our relationship *was* brand new. I had so much more to learn about him.

More coins to put in my pockets. More memories to make us richer.

"You're still sure about this?" I asked him, not relinquishing the grenade yet. "You won't have a job when this is over."

"Remember the dog tags." His lips curved up. "That part of my life is over. You're endgame, Ell. I'd blow up a hundred doors to keep you safe."

I released the grenade, my insides fluttering.

Without further ado, Jackson tossed it, then ducked back into the tunnel, slamming the hatch shut.

A teeth-rattling boom shook the ceiling, and the wail of the alarm followed. Jackson waited less than ten seconds before he flung open the hatch and clambered into the hall.

One by one, the rest of us followed.

Broken lights dangled and flickered from the drop ceiling, and stone debris chipped from the walls dusted the floors. The door to the containment cell was still intact, as expected.

Scott hurried to the door to admit the rest of our team. Once all three bears pushed into the lobby, it got a little crowded. Uncle Alec slid off Gabriel's back to rejoin Violet and me, and we waited as a group for the first of the reinforcements to arrive, Scott on one side of the exterior door with his gun and Gabriel on the other.

"Nobody dies," Jackson reminded his friend when footfalls sounded outside.

Scott sighed. "Yes, Mother."

Less than sixty seconds later, the door opened.

The first soldier got the butt of Scott's gun to his head. Gabriel's giant bear fist slammed the second incoming man into the wall. Having bears on our side, as big and lumbering as they were, turned out to create quite the coup—six soldiers swarmed in, and six soldiers immediately took involuntary naps thanks to furry head-butts, bear slaps, and even one fluffy booty bump.

"Badge!" Scott called out as he pickpocketed an unconscious man's white key card. He strolled to the interior containment door and swiped the badge over the sensor next to the door handle, and we all held our breath. The keypad beeped, the lock unhinged, and Scott pushed open the door with a big grin.

Uncle Alec put a hand on Gabriel's massive, furry shoulder. "You and your men stay here. Don't let anyone in the building."

Gabriel nodded, though I saw him cast a longing glance at the door to Cyndra's containment cell. His striking blue eyes were rather human, and looking into them, I realized Gabriel wasn't just Cyn's friend—he was more than that. But he lumbered over to the open exterior door with his three pals and sat to await the soldiers' inevitable reinforcements.

We needed to hurry.

Jackson and Mateo both grabbed an arm of the man who'd held the Level 1 clearance badge and dragged him into the next chamber. Violet and I helped Uncle Alec limp after them, while KitKat watched our backs.

The next chamber was starkly white and lit by fluorescents so bright they burned my eyes. There was nothing in this room except for another door, this one marked by a fingerprint panel.

Jackson propped the unconscious soldier up while Mateo navigated the man's finger to the pad.

The pad flashed bright red.

Not Authorized.

Mateo dropped the guy's arm with an irritated growl. "This was the right guy?"

Jackson let the soldier slump to the floor. "Thought so."

Scott glanced at the keycard, then tossed it onto the man's chest. "Let's try another one."

They pulled all six men into the room, shooting a dart from

one of the soldiers' stolen tranq guns into anybody who moaned or groaned. They tested every finger in the room with no luck.

Scott planted his hands on his hips and glanced around the pile of snoozing bodies. "Not a single one of these assholes is authorized for entry. I thought for sure they'd send an agent or captain with clearance to check on the security alert."

Violet glanced at me before releasing Alec's arm, then joined Scott at the keypad to try her fingerprint.

Red flash.

Not Authorized.

She shrugged. "I thought maybe since I was medical…"

Scott summoned Jackson with a curling finger. "You try."

"There's no way," Jackson argued. "I've been AWOL. They've wiped all my clearance levels by this point."

Out in the main hall, the sounds of scuffling boots announced backup had arrived. Even though I knew Gabriel and his friends were bigger and stronger, I also knew the soldiers had guns, and not all of them shot tranquilizers.

If Cyndra's boyfriend got killed trying to save her, I'd never hear the end of it.

"We're out of options," Violet said, snatching Jackson's wrist. "Do it anyway."

She yanked him forward and pressed his thumb to the keypad.

Green flash.

Permission Granted.

Jackson's eyebrows rose toward his hairline as the door unlocked with a loud clank. "How in the hell?"

Scott laughed as he reached for the handle, saying, "Don't look a gift horse in the—"

A sharp thwack reverberated around us as Scott took a bullet to the chest the moment the door cracked open. He fell backward with a grunt, and Violet rushed to catch him before he hit the ground.

I ducked instinctually at the sound of gunfire, and something whizzed by my head close enough to ruffle my hair. The bullet slammed into the wall behind me with an explosion of stone and paint.

Everything went too bright and sharp-edged in the chaos, like someone turned up the contrast on a screen. Deafened by the shots and my own heavy breathing, I watched Violet drag Scott away from the door, shouting words I couldn't make out. Mateo tugged Uncle Alec out of the line of fire, and Jackson picked up Scott's fallen gun.

He chambered a round and ducked inside the next room.

No! He wasn't playing lone gunslinger on my watch.

I chased after him into the third, fully furnished lobby that looked more like a teacher's lounge with couches, a fridge, and a coffeemaker. Another round of gunfire ripped through the room and passed like buzzing bees all around me. I couldn't breathe, but I couldn't stop either. Jackson returned gunfire from behind a computer station rigged with a half-dozen surveillance monitors. I didn't know what the hell I was capable of doing to help, but there wasn't a force in the world that could keep me from reaching him.

The two soldiers tasked with guarding this room had flipped their table over and unloaded clips at Jackson, destroying the monitors in an explosion of glass and sparks. The acrid scent of electrical smoke filled the room. The fridge, which appeared to be leaking, sat beside the final door to Cyn's room, on the opposite side of the room from where Jackson was drawing the enemy fire.

"Ellis!" Jackson snarled. "Get out of here!"

Reyes' thick head of hair and square jaw poked over the top of the table, and a gun pivoted toward me.

I only had one place to hide. I dove onto my belly, sliding head-first through a puddle of water behind the fridge like a batter stealing home.

My head slammed into the door of the next room, and gloriously cool water gushed over my fingertips. Gunfire rained out behind me, Jackson called my name, and Reyes laughed.

"Thanks for the promotion, AJ," he shouted over the din. "You have to call me sir now. Too bad I'm going to have to kill your girl.

Maybe I can talk Dr. Hurst into letting you keep her head once he's done poking around in her brain."

"Hurst is dead. You're next," Jackson growled back.

Gunfire banged against my eardrums. A bullet plunked into the stainless-steel fridge and made it rock.

But I'd found water.

It seeped not from the fridge, but beneath the door, as if someone had left a bathtub running with the drain plugged. If I listened closely, I could hear what sounded like a rushing waterfall.

I closed my eyes, my only thought that Jackson was in danger, and dunked my palms into the shallow puddle. It made a faint burbling sound.

More bullets slammed into the fridge, and I heard jars explode inside. Two shots pierced clean through the back, and drywall crumbled onto my head. Fear curled my fingers into claws, and the water began to swirl. I was like a sponge, drawing in more and more water from beneath the door until I was up to my elbows. The water whirlpooled around my body, soaking the front of my dress.

I let the pressure build as another bullet ricocheted off the floor a foot away and struck the wall beside the fridge.

I had no clue what I was doing, but I was going to do something anyway.

When my arms shook with trapped energy, I let it go.

Water arced out from my body like pressurized jets from a fire hose that tipped the fridge onto its face.

Wood splintered and cracked. Reyes and his partner cried out when the mangled table was thrown skyward and struck them both in the head. The second wave of my jets slammed their chests as they tried to run for more cover, Reyes hobbling with his leg brace. The wave sent them sprawling through the air until they bashed into the wall.

I stood and sloshed through the remaining water to Jackson, who was stumbling through the debris toward me, Scott's gun perched on his shoulder.

The chairs had disintegrated. Bits and pieces of cracked wood and splinters lay strewn across the floor. The table was in half near the oddly bent legs of a groaning Reyes. He and his partner had runners of blood pouring down their faces from their heads. Their weapons had been thrown free.

Jackson kicked the two guns further from the injured men. His boots sent another wave of water over my ankles as he reached for me with his free hand. "You hit?"

I shook my head and took his fingers. My knees wobbled a little as I pressed myself to his side.

Mateo peered through the open door, taking in the scene in one sweep.

"Scott?" Jackson asked sharply.

"He's okay," Mateo said, coming further into the room. He pointed his spear at the two downed men. "He had on Kevlar. It's just a cracked rib. Violet's taking care of him." He called over his shoulder, "Alec, it's clear."

Uncle Alec ventured inside. Little by little, I was starting to see bits of him shine through, more of his vigor returning, despite the *shuffle-thunk* of his hard cast with each step.

He paused over the two soldiers and flashed a threatening grin. "Ah, you again," he crooned to Reyes. "How droll."

Reyes' nostrils flared as he tried to wriggle backward on his forearms. "Your shit doesn't work on me, old man. Remember?"

Ha! Reyes really thought he'd gotten a full taste of what my uncle could do?

"You're not going to move," Uncle Alec boomed, his smile wider, vicious.

Reyes stilled and went glassy-eyed, consumed by the power this time.

Uncle Alec relaxed his face and casually scanned the wrecked room, alighting on the fridge and then following the trail of water across the floor to the firewood I'd made of the furniture, landing finally on the splinters embedded in the walls.

"Impressive, Ellis," Uncle Alec said in a firm, approving tone. "We have some work to do to allow you better control, but this is a good start."

I beamed, not caring this probably wasn't the time to bask in the glow of my uncle's praise.

Uncle Alec took in the keypad, knowing we needed access, and smiled at glassy-eyed Reyes again. "Stand up."

Reyes' dopey expression went completely slack as he slowly and awkwardly climbed to his feet, falling into the wall before he was able to lean against it, barely able to put weight on either leg. Had my jets snapped the bone of his unbraced leg? Or had the impact of the wall done that?

But before Uncle Alec could give further instruction, Jackson approached the keypad saying, "Wait. Let me just try."

Brow furrowed, he pressed his thumb to the pad. Green flash. Eyes wide, he withdrew his old badge from his plethora of pockets. He turned it side to side, murmuring, "They told me it was worthless now, but…"

He swiped it beside the handle.

The lock clanked, and the door opened.

I heard that waterfall again, louder now.

A flummoxed Jackson pocketed the "worthless" badge, hefted his gun, and motioned for Mateo to stay with me as he carefully walked through the door into Cyndra's containment cell.

A moment later, his surprised voice came back: "Dr. Craig? What are you doing here?"

37
FALSE FATHER

Dr. Craig?

Had Hurst locked him up here, too?

"Jackson," the doctor's fatherly voice replied. "Took you long enough."

I splashed through the water in the doorway, but as Uncle Alec and Mateo moved to follow, the injured soldier on the floor lashed out a leg that struck Uncle Alec's cast. My uncle slipped like a cartoon character stepping on a banana, slamming into the hard concrete on his back. His head bounced off the ground with a sickening *thunk*.

Mateo let out a sharp yell and launched himself across the room. He swung his spear like a baseball bat, hitting the bleeding soldier with a loud smack across his temple. The man flopped to the ground, out cold.

As Mateo squatted down to check on a motionless Uncle Alec, I whirled on Reyes, ready to attack, but Uncle Alec's manipulation still held him captive. He leaned motionless against the wall, letting water soak his boots.

I heard Jackson's next words as a muddled murmur, drowned by the roar of rushing water. The cogs in my head turned in slow motion, torn between Uncle Alec and Jackson. I couldn't decipher any details of the dark room ahead, but whatever was happening inside wasn't right somehow. That gut feeling told me to choose Jackson.

"Stay with Alec!" I called to Mateo, then darted through the door as Mateo called my name.

My eyes adjusted to the shadowy inner chamber, and I took stock of the situation.

Dr. Craig sat alone on a folding metal chair in the corner of the room, shrouded in darkness. Only his paunch and the gray stubble on his rounded jaw stood in sharp relief, illuminated by the door-way. The single light dangling in the far corner at his back couldn't reach him, but I didn't see any shackles, any bars.

His benign stare drifted away from Jackson when I walked in.

"Ah. Good. Here she is." Dr. Craig tapped his fingers on some-thing long and black in his lap. "Welcome back, Ellis."

I watched his *tap, tap, tapping*, trying to distinguish the object in his hands from the surrounding darkness, but it was like looking though a pinhole.

A... gun?

Why would he be hiding in Cyndra's cell with a gun?

Before I could question anything out loud, however, my atten-tion was drawn to the source of rushing water.

Illuminated by the lone bulb, a waterfall fell over a metal table from the high ceiling. The drops sparkled in riveting patterns as the bulb swung, light turning the water to fire. The water called to me as it spilled over the edges of the table to the floor and formed a river that sloped slightly downhill toward the door. The drain at the room's center couldn't gulp the water fast enough, leaving some of the stream to lap playfully at my ankles and spill into the next room.

A new voice spoke up, sputtering, "It's a trap! He needs us for his deal!"

Refocusing not on the hypnotizing water but the shape within it, I made out strands of drenched red hair, flattened and turned auburn by the waterfall's ceaseless onslaught. Fat droplets of spray bounced off pale, freckle-dotted skin. The waterfall wasn't falling on an empty table.

It was falling on Cyndra.

My sister was strapped to the metal slab on her stomach, her forehead pressed to the surface by the force of the cascade. The thick deluge nearly hid her skinny form. She couldn't turn or she'd get water in her nose; she couldn't even open her eyes.

"Cyn." I sprinted toward her.

Dr. Craig whipped his rifle up and aimed it at me. "Not so fast, Ellis."

Jackson leveled Scott's rifle on the doctor with an authoritative, "Stand down! Put it down, now!" while I slid to a slippery, heart-pounding stop.

I stared down the barrel. I had a supply of water literally at my feet, but I didn't dare use it. One twitchy finger, and I'd be dead.

Dr. Craig eyeballed me and slowly tilted his head. "We need to chat."

I motioned to my sister. "You're hurting her!"

"Water works well for putting out fires before they begin," Dr. Craig said smoothly. "Would you rather I keep drugging her?" He motioned with the barrel of the gun. "Now, back away from the water before I find it necessary to set you on fire. I don't want to hurt you, but I will. They just need you alive."

"They," I repeated, my heart sinking into my stomach. I glanced at Cyn, and her eyes told me the truth in the split second before she had to turn away and breathe. She'd already told me, really.

It's a trap! He needs us for his deal!

All of his notes and obsessions we'd pieced together… Dr. Craig had chased down the "legend" of the Summum Malum. Or maybe they'd found him.

Now, he may as well be one of them.

"Dr. Craig, please. What's this about?" Jackson asked. Though he didn't lower his weapon, I saw his Adam's apple bob in his throat.

Dr. Craig sighed. "Jackson, just put it down. I know you aren't going to shoot me. Not when I have your little *infatuation* in my crosshairs."

Jackson bared his teeth. "That's exactly why I can't put it down, sir." Each word sounded strained, like they were agony in his throat, and sweat beads shone on his forehead.

"Don't force me to use this." Craig propped the rifle up on his lap so he could pat an oblong plastic pendant hanging around his neck. A blue button sat at the upper center, and speaker holes took up the bottom.

Jackson eyed it like it was a detonator.

"I know what you're thinking." Dr. Craig thumbed the button. "Just one click, and your powers are useless. I'd really rather not leave you writhing on the floor. I need you to do your old mentor one last favor."

He kicked something heavy from beneath his chair, and it slid over the concrete to Jackson's feet. In the light of the doorway, I recognized another pair of torturous thermal cuffs.

"Put them on her. Now."

Gun still trained on the doctor, Jackson bent to retrieve the cuffs. He squeezed the metal, a muscle in his jaw twitching, and glared at the doctor.

"Now, Jackson," Dr. Craig barked like a drill sergeant. "That's an order."

Jackson looked at the cuffs, then at me, and cocked back his arm. "Never." He chucked the cuffs into the dark. I heard them smack concrete with a crunch.

Dr. Craig let out a strangled cry, securing his grips on his trigger and the pendant.

Chest heaving, Jackson stared the doctor down, gun back in both hands. "Do what you want to me, but I'm not helping you. But you won't use that gun on her. You said so yourself. You need her alive."

"But not standing," Dr. Craig snarled back, his rifle barrel bobbing as he fought to hold it aloft one-handed. "Or conscious." He dropped his hand from the pendant to lift a little dart pistol from his lap.

I broke through their standoff, biting out an accusation through gritted teeth. "You're working with the Summum Malum." If I could keep him from pushing that button and hurting Jackson, we could get out of this together.

"A recent development. I find it pays to pick the stronger side."

I scoffed. "The Summum Malum don't pay. Any money they promised you isn't coming."

"I didn't ask for money." Dr. Craig eyes brightened with greed, like a junkie who found a secret stash. "No, what they can offer is far more valuable."

I put a hand behind my back and channeled my focus toward the waterfall as I asked, "And what's that?"

"The greatest asset of all. Knowledge."

The stream around Cyn's head thinned to a trickle, and the water around my feet began to swirl, building velocity.

"Knowledge of power beyond the scientific world's current comprehension," Dr. Craig rattled on. "About discoveries that can put a man in the history books. About the keys to immort—" He looked between Cyn and me, blanching. "Back away from the water, Ellis."

I lifted my chin in defiance, summoning the whirlpool up around my ankles to centralize the power. Craig jerked the gun barrel downward.

Bang!

I shrieked and stumbled back as chips of concrete exploded over my arms and legs when the bullet struck the floor an inch from my boots. Like shrapnel, the displaced concrete sliced and stung my exposed skin, and I fell down hard outside the pool of running water. Blood trailed down my limbs.

"Put down the gun!" Jackson shouted, breaking through the fog in my head as he stalked toward Dr. Craig in three big strides. "Don't make me do this!"

Dr. Craig clicked the button, and Jackson went down on one knee, face twisted in agony, teeth clenched.

"Stop it!" I screamed. "What is that?"

"High frequency sound." Dr. Craig gave a simpering, self-satisfied grin. "You and I can't hear it, but Jackson's telekinetic brain has extra sensory receptors. This particular wavelength causes that area of his brain so much distress, his gift is rendered useless. He once described it as white-hot needles to his forehead."

"I can still shoot, you bastard," Jackson ground out. His arms shook, but he kept the gun aloft.

"Do it, and the next bullet hits her." Dr. Craig breathed evenly like he had all the time in the world. Now, as he stroked the trigger of the gun, his fatherly smile looked eerie, plastered on his face—a psychopath emulating an emotion he couldn't feel. How many pictures of famous father figures had he studied to get that smile right?

"You put all of this into motion from the moment you told Dr. Hurst to put me in that tank," I guessed, needing time to puzzle a way out of this mess. "Just to get me here. To get my whole family here."

Hurst's frantic cries came back, unbidden. *It's not me! He led us to you!*

"I'm flattered. But the tank was merely a hunch, after I realized your DNA didn't match your so-called uncle's. When I found his name in your sister Alanna's murder file, I started pulling together the truth. Sisters taken in without following any of the usual legal channels, *collected* by a man with mind control gifts. I'd read the prophecies"—he made air quotes around the word—"of the sisters who would wield elemental powers. I'd read the SWAT team's reports of your fall in the pool. You stayed under longer than should have been possible, and I was certain you could do it again, with a little incentive."

My blood ran cold. "You took off the mask, in the tank. You tried to drown me."

"I tried to unlock your potential, so that you could learn to control it. Wield it."

"For you?"

He deferred with a one-armed shrug. "You're welcome."

"You knew about the relics and her family's powers the whole time?" croaked Jackson. Sweat poured down his face, and I wanted to tear Dr. Craig into pieces for the agony marring his beautiful features. For the betrayal, too.

"I didn't *know*. I thought they were exaggerations, myths based on mutated humans in ancient times." He kept that smile in place but shrank it into a more pitying shape for Jackson. "But when her sister showed up, I knew there was a deeper level of truth to it all. I had fire and water in my grasp, but thanks to you, water slipped through my fingers for a moment. When she told you she had an ally, I chalked your lapse in judgement up to a happy accident. I thought she'd lead me to the other three. Instead, she led me to that motorcycle gang who swore shadow monsters had told them to burn her alive. I knew the stories, but it wasn't until you called to tell me about the relic, an amplifier of a gifted person's... *alternate*'s ability that I believed them. Word for word." That greed burned in his face again and quickened his breath. "Summum Malum. Life after death. Natural elements, the raw forces of nature trapped in stone and wielded by human hands. Immortality."

"They're going to kill you," I said snidely. "The Summum Malum don't negotiate."

"Oh, but I'm not bargaining with them. I am joining them, in brotherhood. They see what a valuable asset I can be. And in return, I will be granted all their teachings, all their texts and abilities and strength."

He was eager to prove himself to allies who weren't even here yet. So eager that he didn't notice the miniature whirlpool I started forming beneath Cyndra's table, waiting for the right moment.

"The government's not going to let you just hand over two assets." Jackson tried to shake his head and winced.

"Alas, no," Dr. Craig said, and though his sigh feigned sadness, his thick lips curled into a more genuine, evil smile.

"You'll be convicted of treason," Jackson said. "All your research will go to waste. The Summum Malum will get what they want, and you'll rot in prison."

"Oh, but you're the one who broke Charlie out both times, son. You're the one who broke into this secure facility and attacked all those guards to retrieve her sister."

My heart stuttered. "You're setting him up."

"Bravo, Charlie." Dr. Craig chuckled and cocked his head at a mocking angle. "Isn't that what I just said?" He clicked the button a second time, and the sound must have stopped because Jackson gasped out an exhale before rising on shaky legs. "Now, boy, let's try this again. Tie her up, tranq her, I don't care how you do it, just put her in that corner over there." He gestured with his head to the corner behind me.

I peeked over my shoulder and saw two stretchers propped against the wall. One for me, one for Cyndra.

Jackson's grip tightened on the rifle, and he licked sweat from his upper lip, repositioning the butt against his shoulder. "You lied to me. All this time. About everything. You're the one who strapped Ellis to that bed and ordered her drugged. You sent me to check in with Scott on purpose, knowing I'd ask him to see the footage of her, want to check on her."

Dr. Craig rolled his eyes. "Must we really do this?" When Jackson's stony glare didn't flinch, the doctor huffed. "Fine. Yes. Hurst didn't want you in his little observation room." Dr. Craig waved a hand. "I had to let you see her on the cameras and piss you off somehow. And you went charging after Hurst and showed your hand, playing the white knight, as I knew you would. And you let her convince you to come free her sister, too, as I also knew you would. So I made it a little easier on you, programming your fingerprints and old badge into this facility's security system." He sighed woefully. "You're such a broken child that you wear your emotions on your face. I knew you'd fallen for her the moment you raced into the desert."

He shrugged, and I noticed his arm wavering. Just a small slip, but enough to tell me his muscles weren't accustomed to the weight of a rifle.

"Hurst didn't hesitate when I suggested he put you in a containment cell," he continued. "I even told him how to fortify it against your gifts." He smirked. "Please tell me you killed that idiot."

I was struggling to split my focus between the doctor and my whirlpool. I didn't know if I had enough energy stored yet. Hell, I didn't even know if that was how it worked. But keeping that water spinning reminded me I was strong. I could get us out of here.

Dr. Craig was locked on Jackson. "Love makes a man do stupid things. Your troubled history of bouncing from home to home, of violence against your own friends, has all been too much for you. You chose these dangerous experiments over your duty to the Marines. I thought you might come here, manipulated by your new girlfriend into rescuing her big sister. So, I headed you off and lay in wait, but when you arrived, you were armed. You threatened my life. And that's why I had to kill you."

Over my dead body.

A water jet fired from beneath the table and smacked Dr. Craig's arm. Eyes bugging, he snarled as he regained his grip and aimed at my knees, squeezing the trigger. Jackson thrust out an arm as the rifle bucked, fingers twitching like he meant to grab the barrel, but it fell from Dr. Craig's weakening hand. I was already midair, leaping for the waterfall's runoff stream.

The gunshot ringing in my ears, I slammed into the water and drew on my powers without hesitation or any real strategy. All I knew was I wanted to get the waterfall off my sister and drown Dr. Craig.

Energy ripped from my core when my body reunited with the water. It raced upstream, up the waterfall, and the pipes over Cyndra exploded. Ceiling tiles fell like rain, along with gushes of water from the destroyed pipe system. With the pressure diverted, Cyndra sucked in a massive breath and raised her head.

But the waterfall didn't sweep away Craig like I'd wanted. It dispersed, and I couldn't gather it fast enough.

Ugh! I needed someone to teach me how to *do* this crap.

A hand touched my arm.

I cried out and whipped around, lashing out with one hand. A pressurized jet shot from me and arced over Jackson's ducking head. The moment I saw his face, the water stream splashed back to the floor.

I glanced past him at the doctor.

The old man was slumped against his chair, an arm bent oddly at the elbow where my jet has dislocated the bone. But the blood pouring from his open chest wound wasn't my doing. He was dead.

"But… I only heard one gunshot," I said dumbly.

Jackson entwined our fingers and wrapped his free arm around my waist to gently lift me to my feet. "I rerouted the bullet." He ran a hand over my fuzzy hair. "No one hurts my girl."

Shock turned my skin cold. "Jax, that's… that's incredible." I squeezed his shoulder. "But are you all right? That couldn't have been easy. I know how you felt about him."

He shrugged, but his gaze dropped almost bashfully, then turned back to Dr. Craig. His mouth worked for a long moment before he managed to say, "I just feel so stupid for not seeing it. I actually believed he cared… you know?"

"Jax, he fooled everyone."

"You know, he should be proud of me." He chuffed out a jaded scoff, but the pull of his frown betrayed the depth of his pain. "I was in complete control when I killed the bastard," he finished, a shadow falling across his dark countenance.

I had no idea what to say to that. Years of love and dedication couldn't be erased overnight. His paternal feelings for Dr. Craig might always linger.

We were still holding hands, standing in the water, when a big bear galloped through the door toward Cyn. The one called Gabriel. A swipe of his claws demolished the straps binding her, and then the bear began to shrink and morph. Within seconds, a tall, muscular guy—naked as a newborn—tugged Cyn off the table and crushed her to his scarred chest. My breath caught and I nearly screamed a warning, but Cyn didn't cry out. His touch didn't burn her. Her relic had fixed it?!

Jackson and I turned away, giving them privacy for their moment of reunion. His hands slid over my injured arms, smearing the bit of blood from my cuts into the water on my skin. He kneeled to check the nicks on my legs. He lifted the hem of my dress, and his fingers were feather-light on my thighs. He brushed over one wound, then another. Even the briefest of brushes sent warm tingles radiating up to my hips, soothing the stings and making my body shiver.

By the time he stood back up with a gruff, "Flesh wounds," my entire body was as hot as if I'd walked through fire.

And then he kissed me.

I melted against his chest as his hands pressed into my lower back, melding our bodies together. Even though the water on my skin and dress was ice cold, his lips were hot, and I wanted to drown in the candied ginger taste of him. Every movement of his lips promised me protection and begged forgiveness without speaking a single word.

He tasted like home.

Enveloped in him, I drew back enough to murmur, "I love you, Jax," against his mouth.

His answering smile lifted my lips, too. "I love you, Ell." One of his hands climbed my spine with an urgency that turned the slow burn of our previous kiss into an eruption. We were pressed together again, and he was everywhere and everything.

Someone cleared their throat nearby.

We broke apart, breathing hard. I blinked through the haze of lust and affection and met my sister's gaze.

Cyndra.

She stood a couple feet away, her naked boyfriend hiding behind her.

Jackson shrugged out of his camo shirt and held it out. "Here, man. Till we find you some pants."

Gabriel accepted the shirt with a nod and wrapped it around his hips. "Appreciate it."

Gabriel was *huge*. Bodybuilder huge, built like a tank. He made Jax look small. His wavy dark brown hair flopped over his forehead toward those clear blue eyes that had stood out so starkly in his bear form, but most striking were the scars that marred his face and chest.

I averted my gaze, not wanting to be rude for staring too long, and beamed at Cyndra. I flung my arms wide and stepped to hug her, but she stumbled back into Gabriel, throwing up her hands to ward me off.

"No!"

I flinched away from her sharp cry and hugged my arms back against my own chest, already halfway to tears. "Cyn?" I said like a mewling kitten.

She softened, eyes crinkling with sympathy, but there was something off about them. "Sorry. I just can't touch other people's skin."

I raised an eyebrow at Gabriel's protective hand on her shoulder, index finger brushing along her tank top strap. "Well, yeah, I know," I said around a lump in my throat, "but I saw him hug you and—"

"He's the only one. We're bonded." She shrugged with an apologetic half-grin. "It's a bear thing."

"Wow. Bonding isn't just a bear thing, but that's amazing."

I took a step back so she'd relax, then let my eyes rake over her. She seemed exposed in the clothing scraps they'd put her in—made of the same thin, synthetic black material they'd put on me in the tank. But she also looked… different. Harder, maybe. She was thin, her limbs taut with muscles. Her fiery red hair was smoothed back from her face, soaked from the water torture, and her bright green eyes were bloodshot. They still didn't look quite right. Or maybe… they didn't look at me quite right.

Beneath her wet shorts, scars marred her pale legs, welted and rubbery like awful burns long healed.

I gasped. "Oh God, Cyndra. What happened?"

"Um. Cassie," she said, shifting uncomfortably to cover her thighs with her palms.

"What?"

"My name's Cassie now," she said with a grimace. "I lost my memories, when I got these scars, and I kind of have, like, this new life, I guess."

"You don't remember me?" I asked, a pang racing through my chest. When she looked at me, she didn't see her sister. That's what was missing from her eyes: all the hugs, all the cat fights, all the inside jokes, all the shared laughs and sorrows of siblings. They'd been erased for her, but I still saw them all in her face, relived them, longed for them.

She shook her head. "No. I mean, I know about you thanks to Vin, but I don't really remember." She hugged herself, rubbing her arms, her teeth chattering. "I'm sorry."

"It's okay," I said firmly, even as the crack in my heart became a canyon. It all made sense now why I hadn't heard from her in so long. "You lost your memory. It's not your fault."

I wondered how burn scars on her legs could cause amnesia, but now didn't seem like the time to dig up traumas.

I took a tentative step closer, hoping to give her one of the careful, clothes-touching-only hugs I'd learned to do before she left, but I hesitated. Would she want a hug? She didn't even know me.

Her green eyes caught mine, and she matched my careful step forward. Reaching out slowly, she brushed her fingertips over my downy cap of hair, careful not to touch my scalp, and smiled. As she let her hand fall, she brought the backs of her fingers a few centimeters from my cheek in a mimed caress.

"I've been told my memories were completely wiped, but I know you somewhere in here." She tapped above her heart.

I felt hot tears gathering in my eyes.

"I can feel it."

She had no memories of me, our family, or her obligations. And yet… "You still came for me." I wiped a tear from my lash.

"Always." She stepped closer.

I carefully looped an arm around the middle of her back, where there was no risk of touching skin, and gave a gentle squeeze. "You know, maybe it's best if you don't remember *everything*."

She laughed. "Why, were you a pain in my ass?"

"Amnesia couldn't erase that feeling, huh?"

Water sloshed near the door, and Mateo helped Uncle Alec into the room, supported with an arm around his waist.

Mateo lifted his chin, ready to say something, but Uncle Alec's wavery, "Cyndra?" cut him off. Tears shone in his eyes as he shuffled toward her, lips pressed tight together so he wouldn't smile. "Or rather, Cassie, now, right?"

Cyndra—Cassie nodded as she left my side to stand before him.

I heard her swallow hard as they stared at each other a long moment, both with hands tucked to their sides. "I might not remember you," she said at last, "but I know what you've done for me and my sisters. You're my best friend's father, and I loved him…" She choked on her next word and let out a tiny, hiccupping sob that, for her, might as well have been a wail. "Um, I'm sorry," she said on a shaky breath. "Do… do you know what happened to him?"

Uncle Alec hung his head for a second, then lifted it with a sharp inhale and a tentative twitch of his lips. "I know he's gone. And I know his last act was to fight for you, as he would have wanted. I'm so proud of him."

Cassie offered a melancholy smile. "I hardly trust anyone, but I trust you."

Uncle Alec's bunched shoulders relaxed. "That means more to me than you can know."

Cassie brightened a fraction. "I'd like the chance to get to know you again."

Mateo cut in softly. "We need to go. KitKat and the bears say more guards are coming."

I caught Jackson's haunted gaze.

He gritted his teeth and looked back at Dr. Craig's motionless body. "They'll have orders to kill me on sight."

"Then we need to run," I said, taking his hand.

"Wait," said Cassie, hurrying to the doctor's chair where she proceeded to rummage around in his pocket. She extracted a thick silver bracelet. "Dr. Dickhead took this from me." She slid the oversized piece of jewelry onto her wrist, where it flopped around, and strolled toward the exit. "Not sure what he thought it was or what he planned to do with it, but Alanna said it helps her find me. Maybe the Malum—"

"You've talked to Lana, too?" I chirped in delight as I followed her out.

"Mm-hmm. Once."

In the guard room, the man on the ground was still out cold and Reyes hadn't moved except to slide to the floor. Uncle Alec paused to flash him another wide smile.

"Give her your shirt," he said, pointing to Cassie.

Reyes shirked off the thick camo fabric and held it out toward Cassie. Gabriel snatched it for her.

"Now," Uncle Alec purred, "You're going to call whoever has authority in the absence of Dr. Hurst and tell them we went south."

Reyes saluted without ever focusing on Uncle Alec. "Sir, yes, sir."

As he reached for his radio on his belt, I prayed to the Priestesses that I'd never see that asshole again.

We hurried into the next room, where Violet had Scott on his feet. He looked a little pale, cradling his left arm—to be honest, so did Violet. She had two fingers on his neck, checking his pulse, and another pair tracking in front of his eyes. She hissed at him to follow the movement despite his low murmurs of, "I'm fine, Vi. Really."

In the front lobby, Cole, Bernard, and KitKat paced around

heaps of unconscious soldiers. Even though I saw some blood splatter on the floor, for the most part, they'd refrained from killing anyone.

As Gabriel stole a pair of pants from none other than Army Kong, lying in a heap with his unconscious fellows, Cole rammed his head into Cassie's chest, nuzzling her like a puppy. She chuckled and nuzzled back, rubbing her cheek over the fur between his ears, "Good to see you, too."

Apparently, fur didn't burn her either.

I half expected Cole to shift back now that the immediate danger had passed, but he and Bernard remained their fluffy bear selves.

Scott was thinking along similar lines. "Can't they change into people like you?" he asked Gabriel, jutting his chin Bernard's direction. "I'd like to shake their hands for all the help."

Gabriel grinned with only half his mouth, the right side dragged down by scar tissue. "Shifting takes a lot of energy. Dad likes to conserve his now that he's of a particular age. Cole has the opposite problem. He's so young that he doesn't have full control of the ability yet; it's easier for him to wait to shift in a safe, relaxed space."

Bernard grunted and held out a paw to Scott, who shook it with a chuckle.

The sun beamed down on the desert outside the containment building. Several UTVs had been parked haphazardly on the dirt, so we piled into them, minus the bears, and took off over the sand.

"Due north, if you please," Uncle Alec said with a little chortle.

Jackson drove our vehicle, with Mateo and KitKat in the back, and Gabriel and Violet drove two more cars while the two bears ran behind us.

I leaned against Jackson as we raced toward the horizon, thinking to myself, *I'm so glad that's over. We're safe.*

Cassie. Uncle Alec. All our new friends.

But my rose-colored glasses shattered when the shadow of a massive bird shot into the sky and unfurled its wings across the

sun, black feathers backlit with blazing orange, like a phoenix rising from its own ashes.

Shadows. Hundreds of them. More than I'd ever seen in my life.

How? Why? *Oh.* I glanced back to the ground. They were here
to watch the show like Romans watching their gladiators fight to the
death. The desert was the Colosseum. Our opposition was a dozen
dark forms on the horizon, their bodies wavy in the desert heat.

At the forefront of the small army was the bear from Guatemala.
He'd found us.

The Summum Malum had come to collect their prizes.

38
CLASH

JACKSON HIT THE UTV's BRAKES, FORCING OUR WHOLE caravan to halt. Dust billowed over the windshield and into the open frame, coating my arms, as Gabriel and Violet's UTVs flanked us. When the bears skidded to a stop and all three engines cut off, the abrupt silence was jarring. Beyond the low howl of the wind, a hawk's cry sounded in the distance.

When the dust cleared, a line of humanoids and giant animals stretched behind the bear loping toward us. Maybe twenty of them total, but the Shadows above had split into a flock of a hundred smaller birds, casting dancing shade patterns that made their force look larger. They were still a half mile away, visible but not close enough to cause any damage.

Yet.

Bernard rose on his hind legs and sniffed the air, big nose twitching.

Mateo leaned forward, draping an arm over the back of Jackson's seat as he murmured, "How did they find us?"

"My dead boss in the containment chamber," Jackson said, glowering. "He told us he intended to hand Ellis and her sister over to the Summum Malum."

"I think that bear has Cyn—*Cassie's* relic, too," I added, glancing at my sister in the passenger seat of the car beside us.

Her green eyes widened, stricken. "The fire relic. He still has it?"

"Still? So you knew?"

Cassie cringed, eyes on the demon bear. "Yeah, he took it from me when I set him on fire."

I grinned. "I should have known."

"Wow, he scarred bad," she said, almost to herself.

"He should've been able to heal those," murmured Gabriel, catching Bernard's large eye.

"Who is he?" I asked.

Gabriel spoke up, gravel in his voice. "My brother. Aaron."

Cole squeezed himself between Bernard and the UTV to lick Gabriel's hand.

Cassie touched Gabriel's leg in a small show of solidarity, then glanced back at me. "Did the relic look okay?"

I nodded. "Whole, as far as I could tell. He had it with him when he found us in Guatemala. I think he used it to locate the water relic like a reverse-engineered guidestone or something. It's the only explanation for how he beat us there. We followed my guidestone to find—" I cut off and slapped Jackson's arm, gripping tight. "Jax, where's the water relic?"

He motioned to his backpack on the floorboard at my feet.

"We can't let him have it." I bent to grab the strap.

Mateo gripped my seat. "I promised my *abuelito* to keep it safe as long as I had breath in my lungs, and that's what I'll do."

"We shouldn't draw attention to it." Jackson put a hand on my arm before I could pull the backpack into my lap. "Keep it in the floorboards and only guard it if they get too close."

Mateo nodded, but he didn't look happy about it. KitKat snuffled his neck, and he wrapped an arm around her.

In the passenger seat of the left UTV, Scott twisted with a pained grunt, reaching behind the seat to pat the pile of rifles and assorted guns we'd jacked from fallen soldiers on our way out. "We've got firepower. My guess is they don't. Gives us a leg up."

Uncle Alec, who was splayed across the backseat of Cassie's vehicle with a cold wet shirt pressed to the bump on the back of his head, chuckled. He nudged Cassie's covered shoulder, though he didn't open his eyes. "Firepower in more ways than one."

Her cheeks flushed as red as her hair.

"I won't be any help out here," I said. "No water for miles. Dr. Craig seemed to think I could just produce my element, like Cyn, but I haven't figured it out yet. It'll be a gun for me."

Uncle Alec squinted open one eye. "I taught you weapons tactics for a reason. I'll be no help either, I'm afraid. Everything's a bit fuzzy at the moment. I can hardly open my eyes."

Gabriel turned around in his seat and reached back to peel open Uncle Alec's eyelid. "It's a concussion. He needs a hospital."

Uncle Alec waved his free hand ineffectually. "I just need a moment to recuperate."

"We don't have a moment," Cassie told him, rolling her eyes. She might not remember him, but she cared for him.

Violet drummed her fingers on the wheel. "We could run. Ride the other way. Well, not south. Scott needs medical attention, too."

Scott scoffed, shoving her lightly on the shoulder. "I'm fine, V."

Violet gave him a withering look. "You're in no shape to be in hand-to-hand combat."

Jackson looked between his friends and my uncle before he blew out a breath and shook his head. "We only have two options. Into that"—he pointed at Aaron's army—"or right back into the military's hands. They'll have more guns, and even if we don't take a bullet, we'll likely wind up locked away."

"Then we fight," I said simply.

Jackson put an arm around me and kissed my forehead. "We need to come up with a plan."

I eyed the pile of guns, then grinned. In all the time we'd been together, he'd been the man with the plan. I'd deferred to his assessments and strategies because I didn't trust my own abilities.

But now...

"I have a plan." I practically bounced in my seat. "We pick them off one by one."

"We have no cover out here," Jackson pointed out.

I patted the narrow dashboard. "Don't we?"

He flashed a wolfish grin that sped my pulse.

It only took us a couple minutes to empty the UTVs, line them up, and push them over onto their sides, creating a fortified barrier with their metal bottoms. Jackson tucked his pack containing the water relic tight beneath one of the seats. Cassie helped me get Uncle Alec settled carefully behind the central vehicle, where I warned him not to move upon pain of a good thrashing by his surrogate daughters and their badass powers. Violet crouched to check him over, asking him questions as she looked in his eyes, felt his pulse, and tested his joints.

Jackson and Scott—enduring his cracked rib without complaint—worked on consolidating ammunition, while Mateo, KitKat, and the three bears stood watch.

I crouched next to Jackson, and he handed me a gun. "You know how to use that thing?"

"An M4 carbine?" I asked with a shrug. "Sure. Easy." I flicked the safety off and chambered a round.

He waggled his eyebrows and leaned in, his lips brushing mine as he said, "I think I love you even more."

He kissed me, and I stopped breathing.

If he noticed that he'd stolen my breath away, he didn't acknowledge it. He pulled back and grabbed another gun, handing it to Cassie. "You know what you're doing?"

I didn't hear my sister's answer because Violet squeezed in beside me and said, "They're picking up speed." She rested her rifle on the edge of the UTV and surveyed the desert through the scope with her one eye. "Hurry up the preparations, guys."

Jackson offered a rifle to Mateo, who waved him off. "I'm more comfortable with my spear. I'll be part of the second wave with the bears."

KitKat nipped at his bare thigh beneath his wetsuit.

"The bears and *KitKat*," he amended, pulling a cross-eyed face at the bobcat.

"Well, I want one," Scott said, selecting another M4 from the dwindling pile.

Our second-wave team began to file out around the UTVs, while the rest of us set up the guns. It had been a while, but holding the rifle came naturally to me, like recalling how to ride a bike after years without. I set the gun atop the edge of the UTV and sighted on the silhouettes growing ever closer.

I wasn't nervous—not really. Not yet, anyway.

As far as I knew, this Aaron guy didn't have any alternates with long-range powers on his side. Our bullets could cut them down before they got close. The only issue might be armored skin. As long we didn't run out of ammunition, I had high hopes we'd get out of this battle fairly easily.

Demon bear fell into a gallop. His cohorts followed suit, racing over the cracked earth and dry scruff.

"Aim and hold," Jackson said quietly.

Bernard stood again and grunted a sorrowful, snuffling sound. I didn't have to follow his one eye to know where he was looking.

Gabriel patted his father's furry shoulder, murmuring, "I know, Dad." He turned to Jackson, face twisted by a war waging inside. "Please, don't shoot the bear. I think I may be able to talk to him once he gets close."

Jackson looked to me, but I deferred to Mateo. It was his family the demon bear had decimated. Mateo kept a white-knuckled grip on his spear as he appraised the bear family, pausing longest on Cole, who'd fixed him with puppy dog eyes that pulled my heartstrings.

"Deal," Mateo croaked.

"You heard him everyone," Jackson barked. "Leave the bear. Take out his army."

I pressed my eye to the sight and picked out an animal directly ahead. Through the scope, I could make out that it was a big cat species—bigger than KitKat, with strange geometric black markings on rust-colored fur. A Shifter, probably, or maybe an ancient species tied to magic, but no ordinary animal, not with that unnatural pelt pattern.

I aimed for the head.

"Get ready." Jackson's elbow brushed my arm as he adjusted his stance.

I braced the gun against my shoulder and fingered the trigger.

The big cat picked up speed. It loomed in my sight, drawing closer.

"Fire," Jackson ordered.

Five rifles exploded with an echoing crack that tore across the desert. My gun kicked back against my shoulder, but my bullet went wide when the cat dodged to the left. I shot again. The second bullet slammed into the Shifter's wide chest, sending them somersaulting.

Squinting one eye, I shot again.

The rising cat keeled over.

I picked another target. One of my old cyclops buddy's clan members. I lined up the singular eye in my crosshairs, and something wet and gooey splattered against the barrel.

Drops sprayed onto my right hand and sizzled like acid. I let out an involuntary shriek, releasing the gun so I could wipe the goopy liquid off on my dress. Except wiping the clear liquid off didn't take the pain away—it only put holes in my dress.

"What the…" Cassie yanked her gun away from the car and stared blankly at the barrel.

The metal was melting, sending up an acrid smoke that burned my nasal passages. The liquid thinned and then evaporated along with the gun.

Right before our eyes.

Shocked, I looked from her gun to mine. Whatever acidic material they'd thrown at us had begun to erode it away, too.

On my other side, Jackson let out a disgusted groan and tossed his gun to the dirt. "It's those frog things. The ones that killed Sofia. They're spitting some new slime."

Frogs. That's what their odd, webbed and pad-tipped fingers had reminded me of that day in the ocean. Fury bubbled in my stomach, and I peeked back over the UTV. Two frog creatures flanked Aaron. The advancing group was way too close now, while our guns were useless.

"Good aim," Scott said irritably as he tossed his smoking rifle butt down. "They took us out in a matter of minutes."

"Two guns left," Jackson said, tossing one of the backups to Scott.

Cassie held out a hand and fire danced along her fingertips. "I'm armed."

Jackson looked past me to Violet and Uncle Alec. "You two stay here. Be ready to throw a UTV back on its wheels and get us the hell out of here when we can break through the line. Got it?"

"I'll be ready, Violet said, squeezing Uncle Alec's wrist.

Jackson glanced over the car, then addressed Gabriel. "If you still want that talk, it's now or never."

Cassie kissed Gabriel's cheek before he rose, hands up high.

"Aaron!" he bellowed over the sand.

A frog man opened his mouth wide, ready to spit acid from the back of his throat, but the demon bear must have given a signal, because he stood down. Kind of. They were still running for us, but they slowed to a jog so Aaron could pull out in front. The Shadow flock swirled faster overhead, agitated. Did they fear Aaron would back down?

Gabriel kept his hands up and his stride long but cautious.

"We know the others might not give up. We know you've made deals. But you don't have to be a part of this. You don't have to fight us again."

"Think he'll really surrender?" I whispered to Cassie.

She didn't tear her eyes from Gabriel as she replied, "Hard to say. I doubt it, but the last time we fought, he gave his guys orders to spare his family from the worst of the violence. Though, he had way less allies to keep control of then. Still, maybe Gabriel can subdue him."

Out in no-man's land, Gabriel slowly spread his arms wide, as if welcoming his brother into a hug. "Aaron, please. You have to know, everything is already forgiven. Just come back to us. Be a family again."

Aaron ran straight for the hug, tongue lolling out of his mouth like a dog returning to his master. On our side of the cars, Cole grunted and scuffed a paw through the dirt.

"Something's not right," Cassie muttered, sparking flames on her fingertips. "Why isn't he slowing down?"

"He feels it, too," Mateo said, jutting his chin at Cole.

Aaron's goofy grin became a snarl, and he lunged, slamming his massive paws into Gabriel's barrel chest and pinning him to the ground.

Cassie gasped. Cole let out the undulating cry of a frightened cub and lumbered around the UTV, breaking out into a run. Aaron roared in Gabriel's face, hovering jaws gaping wide enough to take off his head in one chomp.

A fireball smacked Aaron right in the nose, and as demon bear swiped at his smoking muzzle, Cole rammed into his side. Aaron hit the dirt hard, rolling once. Cole swiveled his fluffy form between his brothers, shielding Gabriel as he started to grow fur of his own. With a low, warbling sound, Cole snuffled the air in Aaron's direction, lowering his big head as if pleading. Aaron shoved to all four paws and tossed his head, grunting back. He took a step forward, and Cole's claws slashed the air in a warning. Aaron didn't flinch, but he didn't retaliate either. Not until his allies overtook the brothers, charging past their standoff with barely a glance as the Shadows circled overhead like angry wasps. Aaron rose on his hind legs and roared, front paws splayed wide.

Jackson leapt to his feet. "Go time! Stay sharp, everyone!"

He and Scott vaulted over the UTV, while the rest of us fanned out around them and sprinted toward the enemy line. Gabriel, now a full-grown bear, mimicked Aaron's threatening stance at Cole's side. I put myself on a collision course with a cyclops, knowing I could take him. I'd done it before. Intense heat warmed my cheek as a wall of flame shot by and slammed into the cyclops and the red cat at his heels. They went up in flames as if they were covered in accelerant, and I halted, chilled by the throaty bellows and high yowls they made in the throes of a slow, painful death.

Cassie raced past me, lobbing more fire at another cat creature that stood in her path to Gabriel. He and Aaron circled each other, still on hind legs and locked in a teeth-baring faceoff. When Aaron struck out first, a fireball blasted his swinging paw, allowing Gabriel an opening for a vicious claw swipe to the Aaron's cheek.

Did Cassie just conjure her flames or draw her energy from the sun? *Holy hell.*

She was a force before. Now she was an avenging angel. Watching her lob fire grenades and dart between Aaron's hench-men, I tried to study how she used her power so I could mimic it.

So, I was distracted when a feral snarl signaled a cat Shifter's pounce. I blocked a swiping paw, tossing the limb away with the force of my arm bone, and punched the muzzle with my other fist. But a claw snagged my shoulder as the cat fell, and the stinging pain lanced toward my neck.

I kicked the Shifter while they were down, square in the soft spot under the jaw—a knockout blow that was sure to bounce the cat's brain around in their skull.

I heard the whistle of a club swinging through the air just in time to duck. I whirled on my new cyclops adversary, agility on my side, and nailed him with a knee to the balls. He grunted but didn't buckle as I'd expected. I spun for a roundhouse kick that struck his wrist and made the club handle fly to the very ends of his finger-tips, but he maintained his grip. I blinked rapidly, transfixed, as his mushy, lumpy skin began to bubble and reform around the club handle until it became part of his forearm.

I backpedaled to dance around him, fists up, but I had a hard time diverting my attention from the club arm. When I threw my next punch, I didn't see his other hand snatch for my wrist. With a powerful tug, he tossed me to the sandy earth and tried to stomp on me. I rolled, but when I popped up, he was already swinging. The club struck my side with rib-cracking force, and pain exploded from armpit to hip. I whipped around from the force and hit the ground on my hands and knees, gasping through the agony.

A gunshot cracked across my consciousness. I flipped around to my butt in time to scoot clear of the cyclops as he tumbled like a felled tree, pouring blood and brain matter from a gaping head wound. Jackson ran toward me, his arm and small pistol still outstretched, the barrel smoking.

Jackson holstered the pistol at his ankle and adjusted the stolen rifle leaning on his shoulder so he could hold out a hand. "You okay?"

"Just a flesh wound," I joked, slapping my palm against his so he could pull me back to my feet.

"Let's stay together," he said gruffly. He aimed his rifle and jerked his head right, away from a ring of Cassie's fire. "This way?"

I nodded, and he ducked back into the crowd.

I stayed at his heels, throwing kicks and punches as we passed enemy alts. But the crowd had grown thick with smoke, combat, and more bodies than I'd anticipated. I moved without thinking, using Uncle Alec's training on autopilot, while Cassie's fire cranked up the heat and gunfire ripped through the smoke.

I was following up with a gnarly punch on a cyclops' misshapen head when someone rammed into me.

I didn't have a chance to catch myself. I slammed face first into the dirt. My nose crunching into the ground. Sharp agony blossomed in my face and blood sprayed out.

My attacker slammed into me again, and my forehead bounced off the hard-packed desert sand.

Snarling my fury, I snapped back my elbow, and the foreign

weight left my spine on impact. The blow left my forearm tingling with pins and needles.

I rolled to my back, panting through my mouth as I waited for the unseen attacker to leap back through the filtering smoke. An orb of light flared to life in the smog. Alanna! I snapped my head toward her and saw a tall, stark naked, spindly humanoid coming at me toothpick-arms first, galloping on all fours like something out of a Dali painting. His fists punched down beside my ears and his bulbous head lowered, opening a leechlike mouth and boring into my soul with glowing red eyes.

KitKat lunged out of the gray smoke and tackled the hell beast with a ferocious growl, yanking on his slender neck and smacking his head into the dirt as blood spurted between her teeth. She clamped down on the spinal cord and rolled along with her prey, right over top of me. The spindly guy's sharp knees caught on my injured side before they cleared my body, stealing my breath and making my vision go fuzzy for a second. I went up on my elbows, trying to scramble to my feet to help her, but I still couldn't draw a proper breath.

KitKat yelped, and I saw her fluffy form go flying. She hit the dirt on her side, skidding a couple feet. Blood welled on her forehead next to her ear, and she lay entirely too still.

Fury and fear launched me to my feet just as the spindly humanoid straightened over the bobcat's motionless body, leaking a dark, viscous blood from a savage wound that should have been deadly—had his anatomy been fully human. I screamed, part anger, part release, and slammed into the alt traitor with my shoulder. We flew away from KitKat, and I made sure every ounce of my body weight landed on top of that piece of crap as we crashed to the earth.

I gripped his round head and slammed it against the ground, once, twice, three times, until his red eyes rolled back into his head.

I left him crumpled on the ground and got to my feet, swaying dangerously as I clutched my tender side, praying I hadn't collapsed a lung. Fire burned in my chest as I gulped for air.

Two more figures loomed out of the smoke, coming right for me and KitKat.

I swallowed.

Maybe this was it. Maybe I was going to die, about to give my life for a damn bobcat that shared some speck of the magic in my blood. KitKat lay deathly still on the desert floor, blood seeping from the gash in her head. But she was breathing. Her fur shook with a ragged inhale.

As long as she was breathing, I'd kill anything that came near her.

The thinner of the dark silhouettes pulled ahead. It looked like liquid as it lunged through the air, bounding in zigzags too fast for my eyes to follow.

I lifted my hands, ready to fight, but then Mateo appeared from the gray clouds, chasing after Alanna's bouncing light ball.

He stepped between the spindly alt and us, his spear sheathed on his back. "Hey, amigo," he said, holding up both palms. "Take a deep breath. Calm down."

The spindly humanoid halted, and its red eyes glazed over.

Mateo smiled. "That's it. Easy does it." He added a string of Spanish, something quick but potent.

I'd figured out that the water race had the ability to "calm" people but seeing it in full effect gave me chills. He was like a Jedi warrior using the Force.

I watched in awe as the spindly humanoid started to back up, herded away from the battle by Mateo's words.

Until the frog man arrived.

No sooner did I see his strange, yellow-spotted, three fingered hands than he opened his mouth to reveal a green tongue and spat a clear loogie into my face.

Standing over KitKat, I took the brunt of the frog's acidic sludge, all over my bare chest and shoulders. A scream I didn't recognize ripped from my aching lungs when the chemical burning began, eating through my flesh.

I staggered backward, swiping at the sludge. Trying to rid myself of the evil. I only smeared it around.

I collapsed backward, barely avoiding squashing KitKat, and writhed through the pain.

Was this how Sofia felt when she died? Her insides on fire. She'd died so fast, coated in a green slime from the frog's hands, but this felt slow. Agonizing. I wanted to scream for Jackson. Scream for Mateo.

Someone make it stop!

The burning spread to my hands as I rubbed clumps of dirt over my chest, trying anything to stop the acid's progress and wipe it off me. *I'm going to die.*

Water.

I need water.

I rolled onto my belly, rubbing my burning palms through the sand, drawing in shallow breath after shallow breath, trying desperately to cling to consciousness. Praying for relief.

But the desert was an overworked mother. She could offer very little.

Dry ground. Dry bodies. Nothing to free me from the pain.

I dug my nails into the cracked dirt, tears streaming down my face.

KitKat was inches away, bleeding to death.

I didn't even know where Jackson was, or my sister. Maybe even Uncle Alec was in danger, a sitting duck behind an eroding UTV.

I'd told myself I'd be stronger. I'd promised myself I would defend them. But what strength did I have without the water bound to me by my relic? The relic had reinvented me, yet I was acting like my old self. Taking the pain lying down. Powerless.

No more. Not this time.

Pressing my forehead to the dry ground, I prayed. To the Priestesses. To the magic inside my relic. To myself—and the warrior that was supposed to dwell within.

Give me strength.

Give me comfort.

Give me the ability to beat this.

Something hard slammed against the back of my head and rolled away over the dirt—a broken hunk of cyclops club. I cried out and held tighter to the ground.

I won't be broken.

Energy swirled through my palms. I embraced the desert, eyes shut to better examine the sensation. Swirling.

Living. Water rushing through the darkness beneath.

I thought I heard Mateo cry out. Then a bear's snarls and my sister's answering cry. Jackson yelled something I couldn't understand.

My friends were in trouble.

The people I *loved* were in trouble.

I refused to lie helpless while their lives hung in the balance.

I refused to be broken.

I refused to give in.

I would fight for their lives.

I dug my fingers deeper into the dirt, reaching for that energy beneath the ground, calling it. I breathed deeply and drew the energy into myself. It swirled in my gut. I focused on my breaths, focused on the slow build of energy between each. *In, out, in, out.* Energy built upon energy, until I lost myself in it.

I invited it in, ready to let go and let my power wash over me. But no, that wasn't quite right. Instead of letting it take charge, I clung to it. I took it in my hands, under my control. Let it carry me high instead of drag me under.

I sought out the water, asked for its obedience, and awakened the underground.

39
FOR LOVE

DIRT EXPLODED BENEATH MY PALMS.

Water as crisp and cool as the Rio Coyolate washed me clean of the frog man's acid. The column parted around me and shot into the sky with phenomenal speed, a powerful geyser that cloaked me in a crystalline barrier.

I blinked against the raining water and looked down at my chest. The outermost layers of skin were ravaged, leaving raw tissue and raised red burns beneath my collarbone. Excruciating, but the pain no longer felt like a savage, living thing. I gingerly touched my throbbing nose, and my fingers came away bloody. Water droplets thinned the blood, washing it down my palm until it dissipated.

I stumbled to my feet at the heart of the roaring geyser and squinted through the watery mirage. My friends still fought in my geyser's downpour. Jackson yelled instructions I couldn't quite hear, and gunfire barked over the chaos. Cassie had moved outside the circle of falling water and tossed fireballs at any enemy who stepped foot outside the gusher. Mateo leapt gracefully through the crowd, his spear slashing and stabbing with a fluid, deadly beauty, as if the water had awakened his ancestors within him.

I swiped at my wet face, then remembered why I'd drawn up the underground spring to begin with.

KitKat.

My heart pounded as I searched the ground for her. What if she'd been caught in the blast? What if I'd hurt her worse?

Frantic, I leapt through the wall of water and spun in a circle.

Another of those spindly, alien alts loomed out of the pouring rain, sharp elbows and knees bent out like skittering spider legs. A halo of smoke from one of Cassie's fires billowed off his burnt scalp as he hissed at me through his toothy leech mouth.

I waved my open hand in an upward motion, slicing through the falling water. A mini geyser burst from the ground and caught the alt in his slender middle. He went flying. I closed a fist instinctually, ceasing the mini geyser, and the alien alt crashed to earth, crushing an arm beneath him. With an angry screech, the alt stood like a man and lunged for me with his good arm, bleeding thick, black blood from the melty ruin of his charred head, steaming when the rain hit it.

I ducked grasping fingers and landed a well-placed kick to his bony back that knocked him onto his face in the mud. I knelt and slammed my hands to the wet ground, then squeezed until the sludge responded to my call and encased my enemy, slurping him underground.

Underwater.

Into death.

Movement caught my attention. I spun, expecting another attack, only to see KitKat's head twitching.

The rain soaked her fur, making her fluffy body look skinnier and smaller. I let out a sigh of relief and crawled to her, tugging her head into my lap so I could check the wound on her forehead.

The jagged edges of the wound cut through one of the white lines between her ears, bleeding profusely. Through the split skin, I could see her skull.

"No," I gasped the word, placing my hand over the injury and pressing down hard. "No, no, no."

She'd gotten hurt saving me.

Her jaws yawned open, gaping like a fish out of water. Her eyes stayed closed, and her limbs never moved.

No. No. Not KitKat.

Hot tears joined the freshwater streaming down my face. I pressed her snout against my thigh and increased the pressure on her wound. While the battle raged around us, I scrambled for a plan. I had to get her clear, had to get her to Violet. Just before I raised my head to search for a path through the fighting, KitKat rippled. The way the desert rippled at the highest heat of the day, making the colors on the horizon fade into one another like an abstract painting.

I thought at first that I'd imagined it. But then it happened again—a ripple that started at her head and raced down her spine.

She began to change.

Her fur receded, and her snout sank into her face. Her torso stretched. Her limbs lengthened and readjusted. Until there was no longer a bobcat head in my hands, but a teenaged girl.

She was tiny, but taut muscles covered her petite limbs. Bloodstained, snow-white hair fell over elfin features.

Familiar features.

Leaving my palm pressed to the wound in her scalp, I gently turned her face to me.

Add a little bit of baby fat to her cheeks and put her pale hair in pigtails…

No. Way.

Aurora?

I said it only in my head at first, then croaked it. "Aurora!"

It was really her. Rori. My precious little hellion. My baby sister. But sixteen now, all grown up.

How had she come to be here right when I escaped the lab?

Better yet, why on earth had she stayed a bobcat the whole time? Never telling me who she was.

I hadn't even known she was a Shifter. She'd been taken too young. Her abilities hadn't shown themselves yet.

Jackson skidded onto his knees in the mushy ground next to

me, breathing hard. He glanced at the girl laying half on my lap, then raised an eyebrow. "Who's that?"

"KitKat," I said, jaw flung wide. "She's my sister."

Jackson blinked, brushed his hand back over his hair to throw off water, then shrugged out of his wet t-shirt. He draped it over Rori's pale body.

Before he could straighten, a massive, brown figure barreled into him.

Jackson went flying with an audible *oof*, and the bear sank his claws into the mud, spinning gracefully around to face me. Jackson fell with a splat, limbs spread-eagled and eyes closed.

The bear tilted his head at me. That angry burn scar wrapped up his neck and face like a thick, frayed rope.

Aaron.

I let go of Rori's head and slapped my palms to the mud.

The water surged at my command.

A thick wall of liquid soared ten feet into the air. Aaron was nothing but a wavy form on the other side, and while I watched, fear trickling in, he began to shift.

One moment, he was a hulking bear.

The next, he was a human silhouette.

"Shut it off," he barked like a drill sergeant.

"No," I called back, scooting away from Rori so I could stand. I planted myself between my sister and the enemy.

Aaron kicked the water, but the pressurized flow yanked his leg over his head and dropped him on his butt with a shout. A vein throbbed in my temple as I concentrated, making a thin jet shoot free and punch him in the nose. Through the temporary gap, I caught a glimpse of a younger, leaner version of Gabriel. The waterfall closed, and I watched him stand in silhouette, sputtering and wiping what I hoped was blood from his nostrils.

"I dare you," I taunted. "Try to come through. Next time, it rips your leg off."

Okay, I didn't *know* if I could make it do that, but it sounded good. And the false bravado helped me push past the knot of fear in my throat.

I chanced a glance over my shoulder at Jackson. He was out cold and far from his gun, but his chest rose steadily.

Everybody else was on the other side of the water wall.

With Aaron.

Two more figures loomed behind him. I couldn't make out what creatures they were through the running water, but the way they posted up next to him told me they were his companions— not mine.

Fire still flashed outside the geyser's range, so I knew Cassie was okay.

But I didn't have eyes on anyone else.

It's just me.

"Drop the water wall," Aaron snapped. "Or I rip the legs off of every one of your friends."

"You wouldn't kill your own family," I countered, remembering what Cassie had said. Plus, alts allied with the Malum in a desperate attempt to save what was left of their ravaged clans, not destroy them.

He harrumphed. "My family," he said in a tone that suggested a sneer I couldn't see through the water wall. "I'm here because of them. Don't you get that?" His voice took on a fevered pitch. "I tried to make them stronger, keep them safe, and no matter what my brother says about them doing anything for me… they won't pay my debts. They're too high and mighty. Too caught up in tradition and all the other idiocy that slaughtered half of us." The tiniest crack ran through his boisterous bravado, and I heard a kid inside it, shaky with fear I'd felt many times.

"They care for you. They just want you back. I've seen it for myself, how much they love you."

"There's no going back!" Aaron thundered, but that fear pitched up the shout. "I'll do whatever I have to, to get what I'm owed. And if that means putting my family in the ground, away from all this, then so be it. Their physical forms don't matter," he said, with more surety. "Not really. For doing the Summum Malum's bidding, I ensure their immortality in the next planes. I do this for all my family, living and dead. They just can't see it yet. Try again, bitch."

How in the hell was I supposed to respond to that? I wasn't going to break through all this dude's rationalizations in a matter of minutes. He'd clearly been telling himself lies way too long.

"Come with me willingly, with your relic, and I'll let your friends walk away," he said amid my silence. "No more alts need to die today."

I swallowed the knot of nerves and checked Jackson again. He was still unconscious, water raining on his face.

I could do it. Turn myself over to Aaron, let my friends get out of here alive. That was a kind of bravery, right? Sacrifice for the greater good.

But that wasn't quite right. The people who had cast their lot with me fought for what they believed was the greatest good. They fought for liberation. They fought for each other. No matter the cost.

To hand myself over to Aaron and the Summum Malum would only cripple their cause and bring them pain.

The right thing was destroying one of the Summum Malum's favorite living puppets. While they searched for Aaron's replacement, we'd have the same opportunity to figure out how to end them.

For good.

Time to keep my promise to myself. I wouldn't hold back any longer. I wasn't a drowning damsel in distress. I *refused* to be that girl anymore. The government could bomb my home, kidnap me, tie me down, study me like a rabid animal. The Summum Malum could throw every pawn they had at me and hunt me for my powers until the day I died, but I would never stop fighting.

I'm strong and capable.

I'll never believe otherwise ever again.

Hope Cassie's boyfriend forgives me for killing his brother. Because Aaron started this fight. He chose the wrong side, and now he's forcing me to protect mine.

I strode to the wall, ready to shove my hands inside, intending to use it as a battering ram—pin Aaron and his minions to the ground, something like that.

But I didn't get a chance to see if I could pull it off.

As I approached, Aaron shifted again, growing larger, turning brown with thick fur. He changed so fast, I almost thought I'd imagined it.

Until his scarred bear form leapt through the water wall.

Right at me.

The wall picked him up, and he roared his discomfort at its punch to his gut, but his thick hide and bulk cushioned the worst of the blow. He cannonballed down on me, giant paws slamming into my shoulders and chest. We hit the ground on my back, and mud closed over my head.

Panic sledgehammered my heart when everything went dark and heavy. I couldn't breathe mud, not like I could breathe water. I couldn't see. I couldn't even move beneath the bear's immense weight, crunching into my damaged ribs with fresh agony. I searched with my newfound sixth sense and found only mud—no fresh water, even though I knew the geyser still pumped nearby.

My hands were pinned against my chest beneath Aaron's sharp claws, so I couldn't dig my fingers in the ground and attempt to draw out more from the spring.

But I felt the cool muck on my bare skin elsewhere. My feet. My legs. My arms. The sundress left most of my body bare. And my power didn't just come from my hands.

It came from inside me.

All of me.

Squeezing my eyes tight, I focused on the ground everywhere it touched my skin. My lungs burned for oxygen. My chest screamed and my broken nose set my face on fire, but I pressed beyond the aches and pains, ignoring them as I searched desperately for the water I knew lay beneath.

A soft, electric tingling tickled my spine.

I homed in on that sensation, letting it fill my body. Energy crackled through me, growing in intensity. It became everything I knew, everything I felt. Power. A force of nature surging through the dirt, barreling into me, growing.

Growing.

Growing.

Bright lights exploded behind my lids. I had to bite my tongue to keep from opening my mouth and drowning in the mud. I needed to breathe.

Finally, the stored energy reached the brim, too much for me to hold.

I set it free.

The water roared like a lioness—a whole pride of angry mothers.

Aaron's weight disappeared, and cold, fresh water soaked me, washing away the mud. I sat up, ignoring the now-broken rib as I quickly wiped my face clean and took a desperate, painful gulp of air.

The explosion had left me in a small trench that was quickly filling with water. I splashed more on my face and chest, grimacing as mud sluiced over my acid burns.

Aaron rolled on his back like a flipped beetle, grunting and stumbling back to his feet. He turned like a drunkard on wobbly knees.

I couldn't let him get the upper hand again.

Swishing my hands in the growing pool lapping at my waist, I drew a deep breath, closed my eyes, and called on my element. Called on my wall. Called on my geyser. And aimed.

My creations merged into a tidal wave that reached for the clouds, arced over Aaron, and crashed down at rocket speed just as the bear stood on his hind legs and raised his front paws to block his face. Solid as a brick wall, it pummeled him with an audible *smack* that dropped him to his belly, legs splayed out.

The bear roared, part pain, part fury, pinned like a butterfly on a board.

I channeled my focus, adjusting the spray to target his wildly thrashing head. To drown him.

I didn't see the frog man until he tackled me.

I splashed into the pool as a frog man's slimy hands gripped my shoulders and groped for my chin.

"No!" I shrieked underwater, making the pool churn to combat and filter the acid before it could hurt me again. The pool gushed over his shoulders, and he clamped his mouth shut to keep it out. "I'm not the enemy! Let me do this!"

But the water was sluggish to respond to me. I was too hurt to fight. Every breath hurt, no matter how I drew it in. The burns on my chest sent sharp, stabbing pain shooting through my nerve endings and incapacitated my hands.

My pool was now a shallow puddle.

"Let me go!" I slapped ineffectually at the frog man's chest, surprised by how human he seemed up close. He held me down with one knee, his acid hands planted in the water. He wore a button-down shirt, so soaked it'd gone translucent. Unlike the cyclopes or the spindly aliens, he could blend with ordinary society. He could have opted to disappear into the regular world if the Summum Malum ravaged his clan's homeland.

He was a human. He was an alternate. No different from me. Not really.

Why had he thrown his lot in with the Summum Malum?

It was not a pact made lightly. Something fueled his denial. Something let him convince himself he wasn't just a disposable tool, used by dark souls who despised him. Only one thing could blind a person so entirely, as it had also blinded demon bear. Love.

Having endured the worst of my meager onslaught, the frog man lifted one hand and reached for my face. I saw green slime ooze from his pores and coat his palm as it drew closer.

Oh god.

I recalled Sofia's puffed face, her body limp in the water. My puddle bubbled as panic seized me, but I met his eyes. Warm brown. Human.

"Whose life did they promise in exchange for my family's?"

The frog man flinched as if I'd slapped him, and sorrow crossed his face like a fleeting shadow. His hand stopped an inch away and retreated.

"My father," he replied, seeming surprised by his own voice. It cracked when he added, "My brother," and some of his weight backed off his knee.

I knew his pain. His loss. "And where is your brother?"

A strange third eyelid blinked on his dark eyes, startling me. I managed not to react.

"Gone," he said in a harsh whisper, looking over my head instead of at me. "But it wasn't them—"

"Where's your mother?" I cut over his desperate denials. "Did they burn her like they burned mine?"

His Adam's apple bobbed. "There is no right choice. We are dead either way," he said, eyes and voice hollow. "You, me, and all we care for. They are coming to claim this world. The only question is whether we get to reunite with our loved ones in the afterlife."

"You can choose to walk away. If their victory is so certain, they don't need you. They've made you empty promises they never intend to keep."

"If I walk away from this cause, my brother died in vain." Any bite the words had died when a tremor slipped into his voice. "Their reward is not assured, but at least it is a *chance* to regain what I've lost. I have no other choice."

"You can choose to stop playing their game. You can live how you want and enter the afterlife with your head held high. Would your brother really deny you that?"

At last, he looked me in the face.

We stared at each other for a long, long minute.

Then the frog man backed away, water sloshing around his

ankles as he stood. He climbed from the trench and took off without looking back.

My heart fluttered, exhausted. *That actually worked? Holy hell.*

I scrambled to get up and peered over the top of the trench. My pounding tsunami was still in place right where I'd left it.

But Aaron was not.

Somehow, he'd shimmied out from beneath the deluge. The soggy bear was halfway across the desert, limping badly on a front paw that was twisted sideways. I thought I saw the white gleam of bone in the shifting fur. The force of my watery fist had mutilated and crippled him, but he'd gotten away.

"Dammit!" I snarled, slapping the edge of the muddy trench. I'd wasted too much time trying to talk some sense into the frog man.

I leaned heavily on my palms, watching the bear hobble away.

His body blurred out of focus.

My head swirled, and black spots seeped into the edges of my vision. I slumped forward, resting my head on the ground.

All the water stilled and fell.

I closed my eyes and gave in to my injuries.

40
FROM THE ASHES

MY EYES FLUTTERED OPEN TO A COOL, DIM ROOM I DIDN'T recognize.

After one jolting thump of my heart, the warmth of Jackson's arm wrapped around me quelled my freak-out. His chest pressed my back with each rise and fall of his deep, even breaths.

I rolled over so we lay face to face beneath a thin blanket. Someone had cleaned me up and replaced my ruined sundress with a pair of loose sweats and a t-shirt. I nestled closer to Jackson, burying my face in the crook of his neck.

"Good morning." His voice rumbled through me.

"Where are we?" I asked, shivering against the chilly air.

"One of Alec's safehouses. New Mexico," he replied sleepily. "Guess this is your room." With eyes closed, he held out a hand and waved it at the closet door, which opened under his influence. With another wave, he extracted a second blanket from the piles inside.

I watched, amused, as the blanket drifted over to the bed, where he grabbed it and tossed it over both of us. He nuzzled my hair with a little sigh.

"I thought you didn't use your powers," I teased.

"This really amazing girl proved to me that we are what we do with our powers," he murmured. He opened his eyes and let them caress my face. "She's absolutely fearless. I want to be like her."

Warmth gushed from my chest and made my breath tremble.

"How'd we get here?" I asked to deflect from my blush.

"A very muddy, crowded ride in one of the UTVs," he replied, cupping my face in one hand. His thumb brushed my cheek as he continued. "Thank goodness Bernard and Cole headed back to their place, or we never would've fit."

"They left?"

"Yeah, something about needing to check up on a cousin who'd run off. They were hoping he'd sent word home by now." He shrugged. "Anyway, your uncle had a van waiting that brought the rest of us here."

"Is everybody okay?"

Jackson nodded sleepily. "Injured, but okay."

"No kidding." I took a deep breath that hurt my side. "I think I have broken ribs."

"And a broken nose." He rubbed his hand over my shoulder beneath the blanket. "A mild concussion, too."

"Guess I should be thankful to be alive."

"I know I am." He kissed my eyebrow, then my cheekbone, careful to move around the edges of the bruising on my nose as he dipped to the corner of my lips. Then his mouth covered mine.

He might not have had the candy for a while, but it was his taste. Wild ginger on his tongue and cinnamon sugar on his skin. I opened my lips to deepen the kiss, making sure not to bump our noses, and dug my hands in his t-shirt to draw him closer. The heat between us banished the chill of the AC. Even without any blood, I could taste and feel his emotions—taste how much he adored me.

How much he wanted me.

He didn't care about the sharp angles my bones created beneath my skin, didn't miss the curves I'd lost, the ideal of beauty I'd been mourning. He didn't know the old Ellis. Jackson only knew this version, and he loved *me*. The whole, not the pieces.

And now, when his fingers explored my body, working around my wounds, I relished the ecstasy of the touch without fretting over what "imperfections" he might find. There was no such thing as perfect. No single definition of beauty. All that crap had made me fear my reflection, hate myself, doubt myself. No more. The next time I saw myself in the mirror, I'd smile and move on, rather than standing around nitpicking or judging. I'd grieved for the old Ellis long enough. I might always miss some things about her, but the woman I'd become deserved love too. She had strength and confidence and new, meaningful relationships that my old self had lacked. Life was about transformation, and I wanted to love every stage.

Someone knocked on the door. "Ellis? Are you awake?"

Cassie.

Jackson huffed as he drew back his hands. He kissed me one more time. "I'll go make some coffee and give you time with your sisters."

"Sisters?" I said blankly.

Oh.

KitKat. No, Rori.

A crooked smile broke over Jackson's face. "I told you she wasn't a normal bobcat."

I grinned and watched in a warm haze of sleepy happiness as he shoved back the covers and got out of bed. He looked lean and powerful in his black joggers and tight black t-shirt. They looked a bit *too* tight, like he might have borrowed them from a closet meant for Vin.

He opened the door and greeted Cassie. "Hey. Be easy on her. She's still weak."

"I will," Cassie promised, assessing him with laser precision.

He glanced back at me one more time before disappearing into the hallway.

Cassie held the door open and motioned for someone behind the frame to follow.

Rori hobbled in.

She looked rough, with two black eyes and stitches in her pale forehead. But when her light amber eyes found mine, none of that mattered.

"Rori," I murmured, shoving aside the covers. I leapt from the mattress, crossed the room in three strides, and crushed my baby sister in a bear hug.

"Rori, I thought you were gone," I said into her hair, careful to avoid the stitches.

"Nope, but you might suffocate me if you don't ease up."

"Sorry." I laughed.

She scrunched her nose at me like she used to as a toddler. "And, if you don't mind… I do like Rori better than Aurora, but I think I'd like to stay KitKat. Or maybe Kit."

I grinned. "Sure. Mom did have a knack for picking the weirdest old names, huh?"

"It's not really that," she muttered, shrugging. Her frown held pain, and she aimed it at the floor, avoiding my eye.

Changing the subject for her, I put my hands on her shoulders and said, "You look good."

She pulled a "Really?" face.

"Well, considering you were unconscious when I last saw you, yeah."

"Cassie and Violet fixed me up good," KitKat said. "Cassie cauterized the wound, and Violet had fluids and stuff in her medical kit. She said if she wasn't so prepared, she might not have been able to stabilize me. Tried to do some cosmetic work with the stitches too. As if I care." She huffed.

I squeezed her again, not caring if she complained. Hot tears stung my eyes. Violet had only had that first aid kit because I'd needed anti-venom. If it weren't for that wandering spider, my sister might not have survived.

Pure dumb luck.

KitKat wriggled out of my grip, grinning. "You look better than I expected. Only slightly like a raccoon."

"Thanks." I stuck out my tongue. "But the bigger question is *why the hell* did you stay a bobcat all this time?"

She shrugged again, dejected. "I was stuck." She rubbed her

arm. "It's kind of a long story, but where I came from, they were forcing me to try to develop powers early. And it just, like, backfired. I shifted by accident and then couldn't figure out how to shift back."

"Well, I promise Gabriel is a much better Shifter teacher than those assholes," Cassie said, patting KitKat's head with a gloved hand. "You'll get it down in no time. Now, scoot, kiddo."

She pinched the back of KitKat's shirt and tugged her aside—a big-sister habit I remembered well but they probably didn't. Cassie crossed her arms and narrowed her eyes in a "don't bullshit me" face I also knew well, careful to leave a foot of space between us. "Are you okay? Really?"

"Tired," I said honestly. "I think there's more internal injuries than external, to be honest."

She nodded, her fiery red curls swinging wildly around her face. "Yeah. I kinda assumed."

"Is Uncle Alec okay?" I asked.

Cassie made a soft sound of assent. "He's resting. He already looks loads better."

KitKat laughed. "Yeah, he looks like he's sixty instead of ninety."

Cassie shot her a scornful look that didn't faze her at all. "He'll be okay," she told me. "I think probably a couple days in bed will restore his energy. As long as Kitty Kat here gives him some peace and quiet."

"What?" griped Kit with an exaggerated shrug. "He talks funny. I like him. He uses big words. And he says I'm *fascinating,* so…" She stuck out her tongue with a sing-songy "nah-nah" sound.

"I think he also said, 'full of untamed energy' and 'coarse,'" countered Cassie.

"Uh, 'delightfully coarse,' thank you very much."

I laughed too hard and had to clutch my aching rib. Cassie's green eyes scanned me as I sank to the edge of the mattress, too exhausted to hold myself upright.

"You got pretty beat up," Cassie said, brushing her covered fingers over a bruise on my shoulder. She squared up in front of me, her gaze raking the rest of my body like a doctor. "It'll be a couple weeks before you can shake the concussion, and the broken ribs are going to be a pain in the ass. But the burns…"

KitKat glanced at the concerned creases around Cassie's eyes, then grinned at me. "They're kind of badass."

I took a deep breath, then tugged my shirt collar down to reveal the acid burns.

They were… red. Raw. Angry.

Kit squinted, mouth twisted into a sideways pucker. "You know, it kind of looks like a phoenix."

I tried to make out what she was seeing from upside down. "What do you mean?"

Kit sat beside me and hovered a finger over the burn, careful not to touch my raw skin. "Look, two wings spread out, the tail down here, the beak open in a victory call."

I followed the outline she traced, and the phoenix popped out. Two wings spread wide, one of them stretching above my collar bone. The starkest part of the burn stretched down my chest, between my breasts, and ended in a fan of feather-like marks on my skin.

Cassie made a small hum of agreement. "I see it now."

Kit took my hand between both of hers and nuzzled it with her cheek. "You're going to rise from the ashes even better than before."

The little motion reminded me of KitKat in her bobcat form, and I resisted an urge to scratch her head.

"It's kinda funny," Cassie mused. "Your ability is rooted in water, but the phoenix is a fire being. It's almost like a sort of balancing symbol."

I pressed my fingertips to the edge of the right "wing" and smiled. A mark of fire, worthy of someone like Cassie. Someone fearless and powerful enough to charge into danger. "Yeah," I said softly. "I kinda like it."

I thought of the Shadows in the desert, rising together in the form of a giant bird. I'd thought it looked like a phoenix on fire. They'd come to burn me, to reclaim their hold on my family. Tried to decimate us. But I was the one who came out of that desert victorious, alive, and made new—and more whole, with two of my sisters back and new friends at my side.

A loaded silence fell between us. I didn't really know how to talk to my sisters anymore. I was rusty.

I studied Kit—the sister I'd thought I lost. I placed my hand on her knee, hoping to say what I needed to in one quick squeeze.

We stayed there, the three of us, in a kind of awkward solidarity. Cassie, with her amnesia; Kit, finally human after being stuck as a bobcat for who knew how long; and me, half the person I once was but somehow stronger than before.

As we stared at each other, relearning the micro-expressions, the postures, the distinct sounds of each other's breathing, the room brightened.

A beam of yellow light sprang into the room. I gripped Kit's hand and stared at the growing light, startled by its sudden intrusion.

Small sparks of white and yellow swirled in the center of the room.

"Uh, you guys are seeing the twinkle lights too, right?" asked Kit.

"Mm-hmm." I stood, still holding my little sister's hand, and the three of us glided forward like sleepwalkers, watching the room flash and adjust. It took a couple moments of quiet before Alanna appeared.

She stood in the middle of the floor, wearing a knee-length cotton dress and a cardigan, dazzling in fifty shades of white and yellow.

"Hey," she said through a mournful smile.

"Holy hell!" Kit said, squeezing my hand tighter as her jaw dropped open.

"Language, missy," Alanna tutted.

Kit let go of me and crept forward, where she gave Lana's transparent belly an experimental poke. "Whoa. Cool!" Kit thrust her whole hand through Alanna's midriff and laughed.

"Are you done?" Alanna asked, always the picture of poise.

Kit withdrew, clasped both hands behind her back, and rolled her eyes up to the ceiling as she droned, "Sorry, Lana." Put her in pigtails and she'd be the spitting image of herself at three after she scribbled in one of Lana's treasured novels. That was one of the only times I ever heard Alanna yell. And boy, had she yelled.

But now, her glowing face softened with a look of delighted surprise. "You remember me?"

"'Course I do."

Alanna broke out in a smile identical to Cassie's. "But you were so little."

"Well, I never forgot," Kit said, low in her throat. She shrugged. "It helped that Ellis talked about you. And until she said you showed up at the lake house, I didn't know you were... gone. But I remember you." A small smile blossomed. "You always played Maid Marian or Joan of Arc."

"And you always played the dragon storming my castle," Lana said, a golden tear gliding down her cheek. She sighed. "I hate that I'm not there with you guys. Alive."

Cassie stepped closer, a smile quirking at the corner of her lips. "You just can't stay away."

Alanna laughed. "Yeah, sure. That's it."

"What are you doing here?" I asked.

"I wanted you to know that Sofia is safe," Lana said in her gentle way. She'd always had the bedside manner of a seasoned nurse, even as a kid.

Even still, Sofia's name on her translucent lips sent me into a tailspin. I struggled to remember how to inhale. "She's... with you?"

Alanna nodded. "You were able to put her body to rest beneath water. She wasn't burned, and her soul reassembled quickly. She's safe with us."

That walloped me in the chest, and I sank to the edge of the bed, struggling to breathe through my emotions. I rested my head in my hands, sucking in air.

Sofia hadn't been destroyed.

Sofia existed on the other side.

She *existed.*

"Us?" Cassie said, cutting through my thoughts, her eyes brighter. "Do you mean Vin? He's with you?"

Alanna's face crumpled. "No. The Malum still have a fragment of his soul in their possession. His ability offers them a valuable energy source." She drew herself back up. "But I'm going to get him back, help him reassemble."

"Ew," Kit said.

Cassie looked green. "Reassemble?"

"He's a soul, not a corporeal form," Lana said on a sigh. "It's not that gruesome. But the journey into Limbo is a rough one, disorienting, and it often leaves a soul scattered. Don't worry. I have allies here. We'll get him back to himself." Alanna took a single step forward. Her translucent foot made no noise. "But I'm not here just because of Sofia or to talk about Vin."

I exchanged glances with Cassie. "What else are you here for?"

Alanna took a deep breath—such a strange act for a dead girl. She gritted her teeth and looked around, as if the generic bedroom might have answers for her.

"The Summum Malum aren't finished," Alanna said quietly, her eyes distant. "They're coming to earth. If their plans succeed, there will be no more Shadows. The horde will come back in physical form to destroy everything. They'll lay waste to this world like they've done in Limbo, devouring life forces—magical, natural, and human—to fuel their power. We have to be ready."

A sharp pang of worry stabbed me in the chest. I pressed my fingertips to the ache and massaged it away. "We'll be ready."

Alanna's gaze pinned me. "Will you?"

I dug my fingers deeper into my ribcage, ignoring the sharp pain. "We will."

"They're not alone," Alanna said quietly. "The Summum Malum. They have help. They have living, breathing men to do their bidding."

"Like Aaron," spat Cassie.

Alanna tightened her jaw. "Yes. And since he stole the empty fire relic, more alt clans than ever before have sold their service in exchange for survival. Seeing a relic in Malum hands has them terrified the end of this war is near, and they want to be on the winning side."

"What can we do?" I asked.

Alanna shrugged helplessly. "Be prepared. Get stronger. The apocalypse is coming, and we can't stop it."

Her yellow lights flickered like a broken radio wave, blinking in and out of existence. She reached for us, her fingertips transparent as a wave of water.

"Don't let your guard down," Alanna warned, her voice a distant, ghostly call. "The time is coming. We have to be strong."

Her light snuffed out and vanished, leaving me, Cassie, and KitKat staring at the empty place where her spirit had stood.

Cassie let out a long breath. "Well. Sounds like we need to be vigilant."

I grunted. "Sounds like we need to sleep with our eyes open."

Silence stretched between us.

Three sisters, so entirely different, yet each recovering from her own personal experience with emptiness. KitKat, with her empty past that I didn't quite understand yet. Cassie, with her empty mind and the amnesia that had changed the course of her life. And me. Lost in the barren desert, emptied of sustenance, dying for water but hungry for blood.

Cassie cleared her throat. "Hey, we'll let you get dressed, okay? We'll be in the kitchen waiting for you. Kit went hunting this morning so there's…" She trailed.

"Blood," I finished with a shrug. "I'm not ashamed of it."

Cassie nodded, a smile curving her lips. "Yeah. You shouldn't be. We'll see you in a few."

"Yeah, hurry up," chimed Kit. "Cassie's giant beefsteak boyfriend found this super creepy book. You gotta check it out with me."

Cassie snorted at Kit's description of Gabriel, making me smile.

"Coming as fast as I can," I promised as they filed out the bedroom.

But I sat on the edge of the bed for several long moments after the door closed. My body *ached* like it never had before. Like I'd been put in a blender and turned into a milkshake. Oh well. If I could recover from the lab, I could recover from this.

I stumbled to my feet and crossed to the closet. Not a lot to choose from, but there were a couple of sundresses. I could see Vin shopping for them now, examining the racks with his fingers, picking by feel first and then examining the cut and color. He had impeccable taste. I picked out a short black one covered in sunflowers, tossing it over my skinny shoulders and letting it settle around my hips.

There was a full-length mirror on the back of the bedroom door. I straightened up in front of it, brushing the wrinkles out of my dress.

I smiled at my reflection, fulfilling my vow to myself, and the moment I did, I liked what I saw a lot better. My hair had started to grow in—just over an inch of thick, dark tresses formed a cap around my skull. It needed a little shaping, sure, maybe into a cute pixie cut. But for now, it was... kinda cute.

Fierce, but still cute.

I hooked a finger into the square neckline of the dress and tugged it down.

The burn looked *bad*. Raw, raised, and shiny. But as I smiled at it in the mirror, I imagined the lines as they would be when the mark healed. My phoenix scar. A reminder that no matter what injustices life threw at me, I could get back up and rise above it.

I could defeat the enemy.

I could breathe.

Air or water.

I traced my pinky along the jagged edges, my smile broadening. The phoenix burn was a mark of my triumph over evil.

It was a part of me.

A *good* part of me.

I released the neckline and strolled into the hall after my sisters. Downstairs, Jackson's deep voice asked, "So, where do we go from here?" My uncle's soothing response was too quiet to make out over Cassie's barked warning. "I swear to God, if that syrup gets on my pants, someone dies." Kitt and Mateo laughed. Violet reprimanded the three of them, while Scott mentioned something about taking his tech skills elsewhere. Gabriel mumbled what sounded like an agreement.

I wasn't alone. I wasn't trapped in a tank or cage of any kind. I'd come full circle from the day that shadowy face had hovered over my helpless form and removed my mask.

You don't need this.

To be fair, Dr. Craig had been correct. I didn't need an oxygen mask. I didn't even need the help I'd thought I did.

I only needed myself.

Despite all the pain they'd inflicted and all their attempts to dehumanize me, that undeserved suffering hadn't made me lesser. Thanks to the person my experiences, choices, and relationships had already made me inside, their mistreatments had only bent and reshaped me a little. They were the ones who had come out twisted and worse for wear. The shame of what they'd done would weigh on them, not me. I brushed my palms over my chest and hips. I was still thin, but I could see where I was growing and changing again. As time marched on, I'd be fitter than ever, stronger. I'd strive to be a force of nature, not some airbrushed feminine ideal.

I could save the world.

"Ellie!" Kit called. "I'm going to eat all your pancakes! I mean, drink all your blood."

I grinned and hurried for the stairs.

We had an enemy to defeat and a world to save.

After breakfast.

END OF BOOK TWO

Looking for more? To receive a bonus scene from Cassie's POV (taking place in the government facility), exclusive updates, and first access to everything in the Five Senses Series, sign up for my newsletter at www.cherylkahn.com.

ACKNOWLEDGEMENTS

This book wouldn't have been possible without the continued support of my family, friends, beta readers, hard-working editors, and critique partners. Thank you all for believing in me and the sisters' stories. I was also fortunate to connect with many wonderful book people on social media since the release of Touch and would like to give a special mention to Ovi (@acourtofspinesnpages) for being such a bright light in the Bookstagram community. Finally, a huge thanks to all the readers who have reached out or left reviews. It means so much.

ABOUT THE AUTHOR

Cheryl once worked as a corporate attorney and yoga instructor, but when the pandemic scaled back her yoga teaching, she reassessed her passions. Following a dream that began in 6th grade when she and her best friend penned a story in a spiral notebook during recess, Cheryl now spends her days crafting stories with care and a lot of heart. When not at the computer, she can be found sweating at the gym with friends, walking her rescue pup, and glued to her Kindle. She lives in California with her college sweetheart, now husband. Connect with Cheryl and receive exclusive Five Senses Series material by signing up for her newsletter at www.cherylkahn.com.